ÆRENDEN
THE CHILD RETURNS

KRISTEN TABER

sean tigh
PRESS

To my husband, who graciously smiles when I dash away from dinner in chase of magical creatures. You are my muse, my balance, my life.

ACKNOWLEDGMENTS

John Donne once penned, "No man is an island" and in this regard, no book is the creation of a single person. Without the efforts of so many, the world of Ærenden would have been no more than black print on yellowing pages, lost to the back of a closet for eternity. I owe a hearty Thank You to my friends, family, and beta readers for their amazing support and guidance. In particular, I must mention my sister and mother for reading and providing daily feedback on work in progress, even when chapters were less than scraps and bones; my husband for refusing to let me stop believing; Jessica Lux, my editor, for her firm hand and never-ending patience; Jaime Palmucci of Debutante Media for having faith in me, and for lending me her expertise and courage; Lisa J. Yarde, the amazing author, my mentor, for teaching me to think of sentences and publishing in ways I never dreamed possible; and, of course, my Grandfather, the man who first introduced me to storytelling and encouraged me to create.

PROLOGUE

THE WALLS fell in first. A flash of light and smoke came next. Or could it have been the other way around? It happened so fast, she could not remember. The air smelled funny, like when Papa put out the fire before bed. It filled her mouth and her nose. It stuffed her lungs and clogged her breathing. Then it turned thick and black so she could not see. She coughed. She tried to stand, to run, but her legs sagged beneath her. Tugging on a curtain, she pulled three times before she grew tired of toppling over, and crawled toward her bedroom. She called for her mama, but heard only the sound of distant screams through the smoke. None of them was Mama.

"Mama? Mama?" she cried again, feeling her way along the floor. Her fingers brushed a rug, soft and cool compared to the stone floor. A glowing fire consumed part of the room, heating the stone. It crept toward her. Fires hurt. Papa had told her she should not touch them. Sometimes she thought about trying to see if he was right, but she did not want to try with this one. It seemed angry. Its flames popped and snarled.

1

The couch began to glow, and then disappeared as the fire swept over it. It folded in half, crashing to the floor with a loud bang. She yelped. Tears stung her eyes and wet her cheeks. Her arms shook. Her legs trembled. She backed away, and found the table that usually stood in the middle of the living room. It must have toppled over too. It lay on its side next to a body that looked like Mama. She knew Mama by her hair. She loved to bury her face in it. She loved to admire the pretty flower smell of it, and the shine.

"Mama!" She still received no answer. Her tears dripped from her chin onto her arms. They felt hot. She reached the body, the strands of hair splayed across the floor, and tugged. Her mama did not move. She pulled again, her hands slipping from her mama's hair. She held them up, wiggled her fingers. They were sticky and red. She knew that color. She had learned it recently. Mama's hair was supposed to be black, not red.

The fire came closer, eating the table with gold teeth, crumbling it into gray ash like the fireplace dissolved the logs on cold days. Heat scorched her face, and singed her hair. It rolled over her body in waves, biting and clawing her skin. She shrank from it and somewhere, somebody wailed. The noise grew louder, closer, filling her with fear. The noise came from her mouth, she realized, and her lungs ached from it. She inhaled smoke and choked on it.

She wanted to leave but Mama refused to carry her. She did not understand why. She reached her arms up, noticing for the first time the soot caking the creases of her elbows and covering her pudgy skin. Then someone grabbed her and she flew.

Firm arms swung her fast through the air and out of the room, down a hallway filled with smoke and outside into the garden courtyard where she had often played with her toys on sunny days.

She rubbed her eyes to clear the tears and the stinging, and felt them burn from the black on her palms. She wailed harder.

"Take her," a gruff male voice said, handing her over to another set of arms. She did not know the man, but she knew the woman who now held her. She knew her orange hair, anyway, but her voice seemed different.

"Is she okay?" the woman asked.

"Meaghan will be fine. She's just scared."

"We all are," the woman replied. "Are they both gone? Were we not able to save them?"

"They're gone," the man responded, his voice heavy with anger and grief. "He betrayed them."

The woman looked away from him, toward the light the burning castle cast into the sky. "So he's won. The kingdom is his."

"Perhaps for now. Has James told you what you need to do?"

"Yes."

"Then go. Keep her safe."

The child wailed again and the woman pressed her close. "Be well, Miles. Give my sister my love."

Miles nodded. "Good luck," he said. Then the world turned white and disappeared from memory.

CHAPTER ONE

MEAGHAN RACED across the yard, blades of grass sticking to her feet as she moved. Frost numbed her toes, but she could not feel it. Her skin burned and her lungs ached. Orange flames chased her, and somewhere in the back of her mind, a hulking shadow waited for her to grow tired. Her heart pounded in her chest and she gulped in cold air to calm it. Then, by sheer will alone, she stilled her feet. The need to keep moving gripped her, but she ignored it to risk a glance over her shoulder, her anxiety dissolving when she saw only the dark windows of her house behind her.

It was a dream. Nothing more. She had known when she had opened her eyes, but the remnants of fire, and the haunting gaze of the dead had soon erased logic from her mind. The images had catalyzed her away from her room toward safety. Toward the only light shining brighter than the stars dotting the night sky—the light coming from the window in the apartment above the garage.

Despite the late hour, Nick was awake. Reading one of the books her father had loaned him, she guessed. The last had been a book on

World War II aviation. A modern mystery sat on his coffee table before that. His tastes were as mysterious as his past.

She blew out a breath, watching as it scattered white droplets into the air, and then resumed her trek to his apartment at a slower pace. The dream began to fade, streaking from her memory like a watered down painting, and she questioned the logic of visiting Nick so late. But the panic she had felt remained and she did not want to be alone.

Racing up the steps for the apartment two at a time, she landed at the top with a muted thud, and then took a moment to push several strands of dark brown hair from her eyes before lifting her fist to knock on the door. A few minutes passed. She shivered and cinched her robe tighter around her body. Her fingers turned numb and she had nearly decided Nick had fallen asleep reading when the thin curtain covering the window shifted. It fell back into place and the door swung open.

For a moment, Nick stared at her, one eyebrow arched in surprise, then his mouth tugged into a frown that cut rigid lines into his soft face. His displeasure hung in the air, thickening it until she felt she would suffocate.

"What are you doing here?" he asked.

She tucked her hands into the pockets of her robe. Her eyes sought his apartment for the familiarity of the threadbare carpet and the worn, green couch, and she longed for the comfort it promised.

"Meg."

Nick's impatient tone brought her attention back to him. Waning moonlight deepened his sandy hair to brown, and darkened his eyes, shadowing ocean blue with sea storms. She longed to find comfort in them, too.

"I just," she hesitated. "I hoped we could talk."

"You know that's not possible. You can't be here."

She knew. It had only been a few days since she had tried to kiss him, since they had agreed to take time apart to allow her feelings for him to die. Her cheeks flared, and so did her fear. She had not realized time apart meant she would lose his friendship. She lifted her chin and set her jaw to prevent tears from forming in her vision. "Do you really think I'd be here without a good reason?" she asked. Removing her hands from her pockets, she crossed her arms. "My last final is in a few hours. Do you really think I'd leave my books unless…"

"Unless what?"

"Nothing," she muttered. Her anger and her fear gave way to embarrassment. Why was she here? Because of a dream? Only children ran from nightmares, not seventeen-year-old women taking advanced classes. "Forget it," she said. Pivoting on her heel, she stopped from leaving when Nick's hand gripped her shoulder. He turned her around to face him again.

"What aren't you telling me?" he asked, narrowing his eyes at her. "If you aren't here to talk about what happened between us, then what did you want to talk about?"

She considered lying and taking a quick escape, but when he squeezed her shoulder in his usual gesture of friendship, she decided to trust him. Moving past the kiss would take effort on both their parts. "I fell asleep at my desk," she answered. "I didn't mean to, but I guess I've been studying too hard and—"

"And you had another dream," he realized. The tension dissolved from his face, and then his body. Stepping back, he cleared the threshold and escorted her inside.

Hot air slammed into her like a wall, assaulting her ice-chilled skin before her body adapted to it. She wriggled her toes to revive them. Her ears tingled from the rush of renewed blood, then her nose and cheeks, but her fingers were slower to respond. She rubbed them together, relinquishing them to Nick when he sandwiched them between his hands.

"You're freezing," he said. His eyes coursed down her body, taking in her robe before landing on her bare feet. He shook his head and let go of her hands. "Are you crazy? You're not wearing a jacket or shoes. It's supposed to snow."

"It didn't cross my mind while I was running for my life."

"Dreams can't kill you," he reminded her, and then chuckled, unfazed by the glare she cast in his direction. "Have a seat," he said. "I'll make you some tea."

"Cocoa," she instructed. Sliding into her usual place on the left side of the couch, she drew her knees under her chin, wrapping her arms around them. "With marshmallows."

"Anything you say." Nick feigned a bow, and then turned to the small kitchenette flanking his apartment to follow her request. His movements were efficient, steady, and it calmed her to watch him. Once he had placed a mug of water in the microwave to heat, he leaned back against the counter, and waited.

She fidgeted with the belt of her robe for a while before she spoke. "The microwave's slow tonight."

The corner of Nick's mouth twitched up. "Give it time. It's old."

"Much like the rest of the place," she said, glancing from the microwave to the outdated wallpaper. Stripes had faded from a once vibrant yellow to sallow gold. "It's overdue for a renovation."

"Perhaps," he said, turning back to the microwave when it dinged. Removing the mug, he set it on the counter. "But it works for me. I'm grateful Vivian and James were between tenants when I needed it. They've been good to me."

"They have," Meaghan agreed. "I'm glad you decided to attend the university here."

Nick cast a glance over his shoulder at her. Shadows returned to his eyes for a moment and Meaghan clenched her teeth, feeling foolish for the slip. Nick diverted his attention back to the mug. "While we're on the subject of school, which final is tomorrow?"

"Psychology," she said. "I wish I had more time. I'll do okay, but I'm not sure I'll get the grade I need to qualify for the advanced program."

"It would be a shame if you didn't," Nick responded. Crossing the room, he handed her the mug before sitting next to her. "You were born to help people."

"Hence the all-nighter. Or rather, the attempt at one." Sighing, she stared into her cup. A few clumps of powder clung to the surface of her hot cocoa and she poked at one with the tip of her finger. Since she was a child, she had understood people's emotions in a way that made helping them feel natural. She did not want to think about how she would react if she failed. She needed the advanced program to funnel her into her Masters and then private practice, as she had always dreamed.

That was, until the nightmares had begun haunting her. For longer than she cared to remember, they had haunted her sleep and clung shadows even to her waking moments. She tightened her hands around the mug as flames overtook her mind again, the heat of it seeming to sear her skin. She stared at one forearm, expecting it to redden, but saw only Nick's hand as it covered her wrist.

"Tell me about the dream," he said. "Was it like the others?"

"Sort of." Meaghan drew in a shuddering breath. Lifting the mug to her lips, she took a small sip, though she could not taste it. "It was like the others and it was different," she said after a moment and set the mug down on the coffee table. "The woman was in it again."

"You mean the dead one?"

"She wasn't dead this time. Not at first, anyway."

"What do you mean?" When Meaghan did not respond, Nick drew his hand to her knee. "What do you remember?"

Meaghan closed her eyes and tried to draw the image of the woman once more. At first, she appeared as no more than a distant ghost, hazed in black and white, but soon she solidified. She smiled, welcoming, and Meaghan caught her breath, preventing a sob from escaping her throat. The woman seemed as real as she had less than an hour before. She stood in a room of stone, but nothing more of the dream surfaced.

Meaghan opened her eyes. "There isn't much."

"Tell me what you can."

She nodded, letting the image take hold of her vision and her memory. "She was elegant," Meaghan whispered. "She wore a gown.

9

A satin ball gown, I think. It was purple. I remember because it matched the amulet around her neck. Her eyes were gold, and her hair was dark like the other times, but braided. At least it started out that way. She let it down to brush it." And it had felt like silk, Meaghan remembered, though her hands had seemed small as she touched it. The thought stalled her breath and Nick's fingers sought hers. She opened her eyes to view compassion in his stare. And worry. When salt water rolled over her lip, she understood why. She had not even realized she had been crying.

"Is this too much for you?" he asked.

Meaghan shook her head. "It just felt real, that's all."

He nodded. "Did she say anything?"

"No. She loved me though. I don't know how I knew, but I did. I could feel it. She held her arms out to me. Then something went wrong."

Nick's grip tightened. "What happened?"

"I don't know. The necklace flashed as if it had light inside it. There was an explosion, fire, then…then…I can't remember." Fear overwhelmed her, reviving her need to flee. She bit her lip to control the reaction, but could not control her tears. She wept, and Nick brought his arms around her.

"It's over now, Meg," he whispered. "I won't let anything hurt you."

She found comfort in his words and in the warmth of his shoulder, and soon her fear faded. He traced his fingers across her cheek, wiping away her tears. "Have you told your parents about the dreams?"

She shook her head, then looked away. Drawing one long breath and then another, she calmed her heart. Her shaking stopped, and she became acutely aware of how close Nick sat. Shifting away from him, she cast him a sheepish smile. "They wouldn't understand. Honestly, I don't know why you do."

"Because I care. But so do they, Meg." He drew his fingers to her chin, guiding her eyes to his. "I realize I gave the wrong impression when you showed up tonight, but I am here for you. Don't doubt that."

"I don't." She reached up to take his hand. Her gaze fell from his eyes to his lips. She recalled the kiss they had shared days before, the excitement she had felt with the contact. She also remembered the pain she had felt when he pushed her away. She started to withdraw from him, but she did not get the chance before he leaned toward her. His lips touched hers, and a fraction of a second later, his fingers closed around her arm and he pushed her back once more. His eyes widened in fear before he stood.

"You have to go."

"But I didn't—" Meaghan started to protest, then lost her words as anger stiffened her lips. She glared at him. "You're the one who made the move this time."

His fear turned to guilt, his complexion to white. He averted his gaze. "It doesn't matter. This can't happen."

"Why not?" she asked, standing to face him. "It's obvious we both feel the same way, so why is this a bad thing?"

When he returned his eyes to hers, but refused to answer, she threw her hands into the air. "Fine. Keep your secrets. But know this.

If I leave now, you won't get another chance with me."

He nodded. Her anger gave way to hurt, but she covered it with a thin smile and exited the apartment, embracing the cold once more.

CHAPTER TWO

NICK AWOKE to the bright stream of the mid-morning sun piercing his bedroom window. When Meaghan had left last night, he had been confused, angry for the way he had handled their encounter. This morning, he knew what he had to do to make things right between them, but rather than bring him peace, his clarity planted dread in his stomach as heavy as a ball of lead. It had slowed his morning routine, stalled his feet as he moved, but eventually he forced his muscles to cooperate.

He left his apartment and crossed the yard, then opened the screen door to the two-story home Vivian and James shared and hesitated, his hand resting on the handle of the back door. Vivian would not be happy with his decision. She would see it as a betrayal, or perhaps even an abandonment of his duties.

He could not blame her. When Meaghan had kissed him, his reaction had been forgivable. Although he had let it go on longer than he should have, he had made his boundary clear. Last night, he had let that boundary crumble. He and Meaghan had been too close.

The warmth of her body had charged him. Her crying had born in him the instinct to protect her. It had been the same need to protect her that had caused him to break their contact before any damage had been done.

But he feared his actions would soon cause damage to his relationship with Vivian. After all, he would not need to make this decision if he had done his job. But *if* meant changing the past and no one had the power to do that.

"I have to do this," he said to reaffirm his courage, and turned the handle, entering without knocking.

Vivian stood at the kitchen island, her focus steady on a cookbook resting on the counter. Waving the wooden spoon in her right hand, she indicated a stool opposite her. "Sit," she commanded without looking at him.

Nick obeyed. Vivian returned the spoon to a bowl resting in the crook of her arm and mixed a light pink batter. She hated interruptions when she cooked and Nick respected that, remaining silent as she worked.

Her movements were fluid, stemming from a natural grace inherent to her lean and limber body. She and her daughter shared the same physique, but otherwise, they looked nothing like each other. Meaghan's hair graced the tops of her shoulders. Vivian's hung to her waist most days, though today she had corralled it into a bun, and the color resembled fire rather than the dark night that belonged to her daughter. Vivian's eyes were green, instead of Meaghan's copper, and they peered at him from a face more angular than Meaghan's, but still quite beautiful.

Vivian let go of the spoon to pull a loose strand of hair behind her ear and the familiar gesture eased his anxiety. So did the smile that tugged at the corners of her lips after she dipped her finger into the bowl and sampled the batter. He knew he should not feel better, not when he still had his news to share, but having a face similar to his mother's to gaze upon eased some of his worry.

"Stop that," Vivian said, setting her bowl aside.

"Stop what? Are those rhubarb muffins?"

"They are. And stop staring at me with that look of terror on your face."

"I'm not. Finish what you're doing."

"Not a chance. I've known you too long for you to fool me so don't bother trying." She leaned over the counter to press his chin between her thumb and forefinger. "Your eyes are sad today, Nickaulai."

Despite the truth in her words, her use of his full name brought a grin to his lips. He took her hand in his and kissed it. "Nickaulai," he echoed. "The last time you called me that, I was in trouble for pulling a prank on our neighbor. Am I in trouble now?"

She laughed. "Hardly. It's nice Meaghan finds comfort in your friendship. She was at your place last night, wasn't she?"

Nick's shoulders stiffened and he let go of Vivian's hand. "She had another dream."

"I suspected as much," Vivian responded with no hint of anger and he relaxed again. "It won't be long before it's time to tell her the truth."

"I'm not sure she's ready."

15

Vivian raised an eyebrow. "It sounds to me like it's you who doesn't feel ready."

"Maybe," he admitted. "She's a handful. She's headstrong and she's too impulsive for her own good."

The corners of Vivian's mouth quirked up again. "I thought that's what you liked about her."

"Except when she doesn't listen to me," Nick muttered. He looked out the window, his attention drawn to the stairs for his apartment, and the memory from last night. He quickly chased it away. "She'll get into trouble."

"That isn't new," Vivian pointed out. "And as usual, you'll get her out of it."

"If she doesn't outwit me. She's smarter than I am."

"Is she?" Vivian asked. Her eyebrow shot up again and Nick realized too late that a drop in his tone had given away his true fear. Vivian laid a palm on one of his hands. He flipped it around to curl his fingers into hers and looked down at them.

"That's far from the truth, Nick," she told him. Her voice turned serious, motherly. "You're as smart as Meaghan. She may like to challenge you, but I have no doubt you'll match her when it matters."

In the back of his mind, he wished she was right, but reality overwhelmed what little hope he held. The facts had presented themselves, and he found them overwhelming.

"She's supposed to be in high school," he said, "yet she's half-way through her second year of college. I'm having trouble getting through my first year. On top of that, when we debate, she always wins. I can't even begin to comprehend her logic."

"You're not from here," Vivian responded. "If you were, you'd have skipped grades the same as she did." She lifted her free hand to pat his cheek and then leaned back, severing their connection. "Your debates are a different matter. You can't follow her logic because you're distracted."

"Distracted? By what?"

"By the reason you came to see me this morning, by your attraction to her."

He swallowed hard. "You know?"

"Of course. Have you forgotten who I am?"

He had not, but he had assumed she would have reprimanded him by now if she had known. "Then you also know why I have to leave."

"No, I don't." Vivian walked around the counter to sit next to him. "I don't see why you have to leave at all."

"Because you disagree with the Council," Nick said, and sighed. "I realize you think they're being overprotective, but the consequences are not their invention. They have centuries of evidence to back their decree."

She nodded. "And you're afraid you'll be subject to those consequences."

"Why wouldn't I be? I can't risk everything we've done and the sacrifices you and James have made because I'm attracted to Meaghan. I have to stay strong to succeed."

"You are strong, Nick. You do an injustice by thinking otherwise."

"I know my limitations," he countered. "I'll be fine once I

17

distance myself from her."

"Maybe," Vivian responded. "But maybe not. Sometimes life isn't as predictable as you want, and sometimes you have to give in to weakness to become stronger."

"I have to…" he repeated, and then pressed his lips together as he tried to decipher what she had said. He shook his head, frustrated. "How can I be both weak and strong?" he asked. "That doesn't make any—"

She silenced him with a kiss to the forehead. Drawing her fingers to his face, she traced a shadow below his eye. "I see the pain you're in, Nick. I understand why you believe it's warranted, but you need to listen to me. Things aren't what they seem. The only way you'll succeed is if you follow your heart."

"My heart tells me what I'm doing is dangerous."

"That's your head talking."

"Stop, please." He took her hand, and tightened his fingers around it. "Please don't make this harder than it already is."

"I'm not trying to," she assured him, and he let go of her hand. "You've made up your mind already, haven't you?"

"Yes."

"All right," she conceded. Standing, she brought her arms around him. He pressed his face into her neck as he remembered doing in childhood. "If this is what you want to do, I won't say any more about it. You have my love, Nick, and my guidance when you need it." He lifted his head from her shoulder and she brought her lips to his forehead once more. "I'll miss you. It's been nice having you around."

"It's been nice for me too," he told her, then frowned when her eyes shot to the door and widened. "She's back?" he guessed on a whisper.

Vivian nodded, responding in a hushed voice of her own. "I should've been paying closer attention."

"Did she overhear?"

"Only the last part," Vivian answered, returning her eyes to his. "But she'll guess you're leaving. You should talk to her."

Nick nodded. His nerves returned as he slid from the stool and exited the kitchen into the living room. Meaghan stood in front of a bookshelf on the far wall, examining a collection of porcelain figurines James had given Vivian to commemorate special occasions over the years. Her guilty pleasures, Vivian liked to call them.

Meaghan traced her finger over the head of a small white dove, and then tensed when Nick put his hands on her shoulders.

"I know you heard," he said. She turned to look up at him. Tears shimmered in her eyes, but he did his best to ignore them. "I wish there was some other way."

"What do you mean?" she asked. He shrugged, tucking his hands into his pockets and she frowned. "This is about us, isn't it?"

"It's complicated," he said, then reconsidered his words as she pressed her lips together. "I wish I could explain, but it's not possible right now."

"Of course it isn't," she said, sarcasm turning her voice hard. She crossed her arms over her chest. "I don't know why I'm surprised by that. You've made a habit of not telling me anything, of pushing me away, and I'm tired of it."

"Meg, please. It's not that simple—"

"It is." Her tears escaped, streaking down her face, but she shoved them away, stepping back from him when he reached for her. "Nothing's so complicated that you couldn't at least try to explain. You just don't want to."

"Meg—"

"Meaghan," she snapped. "Only family's allowed to call me Meg. You've lost the right."

Her words stung more than he cared to admit, but before he had the chance to respond, she turned and stormed from the room.

CHAPTER THREE

A LITTLE more than thirty minutes later, Nick opened his door to find Meaghan standing on his landing, holding a plate of muffins. Heat rose from the muffins in wisps, casting the smell of sweet strawberries and bitter rhubarb into the air. His stomach would have rumbled, if his anxiety at the sight of her had not silenced his hunger.

"I wasn't expecting you," he said.

"Don't think I'm not still mad," she told him. "But I thought we should talk. I brought breakfast."

"I see." Nick chuckled, feeling relieved. Meaghan might be mad still, but she had come, which meant her anger would dissolve in time. He stepped aside, letting her into the apartment, then tucked his hands into his pockets and waited.

After a moment, Meaghan cleared her throat. "Mom and I had a long discussion. It, um," she dropped her eyes to the plate in her hands. "It seems I was being childish."

"Maybe you were," he said, and then held up a hand when her head snapped up, her heated gaze locking on him. "But you're entitled. I'm not exactly the easiest person to be around."

Meaghan sighed and set the muffins down on the coffee table. "That's the thing. You're not as difficult as you think, but you're aloof. I don't understand why."

"You will when you see me next."

"When will that be?"

"Soon," he responded. She stiffened and he brought his hands to her shoulders. "I'd tell you if I knew, Meaghan, but I promise it won't be long."

"Meg," she corrected, and he knew she had forgiven him. He drew her close, and then pressed his cheek to the top of her head when she relaxed in his arms. The next time they met, she would know his secret and their relationship would change, but for now, in this moment, the stillness of the friendship bonding them brought peace.

He wanted to etch the feeling into his memory, but he did not get the chance. Meaghan tensed, and then jerked from his arms, her wide eyes seeking the house over his shoulder.

"There's something wrong," she whispered. She shivered and he gripped her shoulders once more. "There's so much," she gasped. Tears spilled down her cheeks. "Pain," she continued, though Nick could tell she struggled to form her words. Her eyes refocused on him. "It feels so real."

"I don't understand."

"Me neither." She shook her head as if to clear it. "It hurts, but it's foreign. It's like a dream."

Nick's heart hammered when he realized what she meant. "No," he murmured. "It can't be."

"Nick…" Meaghan began, but her voice faded as her eyes found the house again. Her face turned white. Her hands trembled, and Nick grasped them between his own. Closing his eyes, he bowed his head to focus.

"We have to help them," she insisted. "We have to hurry."

Her hands disappeared from his. He felt her brush past him and opened his eyes in time to loop an arm around her waist, preventing her from escaping the apartment. "Don't," he said. "We can't go in there without knowing what we're facing."

"I have to." She pushed against him, but he did not release his hold. She reacted to a drive she could not control and as much as he worried he might hurt her, he tightened his grip to protect her. "Something's wrong," she said. "Please, Nick. I can't—"

"Be quiet," he commanded, his sharp tone silencing her. He shut his eyes and focused again. When he found what he feared most, his eyes popped open in panic. "This isn't happening. I would've sensed them before now."

"Who?"

Rather than respond, he grabbed her hand and yanked her toward the door. He had no time to explain. He had to save her life, even if it meant bringing her straight into danger.

§

THEY FLED from the apartment, down the stairs and across the yard. Meaghan was certain she would have collapsed if Nick had not been pulling her along behind him. She felt weak and useless, overwhelmed by pain she could not understand. She ached from it.

She forced herself to breathe, to think, though her lungs followed the direction better than her brain. She registered the cold air, the grass as it passed under her feet, but she did not notice when Nick abruptly halted until she bumped into his back. Letting go of her hand, he bowed his head as he had in the apartment, then cracked open the back door to the house.

"Is it safe?" she asked.

"They aren't in the kitchen," he responded. "We have to take the chance."

"What chance?" She grabbed his arm. "Nick—"

He finished opening the door and Meaghan's grip weakened, the remainder of her words forgotten. The pristine kitchen her mother treasured looked to have exploded. Colorful mixing bowls and apothecary jars, once stacked on display, lay in shards on the counters, joined by dented pots and pans that used to hang from the ceiling. Drawers gaped open, yanked from their homes, and the refrigerator and cabinets stood empty, their contents strewn across the floor.

A scream came from the living room followed by a series of crashes. Pain surged through Meaghan and she froze, one foot over the threshold.

Nick turned to look at her. "There's no time to stop," he said, and then hardened his tone when she did not move. "Meg!"

She snapped her eyes to his and obeyed. Half-way through the kitchen, he slowed his pace as heavy footsteps thundered from above. He held his finger to his lips and she nodded. She followed him into the living room, freezing once more when she saw the horror that greeted them.

Furniture, upended and broken into pieces, shared the carpet with pages torn from their bindings, cast aside like large snowflakes. Deep grooves in the walls bled drywall and wood splinters. And every figurine her mother had collected had been shattered, turned into pale shards and dust. This was no longer her home, but a nightmare ripped from her worst dreams.

A groan came from the far side of the room and Meaghan turned her head toward it. A man sat on one side of the couch, his body slumped halfway toward the floor. His legs and arms hung at odd angles, and tears in his pants and shirt revealed deep gashes in his skin. Blood poured from a wound in his head, flowing over a face she refused to believe belonged to her father. It sank in places where his bones had collapsed, giving him a hollowed look. She felt sick. Covering her mouth, she sought her father's eyes. They appeared empty, nearly black.

"This isn't real," she whispered. She squeezed her eyes shut. "It's only a dream. I have to wake up."

Another groan came from the couch, drawing her attention back to her father. He moved his lips and Nick ran to him, leaning close to hear. After a few seconds, Nick took something from her father's pocket, then moved to the center of the floor. Lifting a loose floorboard, he pulled a backpack from beneath it.

Meaghan commanded her body to move, turning to her left to pick up the hallway phone. Before she could call for an ambulance, her attention fell on the stairs. Her mother lay stretched across the landing, her unseeing eyes staring toward the ceiling, her back and neck bent at odd angles. Meaghan choked on the scream trapped inside her throat.

"Meg," Nick called to her from across the room. He kept his voice low. "We need to get your father out of here. You have to help me carry him."

She tried to obey him, but her feet refused to budge. She dug her fingernails into her palms, gritting her teeth with the sharp pain, but she still could not believe any of this was real.

"You can't," her father's voice croaked. "You have to leave me here. You have to protect Meg."

"James—"

"Now," her father insisted. His head rose and Meaghan saw a flash of authority return to his eyes. Nick nodded and she stared at him in horror.

"I won't leave him here," she said.

"We have to. You're in danger. Once you're safe, I'll return—"

"I won't go," she insisted. "I refuse to leave him in the house with whoever did this."

"We don't have—"

"No!" she yelled, and then slapped her hand over her mouth, too late to muffle the noise. The footsteps upstairs quickened.

"Meg," her father spoke again and her eyes filled with tears. His voice was no more than a whisper. "Trust Nick. He'll keep you safe."

She nodded, and then shook as her father gathered his last breath. The footsteps reached the top of the stairs. Her father shuddered into stillness, but she had no time to mourn before Nick grabbed her hand and yanked her out the front door.

Cold air bit her face. Black clouds gathered overhead, shadowing the day in darkness. A gust of wind whipped leaves across the yard, building small funnel clouds, but she ignored them. She focused on the back of Nick's head, then on her car when she realized they would need it to escape. They had nearly reached the driveway before she remembered she did not have her keys. She skidded to a stop. Turning back toward the house, she caught her breath when she saw their pursuers exiting the front door.

There were three of them, each taller than the last. Dark brown cloaks covered them from head to foot and they all carried heavy wood clubs stained with blood. They moved with an unnatural speed and disjointed grace, as if they floated instead of touching the ground. A putrid, rotting scent emanated from them in waves. It rolled Meaghan's stomach, pitching her breakfast mid-way up her throat before she controlled the reaction. Nick grabbed her arm and pulled her toward her parents' SUV.

"The keys," she gasped, daring a glance behind her. The creatures grew closer. "We don't—"

"I have them. James gave them to me. Get in the car."

She heard a beep as Nick deactivated the alarm. She ran to the passenger side. Yanking open the door, she slid into the seat while he turned the key.

Releasing the parking brake, Nick threw the transmission into reverse, and then stomped on the gas pedal. The SUV squealed down the driveway seconds before their pursuers reached them. At the road, Nick yanked the wheel, spinning the car onto the blacktop so it pointed toward the highway, then shifted into drive, and gunned the engine once more.

A thud echoed through the vehicle as one of the creatures jumped onto the roof, gripping the edges of the car with long, skeletal fingers that gave the illusion of skin suctioned to bone. Meaghan screamed and tore her eyes from the creature.

"Hold on to something," Nick told her. "I'm going to try to shake him."

She grabbed the door handle with both hands and Nick accelerated again, swerving left and then right before taking a sharp corner at full speed. The creature still held. It inched across the car, moving down the windshield so Meaghan saw his face. The monster staring back at her appeared worse than any of the horrors she had seen in her nightmares. His eyes shone crimson red, pools of blood sunken into ashen skin. His mouth appeared to be no more than a black hole filled with fibrous webbing. A mass of disfigured scar tissue filled the space where his nose should have been. He lifted his fists, then brought them back down, pounding on the window in an attempt to break it.

"Put your seatbelt on," Nick commanded. Heeding his warning, she clicked her belt into place and he slammed on the brakes. The monster flew from the SUV, landing on a car parked in the street. A burglar alarm blared an incessant, alternating pitch that drew neighbors into their yards.

Nick's maneuver halted one pursuer, but the other two had not given up. From the side mirror, Meaghan could see them gaining speed. Nick jammed his foot onto the gas pedal again and headed north, as fast as the roads would allow.

Meaghan kept her eyes glued to the mirror, watching the creatures fade into specks of brown until Nick turned onto the highway. He seemed relieved, but she could not shake her fear.

"They're gone for now," Nick assured her after she had checked the mirror for the fifth time in the same number of seconds. "They're powerful, but they're not very bright."

"They're not very…" she echoed, her voice trailing off when she realized the underlying meaning of his words. She shook her head. "You can't possibly know anything about those things. They aren't real. They can't be. None of this is real."

Nick set his jaw, and for a brief second his eyes met hers before he turned them back to the road. "It's real, Meg. I wish it wasn't, but it is. The creatures are Mardróch. Now get some sleep. You've been up all night and we have a long drive ahead of us. We can talk when we get there."

Sleep was the furthest thing from her mind. She wanted to scream, to run. She wanted to shake Nick and break him out of whatever spell held him firm and emotionless beside her. She wanted to wake, but the pain she had felt when she saw her mother on the stairs, heard her father take his last breath, still ripped through her and she knew this nightmare would never be over.

Only Nick could decipher what had happened, but his white knuckles on the steering wheel and hard gaze on the highway told her there would be no conversation. He remained focused on escape.

Meaghan opted to do the same. Closing her eyes, she let tears ease her into a dreamless abyss.

CHAPTER FOUR

SCREAMS ECHOED across the cold air, startling Meaghan awake and shredding the small amount of peace she had found. Yanking open her eyes, she gasped when blood filled her vision, then eased from her sight in thick, crimson rivulets to reveal the dark wood of her living room floor and the white risers of the staircase, stained pink with her mother's blood.

Logic told her she should be in the car with Nick, escaping to an unknown destination, but her mother's body lay before her, twisted and tortured, bent and bruised in death. Footsteps pounded the floor above her, but she ignored them, dismissing the peril to focus on her mother's pale face and the red hair splayed across her shoulders. Meaghan reached out a hand to brush the strands aside, to feel the softness of them between her fingers, but a stirring of her mother's body froze her.

It had not been much, only the slightest inflation of her mother's chest, and Meaghan would have credited it to imagination except it came again, this time accompanied by rattling breath. Meaghan stepped back, and then froze once more when her mother's eyes opened, fixing Meaghan with a heavy stare.

"Meg," her mother's voice rasped. Red spittle escaped from her mouth, spraying the front of Meaghan's sweater. "Meg," her mother repeated as she lifted her hand, her fingers coated in dark, dried blood.

Meaghan swallowed hard. Her heart raced, but her hand drifted forward on instinct, seeking her mother's comfort.

"Trust him, Meg," her mother's lips moved, though her father's voice escaped them. "Trust Nick."

Meaghan's fingers closed around her mother's. They felt hard, unyielding, like plastic.

"You're in danger, Meg. Danger…There are things…I have to tell you…."

Meaghan fought to hold on to her mother's words, but they faded, lost to the drone of an unseen engine, the sound of rocks crunching somewhere beneath her. Then all sound, including her mother's voice, succumbed to silence. She squeezed her eyes shut, opening them again to search for her mother's face.

She found a black dashboard. Her eyes coasted along the smooth plastic to the car door at her side and the handle grasped beneath her white knuckles. She released her grip, turning her head when Nick coughed beside her. He watched her, his eyes rimmed red, and she knew he was real and what she had just seen had been a dream. Or rather, a nightmare.

Her mother was dead, and any secrets she had held had died with her.

The thought stabbed through Meaghan's heart and her eyes drifted from Nick's face, seeking solace in whatever lay beyond the windshield.

Dark clouds had overtaken the sky, fulfilling their earlier promise with an onslaught of rain and snow. Beyond the haze, she could make out the outline of tall trees and low-lying brush that formed the edge of a thick forest.

"What time is it?" she asked.

"Five," Nick said, his voice as hollow as her mother's had been in her dream.

She nodded, too numbed by her own pain to acknowledge his. "Where are we?"

"North of the house by several hundred miles," he answered. His voice grew stronger and steel returned to it. "We need to go. We have some distance left to go tonight and we need to walk it."

Her focus came back to him. She frowned. "I don't see how we can. It's snowing. I doubt our sweaters will be warm enough."

"It won't be easy," he admitted. "But once we start moving, we should be okay." Taking her hand in his, he offered a thin smile, though it did not hold any encouragement. "I'm sorry. I wish we were better prepared."

"How do we prepare for something like this?" she asked, dropping his hand. "It's not like we could have known," she hesitated, not wanting to say the words that would acknowledge her parents' deaths. "That we would be out here," she finally finished.

Nick pressed his lips together, and then averted his gaze. In guilt, she realized, though she did not understand why. They had found out about the intruders at the same time. They had both seen the carnage and together, they had failed to rescue her father.

The realization stung her heart once again, burning hot tears in her eyes. The tears coursed down her cheeks, splashing onto her hands before she saw Nick's blurry image move closer. She fisted her hands on the back of his sweater, burying her head in his neck as sobs came fast, racking her body. Her grief overwhelmed her until she had exhausted her energy for it and her body stilled. Nick pressed his lips to the top of her head before he let her go.

"I'm so sorry," he whispered. Sorrow hung in his voice and she felt her throat constrict with her own grief. She swallowed to erase the sudden feeling she might choke to death.

"You knew they were there," she whispered, forcing her gaze to his face. His eyes widened slightly and she continued to press him. "You knew, didn't you? When we were in your apartment, when I—"

"Not the way you mean." He placed his hand on the door handle and turned from her. "We need to go."

She grabbed his arm to keep him from leaving. "What happened, Nick? What aren't you telling me? You feel guilty. I can tell."

"Nothing." He yanked his arm from her fingers, facing her long enough for her to see the anger now stiffening his face. "Stop, all right? I'm too exhausted to keep you out right now, so stop reading me."

"Reading you?" She shook her head, confused. "I don't even know what that means. What on earth are you talking about?"

"Forget it. Let's go."

Without waiting for her objection, he opened the car door and stepped outside. She followed his lead, moving around the vehicle to the driver's side.

"What are you talking about?" she asked again, frustration creeping into her voice when he did not answer. "You can't keep avoiding my questions."

"I can and I will. At least until it's safe." He opened the back door of the SUV and pulled out the backpack. When he turned to her again, she felt a cold that had nothing to do with the weather. Despite her talent for understanding small emotional cues, she found his face indistinguishable. His posture appeared impassive, his eyes vacant. His anger had dissolved in an instant.

"What—?" she started to ask what had happened, but did not know how to finish the question. It made no sense.

"I blocked you," he said before turning from her to gather branches from the ground. "Help me hide the car. By now, the police will have found your parents and assumed you've been kidnapped. Their theories on me won't be great, so I'd rather not give them an easy path to hunt us down."

She stood rooted to her spot. "What do you mean 'blocked' me?"

He stacked the branches over the car, creating a nest. "Are you going to help?"

Her hands shook, so she dug them into her pockets to warm them. "Not until you answer me."

"There's no time."

"You promised me you'd answer my questions when we got here. I'm not taking another step until you do."

"You can't be serious," he said, then sighed when she moved to a tree stump and sat down. "We'll freeze to death if we stay here."

"I'll run the car."

"If you do, you'll draw attention. We have to worry about the Mardróch finding us."

"You said we lost them."

He threw another branch on top of the car, and then turned to frown at her. "There's nothing wrong with being cautious, but even if they're gone, we still have the police to worry about."

"I don't have to worry about the police. You do," she pointed out, crossing her arms over her chest when he continued to collect branches without looking at her. "And why do you? Why would they assume you had something to do with this?"

"Because," he started, then hesitated and faced her. "Because I didn't exist until a year ago. The police are bound to realize that when they start investigating."

Meaghan dropped her arms. "That's not possible."

"It is when I'm not from here. To them, I don't exist."

"Of course you do," she protested. "If you changed your name, there's a record. If you didn't and you left another life, there's still a record somewhere. A birth certificate, a school record, *something*. You exist, Nick."

"Not here," he said, returning to his task. "Please help. I don't want to be doing this all night."

She gave in and helped him stack branches along the base of the SUV though the effort seemed pointless. A strong gust of wind would reveal the car in seconds.

Wandering away from him, she returned a few minutes later with heavy tree limbs to stack on top, and picked up the conversation where they had left off. "Unless you were born in the Antarctic to polar bears, you have a birth certificate."

"I don't," he replied. "And neither do you."

"Of course I do. I've seen it."

He stopped his task to look at her. "So have I. Vivian and James did a good job on the counterfeit. It would fool an expert, but it's still fake. So is their marriage certificate. It's all fake, Meg, and the police will figure that out once they realize Vivian and James had no real history either."

The thought tightened Meaghan's throat again, but she shook her head to chase it away. "That's ridiculous."

"It's not. None of us are from here." Nick turned to stack the last of the branches, and then faced her again. "I told you it was too much to explain right now. We have to go."

"Not a chance. Not until I know more, anyway. You sound insane."

Nick shook his head. "Come on, Meg. You know better than that."

When Meaghan met his plea with silence, weariness drew lines over his face, then seemed to emanate from him, turning the air heavy. She felt stifled by the sensation, but ignored it and shoved her hands into her pockets.

"How do I know you're not crazy?" she demanded. "I'm not sure I'm still sane after," she swallowed the rest of her words. Tears burned her eyes, but remembering Nick's guilt from earlier, she backed away from him when he reached for her.

Then her thoughts turned more sinister. She scanned the forest for an escape as her tears dissolved and panic set her muscles in preparation for flight.

"Do the Mardróch even exist?" she asked. "How do I know you didn't slip me something to make me hallucinate and then kill my parents? How do I know I'm not next?"

Nick's eyes widened and pain rolled from him in waves. She felt it as raw as she had his weariness. It drowned her, robbing the air from her lungs and returned tears to her eyes. Sorrow washed over her next, then guilt again. This time the emotion came through clear enough for her to understand it. He had not killed her parents. He felt responsible for failing to stop their deaths, just as she did.

The regret that came last was hers alone. But before she could apologize, he turned his back on her.

"We have a lot of traveling to do before we can rest tonight. You can come with me or you can stay. I don't care which, but know this, Meaghan." He glanced over his shoulder. His eyes and face were devoid of emotion, the wall he had erected earlier to keep her out fixed back in place. "If I had intended to kill you, I would have done so long before now."

He picked up the backpack and walked into the forest.

CHAPTER FIVE

HER FINGERS hurt. Meaghan held them up in the moonlight to examine the red creeping up her skin, and then blew on them in one last attempt to warm them. Shoving her hands back into her pockets, she tried to focus on something else to take her mind off the pain. Her lungs did not help in the effort. She felt like she inhaled steel wool with each breath of cold air. Neither did her feet. They felt like sledgehammers. Too much snow had fallen over the past few hours, burying the path in front of them in white powder so that each step forced snow into her sneakers and soaked her socks and jeans. Before the storm had dissipated, sleet had mixed with the snowfall, coating the trees in tentacles of ice. If she had been at home, warm in front of the fireplace, she would have appreciated the winter storm for its pristine beauty. Out here, subjected to its hostile side, she loathed it. Even the stars resembled tiny icicles hanging in the sky. If they grew too heavy and fell like daggers around her, she would not be surprised. It would be a fitting end to this night.

Although she could no longer sense Nick's feelings, it did not take a special talent to understand his anger. He held his body stiff as he navigated the forest at a brisk pace. At times, she had trouble keeping up, but she thought better of complaining. When he spoke, anger kept his words curt, adding another element of cold to the night. She followed in his footprints, both her steps and movements cautious, and wondered if the trek could be any more miserable.

Despite the long nap she had taken earlier, tiredness plagued her. Her muscles had grown stiff, making it difficult to move. She stifled a yawn, glanced up at the sky again and froze, horrified when the stars moved. They swayed, ebbing closer, inching away, taunting her. She closed her eyes, felt the world spin, and then met darkness.

§

"MEG, WAKE up."

Nick's voice came from far away, and Meaghan ignored it. The darkness enveloped her, a warm and welcoming friend, and she hated to leave the comfort of it for the frigid wilderness she would have to face if she opened her eyes.

"Come on, Meg. I know you can hear me. I need you to wake up now."

He sounded closer this time. The air smelled of mildew, wet hay, and dust and though it still held the edge of chill, it no longer bit her skin. She stirred, turning so she felt something tickle her cheek. A blanket, she realized, and drew it up to her chin. A pair of arms tightened on the outside of it.

"That's it, Meg. Not much further. Open your eyes for me, okay?"

Her eyelids felt like cement and it took all her effort to pull them

39

open. When she did, a flickering light assaulted her. It seemed unnatural after the past few hours spent walking in the dark and she turned away from it. She felt the soft wool of Nick's sweater brush her cheek, and looked up at his worried face. She lay nestled in his lap, her head cushioned against his chest as he held her.

He smiled. "Welcome back. You scared me for a while there."

"I'm sorry," she muttered. Turning her head, she tried to gauge her surroundings. A scan of the room revealed a packed dirt floor. Hay tufts littered the floor in spots. In others, the hay had been stacked into bales and piles. Exposed beams framed a high roof, though holes marred its protection, baring a near-black sky. In front of them, a small bonfire provided a barrier against the cold as it cast flickering light into the far corners of the barn.

She sat up, felt her world pitch, and succumbed to Nick's arms when he eased her back down.

"Not so fast," he said. Retrieving the plaid blanket she had tossed aside, he drew it over her. "Rest for a while. I have something which will help you." He picked up a tin cup at his side, and then eased her up so she sat. Keeping an arm behind her back to steady her, he handed her the cup.

Taking a sniff of the liquid in the cup, she wrinkled her nose when the smell of rotting dandelions assaulted her. "What is this?"

"It's a root," he responded, "made into tea."

She sat up fully, propping her elbows on her knees so she could hold the cup between her hands. "What's it called?"

"Jicab." Nick stood and walked to the fire. He picked up a stick and then tapped it against several logs, moving them so the flames blazed higher. "It's used as medicine for everything from headaches to stomachaches, or in your case, exhaustion. You passed out. It should help you feel better."

Meaghan sniffed the drink again and had her doubts. Steeling her stomach, she took her first sip. Its flavor did not improve much over its smell. It moved from sour to bitter, visiting salty in between, and finished with a licorice undercurrent which made her never want to eat the candy again. She gagged in the effort to swallow the first mouthful.

Nick grinned. "Terrible, isn't it? I wish I could say it gets better, but it doesn't. You'll get used to it though."

"How much do I have to drink?"

"All of it."

Her eyes fell to the muddy liquid. Her stomach rolled with the thought. "Are you serious?"

Nick did not respond, but a quick glance at his stony face gave her his answer. She sighed, corralled her bravery, and took a large gulp. The tea overwhelmed her tongue and she almost spit it out. Pinching her nose before she lifted the drink to her lips again, she closed her eyes, and tossed back the cup, chugging its contents. It burned going down, but the pain lasted only a moment before the warmth began. Her toes heated first. Her fingers warmed next. The throbbing eased from her head, and then the heaviness sitting deep within her muscles disappeared. No medicine had worked this well for her before and those that had come close had left her feeling hazy and sleepy. This tea had the opposite effect. She felt energized.

She stared at her hands, at the natural shade that returned to them, and smiled. "This stuff is amazing. Where did you get it?"

Nick slid his hands into his pockets. He nodded toward the backpack resting a foot away from her on the floor. "From there, with the cup."

"My father packed it?" she asked.

Nick nodded. "As well as a few other things. Matches, some energy bars, and a medical kit."

"How did he know we'd need it?"

Nick shrugged. "Who knows? It doesn't really matter, does it?"

It did to her, and she had a feeling Nick knew the answer, but she did not want to start another argument. At least not until she had fully recovered. She looked down at the blanket and ran her fingers along the frayed edge of it. "Did he pack this as well?"

"No," Nick answered, and sat down beside her. "I found it in the back of the barn."

Meaghan placed the cup beside her and drew the blanket around her shoulders. "I don't remember having jicab before," she said.

"That's because you haven't had it. Vivian and James kept their supply for emergencies. Since the medicines here are adequate, they never needed to use it."

"It's not from here, like you claim they aren't." He nodded and she turned to study the fire. "You said you'd answer my questions. Will you tell me where it's from?"

"Soon," he told her. "Once we get to our destination."

Her eyes found his, and they appeared dark to her, much as they had the night before when she had showed up at his door. The moon was not shadowing them now, and she wondered if it had not been last night, too. "You said you 'blocked' me earlier. You're doing it now, aren't you?"

He nodded. "It's necessary."

"Why?" she asked, and then pushed out a breath in frustration. "Never mind. I'd rather know what you're doing first. I'd think you were crazy if I weren't feeling the result of whatever you're doing. You seem empty to me."

"Is that what it feels like?" He took her hand in his. "I'm sorry. That has to be frustrating for you."

"Not as frustrating as not knowing what's happening. I don't know what you're doing. I don't know where we're going. I don't even know who my parents were, if you're telling me the truth and they were lying about their past." She removed her hand from his. "You want me to trust you, to follow you, yet you won't explain anything. Trust goes both ways."

Nick clasped his hands together. "Everything you want to know is related. It's also complicated, and it's going to take some time to explain."

"We have time," she responded. "I have no intention of walking through any more snowdrifts in the dark, so as far as I'm concerned, you have several hours until daylight to explain."

"Fine. If you want to hear it now, I'll tell you, but you have to promise you'll listen to everything before reacting."

She nodded and waited for him to continue.

"You're an Empath. You sense people's emotions."

She stared at him, certain she had misheard him, but when he said nothing further, she had no other choice but to acknowledge what he had said. "An Empath?" she managed. "Are you trying to tell me I can feel other people's emotions?"

"Exactly."

She shook her head, wondering if the tea had developed side effects after all. "I was wrong. You are crazy."

"I am not," Nick protested. "I realize this is difficult to comprehend, but—"

"Difficult doesn't begin to cover it," she interrupted. "Empathic powers and psychic abilities don't exist. They're not real."

"Then how do you always know what people are feeling, even when they're trying to hide their emotions? Isn't that why you chose to study psychology?"

His question stopped her argument for a moment. She wanted to respond that she could read body language, as she had always thought, but she knew better now. "There are case studies," she told him. "We reviewed them in one of my classes. Most of the people who claimed to have those abilities were exposed as fakes. There has to be another explanation."

"Most of them were," Nick said, "but not all of them. What about the ones who weren't proven to be fakes?"

She shrugged. "They fooled the testers or the test results were inconclusive. It doesn't mean the abilities exist. It means the explanation wasn't available."

"Or the explanation was outside the realm of common understanding." Nick grabbed Meaghan's hand when she tried to pull away from him. "Keep an open mind, please. I'd think after today you wouldn't find the abnormal so easy to dismiss."

"I wouldn't if the explanation wasn't impossible." Or rather, if the possibility meant a future she could face. She shook her head, refusing to believe Nick, refusing to allow images of the creatures and what they had done to her parents to surface in her mind. She had to hold on to logic. She had to believe she could return to her life. Her normal life. "There are always valid explanations for things which appear abnormal."

"The explanations for today and for your ability may not be what you'd consider normal, but they are valid. Your ability stems from a power, and my ability to block you from reading me also stems from a power."

"Right," Meaghan scoffed. "So you're saying I'm magical and so are the other people who claim to be empathic or psychic."

"Not quite, but close. Your ability is a true power. It's stronger and it works differently than the ones you learned about in the case studies."

"I see. So those people don't have powers."

"Their ancestors did. They have the ability because it stems from a rare, genetic variation of your power."

She stood. "This is nuts."

"It's not."

"It is. I don't know what game you're trying to play, but I'm not a child. I stopped believing in the supernatural a long time ago. Powers don't exist except in comic books and magic belongs to rabbits in top hats."

"And you and me," Nick said, standing to face her, "as well as Vivian and James."

Meaghan shook her head again and scanned the barn for a way out. She felt more certain now than ever that Nick had grown delusional. He may not seem dangerous, but his behavior could escalate. If he believed he could perform magic, there would be no limit to what he might attempt.

The heavy, wood doors at the entrance to the barn would be impossible to open quickly enough to provide an escape, but the side door would work, if she could figure out a way to get around Nick. He blocked her path to it.

She walked to the fire, feigning interest in the flames, and in the conversation. "What powers did Mom and Dad have?"

"James could control electricity," Nick answered.

"That's handy," Meaghan commented. "So he was stealing it all this time instead of paying the electric company?"

Nick narrowed his eyes at her. "You're the one who wanted to have this conversation."

"I wanted the truth, not some tall tale. Next, you'll tell me Mom's baking skills stemmed from a power. Why are we out here, Nick? Is this some sort of joke you and my parents cooked up? If so, it's not funny."

"It's not a joke," Nick said. He came to stand beside her and though his body was stiff, his voice remained soft. She could hear pain in it, but she still could not read the emotion on his face. "The powers are real, Meg. You can sense people's emotions and I can sense people, too, but in a different way. I can feel the presence of their powers, and I can tell when they're dangerous. I can also block people from sensing me, which is why my power works against

46

yours."

"And Dad could control electricity," she stated. "Or so you claim. I never saw him do anything out of the ordinary."

"Some powers don't work here. His didn't, and our sensing powers weren't as strong."

"Our?"

"James', Vivian's, and mine. We all had the same sensing powers, but we each had different personal powers."

"I see." Meaghan glanced at him, and then past him to the door. Taking a step away from the fire, she positioned her feet to run. "Did Mom's personal power work?"

"For the most part. You would have considered her a psychic, but where we're from, she's a Seer. She could look into the future and make predictions."

"A Seer?" Meaghan's eyes snapped to Nick's.

"Yes. She was gifted. One of the best Seers I've ever—"

"She couldn't see the future," Meaghan insisted. Her hands balled into fists at her sides. "That's impossible."

"As impossible as you sensing emotions," Nick countered. "Damn it, Meg. I'm getting tired of this conversation. If you don't believe me, fine, but—"

"She couldn't," Meaghan repeated. Her voice wavered and she closed her eyes over tears. "If she could, she would have seen. She would have stopped..." her voice failed her and so did her control. Visions of the attack filled her mind. She could see her mother stretched over the stairs, eyes vacant in death. She could see her father taking his last breath, could hear it as if it had just happened. If

47

Nick told the truth, how could her mother have seen the horror in advance and allowed it to happen?

Nick put his arms around her. "Vivian didn't know she and James would die," he whispered. "Seers can't control their visions."

Meaghan turned her face into his shoulder. "Then what good is being able to see the future if she couldn't prevent her own death? It isn't right."

"No, it isn't," he agreed. "I've wondered the same thing since we left their house, and I've wondered what good my powers are if I couldn't use them to save Vivian and James. I'm supposed to be able to sense Mardróch, but I couldn't when it mattered most." He pressed his forehead to hers. "I loved them, you know."

"I know," she responded. "You became close to my parents over the past year."

"It's more than that." He drew his fingers down her arm, taking her hand in his before stepping back. "Vivian and James were my aunt and uncle."

"Wait." Embarrassment warmed Meaghan's cheeks as she remembered the kiss they had shared. She removed her hand from his. "We're cousins?"

"No." Nick drew a deep breath. "Vivian and James weren't your real parents. They protected you after your parents died. They brought you here with the intent of telling you the truth when you turned eighteen."

"Here?" she echoed, and the word tasted heavy in her mouth. He had used it several times tonight, but it had not occurred to her until now he had meant something other than a different country or maybe some tribal island few had mapped. "By here you mean?"

"Earth. We're from another world."

Meaghan's mouth dropped open and though she wanted to argue, her voice failed her. What could she say? Even if she could accept the rest of what Nick had said, this fell so deeply into the realm of the impossible that she could not even begin to entertain it. Her parents had loved her too much to not be her own. And Earth was the only world which could sustain life. No other world could exist to allow Nick's explanation to be true. Everyone knew that.

So why did she feel sick?

Nick walked away from her, clearing a direct path to the door, but she could move no easier than she could speak. He picked up the backpack from the floor, opened it, and then pulled out a velvet pouch. "James packed this, too. He and Vivian intended to give it to you when they told you the truth. Vivian felt it would help you understand."

"Understand what?" she choked out.

He pressed the pouch into her hand. "Just open it, okay?"

Her eyes dropped to the item. It felt heavy. So did her head. A haze descended over her, muting color and sound. Her mouth grew dry. Her tongue felt swollen. She swallowed air past it, but could not manage much else.

"Meg," Nick begged, covering her hand with his. "Please."

The soft material rubbed against her skin, the sensation of it breaking through her numbness and she did as he asked. She fumbled with the string, untying it after several attempts, and then tipped the pouch over. A large, silver amulet slid into her palm. From the center of its intricate flower border, a purple stone glistened by the firelight. She gasped. "It can't be."

"It is," he confirmed. "It's the one from your dreams."

"It was my mom's?" she asked and looked up at him. "Is that why I dreamed about it?"

"Yes and no. It was your mom's, but not Vivian's. You weren't having dreams, Meg. You were remembering our world. You were seeing your birth mother."

She stared at the amulet again. "I don't understand. Some of those dreams were nightmares."

Nick brought a hand to Meaghan's shoulder, drawing her close again. "You were young. We weren't sure what you would remember, if anything. You were with your mother when she died."

"The woman with the black hair was my mother?"

"Yes."

"It's not true," Meaghan protested, though she could not find conviction in the words. Her life had been a lie. The people she thought were her parents had been strangers. But the love she had felt from the woman had been real. And it came to her through a nightmare.

She pushed from Nick's arms. "They were dreams, and I refuse to let you use them to convince me your delusion is real."

"Then why are you holding the necklace from your dreams in your hand?"

"Dreams use memories from our subconscious. I remember Mom wearing it from when I was a kid. That's all."

"And the Mardróch? How can you explain them? They're not

from this world either."

"They could have been from a military or science experiment." She crossed her arms over her chest. "Or you could have drugged me. I still think that's the most likely scenario."

"So it's easier to believe I'm a psychopath or creatures escaped from some sci-fi experiment than it is to believe the truth?"

"That I'm from another world that can't exist? Yes." She tossed the necklace aside. It landed with a thud on the ground, then skidded a short distance, leaving a groove in the dirt. "It's a trinket. It proves nothing."

"It's not a trinket." Nick retrieved the amulet from the ground, dusting it off before pressing it back into her palm. "Our world does exist and it's similar to Earth in a lot of ways. But where you have technology, we have powers. The people of Earth can't visit our world, but we can travel here. We use portals. When you were a child, Vivian used one to save your life."

Nick tightened his fingers over Meaghan's, forcing her to hold the amulet. "This is an heirloom. It's been in your family for a thousand years. It holds the emotional energy of your ancestors, and like them, you have magic. You may not like it, but it doesn't change the truth. Your Empath power should allow you to sense the emotions in the necklace."

"Forget it," she snapped, yanking her hand from his to free it. "I won't play your game any longer. If you want to kill me then do it. Otherwise, I'm leaving."

She stood her ground, expecting Nick to argue further, but he nodded instead. Retreating to the blanket, he dropped his head into his hands, and she saw her chance. She ran for the door, freezing halfway when sorrow washed over her. It overwhelmed her, stalling the breath in her lungs in the same way it stalled her legs.

"I'm sorry, Aunt Viv," Nick whispered behind her.

The sorrow swelled. Nick no longer blocked her, and even though Meaghan could not see him, she could feel him. It made no sense, but in the intensity of his emotion, she knew the truth. She also realized that whatever power she owned was growing stronger.

She looked down at her hand, at the amulet still clutched within it, and felt a low vibration coming from the metal that she had not noticed before. She would not consider it an emotion, but it did speak to her. It contained a historical presence, as if the amulet had stored memories. Wide-eyed, she turned to face Nick and felt relief wash over him before he blocked her once more.

"What was my mother's name?" she asked.

"Adelina."

"And my father?"

"Edáire. We called him Ed."

A foreign world with a familiar name. She smiled, finding that somehow comforting. She returned her gaze to the amulet and memories trickled back to her. "Adelina never took this off," she said. "Every time I remember her, she had it around her neck. But it glowed then. Now it's dull." Tracing her finger over the stone, she frowned. It felt too smooth. "It's glass," she realized. "I thought it was an amethyst."

Nick stood and approached. He pressed his finger on the glass, opening it to reveal a shallow compartment. "It held a stone once.

Someone stole it. Are you all right?"

Meaghan nodded. "I'm sorry I doubted you."

"I understand. It's a lot to absorb." He closed the necklace again, and then lifted it over her head, releasing it so it hung against her chest. "Keep this safe. It's the only thing left of your mother."

She tucked it under her shirt. "What do we do now?"

"Sleep," he answered. "We can set out at first light."

"Where are we going?"

"Home," he replied. "It's time to bring you home."

CHAPTER SIX

ANTICIPATION GREW, building within her until it hardened her muscles with tension. It overwhelmed both the excitement and nervous energy that preceded—preceded what exactly? Meaghan did not know. She also did not know the source for the sudden rush of emotions. She reacted to them. Her muscles trembled. Her nerves tingled. Her breath came short and shallow. Her mind felt the flush of adrenaline and stood on guard for whatever came next, but the reaction did not belong to her. At first, she thought it stemmed from a dream, but when she opened her eyes and excitement remained, she realized the danger in it.

The fire flickered in front of her, casting shadows across the barn walls. Though the flames had dwindled, their presence told her she had not been sleeping long. The foreign emotions intensified, hammering through her mind like overlapping percussions, and she felt her own fear rise in response. She rolled onto her side to wake Nick, surprised to find he no longer lay next to her. She sat up, scanned the room, and discovered him by the barn door holding a bucket. He brought the bucket to the fire and set it down.

"Can you feel them?" he asked, keeping his voice low.

She threw off the blanket and stood. "I can feel their emotions. Anxiety, tension, and excitement, mostly. Who do they belong to?"

"The police. I'm guessing they found the car." He walked over to her, then picked up the blanket, and folded it. "Do you have your mother's necklace?"

She brought a hand to her throat. Finding the thin silver chain, she traced her fingers down to the amulet and nodded. "It's safe."

"Good. Keep it on for now. We need to open the portal."

"I thought you said we had to travel more." He did not respond and she studied his face, trying to gauge how he felt. "How far away are we from where we need to be?"

"I'm not sure. I left a pulse stone at the portal location where I landed when I first came to Earth. It emits a magical beacon." He located the backpack on the ground, and tucked the blanket inside. "We're at least five miles away."

"Can we sneak out of here without the police seeing us?"

Nick shook his head. "I'm sensing people from every direction. What about you? Can you focus enough to tell where the emotions are coming from?"

She frowned. "I'm afraid not. It's all a big jumble. They're confident, though, and the anticipation is mounting. That's not a good sign."

"No, it's not."

"They're coming," she added, focusing her attention toward the door. "The emotions are getting closer."

"I know. Are you ready to cross over?"

"How?" Meaghan turned her head to stare at him. "If we're five miles away—"

"Portals can be opened anywhere. It would've been more convenient to reach the pulse stone before we opened one, but we have no other options. Not unless we want to try opening one from jail." Nick handed her the backpack and picked up the bucket again. "It's time."

She slung the backpack over one shoulder. "What do you mean by 'more convenient'? What aren't you telling me?"

"Nothing that can't wait." He tipped the bucket. Water rushed out, turning the fire into hissing embers. Only moonlight remained to cut the darkness, filtering through the roof in faint streams.

The door burst open. Four men in black clothing and bulletproof vests ran into the room, their guns and flashlights drawn and pointed at Nick.

"Freeze," one man yelled. "You're under—"

Nick grabbed her hand and the barn dissolved into white.

§

SHE EXPECTED to feel weightless, like she drifted on air, or to feel compressed and torn as her new world ripped her from her old one. At the least, she expected nausea to accompany her journey. She had read enough science fiction novels and had watched more than her fair share of space-themed television shows to know crossing from one world to another should disrupt her body and shake her mind. Yet she felt nothing.

They had not leapt into a wormhole. Nick had not tugged her

after him into a swirling vortex. She had simply stood in place, the ground solid beneath her feet as the barn disappeared, its wooden roof yielding to an endless sky decorated with brilliant stars and a low hanging moon. A large clearing replaced wood walls and tall trees replaced the policemen. Even the frigid weather warmed to a manageable temperature.

"That was anti-climactic," she quipped.

Nick grinned and let go of her hand. "I'm afraid reality can't compare to fiction where portal travel is concerned."

He turned to scan the horizon and his grin dissolved. She tried to sense the emotions behind the mood change, but he blocked her still. Inhaling a deep breath, she used the motion to calm her mounting anxiety. Today had been more than she could handle. She chased a tear away from the corner of her eye, and then tucked her hands into her pockets when Nick turned to look at her.

"It's not as cold here," she said. "Is the climate more temperate?"

"It's about the same," he responded. "We're a season behind where you lived on Earth. It's autumn now. It'll start getting colder soon, but it should be better travel for us."

"That's good." Rocking back on her heels, she glanced away, toward the distance where she thought he had been looking. Through the darkness, she could see the faint outline of a mountain range. "Can you sense any better how far we have to travel?"

He shook his head. "I won't be able to tell where we are until daylight. We'll need to stay put for the rest of the night."

The apprehension in his voice drew her gaze back to him. She scanned his face in an effort to sense what he felt, but again found emptiness. He walked to a fallen tree and sat down.

"I think it would be best for you to get some rest," he told her. "If you lay the blanket on the grass here, you should be comfortable enough to sleep for a few hours. I'd like to be moving again at dawn."

She slipped the backpack off her shoulder. Opening it, she removed the blanket and spread it on the ground before joining him on the log.

"You need sleep too," she said.

"I slept enough. I'll stand guard. I'll wake you when it's time to go."

She frowned, then clasped her hands in her lap and closed her eyes, attempting to see if she could force her power past his block. She soon realized the effort was as useless as trying to speak a foreign language without taking any lessons. The ability to read emotions came naturally to her and as a result, she knew nothing about controlling it. She tightened her hands in her lap and turned her gaze toward the mountains again in an effort to hide her growing frustration.

There were four peaks. They followed each other, black against the night sky so that she almost could not make out the last one in the distance. They reminded her of the mountains near her home where she and her parents had camped every year since she was a small child. Their most recent trip had been at the end of the summer. She could still smell the campfire and hear her mother laughing at her father's ghost stories. It had been one of their best trips, although they had had to cut it short so Meaghan could meet with her advisor at the university. The appointment had seemed important then, but now she wished she had moved it to have more time with her parents. Grief stabbed through her and she closed her eyes against it.

"What's wrong?" Nick asked. She opened her eyes, but did not respond. "Meg, talk to me."

"I'm fine."

"You're not." He placed a hand on her arm. "You're upset. You're trying to hide it, but I can tell. What's going on?"

"I'm…" she hesitated, and then sighed, "frustrated. I don't like this."

He raised his hand to her cheek. "I realize the situation is hard, but by tomorrow we'll be able to—"

"I can deal with the situation." She brushed his hand off and stood, turning to face him. "I don't like you blocking me. I miss my parents. I'm still having a hard time believing I'm on a different world, and this blocking thing makes me feel odd, like there's something missing."

"That's because there is," he told her. "Your power is a part of you and having it blocked is unnatural. I promise it's for the best."

"Why?" She crossed her arms in front of her. "What are you hiding from me?"

"I'm not hiding anything."

"You are. I know you're not telling me something, and now you can sense what I'm feeling."

"What makes you think I can sense your feelings?"

"You said you knew I was upset. How else could you know?"

He laughed, and she narrowed her eyes at him. Her frustration gave way to anger. "You think this is funny? You drop me in the middle of nowhere, then you take away my power and you think it's *funny*?"

He stopped laughing. Standing up, he bracketed her shoulders with his hands. "Your power is still your own," he told her. His eyes met hers and she sensed him again. Although she felt anxiety and sorrow in him, humor overpowered those emotions. The warmth of it almost brought a smile to her lips. She fought the reaction, still irritated he found her anger humorous. "See?" he said, blocking her again. "I haven't taken your power."

"So why do you block it? What are you afraid I'll discover?"

"Nothing." He dropped his hands from her shoulders. "Your power is stronger here and I'm afraid my emotions will be overwhelming for you."

"You can't be certain, not if you don't let me try."

"I already know what will happen," he responded. "I wish you'd trust me."

"How am I supposed to trust you when I can't tell what you're feeling?" she countered and then frowned when a smile returned to his lips. "You're laughing at me again."

"Not quite, although I may be soon if you don't stop complaining. You don't get the humor in what you said, do you?"

Meaghan glared at him instead of responding and he sat down on the blanket. "Sit, please," he said, patting the area beside him. When she refused to move, he took her hand and pulled her down. "I'm tired of battling with you. We're still friends, aren't we?"

"That has nothing to do with this."

"It does. You're not acting like it right now."

"That isn't fair." She crossed her legs and then her arms. "I'm entitled to be upset over this."

"You are," he agreed. "You've been through a lot, but I'm not your enemy. I'm trying to help you, so please stop fighting with me." She nodded and he lifted a hand to her arm. "I can always tell when you're upset, you know. You get tense and you draw into yourself. Your shoulders tighten toward your ears," he brought his hand to her shoulder and she noticed the tension in it for the first time. She exhaled a slow breath, forcing her muscles to relax. "And you bring your arms in. You cross them or you clutch them in front of you."

"I didn't realize."

"I did," he said. "I've learned your cues over the past year, and not the ones only associated with negative emotions. Your eyes crinkle when you're trying to hold back a laugh, like the time you played that prank on Vivian last fall, replacing her pumpkin pie with a salted one. And you narrow your eyes right before you make a joke or a sarcastic comment. It's cute, and it's one of the clues anyone without your power would have to learn in order to gauge your emotions."

"So you think it's funny that I have to learn to be like everyone else," she realized. She dropped her arms and he took her hand in his. "I guess I can see that, but it's frustrating for me. I thought I was good at reading people and it turns out I don't know how to do it at all. I wish I could. It would make this world easier for me to understand."

"Why?"

"Because there's too much to learn." She let go of his hand. Lifting her palms to her face, she rubbed away more tears. "It would be so much easier if I didn't have to learn how to read you. If I could sense your emotions, I would know more about what's happening."

"That would be true if you were a mind reader, but you're not. You don't know what's happening. You guess. You guessed right more often than not on Earth because you were familiar with your environment. You don't know anything about this world and being able to read my emotions could lead to bad guesses, which could get you hurt, or worse. I can't have that. It's my job to protect you and I won't let anything happen to you."

"What if I promise not to guess?" she asked. "I can—"

"You can't," he said, then took her hand in his again when she looked away. "It's second nature to you, and until you learn to control your power, you'll fall back on that habit." He brought his fingers to her chin and guided her eyes back to his. "I'm sorry I found this humorous. I shouldn't have. It was difficult for me to learn to live in a new world with stifled powers, and I'm sure it's not any easier for you. It will get better though."

"Are you certain?"

"Absolutely." He withdrew his hands and stood, reclaiming his seat on the log. "I think it's time for bed. Starting tomorrow, I'll answer all your questions, so ask me instead of wondering, okay?"

Meaghan nodded and stretched out on the blanket. Silence descended over the forest, interrupted only by the passing song of a few crickets and the occasional curious hoot from a distant owl. She turned onto her stomach, propping her head up on her fists to look up at Nick. "Will you answer one question for me tonight?" she asked.

"Sure."

"What did you mean when you said it's your 'job' to protect me?"

He leaned forward, propping his elbows on his knees. "I guess the simplest way to explain is I'm part of a special group of people with a rare combination of powers. Our powers are designed to protect. Some of us are assigned to protect specific people and others are assigned groups of people."

"And you're assigned to me?"

"Yes. Shortly after you were born, I began training for that purpose. Vivian protected you when you were on Earth and now it's my job."

Meaghan yawned and flopped onto her back. "Why was I on Earth?"

"That's your third question and I only promised to answer one. I'll explain it all in time, but not tonight. You need to sleep."

"One more question," she said, then pushed forward when he did not object. "Does your group of people have a name?"

"Guardians," he replied. "We're called Guardians."

CHAPTER SEVEN

DAWN CAME too soon. Meaghan watched the sun push a crimson curtain through the sky, then waited a few extra minutes before she turned on her side to search for Nick. He stood over her, studying the forest with an intensity that left her wondering if the shadows blanketing his face had little to do with the disappearing night. Her sleep had been plagued with dreams of her parents and she had woken several times with tears soaking her cheeks. Nick had stirred beside her each time, drawing an arm around her body to offer comfort, and she doubted he had slept any better than she had.

His eyes drifted from the trees to meet her gaze. Understanding passed between them before he sat down next to her, taking her hand with the movement.

"Is it time to go?" she asked, sitting up.

He nodded, squeezing her hand before standing and pulling her up with him. "I found some fruit for breakfast. It's over by the log. Why don't you go eat while I fold the blanket?"

She did as he asked, and soon they found their way deep into the forest. The leaves overhead formed a canopy so dense Meaghan felt dawn had slipped back into twilight. There appeared to be no set path and at times the vines and overgrowth made passage slow. Nick used a stick to push limbs out of their way as they moved. Only an occasional noise greeted them from the depths, the warble of a bird or leaves rustling as a small animal ran from them, and it added to the darkness pressing down on Meaghan's senses.

Her heart ached, squeezed by memories of her parents' deaths and she gave in to the pain, allowing a sullen mood to fill the hours. Neither of them spoke until Meaghan caught sight of a bright blue bird flying overhead. By the time a second and a third darted past, recognition had brought a smile to her face. "Those look like blue jays," she said.

Nick glanced up without breaking their pace and nodded. "They are. I'm surprised to see them. They're usually skittish around people."

A noise rustled to their left and Meaghan turned in time to catch the tuft of a white tail. A few seconds later, a flash of brown bounded in front of them, almost knocking Nick over. The brown paused long enough for Meaghan to recognize it as a deer before it disappeared into the forest as fast as it had appeared.

She took one look at Nick's ashen face and the oppression that had eclipsed her all morning dissolved into laughter.

Nick scowled at her, and then chuckled as he rubbed at the back of his neck, his cheeks flush with embarrassment. "I should've seen that coming. I was concentrating too much on sensing my way, I guess."

"You couldn't sense him?"

"Sensing deer is not one of my skills. I didn't know he was there until he jumped in front of me. I think we scared him."

"Not as much as he scared you," Meaghan teased, and then curbed the urge to laugh again when Nick narrowed his eyes at her. "I didn't realize so many of the animals would be the same here. It's comforting to think this world isn't so different from my own."

"Some of them are the same, but some aren't, even if they appear to be. You need to be cautious until you're certain of what you're facing."

"What do you mean?"

"I mean being too comfortable with something which appears familiar can get you hurt." Nick placed his hands on her shoulders and turned her around. "Look into the higher branches."

She scanned the trees surrounding them. When a blue bird twittered at her from a high branch to her right, she frowned. "Are you trying to tell me the jay is dangerous?"

"Not the bird. That," he pointed at a spot above the bird. At first, Meaghan saw nothing, but then a flicker caught her attention. A small monkey, no bigger than the size of a kitten, hung from a branch by a long, thin tail. It watched them, cocking its head back and forth with interest. She took a step toward it, stopping when Nick's hand tightened on her shoulder.

"Don't get too close," he said.

"Is he really dangerous?" she asked. "He doesn't seem big enough to cause harm to anything larger than a banana." She took another step so she stood underneath the tree. The monkey swung on top of the branch, scurrying away from them. "Darn it. I scared him."

"Not quite," Nick said. The monkey reappeared in a lower branch, only feet from Meaghan. It crept toward her, and then froze again.

"I've never seen a monkey this close before," she said. The monkey chattered in excitement. It extended a small paw toward her and she reached up in turn.

"Don't!" Nick snatched her hand from the air seconds before the monkey's fingers had the chance to close around her wrist. The animal leapt from the tree limb, catching the branch with its tail so it swung in front of them before it turned its focus on Nick. Its eyes glowed red and it hissed, baring a mouth full of jagged teeth.

Meaghan jumped, and then clutched her hands in front of her heart as the monkey swung back onto the branch, screeching in anger.

"That's not a monkey, is it?" she whispered, refusing to take her eyes from the animal. It spotted the jay moving through the tree and swung after it, an unnatural silence masking its movement.

"It's a type of monkey called a dranx," Nick answered and put an arm around her shoulder. "Are you okay?"

"Yes," she assured him, though her voice shook. "Could it have hurt me?"

"Its teeth are laced with poison. It wouldn't have killed you, but it would have made you ill for a few days."

Meaghan trailed her eyes to a limb further up the tree where the bird had found a new perch. The dranx landed in front of it.

"You'll want to look away," Nick told her, though the warning came too late. The dranx pounced on the bird, sinking its teeth into the feathered body of its prize before disappearing with it into the canopy of the tree.

Meaghan gasped, and then turned, burying her head in Nick's chest. "That was terrible," she said, her voice muffled against his sweater. He wrapped his arms around her.

"I'm sorry. I needed you to understand the danger here, but I didn't mean for you to see that."

"Not everything's the same," she repeated his previous warning and stepped out of his embrace. She glanced toward the tree once more to ensure the dranx had gone and then returned her attention to Nick. "Why didn't the bird fly away? It had time."

"It couldn't. The dranx monkey has the power to paralyze its victims when they look into its eyes."

"But you looked at it and you're fine."

"Its power is in proportion with its size. It only works on birds and other small animals. Its poison is deadly to those animals as well."

"Oh." Meaghan crossed her arms over her stomach, controlling the shudder that crept up her back. "So it's poisonous and it has the ability to paralyze its victims. Can it do anything else?"

"It can move without making any sound, which is why you didn't notice it at first. This particular dranx has been trailing us for a few miles. We heard it only when it wanted us to hear. Let's start moving again," he said. "We have a long walk ahead of us today."

Meaghan nodded and he turned, leading the way again. She stayed close behind him, scanning the forest with more vigilance and wariness than she had when they had started out in the morning. Although she could no longer see the monkey, and she had no doubt it had fled the area, it refused to leave her mind.

"How did you know it was there?" she asked after a minute. "If you couldn't hear it, how did you know?"

"My ability to sense things isn't limited to people," he answered. "And it isn't random. I can tune into magic when I want to, like the pulse stone I left at the portal, and danger triggers that sense automatically." He glanced at her over his shoulder. "Even the smallest forms of malicious magic can trigger my power."

Worry lines creased Meaghan's forehead, and Nick stopped again. "What's wrong?"

"I'm confused," she said. "Is your village magical?"

"Not to the point where I can sense it from here."

He reached a wall of vines. Tapping them with the stick, he waited a moment before parting them with his arms. He let her through and then followed.

"But you know where you're going," she said when he took the lead again. "You told me last night you weren't sure where we were, but it was dark. You seemed more certain this morning, so I assumed you were following the trail again, like you followed the pulse stone at home." She hesitated. "You do know the way, right?"

"Not exactly."

They stopped at a tree lying across their path. Its trunk rose higher than Nick's shoulders. Its length disappeared in both directions through the thickening forest, its ends nowhere in sight.

"You need to boost me over," Nick decided. "I'll pull you up from the top."

"All right." Meaghan crouched on the ground and cupped her hands, launching him into the air when he stepped his left foot into her palms. He straddled the tree before leaning down to grab her hand, and hoisting her up beside him.

She faced him, swinging one leg over the tree to mimic his posture. "What do you mean by 'not exactly'?" she asked. "When we were on Earth, you said we were five miles away from the portal to your village. We've travelled at least that far today, so we should be close by now. Are you lost?"

"Not exactly," he repeated. He looked over the side of the tree and she followed his gaze. Thick underbrush hid the ground, as well as any rocks that might pose a danger to their landing. He frowned. "I think it's best if I—"

"Stop," Meaghan begged. She pressed her hands into the tree and leaned forward, not caring about the pain the rough bark brought to her palms or the surprise that overtook Nick's face. "You promised you'd answer my questions. 'Not exactly' doesn't answer anything. Are you lost or not?"

"I'm not lost," Nick responded and then sighed when she raised an eyebrow at him. "I'm not," he reassured her. "I just have no idea where we are."

She sat back. "How can you be both?"

"Portals don't work the way you think," he answered. "Each location here is linked to a specific location on Earth. A portal connects those two locations but the geography doesn't line up. I could open a portal here and one a mile away and they could be next to each other on your world or fifty miles apart. There's an intricate formula which would tell me where we are, but I don't have it memorized."

Her mouth went dry. "So we could be half-way around the world from your village?"

Instead of answering, he dropped his gaze to the ground again and Meaghan touched his hand. "Please, Nick. Tell me that's impossible."

"Theoretically, it's possible," he responded. "Although I'd prefer to think we aren't. I'm not in the mood to find our way across three continents and two oceans."

"Me neither," she said, and then swung her other leg over the tree when he jumped down from the trunk. He extended a hand to her and she took it, landing beside him in the brush. She stepped from the greenery, following him through the forest once more.

"So we're stuck wandering around here until something looks familiar?" she asked.

"Not quite," he told her. "As I said, I'm not lost. I recognize the mountain range we're walking toward, but I think we're on the wrong side of it." He helped her over a smaller tree lying in their path, and then dropped her hand as they kept moving. "We should be at the base of the first mountain by tomorrow night. If I'm right, we'll reach my village in a couple of weeks."

"Weeks," Meaghan echoed, barely managing to form the word. She crossed her arms over her stomach, slowing her pace and then stopping so Nick could not see her tears. She closed her eyes to chase them away.

She had never minded being in the wilderness and had often enjoyed it, but weeks without proper food or a shower, weeks without a comfortable bed, and weeks dealing with evil-looking animals and aching muscles did not thrill her.

Getting lost did not either. She opened her eyes as a soft wind tickled her cheek, and scanned the forest ahead. She caught sight of Nick, his form no more than a distant outline scattering leaves, and she chased after it.

"The wind brought me here on a gust of luck, I'd say."

A breezy tenor stilled Meaghan's feet. She spun around, looking for the source of the voice, but saw only the movement of loose vines dancing in the wind.

"Jumpy, aren't you?"

She snapped her head to the left. An echoing laugh followed. She turned a full circle, watching for any movement or a potential hiding place that would give away the man's location, but she found nothing.

"Earth, water, fire, and air," the voice sang as the breeze gusted stronger, swirling leaves in a vortex around her. "They are your friends, but you'd best beware. The forest path you travel along will soon bring you to a deadly wrong. Find the way the water leads you, and you will find the man who sees you."

The words came from every direction. Meaghan's heart raced in her chest and she followed its lead, speeding after Nick through the forest. Fire scorched her lungs and panic froze her mind.

She had almost caught up with him when pain ripped through her, a bolt of electricity that sent her screaming to the ground.

CHAPTER EIGHT

HER PALMS hit the ground first in time to prevent her forehead from landing on a rock in the path. She heard thrashing close by and somewhere in the distance, footsteps running toward her. Pain shot through her again as something yanked on her ankle. She screamed and tried to turn over, but her legs refused to budge. Pressing up on her forearms, she felt something hit her on the back and fell to the ground. She struggled against the pressure, wiggling and flailing to get loose, but her attacker's grip tightened. The tightness slid up her legs, pinning down her waist before latching onto her wrists.

She yanked them forward so she could see her attacker and then caught her breath in disbelief. A vine writhed, thickening along her arms. It crawled over the ground toward her head, slithered up her shoulders onto her neck, and constricted. She opened her mouth to cry for help, but no noise escaped. Blackness closed her vision into a narrow tunnel. She dug her nails into the vines on her neck, tearing at them with the last of her strength, and then dropped her hands, surprised when the vines went limp.

Air rushed back into her lungs, sweet and powerful. She held it. Her eyes cleared and the pressure eased from her body. She turned her head in time to see the vine slither into the underbrush, trailing a thick liquid that looked like dark blood. It coiled into a pile and stilled.

She saw the glint of a silver knife in someone's hand. It disappeared, then she felt arms slide underneath her body. Too weak to struggle, she closed her eyes and succumbed to them as they lifted her. When she felt a wool sweater brush against her cheek, she opened her eyes again, relief flooding through her when Nick's face filled her vision.

"You have the worst luck," he muttered. He sat her on a stump so he could examine her wounds. His cursory review seemed to miss nothing. His fingertips coasted over the scrapes on her palms, then parted a tear in her sleeve to reveal a long cut from her elbow to mid-way down her forearm. Red welts along her skin had already begun fading, but his fingers tested them anyway, and she knew they would turn into bruises by tomorrow. He ran his hands down her legs to look for breaks, stopping at her ankle when she released a sharp hiss of air.

He moved her ankle back and forth and side to side. "Does this hurt?"

"Yes," she groaned. He pushed harder and she pitched forward from the pain. "Don't, please."

He let go. Lifting her pant leg, he pulled down her sock to view the skin puffing over the edge of her sneaker. He removed the sneaker, then resumed his light prodding.

"Does this hurt much?" he asked. She shook her head and he sat back on his heels. "The color isn't changing. That's good news, though I think it's sprained. I'll bandage it for now and we'll know more by tomorrow morning." He removed the backpack from his shoulders, pulling open the zippers before glancing at her again and frowning. "You're not wearing your mother's necklace," he said. "Do you have it?"

Panic swelled a lump in Meaghan's throat. She reached for her neck, searching for the amulet with frantic fingers. When she felt its thin chain and realized it had flipped around to her back, she sighed in relief. "It's here," she said, tugging it forward. "It's safe."

"Good. We'd better keep it in the backpack for now."

She pulled it over her head and handed it to him. Nick found the amulet's velvet pouch inside a front pocket of the backpack, stored the necklace inside, then removed a plastic first aid kit from another zippered compartment. After wrapping Meaghan's foot and ankle with a bandage from the kit, he tended to her other wounds, covering them with gauze and antibiotic cream. Once he had finished, he sat back to study her.

"I know it hurts," he said, "but I can't light a fire to make jicab tea right now. As soon as it's safe, I will." He stowed the first aid kit and her sneaker, then stood and slipped the backpack over his shoulders again. "I'm afraid your injury will slow us down, so we don't have time to take a break. Do you want to lean on me?"

"I can try." She took his hand and allowed him to pull her up from the stump. Balancing on her good foot, she leaned against him. He slung an arm around her waist. At first, their movements were tentative and slow, but as they developed a rhythm, matching each other's steps, they were able to move at a quicker pace through the forest.

Meaghan focused on the ground in front of her, careful to avoid tripping over rocks or roots. She did not want to slow their progress even further. When they approached a thick curtain of vines, Nick tapped them with his stick, waited a moment, and then started to walk through them. She hesitated and he tightened his grip on her waist.

"They won't hurt you," he said. "They didn't react when I touched them. They aren't creeper vines."

"Creeper vines," she echoed. A chill ran through her. "Why do you have to test them with the stick? Why can't you sense them?"

"Because they aren't magical." He urged her forward with the slightest pressure from his arm. "They're a different species of vine which can think and react. They attack when they're provoked. You must have stepped on one."

"I was running. I," she hesitated, swallowing hard when a vine brushed her cheek. "I tripped."

"Why were you running?"

"The man. He scared me and…" her voice failed her as another vine brushed her shoulder.

"What man?" Nick stopped and stared at her. A breeze stirred the vines. They swayed around her, brushing her head, her cheek, and her neck. She felt sick. She wanted to run, but her ankle throbbed and she knew it would not hold her.

Fear quickened her breathing. "Please. The vines. I can't…"

He scooped her into his arms. The vines cleared from her sight as he carried her through the curtain, setting her down on the other side in front of an oak tree. She leaned against it, closing her eyes to calm her speeding heart.

"I'm sorry," she said.

She felt Nick's hand on her cheek and she opened her eyes. "I'm the one who should be sorry," he told her. "I'm not doing a good job of protecting you, am I?"

"So far, I'd say you are." She covered his hand with hers and smiled. "I'm still alive, despite my tendency for getting into trouble. At the rate I'm going, you'll wish you'd never met me by tomorrow afternoon."

"We'll see." He chuckled, and then broke their contact, his face turning serious. "Tell me about the man."

"I trailed behind," she confessed, lacing her hands together in front of her. "I shouldn't have, but I did. That's when I heard him. His voice came from every direction. It made it impossible for me to find him, but he had to have been hiding someplace nearby because he said he was watching me."

"This happened right before you ran into the creeper?" he asked. She nodded and he slid a hand between hers. "Did anything else odd happen at the time? Was there wind or water?"

"There was wind," she answered. "The more he spoke, the stronger it got. When it swirled around me, I ran."

"He came on the wind," Nick said and to her surprise, he smiled. "That's fantastic news. We've had wind since, which means he's following us."

"I don't understand. What do you mean?" She stood up straight. He brought his hand to her waist to steady her. "Why is that good news?"

"Because the man you heard has a power I've been trying to sense since we set out this morning. He can use the four elements to send his presence somewhere else. He can also use those elements to see, sometimes for miles."

"So he could see me and talk to me, but he wasn't there?"

"Right."

"Can he see the future?"

"No," Nick responded. "He's not a Seer. He's a Guide. He can't see the future. He can only see what's happening now. But now that he's found you, I can stop concentrating on finding him. He'll lead us to him."

"That is good news then," Meaghan decided, though she had trouble finding relief when her first meeting with the Guide had instilled her with so much fear. "Why did you need to find him?"

"He'll be able to tell us where we are and what the safest route of travel will be."

"I see." This time she allowed relief to take over. She met his smile with one of her own. "That's the best thing I've heard all day. You said he uses the four elements. Do you mean Earth, Water, Fire, and Air? He used those words when he spoke to me."

"Those are the four," Nick confirmed. "What else did he say?"

"Something about water and our path not being safe." She hesitated, trying to focus on her memory of the Guide's song. She could hear the melody in the back of her head, but found the harder she tried to remember the words, the more they stayed out of reach. Her smile faded. "I can't seem to remember. I was scared. All I could think about was escaping from him."

"I understand." Nick squeezed her hand. "I suspect you remembered the most important part. If he said our path isn't safe, we need to be careful. As far as the rest, he'll make sure we get the message again when we need it."

She leaned into him and hoped so.

§

THAT NIGHT, they set up camp in a small clearing, both of them taking shifts watching for danger. The dense forest surrounding the camp permitted a small fire for a short time, so Nick made her a cup of jicab tea and a poultice from wide leaves he found in the forest. The tea eased the pain and the poultice reduced the swelling so that by morning, Meaghan could wear her sneaker again, even if she had to remove the laces.

They ate the last of the energy bars and Meaghan choked down another cup of tea. The tea allowed her to walk most of the day on her own, but by mid-afternoon, she needed Nick's help again. Although a gentle breeze greeted them several times while they travelled, they did not hear from the Guide. Nick remained unconcerned, but Meaghan worried she had ruined their opportunity to find the elusive man.

By late afternoon, a fine mist fell from the sky, turning the soil to mud. They took a break underneath the branches of a tree, picking its orange nuts to satisfy their hunger. Nick called them túrú nuts. He shelled and devoured them by the handful, but she ate them one at a time, savoring the flavor as it moved from rustic and earthen to sweet in her mouth.

After they finished their snack, they continued. The rain fell harder, creating rivers in the forest. Nick led her at a slower pace, cautious of the softening earth. Their clothes and hair stuck to their skin. Their feet sank into the ground, leaving deep impressions behind them as they moved. The sky continued to darken and soon they had trouble seeing in front of them. The forest thinned, giving way to rock outcroppings and large boulders and Meaghan knew they were nearing the mountains. Spotting a clearing up ahead, they hastened their pace, hopeful for a place to rest for the night. Nick froze steps from their goal.

She started to ask if everything was okay, but stopped when he covered her mouth with his hand. He kept his eyes locked on the clearing as he pulled her into a thicker part of the forest, then he pressed his lips to her ear. "Mardróch," he whispered.

In the waning light, she had missed them, but their rotting stench sat in the air. They skulked along the edge of the clearing. One paused, turning his hooded head toward Nick and Meaghan's hiding place, and then glided partway into the forest. She shrank a step back, stilling when Nick tightened his hand on her shoulder. An almost imperceptible shake of his head kept her immobile.

She held her breath. The creature moved closer, raising and lowering his chin in a way that reminded her of a dog sniffing for food. He paused, glided closer, and then turned away. Relieved, she exhaled, but found it impossible to move when the creature raised his hand to signal the others. Three Mardróch charged on Nick and

Meaghan's hiding place. One of them raised his arms and Nick pushed her toward the clearing.

"Run!" he commanded as bolts of electricity shot from the creature's hands, exploding their hiding place. Wood and dirt flew into the air. Despite her protesting ankle, she propelled forward, launching over rocks as she fled. She heard Nick panting close behind her.

Out of the corners of her eyes, she saw the creatures flanking her. They moved faster, unimpeded by the rocky terrain. The electricity they threw into the field corralled her and Nick rather than hitting them. Soon, Meaghan faced a rock wall on the side of a mountain, a dead end. She veered toward one of the creatures in an effort to find another route, and then came to a halt when she realized Nick no longer followed her. She turned and spotted him a few yards away. A Mardróch had blocked his path.

The creature faced Nick, who stood stiff, his feet planted and sinking into the mud. His arms hung at his sides. His face showed no emotion.

Meaghan did not understand why he did not move or try to escape. The creature had not attacked. Nick could fight, yet he did nothing. She took a step toward them, but froze when a wave of fear struck her. Her own terror flooded her brain, masking the foreign emotion at first, but once she felt it, she knew it was Nick's.

She heard a whispering movement behind her and turned her head to see the other two Mardróch approaching. One raised his hand to his hood and she understood. The dranx's eyes had been red because of its power, and so were the Mardróch's.

She averted her eyes when the creature removed his hood and then she took off running. She headed straight for the Mardróch guarding Nick, tackled him, and sent him sprawling to the ground. His body felt denser than she had expected, and she scrambled away to prevent him from flipping her over. He whipped his red eyes toward her, but before he could catch her gaze, a hand grasped her own, yanking her away.

Nick pulled her behind him as they fled from the field toward the mountain. The creatures pursued, howling in anger, a mournful, high-pitched wail that hurt her ears. This time, the electricity cascading from their hands did not aim to miss. Rocks exploded beside them as they charged up the mountain. They dodged around a boulder, then up a dirt path hidden behind it. When Nick spotted a cave large enough for two people, he tugged Meaghan into it, pulling her down at the entrance so they could view the trail.

"They'll see us," she protested, tugging on his hand. "Nick, please," she tried again, quieting when he held his finger to his lips.

The Mardróch circled the boulder. They stared toward the cave and Meaghan tensed for a fight, but the creatures kept moving without slowing down. She shrank back as they glided past, their cloaks swirling into the entrance of the cave inches from touching her arms. They continued up the trail, and then disappeared around a sharp bend. Meaghan waited several minutes to ensure the Mardróch would be out of earshot before she spoke.

"Why didn't they see us?" she asked, keeping her voice low.

"They couldn't," Nick answered as he shifted out of the backpack. He opened it, smiling when she raised an eyebrow at him, but did not continue to explain. He pulled out the blanket and unfolded it. "I realize we'll be a little crowded, but it's safest if we sleep here tonight." He spread half the blanket on his side of the cave, and then flipped the other half in her direction so she could do the same. He sat down. "Tonight, we can get a full night's sleep. It isn't necessary to remain on watch."

"I still don't understand why," she said and sat down opposite him, crossing her feet in front of her. He grinned and she sighed. "You're being juvenile."

"Probably." He chuckled. "It's a relief to be here, and I guess I'm having some fun at your expense." He pointed to the entrance of the cave where several small, white crystals hung from the ceiling. "Those crystals are used for protection. Guardians hang them around cabins and caves throughout dangerous areas to provide safe havens for travelers. The hiding places appear to Guardians or people in need of them. To anyone else, this cave looks like part of the mountain. We're safe for now, but the Mardróch know we're in the area so from now on, we need to be on guard and more discreet about our travels. Tonight, though, there's nothing to worry about."

He stretched out, lying down along the back of the cave and she did the same, filling the space in front of him. Though the rain brought a chill to the air, the small cave consolidated the warmth from their bodies. By morning, she knew their clothes would be dry.

Feeling safe for the first time in days, Meaghan smiled and rested her head on Nick's arm. His steady breathing soothed her and soon she drifted to sleep.

CHAPTER NINE

CLOUDS CONTINUED to blacken the sky as the night's storm persisted, denying morning its rendezvous with the rising sun. Nick could hear the rain pelting the soil, muted thumps hinting of large, skin-soaking drops. The thought of slogging through another mud-filled day did not thrill him, nor did the idea of trying to scramble along narrow mountain paths with limited visibility. Though the forest had been unpleasant, a dense canopy had kept some of the rain at bay. The mountain would not provide the same protection, and the slick rocks would be treacherous with Meaghan's injury.

He considered staying put until the rain subsided. He felt warm, comfortable, and somehow content despite the fact the cave left them little room to move and the floor remained hard and unforgiving underneath the blanket. He guessed it had more to do with the company than the cave. During the night, he had awoken to find Meaghan shivering and had taken her into his arms to warm her.

Although holding her had filled a functional role, he could not deny the pleasure it had brought him. She had curled into him, pressing her face into his neck, her soft breath tickling his skin, and he had fought the urge to stroke her hair in return. She had shifted and he had tightened his arms, drawing her close, but had stopped short of caressing her back. And once, while she had remained lost to a dream that curled a soft smile onto her face, she had lifted her mouth to his.

The electricity he had felt when they connected jolted him backward, knocking his head against the rock wall. He had not been able to decide if he had seen stars in front of his eyes or the crystals flickering against the black night, but the pain had been enough to bring him to his senses. He let her go. Shivering would not harm her and it seemed better than the alternative.

Even without the direct contact, the confined space had left her too close to him. The slightest movement had brought light touches and brush-ups that had elevated his heart rate and bred excitement. Although he hated to admit his weakness, he knew he could not withstand a full day in close quarters with her. Travelling in the rain would be safer than staying in the cave and risking a different danger he never wanted to face. Placing a hand on her back to wake her, he frowned, sensing something from her he did not expect.

He shook her and she opened her eyes. They seemed cloudy. His worry increased, but he kept the emotion from his voice when he spoke.

"Tell me what's wrong."

"I'm fine," she said, sitting up. For a moment, he wondered if he had misunderstood what he had sensed, but then she crossed her legs, the movement bringing a grimace to her face, and he knew she had lied.

"You're not fine," he said. "I can feel your pain, so don't bother denying it. Let me see your ankle." She uncrossed her legs and he lifted the injured leg, setting it on his lap before he began unwrapping the bandage. She closed her eyes, her breath growing shallow as each movement brought tension to her face. When he saw her ankle, he understood why. It had swollen to twice its normal size. A large, black bruise stretched from the top of her foot to a few inches above her ankle. Where the bruise ended, the bandage had rubbed her skin red. "Meg," he sighed, covering her ankle with his hands. It felt warm to the touch. He looked up at her. "Why didn't you tell me?"

She shrugged. "I didn't see the point. We can't light a fire, so we can't make tea. Until we're able to, I can walk on it well enough to make it through."

He stroked his thumbs across her skin. Although he kept his pressure light, she still winced. "You'll be lucky if you can stand on it," he told her. "Is this from running yesterday?"

"Yes." She leaned her back against the cave wall. "Now what? We can't stay here all day."

"No, we can't," he agreed, "but we can stay a while longer." He slid her leg off his lap and set it down on the ground, careful not to bump it. "I'll find breakfast and something to help you. Rest some more."

He stood, and then stepped into the rain.

§

THE DOWNPOUR continued, pattering rocks outside the cave in a steady rhythm and Meaghan counted time by the noise until Nick returned some time later, holding a thick, pointed leaf in one hand and his sweater tied up in the other. Both his jeans and his white undershirt stuck to his skin, and his hair, heavy against his head, released rivulets of water down his body. He flipped the blanket away from him, and moved to sit on the bare floor.

"You need this more than I do," Meaghan said, and though pain charged through her with the effort, she struggled to her feet. Collecting the blanket from the floor, she offered it to him. "If you don't dry off, you'll get sick, and I'm pretty sure there's a rule that only one of us can be sidelined at a time."

Nick chuckled and accepted the blanket. Running it over his head, he shook as much of the water from hair as he could, and then draped it over his shoulders.

Meaghan eased back to the floor. Untying Nick's sweater, she discovered a pile of apples. After handing one to him, she grabbed another and feasted on it, easing the rumbling in her stomach. A second apple went down with the same speed, but she slowed her pace for the third, taking the time to enjoy the newness of the fruit. The intensity of the aroma was heavenly, sweet and alluring, and the flavor, crisp and tart, danced along her taste buds. Or perhaps, she thought, she appreciated the food more when she had to go so long without it.

She finished her last apple, and then stretched her leg out in front of her. As she waited for Nick to finish eating, she focused on the storm again, allowing it to distract her from the pain. The gray sheet the rain cast across the horizon blurred the shapes of the rocks and trees in her sight, blending them into a muted painting that served as a fitting accompaniment to the patter of drops against the rocks. Lulled by it, she did not realize Nick had moved until she felt his hands on her leg.

"I'll try my best to do this without hurting you," he said and rolled up her pant leg. "I found an ice bush. It should help with the swelling, but the salve has to be rubbed in to work and I'm afraid that won't be pleasant at first." Picking up the leaf, he snapped it in half. It oozed a pale yellow gel. "Are you ready?"

"As ready as I can be."

He squeezed some of the gel into the palm of his hand, and then spread a thin layer of it onto her skin, covering her leg from her foot to halfway up her calf. He rubbed, his pressure light at first, but then he increased it, kneading her muscles with steady fingers. The pain ran up her leg as a stream of fire. To keep from screaming, she curled her fingers into her palms.

"It should start working soon," he said and a moment later, she understood what he meant. Her skin tingled and then cooled, almost as if he had applied ice to it. She uncurled her fingers from her palms. He continued to massage her leg, but she felt numbed to it now. She relaxed against the wall.

"How did you know I was in pain?" she asked. "I thought you said you couldn't sense emotions."

"It's complicated."

"Everything here seems to be," she responded and smiled when he glanced up at her. "Try me."

He nodded. "I think it's best to start from the beginning. As I mentioned before, I've trained my whole life to be a Guardian, but there's a big difference between learning about it and doing it." He picked up the leaf. After squeezing more gel into his hands, he continued massaging. "Before Guardians receive their first charges, they're given a co-duty, taking over with experienced Guardians for a year. You'd know it as apprenticing. It allows Guardians to benefit from the knowledge of their mentors and it also gives less experienced Guardians the chance to practice things they may have forgotten from their studies." He stilled his hands and looked up at her. "Does that feel better?"

"You can't tell?"

"My ability to read emotions is limited. It's not as fine-tuned as yours. I can sense your pain when it's strong, but I can't tell how bad it is. Is it better?"

"Yes."

He reached for the cloth bandage and wrapped her ankle again. "Please don't think I lied to you," he said. "I forgot I could read emotions. It's one of a dozen smaller Guardian powers. It stems from my sensing abilities. I learned about it ten years ago in school. This morning is the first time I've felt it." He tucked the end of the bandage under itself and pulled down her pant leg. "That will help for now, but the ice bush isn't as effective as jicab. You won't be able to walk on it. We'll go back to moving in tandem, but I want to stay here until the rain subsides some. Visibility is bad."

Meaghan hated the idea of waiting, but nodded, deferring to his judgment. He picked up the blanket again, drying his hands and she continued their conversation. "I'm confused. How could you forget you can read emotions? Even if you can't read the degree of an emotion like I can, you've been around enough people to use the power on a regular basis."

"A Guardian can't read everyone's emotions," he told her, "only the emotions of the person he or she protects. And even then, only certain emotions."

"So you can only read my emotions?" she asked. He nodded. "But you said you'd never used the power before. Weren't you able to read the emotions of the other person you protected?"

"What other person?"

"Your internship charge." He refused to meet her gaze and she frowned. "Nick, what aren't you telling me?"

"I've never had a charge before."

Dropping the blanket, he rose to his feet, then picked up his sweater and put it back on. Although it was still wet, he did not appear to notice. Leaning against the wall at the entrance of the cave, he stared at the horizon. Several minutes passed before he spoke again.

"This isn't how we planned things for you," he told her, though he still faced the rain. "Once it was time to transfer your guardianship, Aunt Viv and I intended to take more than a year to do it. Because she raised you, she knew you better than most Guardians know their charges and she wanted to pass her knowledge on to me. We thought it made more sense than performing a co-duty so I was never assigned one." He turned his head. His eyes met hers. "I'm your Guardian now because I was the closest living Guardian to you when Vivian died."

"It transitioned to you automatically," Meaghan realized.

Nick nodded. "I'm sorry. I still had a lot to learn, but I never had the chance."

Meaghan did not say anything as she studied his face. His brows drew together, forming lines in his forehead. His mouth turned down at the corners, grim and set. His eyes appeared strained and shadowed. She did not need access to her power to understand what emotion plagued him. She had seen grief on his face too many times over the past two days not to recognize it.

She stood. Although the pain had subsided in her ankle, it still throbbed when she applied weight to it. Gritting her teeth, she pushed forward so she could stand beside him. She wrapped her arms around him. He accepted the embrace, but only for a minute before letting her go. He turned his attention back to the trees.

"You deserve better, someone with more experience," he said. "Once we get to my village, I'll make sure you're reassigned. For now, I'll do the best I can."

"Is that so?" she asked, frowning. "What other emotions can you read from me?"

"Not many. Only the ones which indicate if you need help, like distress or intense fear."

"So you can't tell what I'm feeling now?"

He shook his head. "Why?"

"Because it would be easier for me if you could sense the depth of my anger. It would feel a bit more like justice."

He retrained his eyes on her. "You have a right to be mad," he told her. "The situation isn't ideal for you. After everything you've been through, you deserve someone who can—"

"I don't care about the situation," she interrupted. "I care about the fact you're planning on pawning me off on someone else."

"That's not fair."

"And you abandoning me is fair?"

"I'm not abandoning you," he protested. "I'm trying to help you. You need someone who can protect you better than I can. I have no experience."

"You've saved me four times now," she pointed out. "Once at home and three times here. I consider that protecting me."

He sighed. "It's not. In each of those cases, I screwed up. An experienced Guardian would never have let you get so close to danger."

"You don't know that," she countered. "But you do know me, which makes all the difference. I trust you, Nick. It's the only reason I'm here. No one else could've convinced me to follow him into not one, but two strange forests, let alone another world. No one else would've had the chance to guard me. I would've ignored him and gone home. To my death, I'm certain."

Nick smiled, though the gesture held only sadness, and he brought a hand to her cheek. "I know you trust me," he said, "but there's a lot you still don't understand. If Aunt Viv had known her future, she wouldn't have brought me over. She would've had another Guardian assigned to you. You would've known him and trusted him. Maybe not in the same way you trust me, but enough to let him help you."

"Mom wouldn't have done that."

"Meg, I realize you mean well, but Aunt Viv's priority was your safety. There's no question she would have—"

"She knew."

Meaghan only whispered the words, but the impact of them widened Nick's eyes. "What?" he asked.

"She knew," Meaghan repeated. A tear rolled down her cheek and around Nick's thumb. He brushed it away, and she covered his hand with one of hers, pressing her face into his palm. "I realized it when you told me she was a Seer. She told Dad to pack the backpack, didn't she?"

"Most likely, but that doesn't mean anything. She could've had that ready for years, just in case."

"Maybe, but I don't think so. The morning she died, when she and I talked, she told me to remember she loved me. I felt sorrow in her then. I thought the emotion was mine, because it was right after you'd told me you were leaving, but it wasn't." She withdrew his hand from her face. "Mom knew she was going to die, Nick. She knew and she let it happen."

"You're certain?"

Meaghan nodded. "If you trusted her as a Seer, then you have to trust she kept you as my Guardian for a reason."

Nick turned his attention to the rain again. When Meaghan realized he was considering her words, she continued. "You're right. Mom wouldn't have put me in danger, so I know I'm safe with you. I can't say what her reasons were, but I think we'll find out in time. At least, we will if you don't give up on me."

"All right," he agreed and returned his eyes to hers. "But if you change your mind when we get to my village, I'll understand."

"I won't." She reached up to give him another hug, and then stepped back. Her foot sank into a puddle, soaking her sneaker and her jeans. She jumped away from it, regretting the movement as soon as her ankle buckled with pain, refusing to support her weight. Nick looped an arm around her waist to keep her from falling backward.

"We're flooding," he said, turning her so she could see the stream flowing into the cave. It pooled in the center of the floor then flowed back out, exiting the opposite side of the cave from where it entered. "There must be a groove in the floor causing it to do that. I imagine it will spread soon, which means we need to start traveling before the rain eases."

He grabbed the blanket from the floor, stuffing it inside the backpack before handing the bag to Meaghan. She clutched it at her side, but remained rooted to her spot as she watched the stream. The water gurgled when it hit small pebbles in its path, creating a soft melody and triggering a memory in her mind. She frowned and dropped the backpack.

Nick rescued the bag from the floor before the water claimed it. "Are you okay?" he asked.

"Yes." She grabbed onto his arm. "Nick, it's not natural."

"What isn't?" He raised a hand to her shoulder. "Meg, are you sure you're okay?"

"The stream." She pointed toward it. "It's not natural. It's magical. It's flowing uphill."

He stared from her face to the stream and back again. "The Guide," he realized. A smile spread across his face. "He's controlling it."

"I believe so. And I remember now what he sang in the forest. He told me we had to follow the water." She watched the river bend, beckoning to them. "Nick," she said. "The water is leading us up the mountain."

CHAPTER TEN

THEY FOLLOWED the stream for several miles. It deviated from the mountain path at times, detouring up steep slopes and across jagged terrain, wandering under bushes and behind boulders. Nick supported Meaghan when he could, and tested off-trail paths ahead of her when he could not. In silence, he pushed them forward.

As rain pelted harder on their heads, the river swelled, stirring red silt with mud. The resulting orange flowed down the gray mountainside, reminding Nick of rust on steel. He enjoyed the beauty of the scene for a moment, but his joy soon disappeared when the river took a path he knew Meaghan could not manage. He refused to follow and familiar clouds gathered in her eyes.

"We need to," she insisted. She sat down on a boulder beside the path and crossed her arms over her chest. "Going up that hill is the only way we can get to the Guide."

"I wouldn't call it a hill. It's practically a cliff face. I can't even figure out how the river's getting up there."

"There has to be a way. He wouldn't lead us here if there wasn't."

"We can't take the risk." Nick sat next to her and lifted her leg onto his lap. The bandage wrapping her ankle, like everything else they wore, dripped water. It slipped in places, exposing swollen skin. "We need to take it easy. Your ankle is bad again. We'll follow the path, and the Guide will have to get us there another way."

"Nick—"

"You said you wanted me as your Guardian, so now you're getting what you wanted. The path isn't safe. We're not taking it, and that's final."

She opened her mouth to argue, but shut it when he shot her a warning look. He began unwrapping her bandage and she sighed. "I think I'm beginning to regret my choice."

He chuckled, continuing his task. After wringing out the bandage, he rewrapped her leg and stood. "Are you ready?" he asked.

She nodded and he helped her to her feet, tightening his grip on her arm when she tensed. He did not have to ask what had caused her reaction. He already knew.

"Mardróch," he muttered. "They're close."

Meaghan pressed a hand to her nose. "That smell is unmistakable."

"What smell?"

"Their odor. It's like rotting meat and composting garbage mixed together." She stared up the path. "They're coming from up there."

"I can sense them, but they don't give off an odor."

"They do," she insisted. She frowned at him. "I don't see how you could miss it. It's vile. It makes me nauseous."

Nick's brows knit together. "I've never heard that before."

"I don't see why not. They…" she grimaced and pressed her fingers to her lips. Nick put an arm around her shoulders.

"Are you all right? You look pale."

She nodded and dropped her hand. "I'm sure I'll get used to this after a while, but it's hard for me to ignore today."

"Because you're in pain," he said. "What emotions do you sense from them?"

"They don't have any." She turned her attention toward the stream. "We can't stay here. Is there any way we can follow the Guide's path? Or should we try to head back down the mountain?"

"There's no place to hide if we retreat. The slope may be our only option." Looping an arm around her waist, he supported her as they walked the short distance to the point where the stream began flowing uphill. "I can climb using the rocks as hand and foot holds, but I don't see how you could. Your ankle will never support you."

"I have to try. The Mardróch will be here any minute."

Nick glanced down the path. "If we went that way, I could carry you."

"You can't outrun them normally," she pointed out. "Adding my weight would only slow you down."

"The only other option is to fight."

"That's not much of an option."

"I'm aware." Nick moved around her, blocking her from the unseen Mardróch, then looked back at her. Her eyes locked with his, the hardness of her determination matching his, and he realized she would fight with him. But they would both die for their efforts. There could be no other outcome. His attention trailed from her to the Guide's stream, which still babbled an oblivious song in the face of their danger. It had been a trick. The Guide had been a traitor, promising safety while leading them to their deaths. Nick scanned the length of the river, his stomach turning sour as he traced the impossible path. He saw only several large rocks hindering their escape. His eyes fell on one, and then his heart jumped when he realized what he had missed before. He took off running toward the hill.

"Nick!" Meaghan cried after him, but he ignored her. Her panic spiked. It grew strong enough for him to sense it, but he ignored that, too. He had no time to explain what he had found. He had no time to point out what the Guide had been trying to show them. Hand over hand, foot over foot, Nick focused on grabbing the next rock, the next hold, pushing his muscles to work harder until he reached the ledge halfway up the hill. Blocked by a large boulder, the Mardróch would never see them there. He only had to bring Meaghan up in time.

He reached into the river. The flow broke, and then disappeared, revealing a flash of angry green. Tightening his fist around the creeper vine, he whipped it toward Meaghan, and let it do its job. It twisted around her waist, but before it could tighten any further, he yanked on his end, pulling her up to the ledge.

Retrieving his knife from his pocket, he cut her loose before pulling her behind the boulder. She shook from fear, and panic turned her face white, but she was safe. He held her as the Mardróch rounded the bend and continued on their way down the path. Without the river to guide their focus up, they could not see their prey only feet above their heads.

Nick shut his eyes, sensing them until they were no longer close, then he forced his heart to calm. Meaghan stirred in his arms, pressing her face into his neck. Tears wet his skin and he buried his hands in her hair, consoling her until her crying stopped.

"I'm sorry," he said when she lifted her head. "It was my only option."

"It had to be a creeper vine," she muttered, wiping the last of her tears from her face. "That was too close. I thought for certain I'd be learning what it's like to be frozen by them."

Nick slipped the backpack from his shoulders and rested it against the rock. "It's not pleasant, but I don't think you'll ever experience it. I have a feeling you're immune."

"Why would you think that?"

"Because you can smell them." He opened the pack, then pulled out two apples and handed her one. "Their power works by transmitting fear through their eyes. It's so intense it's paralyzing."

"And?"

"And you can't sense emotions from them. You said you didn't think they had any, but they do. They're malicious creatures and their emotions match their intent. Given your power, I imagine sensing them would be overwhelming for you."

"I see," she said. "So I can't sense them, but I still don't understand why I would be immune to their power."

"I didn't say you can't sense them." Nick set his apple down and took her hand in his. "I said you can't sense their emotions. At least, not in the same way you do everyone else's. With regular emotions, you can understand and interpret them because you experience them. With the Mardróch, you have no way of understanding the depth of their evil, and the emotions stemming from it. Your power receives them, but it has to translate them into something you can recognize."

"The odor comes from my power?"

"As you said, you think of their odor as vile and rotten, which is what they are. The smell is your power's defense mechanism. Without it, you wouldn't be able to function when the Mardróch were around. The same defense mechanism should block their freezing power by filtering out the fear they project."

"So they don't smell?" she asked. He shook his head and she took a bite from her apple, chewing with slow purpose and swallowing before she responded. "Your theory makes sense, but if you don't mind, I'd rather not test it."

He laughed. "I'd rather you didn't as well. The stream has started again." He pointed toward the middle of the ledge. Water flowed around another, smaller boulder into a break in the rocks they had missed before.

"A hidden path," Meaghan said. "It looks like we can avoid climbing the rest of this hill."

"And the creeper vines," Nick remarked, grinning when she glared at him. "Shall we get going?"

§

THEY TOOK the path, a narrow shortcut through a section of the mountain, and then followed it as it descended into a valley. From the crest, Meaghan could see a column of smoke rising through the rain. The stream twisted, leading them around several small groves before deviating into a lake on the far side of the valley. Meaghan started looking for a way to cross it, and then the rain stopped. The stream shrunk to the size of a creek, disappearing a few minutes later, and she realized they had reached their destination.

They searched the area for a clue to the Guide's location, but after a fruitless half hour, Meaghan gave up and sat down on a rock. She stared at the dirt slope leading up the side of the next mountain and fought to remain positive, but as the throbbing in her leg grew stronger, her resolve waned. "There's nothing here," she whispered. "It's a dead end."

"It's not," Nick promised. He crouched in front of her, removing her sneaker to ease the pressure on her ankle. "The smoke came from over here. I'm sure the Guide has chosen a well-hidden home. There aren't many people with his power, and the Mardróch have set out to eliminate all of them. It's only a matter of finding the next clue to his hideout."

"All right," she agreed. She pointed to her left where several dozen dense trees created a small forest. "Let's check there next."

He nodded, and she attempted to stand, crumpling as soon as she applied pressure to her foot. Nick caught her, and then eased her back onto the rock.

"Rest first," he told her. He sat down in front of her, taking her foot into his lap to release the bandage. She turned her head to hide the tears streaking down her face and he frowned. "I don't like the look of this swelling. I'll keep hunting for the Guide. Hopefully he'll have medicine or at the least, we can use his fire to make you some jicab tea. Stay here and yell if you need me. I won't be far away."

He handed her the backpack before disappearing into the forest. She wiped the tears from her face with her hand and gave into the weariness weighing down her eyelids, allowing them to drift closed. A tree branch snapped behind her and she jumped up, whipping around to face whatever had made the noise. Pain screamed through her leg with the effort.

A man stood less than twenty feet away, his emotions warring with hers for attention. She sensed a combination of curiosity, happiness, and relief in him, and when he smiled, she sat back down on the rock. His shoulders were broad, his arms and legs looked like tree trunks, and his long hair and full beard constructed of bristles streaked with black and gray. But his face matched his emotions, belying his rough appearance. Etched with laugh lines, it held only kindness, as did his pale blue eyes. The familiar color and shape of them filled her with sorrow, and she knew the emotion belonged to him as well as to her.

He covered the distance between them, knelt in front of her, and offered his arms. She accepted the embrace, returning it in kind. It felt fatherly, appropriate from a man whose eyes mirrored her dad's. He patted her back, a gesture also fatherly and familiar, and let her go. Tears shimmered in his eyes as he took her chin between his thumb and forefinger, lifting her face to peer into it.

"I haven't seen you since you were a small child. You've grown into a beautiful woman, quite regal."

A cough came from nearby. The man turned on his heels to view Nick. They exchanged a look Meaghan could not place, and then the man nodded, and stood. He strode over to Nick and engulfed him in

103

a hug.

"You're a foot taller than when I last stood in your presence, lad," he said. "But I guess a decade or so will do that to a man."

"I didn't realize it was you leading us or I might have reconsidered following," Nick responded, though his broad grin announced his own joy at the reunion. "I'm glad to see you've been able to avoid the Mardróch."

"Don't insult me. I used to guard the King. I didn't get my position for lack of skill. I earned it."

"That's funny. I heard you won your position from the King's old Guardian in a lucky hand of cards."

The man scrubbed his hand through his beard, and then chuckled. "Well, I suppose that might be true, but the King's old Guardian was a bore. The King much preferred me."

"He wasn't the only one," Nick remarked, then nodded toward Meaghan. "I see you've met my charge."

"Not officially." The man faced her again and extended a hand. "I'm Caldon. People call me Cal."

"Meaghan," she responded and shook his hand. She tried to stand, but lost her balance when the pain shot through her, dropping her back onto the rock.

"She's injured," Nick said.

"Time to get her inside, then," Cal responded, scooping her into his arms. Trees streaked by as he moved, then turned into a low border of overgrown bushes. He charged toward the dirt slope without slowing down and Meaghan thought for certain he would run into it, but as he grew closer, the slope shook, sliding out of the way to allow them into a narrow cave.

Faint light glowed in the distance and he followed it, exiting the smaller cave into a larger one. A fire blazed in the center of the floor, its black smoke drifting through a hole in the ceiling. Cal glanced at the smoke and frowned. "They've found us now," he said, and it took Meaghan a minute to realize he had spoken to the fire. "The Mardróch aren't far. Don't give us away." The smoke turned almost transparent and he nodded. "Better."

He set Meaghan down on a bed made of moss and soft leaves before turning back to the fire to pull a pot from the embers at the bottom. Tipping it, he poured dark liquid into a cup and held it out to her. "I trust you're familiar with this?" he asked. She took the jicab tea from him and nodded, grateful for once to drink it.

It took half the cup before her head cleared of pain. By the time she emptied it, the throbbing had eased enough for her eyes to drift closed again. Nick and Cal's voices became lullabies to her dreams, wordless melodies playing in the background. Only a single sentence broke through, brought to her attention by a strong disbelief that alerted her power, "You haven't told her yet?"

Although the question wrested her from the depths of unconsciousness, it failed to keep her awake long enough for her to comprehend its meaning.

CHAPTER ELEVEN

SEVERAL RABBITS roasted on a spit over the fire. Wild potatoes and carrots baked in the coals. Meaghan still slept, so Nick agreed to leave her when Cal grabbed a brown jug and two mugs from a makeshift shelf on the far side of the cave and held them up in silent offering.

Nick trailed him to the entrance. The ground moved again, revealing the deep blue evening sky, and Cal strode through the opening he had created. Nick followed. No trace of yesterday's storm remained, not even the faint wisp of a cloud to hide the stars appearing overhead. Though it would soon cool, the air remained balmy from the sun's late afternoon caress and it warmed Nick's skin, though it failed to ease the chill that had formed between he and Cal after Nick had halted their previous conversation.

Cal walked to a slab of rock and sat down. "It's nice to have dry weather again," he said, setting the mugs and jug down at his feet. He gestured toward a spot next to him. "Are you joining me?"

Nick remained standing. "I thought you brought the rain."

"You know I can't create it," Cal responded.

"But you kept it going."

"It would've dissipated after a few hours if I hadn't. I thought your safety was more important than following the Guide's primary rule."

"You mean 'don't change the environment on a large scale'?" Nick asked.

Cal chuckled. "That's the one. It's nice to know your studies stuck with you. I don't think my meddling affected anything though. The weather's already returned to normal."

But the man who had spent two days controlling it had not. Cal looked pale. His eyes appeared dull, the corners of them drawn with deep lines. Nick frowned. "The rule is meant for more than environmental protection."

"I know," Cal said and picked up the jug at his feet. He uncorked it and poured two fingers worth of liquid into each mug. "I'll be fine soon enough. I can't say you would've been if I hadn't intervened."

"I suppose not." Nick sat down next to Cal, accepting a mug. He passed it under his nose. "Is this what I think it is?"

"The famous spirit," Cal confirmed. "I promised you a drink when you were old enough, didn't I? It's a bit delayed, but nevertheless." Raising his mug, he tapped it to Nick's and then took a large gulp from it. When he lowered it again, his cheeks had taken on a rosy glow. "It's a shame I had to abandon my still a few months back. This is the last jug I have."

Nick examined the spirit. It was colorless, reflecting only brown from his clay mug, and other than the fumes bearing the weight of high alcohol, it was odorless. He raised it to his lips and took his first, careful sip. It warmed his throat and settled into his stomach, calming his nerves within seconds.

He had always heard Cal made the best spirit. The Guide guarded his supply well, offering it as a gesture of friendship only to those he deemed worthy. As a child, Nick had hoped to earn the honor someday, but after the Mardróch grew more aggressive and his mother deemed it unsafe for him to visit Cal, Nick let go of his hope.

He took another sip, relishing in the complexity of the spirit, and felt his heart warm from the memories it brought back to him. He could recall James' laughter as Vivian had tried the spirit for the first time, curling her nose up in disgust at the taste. He remembered his mother's enjoyment of the same beverage, and his father's. He could see the fireplace in his house as it blazed in the late winter hours while Cal and a woman who had all but escaped Nick's memory passed the jug to family members who had yet to know the pain of war and death. He could recall their laughter and joy as he watched from the stairs, too young to comprehend the scene below him, but comforted by it nonetheless.

They had thought he was asleep, as a five-year-old boy should be, but he had stayed up to watch them, and that night had made a lasting impression.

He wondered if it was because it was the last night he had seen them all together. The woman whose face had faded in his memory would not live much longer, and James and Vivian would soon be gone, spirited to another world by a magic Nick had yet to understand.

A world James often lamented had nothing close to Cal's masterpiece. Nick took another sip from his mug and marveled at Cal's talent with a still. Although the spirits Nick had enjoyed on Earth were more polished than this, the unusual mix of spice, sweet flowers, and smoke smoothed the rough edges.

Cal finished his own drink, and then refilled his mug before adding more to Nick's. He set the jug down. "What do they call this on Earth?" he asked.

Nick rolled the liquid over his tongue, contemplating. "I think the closest they have is called whiskey, but it's a brown color and they don't have anything of this caliber." He clutched the mug between his hands and stared at the sky, inhaling the fresh air with an appreciation he had not understood a year before. "It feels good to be home. Earth was too much for me."

Cal raised an eyebrow. "You didn't care for it? Vivian told me she loved it."

"I suppose if I'd stayed a few more years, I might have acclimated to it like she and James did, but I never had the chance. Too much of the world is different than ours."

"Like what?"

"It's easier to tell you what isn't different," Nick responded. "Their lives are filled with gadgets and electronics, with noise and lights, and it's hard to keep up with them. I couldn't figure out how they were able to deal with all of it at once and stay sane."

"I'm not sure I understand."

"I didn't either at first. Too much is foreign. Instead of commcrystals, they use things they call telephones to talk to each other and instead of walking or using horses, they ride in planes and cars. Cars are sort of like wagons and planes fly through the sky like birds. Everyone has a car, so I had to learn how to drive one. It wasn't easy." He sighed. His head started to ache, so he lifted his mug and took another sip from it. "On top of that," he continued, putting the mug down on the ground, "everyone had a television and a computer. Televisions transmit plays, and computers allow people to write without paper and perform research without books. It's complicated."

"Sounds like it," Cal agreed. "I can't believe Viv liked it there."

"She found it convenient," Nick said. He clasped his hands together between his knees. "It was overwhelming at first, but once I understood it, I could see why it appealed to her. Telephones, despite their constant beeping and ringing, allow people to call and have food delivered to their doors. They only have to hunt if they want to. In a similar way, people use computers to order items like clothing, and cars and planes can travel large distances in a short amount of time. If I had one of those here, I'd be home by now."

Cal shrugged. "I suppose so. But I doubt you'd stay hidden long, and I highly doubt they're faster than teleporting, so we win on convenience there."

"When we can use that power," Nick pointed out. "Are the Mardróch still monitoring it?"

"For the most part, but I can show you a place tomorrow where it's safe to teleport. That should cut some time off your journey."

"Good." Nick smiled when a streak of white shot across the sky. Another star followed it, and then a third. "I think I missed this the most. The stars were hard to see on Earth, except when we visited the mountains. The lights from the cities block them."

Cal drained his mug again and set it aside. "Earth wasn't your home," he said. "You belong here."

Nick nodded, and then closed his eyes to block out a sudden wash of pain. "Aunt Viv and Uncle James belonged here too," he whispered. "They should have come back with me."

"I know." Cal laid a hand on Nick's shoulder and Nick opened his eyes to look at him. "The river was in the cave with you and Meaghan this morning," Cal continued. "I heard your conversation."

"All of it?"

"Yes. Meaghan's right, Nick. Vivian had a vision about this, but it wasn't recently. She had it her first night on Earth fifteen years ago."

"I don't understand."

"She's known all along when she and James would die. The last time I saw her was about four years ago. It took her a week to find me. The Mardróch were on my trail, so I lived deep in the mountains, but she went through the trouble because she wanted to tell me what she had seen. She needed me to know what she and James had decided. They had the option to return earlier, to bring Meaghan home after her fifteenth birthday, but they chose not to."

Nick stared at Cal. "Why? If they knew, why didn't they come home? They could have prevented this."

"Because Vivian was a gifted seer. Some say she was the best this world has seen in hundreds of years. I agree. She understood that saving her own life meant jeopardizing our future. She knew she and James had to die for our cause to succeed."

Nick rose to his feet. Unable to stay still, he paced as he mulled over Cal's words, then turned to frown down at the older man. "They didn't have to be martyrs," he said. "They should have told me. We could have worked something out, figured out another way. Instead, they let me believe I was there to integrate myself into Meaghan's world. I wasted so much of my time—"

"Getting to know her," Cal interrupted. He stood and placed his hands on Nick's shoulders. "Viv was never wrong. If she said that's how it had to be, then that's how it had to be. If she'd told you what she had wanted to do, you would have tried to stop her, and you wouldn't have done what you needed to do to keep Meaghan safe. You had to get to know Meaghan for her to trust you."

Nick shoved his hands into his pockets. He looked away and Cal tightened his grip. "Nick, listen to me. Viv kept this secret to protect you."

"How?" Nick countered. Pain shadowed his voice and tears filled his eyes, despite his best efforts to control them. "Because she kept her secret, I wasn't prepared to take over. I'm not ready for this, Cal. Meaghan's too important for this world to lose, and I don't know how to protect her."

"She's too important for *you* to lose," Cal corrected. "And you're scared. I understand, but don't let fear control you. You're ready. You may not have the experience you think you need, but you're meant to be her Guardian."

Nick's eyes came back to Cal's. "You don't know that."

"Actually, I do." Cal dropped his hands. "I'm sure your mother never told you, but you weren't slated to guard Meaghan. It's rare for the Elders to assign a charge to a Guardian of the opposite gender. I can understand their reasons, but they had no choice once you developed your personal power and she developed her power. It's fate. If they couldn't dispute it, I don't see how you can."

"I don't believe in fate," Nick argued, then blew out a hot breath when Cal grinned. "Fine, let's call it fate, but it doesn't make me feel any more prepared."

"Maybe not, but you'll get there. In the meantime, don't let on. The Elders may not have been willing to argue against fate back then, but Viv and James' deaths will alter their views. You may have to fight to stay as Meaghan's Guardian, and I expect you will. Meaghan trusts you. Don't fail her."

"I won't," Nick promised.

"Good. While you're at it, you need to learn to trust her."

"I trust her."

"Not fully. The hardest part about being a Guardian is letting your charge make mistakes. You can't protect her from everything or she'll never learn. And if she doesn't learn, she won't develop into the person we need her to be to succeed."

"What if she gets hurt?" Nick asked. "What if she...?" he faltered, incapable of completing the thought.

"She won't get killed," Cal assured him. "You won't let her. As far as getting hurt, it's okay. She was tough enough to make it all the way here on a sprained ankle, so I think she can handle injuries." He picked up Nick's mug and handed it to him. "She can also handle the truth."

Nick frowned. "We've already had that conversation."

"We started it, but we never finished. You ended it when Meaghan stirred."

"She didn't need to find out about it by overhearing us."

"I agree, but she does need to find out, and soon." Cal nodded toward Nick's mug. "Drink up. I'm on guard duty tonight. You need a break."

Nick did not feel like drinking any longer, but he pressed the mug to his lips anyway. An awkward silence stretched between him and Cal, but as the liquor settled into Nick's stomach and added a film of haze to his mind, the tension eased, and so did the conversation.

"I've always been told I was assigned to Meaghan from her birth," Nick said. "It's funny how stories change over the years."

"Funny had nothing to do with it," Cal responded. "May wouldn't allow the story to be told any other way. Your family has been protecting Meaghan's for generations and your mother wasn't giving up your family's heritage no matter what the Elders said." He chuckled. "Of course, while you were gone, May was promoted to Elder status. I think there's justice in that."

"No kidding?" Nick asked, pride spreading a grin across his face. "That's fantastic news."

"It is," Cal agreed. He picked up the jug and uncorked it. After topping off Nick's mug, he poured another sampling into his own. "Welcome back, Meaghan," he directed toward the mouth of the cave. "You've been asleep for a while. Do you feel better?"

"Yes, thank you," she responded. She exited the shadows of the mountain and joined them at the rock. Although she still limped, Nick was relieved to see that pain no longer lined her face.

Cal handed her his mug. "This will help, though it's not quite medicine. You'll need to see a Healer soon or you won't get much further. There's a village with one not far from here."

"We'll detour there tomorrow," Nick decided. He sat down on the rock, pulling Meaghan down with him. "For now, stay off your feet as much as you can."

She nodded and took a sip from the cup in her hand, choking before Nick had a chance to warn her about its contents. He had seen her drink less than a half dozen times, and only beer or wine Vivian and James had given her, never liquor. Her eyes widened and she turned them on Cal.

"What is this?"

"My famous spirit," Cal beamed. "Do you like it?"

"It's," she hesitated, "strong."

Cal laughed. "I was telling Nick about May's promotion. She's an Elder now."

"Who's May?" Meaghan asked. "And what's an Elder?

Cal knit his brows together in confusion before he turned the look on Nick. "Geez, lad, you haven't told her anything. Does she think she's still on Earth, too?"

"Don't be sarcastic," Nick muttered before addressing Meaghan's question. "The Elders are a panel of five Guardians who regulate the Guardian community."

"They're down to four now," Cal said. "The Mardróch got two of them a few months ago. May was the only one they trusted enough to promote, so they're staying short one Elder for a while."

"Who did we lose?"

"Silus and Morgan, but I'm sure that's no surprise to you. Those two have been pushing an aggressive agenda for too long. Their Mardróch nighttime raids were bound to catch up with them eventually."

"It's not a surprise, but it's a shame," Nick responded. "There aren't many Guardians with active powers left. Silus' ability to bend matter and Morgan's pyrokenesis would have been helpful in the final plans."

"If we could trust them to stick to the plans," Cal countered. "I don't know if we could have."

"There's no way to know now," Nick said and turned back to Meaghan. "May is my mother. Her full name is Maiyahla. She was Vivian's sister." He hesitated, debating if he should tell Meaghan any more, but decided to trust her as Cal had recommended. He took her hand in his. "You should also know they were identical twins. You'll meet my mom soon and it may be hard for you to see her."

"I'll be all right," she assured him. She squeezed his hand before letting it go. "I did fine with Cal, didn't I? He looks a lot like my father."

"I should," Cal told her. "James was my younger brother."

"I thought so. You and Dad have the same eyes."

"As did our father," Cal said. A smile crossed his face. It only lasted a moment before fading. "James was a good man and I'm sure he made a fine father."

"He did."

Cal nodded. "But I'm afraid you can't address him by that name on this world."

"What name?" Meaghan asked.

"You can't call him your father. I know he was to you, but to the people on this world, he wasn't."

"Why should anyone care what I call him?"

"It's," he rubbed the back of his neck, "complicated."

"And Mom?"

"You should call her Vivian."

"I see." Meaghan tightened her hands around her mug and drew them into her lap. Her shoulders stiffened, but she did not press the issue. Nick realized her leniency for Cal would not extend to him when they were alone later. "I'll be mindful of your request," she told Cal. "It won't be easy to remember to call my parents by their proper names. I've been calling them Mom and Dad almost my entire life. But I'll try."

"I appreciate that," Cal said. "Let's leave the serious topics alone for the rest of the evening. Dinner should be done soon and I imagine you two are starving."

"And then some," Meaghan agreed. "It smells heavenly, by the way. I don't even care what it is. I want to eat until I can't move."

Cal laughed and scooped her into his arms, shaking his head when she started to protest. "No walking," he reminded her. "You'll have plenty of time to agitate your injury tomorrow. Tonight, let's feast. And when we're done, let's empty the jug of its spirit. It's time to celebrate your homecoming."

CHAPTER TWELVE

TONGUES OF fire cast halos into the abyss, commanding them to their deaths in the near endless dark. Where the light found a place to settle, it revealed more than Meaghan wanted to see. The walls bled water, a slow seeping which trailed mineral formations behind it. Thousands of years had crafted the formations into shapes. Some became distorted animal outlines while others twisted into writhing ghosts. Where water oozed from the ceiling, it hardened into sharp, gray icicles that reached for her when she passed beneath them. Although she knew the sinister shapes were only a betrayal of her imagination, fright still kept her within a step of Cal. At times, she trailed so close she almost ran into him when he stopped.

They had been traveling through the caves since morning. Their route traversed narrow passageways and cramped rooms, forcing them to stoop to pass. They wandered up steep slopes and down into valleys, over rivers and beside canyons. She had never realized caves could be so complex, but Nick explained that hundreds of miles of cave systems interconnected the mountains. They could be dangerous for those who did not know them well. Folklore told of fierce warriors driven into them by advancing armies, lost forever. Nick shared some of those stories. While they frightened Meaghan, Cal chuckled at the story, unconcerned as he led them through the underground maze. He stopped every so often to lay a hand on the wall, nodding in the direction they should follow.

In his other hand, he held a torch fashioned from a short tree limb wrapped in cloth. Nick carried a similar torch. Both torches burned steadily, never waning despite the hours they wandered. Mesmerized by the limitless flames, Meaghan watched the fire dance in front of her, and marveled at Cal's command over his power. She hoped someday she could gain the same control, but she had her doubts. Since she had met the man, his emotions controlled half her mind. She fought to separate them from her own, but found the chore exhausting. Her power continued to grow stronger on this world and she had yet to figure out how to manage it.

After they stopped for a lunch of leftovers, they entered a cavern so large Meaghan could not see the ceiling. An eerie glow emanated from above, bathing the room in faint light. To their right, a landslide of boulders and small rocks blocked the path. And to the left, a pebble-laden shoreline descended into the ink-black waters of a lake. The lake stretched out in front of them, its far shores obscured by dark and distance. She could hear splashing as fish leapt from the water and dove back under the surface. An occasional ripple indicated movement. She watched several dance in succession close to the shore, and then a large one drifted toward them.

Cal moved in front of Meaghan as Nick stepped forward to do

the same. A line of spikes broke the water from the center of the ripple. Following the spikes, a head emerged. Two round, milky orbs came next, protruding from a bulbous face covered in scales. Metallic colored lids descended over the orbs several times in quick succession and Meaghan realized the creature was blinking. A serpentine tongue flicked from its gaping mouth as it rotated its orbs to focus on Cal, then it climbed onto the shore, revealing a toad-like body and elephantine legs. Although it stood the height of a large dog, its body held twice the mass. It pawed thick, webbed feet into the dirt, and then settled them.

"What is that thing?" Nick asked.

"I don't know," Cal responded. "There are a lot of weird beasts down here that don't exist on the surface. Keep your eyes on it. I'll try to clear the path."

Cal managed only a few steps toward the rockslide before the creature let out a high-pitched howl. Cal froze, but the effort came too late. Without any further warning, the animal charged toward them, its massive legs spraying rocks behind it.

Nick lowered his torch and swung it at the creature. He missed, and the beast circled, its speed quickening. It lowered its head, pointing its sharp spikes at Nick's stomach, and then let out a pig-like squeal when Cal's torch met its backside. It reared up, rounding to face its attacker.

Cal took a step back as the animal continued to stand on its hind legs, using its webbed feet to try to push him down. He fenced it off with his torch, the fire trailing and leaping as he swung it through the air, then he waved a hand toward the rockslide and the earth rumbled. Rocks fell, rolling away from the path to reveal a small opening.

"Go," Cal commanded. "I'll catch up."

Nick pulled Meaghan onto the pathway. He ran, but she planted her feet, tearing her arm from his grip when the steady fear she had sensed from Cal changed to pain. She turned, hurrying back into the cavern before Nick could stop her. Cal lay on the ground, his torch several feet away. The beast advanced on him and he struggled to his feet only seconds before webbed paws knocked him back down. Meaghan felt his pain spike.

The creature reared up, and she dove for the torch. Brandishing it, she attacked the animal, knocking it away from Cal before it could crush him. She rolled with it down the embankment, and then felt her leg snap when she hit a rock. Her own intense pain joined with Cal's in her mind. She opened her mouth to scream, but inhaled water instead as the lake swallowed her and the creature, halting their descent.

Weighted by her clothes, she sank below the surface. She let go of the deadened torch and struggled to find the lake floor with her feet. She felt only a current as the beast moved underneath her. Thrashing her arms, she tried to swim but her sweater weighed her down. She stripped out of it, kicked again, and found purchase when her feet struck the creature's back. Using all of her energy, she launched up, breaking the surface of the water.

Air rushed over her skin. She gasped a large breath before teeth clamped around her injured leg and pulled her back down. The urge to scream almost forced her to take another breath, but she curbed the reaction in time.

Black water blinded her eyes. She heard nothing but her own frantic heartbeat and the whoosh of the creature's body as it descended with her into the depths. She struggled, and then renewed pain shot through her as the grip on her leg intensified. Cal's emotions muted. Her lungs burned. Instinct finally forced her to inhale water as the black haze of unconsciousness fringed her vision. Death would not be far behind. She lost her strength and then a roar filled her ears. She flew upward, floating, spinning in a whirlwind of pressure, and then she fell.

Her back hit the ground. Too weak to move, she stopped fighting and accepted whatever came next. Softness pressed against her lips, separating them. Air filled her lungs. She choked, coughed, and then hands pulled her onto her side. The water in her lungs rushed out, and she succeeded in taking her next breath on her own. Although labored, it felt like the greatest accomplishment of her life. She struggled to rise, but failed when dizziness overcame her.

"The beast is coming back," she heard a distant voice say. "The water spout didn't deter it."

"Take her," someone else responded. She thought she recognized the second voice as Cal's. Arms lifted her and she floated through the air again.

She forced open her eyes. Nick held her. Cal ran close by. They fled into the passageway. Cal raised a hand, flipping it toward the opening and the stones tumbled back into place. Seconds later, darkness descended around them.

Meaghan heard the sound of stone scraping stone. A spark shot from the wall, then turned to fire as it caught the cloth on the remaining torch. Frantic scratching and scraping emanated from the pile of rocks blocking the entrance and Nick and Cal continued running. Up ahead, the pathway glowed from another opening. Rocks scattered behind them, tumbling from the pile as the creature made progress. Cal directed them into the new opening, and then waved his hand to seal it.

Brightness seared Meaghan's eyes. After half the day spent in shadows, they burned from the light, and she squinted to allow them to adjust. The walls and ceiling of the cave sparkled with hundreds of multi-faceted crystals in varying sizes. Each cast a soft white glow from its center, turning the darkness of the deep earth into daylight.

Nick set her down on the ground. He tried to be gentle but the slight movement brushed her leg against his, sending pain shooting through her body and she clenched her teeth to avoid screaming. The pain, coupled with Cal's fear, drove her heart into frantic beats. She felt sick and squeezed her eyes shut.

Fingers slid down her face. She could hear Nick's voice, but through the intensity of the emotions, she could not make out what he said. She opened her eyes. Nick laid a hand on her brow. His lips moved and she concentrated on them until his words made sense. "Focus," he said. "Focus on my emotions. Feel my power, Meg. Focus on it."

She stared at him, not understanding. The emotions swirled within her. The pain held her captive. She could not focus on anything else. He laid a palm against her cheek, and then dropped the block he held over her power and allowed her to share his emotions.

His worry overshadowed all other emotions. Slowly, he withdrew it. As it dissipated, she felt warmth in its place. It was his power, she realized, and allowed the warmth to flood out Cal's emotions, leaving only her own. She covered Nick's hand, pressed her cheek into his palm and he understood. He turned from her to roll up her pant leg, his hands gentle and slow.

"How do your lungs feel?" he asked after she had propped up on her elbows to watch him.

"Okay, I think," she responded, attempting a deep breath. She coughed on the air, but managed to take another with better results. "I'll be fine."

"Good." He finished rolling up her pant leg, careful to keep the wet material from tugging on her skin, then removed the bandage, frowning when a gash a few inches above her ankle revealed a splinter of bone. "This won't be though. I can see why I'm sensing so much pain from you." He turned to Cal. "We have to get her to the village soon. I can't help her with this."

Cal walked over to them and examined the injury. "At least she hurt the same leg. She'll still be able to move. Do you have any jicab root?"

"In the backpack," Nick responded and slipped it off his back. Digging through it, he found the portion of root they had left. "We can't build a fire," he said, handing it to Cal. "This space is too enclosed."

"I don't intend to," Cal responded. He took a knife from his pocket and cut off a small chunk of the root. "Open up," he told Meaghan, slipping it between her lips when she followed his direction. "It will taste horrible, but chew it. Don't swallow, or you'll be having visions for the next three days."

He handed the root back to Nick.

"You didn't take the bark off," Nick told him. "I thought it was poisonous."

"It's not. It's the most concentrated part of the root. The Healers say it's poisonous because swallowing it can have hallucinogenic properties, and because too much can be deadly. But it's useful in some situations. Just don't tell anyone I taught you that trick and don't ever use more than half a thimble's full."

"Good to know." Nick put the root away. "How far are we from where we can teleport? I think we need to—"

"Teleport?" Meaghan interrupted. She blinked several times, trying to clear her vision. Nick and Cal looked fuzzy. "You mean like Star Trek?"

"Sort of."

"Cool." She grinned, and then realized her leg had stopped hurting. "So you're from space."

"Uh….yeah," Nick responded. He narrowed his eyes at her before turning a censuring look on Cal. "What did you do to her?"

"I took her pain away," Cal responded. Meaghan giggled and he tapped her on the arm. "Sit up all the way, please. I need to set your leg."

"Won't it hurt?"

"You won't feel much," he promised. When she did not move, he took her arm and pulled her into a sitting position. "Brace her," he told Nick. "And give me your backpack."

Nick handed the bag over and sat behind her, scooting her between his legs. She flopped back against him, giggling again.

"Do you think maybe you gave her too much?" Nick asked.

"Not at all," Cal responded. He opened the backpack and pulled out the first aid kit. Removing gauze, tape, and a small pair of scissors from the plastic container, he set them by his side. "That's what happens when you chew the root, which reminds me," he held out his hand, palm side up. "You've had enough. Take it out of your mouth."

Meaghan shook her head. She felt too good. She did not want to let go of that yet.

"Meaghan," Cal warned, his tone stern as her father's had been when she was a child. She frowned. "Now," he added and she did as he asked. She spit the root into his palm. He sighed, tossed it aside, and then wiped his hand on his pants. "I guess it's obvious why we're not supposed to use it that way."

"I guess so," Nick muttered. Meaghan lifted her fingers to touch his cheek, stopping when his hand met hers. "I've never seen her like this."

Cal chuckled. "It's the bark, and it's only an initial effect. It's flooded her system so it mimics drunkenness, but it'll wear off soon. I need to get this done before it does. Do you have a good hold on her?"

Nick brought his arms around her and nodded. Cal began working, cutting a length of wood from one side of the torch with a pocketknife before setting the torch and wood aside. Feeling along her leg, he pressed to gauge the extent of the break. Although the pain was not severe, she jerked, and then quickly forgot about it. She watched, fascinated, as Cal placed his hands on the wound and snapped the bone back into place. Needles ripped into her awareness. She inhaled a sharp breath and tried to push away from him.

"Nick, keep her still," Cal commanded. "I have to finish this."

Nick tightened his arms, locking her against him. She struggled, and then went limp. Tears coursed down her cheeks. "It's all right," he whispered when she whimpered. "It's almost over. Hold on."

Cal quickened his pace. He wrapped the wound in gauze, and then laid the stick against her leg to brace the bone before immobilizing it with another layer of gauze. He secured the bandage with tape before leaning back to examine his work.

"It's not bad," he decided. "I'm sure a Healer could do better, but it only has to last a few hours."

"It's better than most people could do," Nick agreed. He released his tight hold on Meaghan, but did not let her go.

"How are you feeling?" Cal asked her.

"Loopy," she responded. She smeared the moisture from her cheeks with her palms. "I think it hurts, but I don't care."

Nick sighed. "You may not care, but your body does." He addressed Cal. "She's in enough pain for me to feel it. I'm glad she doesn't recognize it. Where did you learn to use jicab that way?"

"From your mother. She taught it to me during the Zeiihbu War. It came in handy more than once during battles." Cal put the supplies away and zipped up the backpack. "So what's Star Trek?"

"It's something they have on the televisions on Earth, kind of like a weekly short play."

"No kidding? I didn't realize they knew about teleporting."

"They do but they think it's fake, and when they pretend to do it, they don't do it the same way we do."

"What do you do then?" Meaghan asked. "Can I do it too?"

"Only when you're with a Guardian," Nick answered. "Teleporting is like using a portal, but Guardians can do it by themselves. It's one of our powers. We can travel from one spot to another within a limited distance."

"Are you sure?"

"Of course I'm sure. I've been doing it since I was a kid."

"Then why are we walking?" She crossed her arms in front of her. "Why don't we teleport to your village?"

"I wish we could," he answered. "The Mardróch can sense the signature trail teleporting leaves behind and they can follow it. We'd be caught right away. The only way to do it safely is in a large group where everyone is going somewhere different. It mixes up the teleporting signatures so the Mardróch can't follow them."

Puzzled, Meaghan looked to Cal, then back at Nick. "But we're a group."

Nick chuckled. "Not quite a big enough group I'm afraid."

"There's another way," Cal told them. "These caves prevent the Mardróch from sensing the signature. It has something to do with the crystals, I think. There are caves like this all through the underground in this part of the kingdom. Provided you teleport from one to the other, the Mardróch will never catch you. We can jump from here to one closer to the village."

"Let's do that now," Nick decided. He nodded toward the bruises and cuts on Cal's arms. "I think you should come to the village with us. It wouldn't hurt you to have a Healer look at you."

"He'll come. He's in pain too," Meaghan muttered. Leaning back, she rested her head against Nick's chest. "And he feels love and excitement when you mention the village. There's someone there."

"No use hiding anything from her," Cal responded with a lopsided grin. "I guess it's a good assumption she isn't focusing on your power anymore." He handed Nick the backpack and picked up the torch. "Ready?" he asked, then without waiting for a response, he placed his empty hand on Meaghan's back and for the second time in short memory, her world dissolved into white.

CHAPTER THIRTEEN

A SECOND cave appeared around Nick, its size and layout so close to the first he wondered for a moment if Cal had been unable to make the teleport. Similar crystals flashed brilliant light from nearly every surface. Large boulders of the same size and shape lined the walls. Even the dirt floor seemed to be the exact shade of the floor in the cave they had left behind. But unlike the first cave, a single beam of yellow sunlight descended from the ceiling, painting a circle in the center of the room. Cal moved to one wall to study the boulders and Nick stood, drawing Meaghan up with him.

"There's a tunnel to the outside," Cal told him. "We'll need to crawl through it."

"Can you manage it?" Nick asked Meaghan. She wobbled her head and he took it as a nod. "Where is it?" he asked Cal.

"It's," Cal paused, took a step forward and pointed to a boulder on the far wall, "there." The boulder slid away from the wall, revealing a small opening.

Nick crossed the floor toward it, but Meaghan did not move.

"Meg," he said. "We need to get to the village."

Her eyes widened and she shook her head.

He sighed. "Look, Meg, I know you're under the influence of the jicab, but you have to—"

"It stinks," she interrupted. She tore her eyes from the hole, bringing them around to meet his. The cloudiness he had seen in them after Cal had given her the jicab root had started to clear. "They're coming," she said and turned to Cal. "Close it. Quick. They're not far."

Cal raised an eyebrow at Nick. "Do it," Nick responded to Cal's unspoken question. "Now!" he insisted when Cal hesitated.

Cal flicked his hand and the boulder slid back into place. Nick slipped his arm around Meaghan's waist. She shook. He walked her to a nearby boulder and sat her down, then he focused his power on sensing what she feared, but found no danger.

"I don't feel them," he told her. "Are you sure of what you sensed?"

She nodded. "They smell terrible."

"Smell?" Cal asked. He moved in front of her, crouching down to study her face. "Did you swallow any of the root?"

"No," she said. "You told me not to."

He turned to Nick, frowning. "I'm not sure I believe her. I think she's hallucinating."

"She's not. It's how her power translates Mardróch emotions." Nick's eyes trailed to the circle of sunlight on the floor then up to the hole that allowed light through the mountain. He pointed to it. "Can you use the hole to see outside?" he asked. "We need to know if they're here."

"Sure. I can use smoke from the torch. I don't see the point in it though. We're not sensing them."

"Do it, please. I'll explain later."

Cal shrugged and walked to the center of the room. He held the torch under the hole. The fire blazed, emitting a thick smoke, which turned opaque as it neared the ceiling. It floated up the hole, escaping into the sky in a long, continuous trail. Cal narrowed his eyes. "Turn around, twist and ride; seek to see what others hide. Around the bend, now there's a friend, around the wall, tell me all."

"He's singing," Meaghan whispered to Nick. "He did that when he first spoke to me in the woods. Why? He doesn't normally."

"It's a focusing technique Guides learn in school," Nick responded. "Most of them stop using it once they graduate, but Cal finds it helps him concentrate sometimes."

"Quiet," Cal said, turning his head to cast an irritated scowl in their direction. The smoke waned. "It's not as easy as it looks."

"Sorry," Nick muttered.

"Past the mountain, round the trees," Cal recited, trying again. "Show the way if you please. To the village, do as I say. Don't let the breeze make you stray." The smoke thickened again. Cal closed his eyes. Silence filled a minute and then another before he opened his eyes again and the smoke disappeared. "I'll be damned."

"You saw them?" Nick asked.

"Yes." He set the torch on the ground, and then waved his hand over it. It dimmed to gold embers. "There are about ten of them. It's a hunting party. They're in the field looking, but they won't find it."

"Find what?"

Meaghan leaned forward and answered. "The village. His words don't match his emotions. He's afraid they'll find it. He's worried about her."

"Stop that," Cal snapped. "You're not helping." He clutched his hands behind his back and cursed. "You need to teach her to control her power, Nick, or at least to control her tongue. I don't like having someone announcing what I feel all the time."

"She didn't mean—"

Cal ignored Nick and turned on Meaghan. "Just because you have a rare power doesn't mean you can say what you please. I know plenty about you I shouldn't, but I don't announce it. And just because you're—"

"Enough!" Nick stood to square off with Cal. "You have no right to talk to her like that. The jicab root's effecting her actions and you're the one who gave it to her, so deal with it." He held his position long enough for Cal to gauge his anger, then turned back to Meaghan, kneeling in front of her. Her face remained still, but shame flushed her cheeks a light shade of pink and held her eyes to the floor. He took her hands in his.

"I'm sorry, Cal," she whispered. "I didn't mean to say it."

Cal sighed and sat down next to her. Draping an arm around her shoulders, he pulled her against him, and then tucked a knuckle under her chin, lifting it so she would look at him. "Nick's right. It's the jicab root talking. And you're right too. I'm worried. I'm taking it out on you, that's all. I should be the one to apologize."

"Or we could forget about it," she offered with a smile. "I'm sure

I won't remember it in ten minutes anyway."

Cal laughed, squeezing her shoulder before letting her go. "It's a deal. I suspect we'll be here a while. Why don't you sleep while Nick and I figure out what to do?"

"I think that's a good idea," Nick said before she could object. He knew she would want to help, but he doubted Cal would be able to tolerate her jicab-influenced state much longer. The worry on the man's face grew with every minute.

Meaghan frowned, and folded her hands in front of her, but she nodded. Nick removed the blanket from the backpack and spread it out in a corner of the cave. Laying the backpack at one end of it, he picked her up and set her on the blanket. "We'll wake you when it's time to go."

She offered him a crooked smile as she stretched across the blanket and settled the backpack under her neck as a pillow. Reaching a hand up, she traced her fingers along his cheek, then pressed her fingertips against his lips. "I liked what you did with these, you know. It felt good." She removed her hand, bringing it to her own mouth to stifle a yawn, and then closed her eyes. A moment later, her breathing deepened in sleep.

Nick took a moment to erase the excitement her words and touch had brought him before turning to face Cal. He could not tell if the man's half-smile and owlish expression stemmed from censure or curiosity, but he did not care. They had more important things to discuss.

He crossed the room to sit on another boulder and waited for Cal to join him. "Is the village in danger?"

Cal shrugged. "They have the standard protection. They should be fine."

"Yet you're still worried."

Cal nodded. "The Village at Three Points was destroyed last week."

Nick hissed in a breath. "There's no reason Garon would've wanted that village. It had nothing to offer him."

"Morgan's daughter was stationed there. Things have changed in the time you were gone, Nick. Garon isn't only targeting people with strong powers. He's targeting specific people to prove a point. No one is safe from him."

"I take it a traitor lived within the Village at Three Points."

"There seem to be more of them every day." Cal tightened his hands into fists and stared down at them. "Garon has become aggressive in his recruiting. Some sway to promises of power. Others fear torturous deaths. He's left enough bodies behind to serve as examples of what he can do to those who refuse him."

"It only takes a single person inside the village to let the Mardróch in," Nick said.

Cal nodded again and stood. He walked to the center of the room, and then glanced up at the hole. "I wonder if I should look again. Maybe there's a way to sneak around them."

"I can't take the chance with Meg."

"You're right," Cal said and rejoined Nick on the rock. "It was a stupid suggestion."

He clutched his hands together in front of him, and then leaned over his knees, and Nick could not ignore the nervousness in the gesture. Cal, the unshakable mountain, trembled.

"Who is she?" Nick asked.

"Her name's Neiszhe," Cal answered and drew his hands under his chin. "She's beautiful. She's smart, kind, and I don't know why she puts up with a fool like me." He smiled. "Maybe it's because we don't see much of each other. She hasn't had the time to get sick of me yet. The Mardróch are relentless about finding me and I don't want to put the village at risk."

"You love her," Nick guessed. "Are you wed?"

"It happened soon after we met. From the start, I had no doubt she was for me." Cal sat up straight. His hands tightened in his lap. "I can't lose her, Nick. With this war, with the Mardróch after me, I worry every day I will."

Nick lifted a hand to squeeze Cal's shoulder. He wanted to offer words of comfort, but he knew they would be false. In this world, fear belonged to everyone and no person could guarantee who would live to see tomorrow. Death was the unvarying consequence of war. It left no one free of its numbing grasp. Nick had learned that firsthand at too young of an age.

"Listen to me carrying on," Cal said, standing up. "She's safe now. I have to focus on that. I'm going to check on the Mardróch." He picked up the torch again, then extended his arm to hold it below the hole. His lips moved, uttering silent words and the fire flamed again. A few minutes later, he set the torch down again. "No change."

"We'll set out as soon as they're gone," Nick promised, "even if it's in the middle of the night."

Cal sat back down. "It's a good thing she sensed them or we would be dead now."

"I know," Nick said. Meaghan stirred in the corner, and then settled again. He watched her, waiting for her breathing to resume a deep rhythm before continuing. "Her powers are getting stronger. She couldn't sense them this far away when we crossed over."

"It's expected," Cal told him. "Our powers stem from the world. She's growing accustomed to being here and opening up to more power as a result."

Nick tore his eyes away from Meaghan to focus on Cal. "Are you sure?"

"Positive. It's not anything you did."

"I don't know what you mean."

"You do," Cal said. "You forget I was watching you through the rain. I saw everything."

He saw the kiss, Nick realized, and felt panic rise in his throat. He swallowed hard to control it. "Are you going to report me?"

"It's not the Elders' business, despite what they think," Cal told him. "Was that the only time?"

"No." Nick rose and walked to the center of the room, to the patch of sunlight and stared down at the circle it traced on the floor. It had been no more than a handful of days since it had happened, but it felt like a lifetime ago. Still, the joy and agony of it remained.

"How many times have you kissed?"

"Only once before, on Earth shortly before Uncle James and Aunt Viv died." Nick turned to face Cal. "I know what you said about Viv's vision, but I also know I could have prevented it."

"Somehow I doubt that," Cal responded. "You've always been the type to take on responsibility that wasn't yours. Sometimes that's a good thing, but in situations like this, it's not."

Nick clasped his hands behind his back. "I got your brother killed, Cal. You shouldn't be trying to comfort me. You should be angry at me."

Cal raised an eyebrow. "Is that so? Let's hear your reasoning then. I'm assuming it has to do with this forbidden kiss?"

Nick nodded and his eyes drifted to Meaghan. She lay before him, so beautiful it made his heart jump, and so unreachable it made him ache. "I didn't think it would matter on Earth," he said. "It was irrational to think that way. I realize that, but I wanted to know what it felt like to touch her. Although the kiss lasted less than a minute, it was long enough. It seemed to have had a lasting effect. When the Mardróch attacked, I couldn't sense them in time." He passed a hand over his eyes, and faced Cal again. "It's been difficult to sense them since."

Cal stroked his beard. "So you think your powers have grown weak because you kissed her?"

"Yes."

"They haven't." Cal stood and met Nick in the patch of sunlight. Raising a hand, he clasped the side of Nick's neck. "Feel what you feel, Nick. It'll work out. I promise."

"You know the dangers as well as I do."

"I do. Maybe more than you do. That's the curse of age, but the benefit is wisdom. I realize you think you lost some of your power to her, but you didn't. When that happens to you, whichever girl it happens with, you'll understand. It's all or nothing. There's no such thing as part-way."

Nick searched the sincerity in Cal's face and the fear that had resided as a steady fist around Nick's heart since his last day on Earth dissolved on an exhale. "Then what's wrong with my sensing power?"

"It's not only yours. Garon found an ancient spell that mutes a Guardian's ability to sense danger from a distance. It took a large amount of power to cast, but he has enough Mardróch now to do it. Most likely, the spell is one of the few that works on Earth." He picked up the torch again and it flared in his hand. "I couldn't tell you why we can't sense them now, though. A few of them are close enough. I hope they haven't found a spell that blocks our ability to sense them entirely."

"I don't think they have," Nick assured him. "Our sensing powers work on the same frequency, no matter what we're sensing. My guess is that the crystals don't just block the Mardróch's ability to sense teleport trails, they block all sensing. Since Meaghan's power works differently, it isn't blocked."

"That never occurred to me," Cal confessed. "But you were always the logical one. At least now I know to check before I leave the cave. Speaking of, if you don't mind keeping quiet for a minute, I need to take another look."

He picked up the torch and closed his eyes.

§

THE MARDRÓCH search party remained until late afternoon. Nick made them wait a half hour longer before deciding it would be safe to travel, then Cal pushed the rock aside, opening the tunnel once more. Nick crawled in first, pushing the backpack in front of him, and Meaghan followed. Cal went last, closing off the tunnel entrance behind him.

Although the jicab root still kept Meaghan's pain manageable, it helped little in the tunnel. Every shuffle felt like sandpaper dragging across her leg. Each pebble became a searing knife, stabbing her as she crawled over it. Even her own weight became intolerable, forcing agony through her body whenever her injured leg had to bear it. Although it took only minutes to travel the tunnel's short distance, it felt like hours. By the time sunlight touched her face, it met tears. She sat on the ground and worked hard to control the urge to scream.

Nick checked her bandage to ensure it remained tight, and then turned to Cal. "She can't walk," he said as he drew the backpack over his shoulders, securing it in place. "We'll take turns carrying her. How far do we have to go?"

Cal pointed to the south. "About two miles through the field. Unfortunately, it's all open, so we need to move fast. Should I give her more jicab root?"

"Not a chance," Meaghan responded. She managed a smile and wiped the tears from her cheek with the back of her hand. "Not if you're carrying me. You'll want to throw me if I take that stuff."

Cal chuckled and picked her up, cradling her in his arms as they set out across the field. He and Nick traded carrying her every quarter mile and they made good progress, covering the distance before the sun had finished hiding behind the horizon. Dusk turned trees into silhouettes of black against a deep red sky, and a mild breeze tickled daisies as it passed. The breeze brought a chill and Meaghan shivered, wishing she still had her sweater. The short-sleeved t-shirt she wore did little to keep her warm.

Cal stepped onto a slab of granite flush with the ground and stopped. "Put her down," he instructed Nick. "We're here."

Nick eased her onto her feet, leaving an arm at her waist to give her support. Her leg throbbed, but she did her best to ignore it. She leaned against him, balancing her weight on her good leg as she scanned the area. Tall grass bloomed into weeds in front of them, its endless expansion broken only by the occasional tree or rock.

"I don't see anything," she said.

"You will," Cal assured her. He puckered his lips, whistling one long, high pitch followed by two short, low ones, and then waited.

A minute passed, then another. After a third had come and gone, a woman stood in front of them, seemingly created from air. She paused for a minute. Her jet-black hair danced along the breeze while she scanned their faces in the thickening darkness. When she saw Cal, she approached them, a large smile floating on top of full pink lips. Her smoke colored eyes twinkled in greeting. Her emotions welcomed with joy. And love, Meaghan realized. She felt the same love flowing from Cal.

The woman took Nick's hand and held it between her own. "You are welcome here, Nick," she said, her voice soft and melodic. "You won't recognize me, but I know you. I apprenticed under your mother when you were young. I'm Neiszhe. It's good to see you again."

"Likewise," Nick said. He nodded and she returned the gesture before releasing his hand.

She moved to Meaghan next, taking her hand in the same manner. "You're hurt," she said. "I can feel the intensity of your pain, but it won't last long. You'll be healed by morning."

Meaghan almost wept with relief at her promise. "Thank you."

"It's my gift. It's my pleasure to share it with you, though I'm afraid I don't know your name."

"Meaghan."

Neiszhe's eyes widened. Awe and respect emanated from her. "I apologize, my Lady. I didn't know. It's an honor, a true honor." She let go of Meaghan's hand, then took a step back and curtsied.

Confused, but not wanting to be impolite, Meaghan moved to mimic the gesture, stopping when Nick tightened his hand on her waist. "Don't," he whispered in her ear. "If anyone bows to you, nod in return." He loosened his grip. "I'll explain later. Don't keep her waiting."

Neiszhe remained frozen in her curtsy and Meaghan took Nick's advice, nodding to the woman. Neiszhe offered another smile before straightening up and taking Meaghan's hand in hers. "You are welcome here, my Lady," she said, and then moved on to greet Cal with a kiss.

Meaghan opened her mouth, intending to ask Nick for his explanation, but shock robbed her of the words. In front of them, the field began to ripple. Ripples dissolved into shimmers, blurring the landscape until the field no longer existed.

In its place, an entire village materialized.

CHAPTER FOURTEEN

STREET LIGHTS illuminated their path as they threaded their way through the village along packed dirt roads sprinkled with thin layers of gravel. Cal led the way, using side streets whenever possible. Even though Meaghan did not see many people, she sensed all of them, their emotions impossible to manage on top of her own increasing pain. She focused on Nick's power again, and then sighed in relief when it worked to shut out their emotions almost as well as it had Cal's.

Cal managed to avoid all but a handful of villagers, but those people they encountered welcomed him back with a wave and an eye of curiosity for the woman in his arms. He responded to them, nodding or calling out a quick hello, but did not stop.

The village consisted of twenty or thirty houses that would have fit well in a quaint New England town. Cheerful paint, clapboard siding, and wood shutters greeted them from one and two story homes maintained with pride. Meticulous lawns and bright flower gardens mimicked magazine photographs, creating a sense of cozy warmth cities of steel and glass skyscrapers could never accomplish. In front of some of the houses, small wood signs advertised shops. A tailor resided across the street from a General Store. A grocer faced a carpenter. And near the end of the village, they turned at a sign advertising medicines and herbs.

A small stone path led them to the front door of a one-story cottage painted in baby blue with white trim. They entered into the main living room of the house. A plush tan couch and hardwood rocking chair offered inviting places to sit. Blankets and pillows tossed on furniture added warmth and color. And shelves lined with hard cover books showed varying interests in medical practices, baking, history, and gardening. They passed from that room into the kitchen. Cal set Meaghan down in a chair at the dining table before turning to a wood cooking stove monopolizing one wall of the room. He picked up several logs from a bin next to the stove.

"I'll light a fire," he told Neiszhe. "It feels like it'll be a cold night. Shall I assume it'll also be a long one?"

"I believe it will be," she responded. "When you're through building the fire, can you make Meaghan some jicab tea? I'm going to set up in the living room. If you can bring her when she's done drinking, I'd appreciate it."

"Of course," he agreed and she left the room. Nick took a seat at the table opposite Meaghan while Cal finished lighting a fire in the stove and put the kettle on to boil.

Meaghan closed her eyes, hoping the tea would not take long. The jicab root no longer worked. She tried to focus on something other than the pain echoing through her body, but had little success. Her mind flashed to her meeting with Neiszhe. Nick's explanation of the woman's reaction would prove a good distraction, but Meaghan doubted she had the energy for it. Instead, she focused on the next question running through her head.

"How do you buy things?" she blurted out, and then grimaced when Nick raised an eyebrow at her. "I saw the shops," she told him. "But I don't know how commerce works here. Do you have some sort of currency?"

"Currency?" Cal asked, sitting down at the table with them. "What's that?"

"Money," she told him.

Cal's blank stare was uncomprehending, and Nick chuckled beside him. "Money is pieces of paper and metal discs," he explained. "The people on Earth work for them and then exchange them for what they need, like food."

"Got it." Cal smiled. "So it's like bartering."

"Sort of. They call it buying and selling. Someone who wants the product is buying and someone giving it is selling," Nick said. "And it's required and not optional. If they don't have the money, they don't get what they need, no matter how much they need it."

"Odd," Cal muttered, standing up when the kettle whistled. "I'm glad we don't do that here. I'd be in trouble. I'm not able to make enough spirit to get everything I need."

"So what sort of system do you use?" Meaghan asked. "You have shops, so you must have them for a reason."

"They aren't shops," Nick responded. "Though I can see how you would think that. They're houses, like Neiszhe's. The owners put up signs so people can find what they need. We don't buy or sell things. We get them for free."

Meaghan frowned, considering what he had said. Money served the purpose of controlling supply and demand and this system did not seem to have any similar controls built into it. On top of that, she could not picture anyone working for free. "Aren't people unhappy?" she finally asked. "Without payment, don't they feel like slaves?"

"Not at all," Nick said. "What we do for work is natural to us. It extends from our powers and using our powers to benefit society as a whole benefits us, too. A shoemaker is gifted at making shoes, but not clothing, so he trades in a way. He gets the clothes whenever he needs them and the seamstress gets her shoes whenever her old ones wear out."

"Then how do you keep track?"

Cal set a mug in front of her. Steam rose from it in curling tendrils and she clasped her hands around it, absorbing the warmth.

"We don't," Cal answered her question. "There's no point. People don't take what they don't need." He sat back down and nodded toward her mug. "Drink your tea."

She raised it to her lips, blowing on it before taking a sip. It was all she could do not to spit it out. Squirreling her face, she gagged down another sip before continuing the conversation. "I suppose if you've been brought up to respect that tradition, it could work. But if everything is free, when do you barter?"

"When we have something rare someone else wants, such as decorative items—"

"Or my spirits," Cal interrupted.

"Right." Nick chuckled. "Exactly. And we barter when we're in other kingdoms. Since we aren't giving back to those societies on a regular basis, we either exchange goods or we perform services to make things even."

"Kingdoms?" Meaghan asked. "You mentioned a King before, but I thought he was a figurehead. He's not?"

Nick shook his head. "A single family line has ruled this kingdom for well over a thousand years."

"No kidding," she muttered. She lifted her mug, taking another sip. "That seems archaic to me."

"Does it?" Cal asked. He braced his hands on the table and leaned toward her. "I wouldn't be so quick to judge if I were you. What we have certainly works better than what I've heard of your world. You have money which makes people starve, gadgets which keep people distracted and in a hurry, and no stars to look at during the night. Do you want us to turn into that?"

His question hung heavy in the air and Meaghan realized too late how insulting her words had sounded. She set her mug down.

"That's not how I meant it. Where I grew up, we overthrew a monarchy because it didn't keep the people's interests in mind. A majority vote now determines who runs the country. Despite how it appears to you, that type of government does work best for us."

"It works best for *them*," Nick corrected. He took her hand in his. "You aren't part of that world anymore, Meg. Here, the monarchy works best. Or at least it did, and it will again."

"Did?"

"The royal family was overthrown, but when they were in charge, they were excellent rulers. They took care of the people and they were well-loved."

"By everyone except Garon, a pig of a man who murdered the King and Queen," Cal interjected. "He has no head to rule except by his own whim and the kingdom has suffered since."

"Garon was the royal advisor," Nick explained, his voice matching the steel in Cal's tone. "And he was a Guardian. He may have declared himself King, but we aren't powerless to stop him. We didn't need a democracy to wage war and we don't need one to overthrow him."

"I understand." Meaghan shifted in her chair to direct her next question at Cal. "You were the King's Guardian at the time, weren't you?" He nodded and she covered his hand with hers. "That must have been difficult for you."

"You can tell," he responded. He drew his eyes up and she thought she saw mist coating them. "If you choose."

She dropped her hold on Nick's power. Anger and pain washed over her with such strength she held her breath. When she had felt enough, she forced an exhale, and welcomed Nick's power again.

"Your pain is deep," she said, "and your anger's equally strong. Were you close to Garon?"

"Yes." Cal stood and went to the stove. Picking up a poker, he opened the door to the firebox and shifted the logs. "He was a close friend, or so I thought. In the end, he cost me many of my real friends, and my first wife, Alisen." He put the poker away. "She was a member of the castle guard. The worst part is none of us saw it coming."

"I'm sorry," Meaghan whispered. "I truly am."

"A monarchy can be a good thing," Cal told her, turning back around. "When the right people are in charge. You'll learn in time. For now," he nodded toward her cup, "drink. You'll learn nothing if you aren't healed."

§

SHE SCREAMED. She did not mean to and she feared someone outside would be alarmed by the noise, especially so late at night, but she could not help it. She kept it stifled as long as she could and then it forced its way out of her, a cyclone of power and velocity. It had been hours since they had started the healing process, hours in which Neiszhe's power had burned through her ankle, knitting tendons and muscles back together. Meaghan understood the necessity of it, but she could not control her own human reaction. Neiszhe's power seared her to the core. Each time the Healer forced more energy into Meaghan's wound, pain flashed again, fire upon fire, until she had no other choice. She screamed.

Nick took her hand. He said nothing when she gripped him with such strength she felt certain she had crushed his bones. He only held her as she cried.

Neiszhe's hands moved from Meaghan's ankle to her pant leg. Lifting it, she frowned at the bandage underneath.

"You did this?" she accused Cal.

He rubbed the back of his neck. "I did my best, love. The bone broke the skin and I had to move her. I reset it, but I can't sense the injury like you can."

"The reset is fine. You did a good job. It's your bandaging that needs practice." She unraveled the gauze. Dirt fell to the floor with each layer. "Something got into the wound. She has an infection. It isn't bad yet, but it's there. How long has her leg been broken?"

"Since early afternoon," Nick answered. "She saved Cal's life by tackling a monster in the caves. Both she and the beast went into the water."

Neiszhe's head snapped up. Panic froze her eyes wide as she tore them from Nick to Cal.

"I'm okay," he assured her. "I have cuts and maybe a bruised rib or two. It can wait."

She nodded and returned her focus to Meaghan. "What color was the water?"

"Black," Meaghan muttered. She struggled to sit up, losing the will when Nick pushed on her shoulders to keep her down. "Black. The monster, it," she hissed a breath of pain. "It bit my leg."

"The water may have had something in it," Neiszhe said. "Though it's usually green we have to worry about. More likely, the creature's mouth caused the infection." She found the stick Cal had used as a brace and sighed. "Or this might have."

Cal shrugged. "It's the best I could do, given the circumstances. We had to get her out of the cave somehow."

"It's all right. It just doesn't make it easier for her." Neiszhe removed the last of the bandage, and then looked up at Nick. "Be sure to hold her still and keep a hand in contact with her skin. Healing her ankle was painful enough. Fusing bone is worse, and the infection complicates things. Speeding up her healing will cause it to speed up, too. If her fever gets too high, we'll need to take a break."

Nick raised Meaghan's shoulders and slid her onto his lap. Then he pinned her with his elbows and placed his hands on her forehead.

Neiszhe interlaced her fingers and rested them over the wound, closing her eyes to focus. Beads of sweat began rolling down her face. Meaghan's skin tingled. She squirmed and Nick tightened his hold moments before the pain resumed.

It did not take long before Meaghan's mind burned with the heat building within her. They stopped for ten minutes and then began again. The process repeated a dozen times during the night until both Neiszhe and Meaghan's clothes were soaked in sweat. When Meaghan became too tired, she slipped in and out of awareness.

Finally, when the sun danced its first tendrils of color over the horizon, Neiszhe lifted her hands and smiled. The small effort chased the lines from her face.

"It is done," she said.

CHAPTER FIFTEEN

IT WAS not the first time Nick had experienced the healing process. Several times, injuries and broken bones had placed him on the receiving end of that pain. He had also witnessed it many times before in his mother's house, and had assisted her in her duties once he had grown strong enough to keep her patients steady. He thought he had built an emotional callous to it, but tonight had taught him otherwise.

Perhaps his ability to sense Meaghan had made it worse. The intensity of her pain had washed through him, a steady ache he could not relieve or abolish. Or perhaps it had more to do with how he felt about her. Whatever reason, he had despised the process by the time it had finished. As Meaghan lay unconscious in his arms, he fought to control the anger surging through him.

Despite how he felt and despite his desire to find someone to blame for Meaghan's suffering, he could not fault Neiszhe for the necessary evil. Meaghan's injuries had been severe. The power needed to heal them drained extensive energy from its host and

Neiszhe bore the signs of that labor. Her movements were slow and stiff. Her eyes looked tired and dull. And her cheeks appeared flush beneath a thin layer of sweat.

Cal helped her to bed, and then returned to the living room where he sat on the floor next to Meaghan. He laid a palm on her forehead.

"Her fever's gone," he said.

Nick nodded, but he kept his arms locked tight around Meaghan's body.

"I see the look in your eyes," Cal continued, "and I know it well. The first time I had to watch Alisen go through this, I wanted to kill the Healer for it." He squeezed Nick's shoulder, a gesture born more from camaraderie than comfort. "That time, she had broken her hand in a sparring match in school. The second time, she broke her arm falling off the vines on the side of the castle. My fault," he said, chuckling when Nick raised an eyebrow at him. "I dared her to climb them. It's not something you'd expect for the maturity level of a couple of twenty-something Guardians, but in my defense, the King was the one taking bets on the endeavor." He shrugged, turning serious again. "I'd like to say going through this gets easier, but it doesn't. Focus on the fact Meaghan is healed and remember to thank Neiszhe when she wakes this afternoon."

"I will," Nick promised. "She's talented. This should have taken longer."

"Yes it should have," Cal agreed. "You should get some sleep."

Nick made no effort to move. He studied Meaghan's face then lifted a hand to her cheek. It remained pale, but Cal was right, her skin no longer burned. "Do the villagers know who she is?"

"None of them know her by sight, only by name, and Neiszhe will keep Meaghan's identity a secret. Still, I recommend staying hidden until dark and then you can start travelling again. You have two days of open fields to go through before the next protected area, so night travel will work best for a while." He stood, casting a glance down at Nick. "You know you need to tell her soon. She should hear it from you, but she'll hear it from someone else if you're not careful."

Nick sighed. "It's not an easy thing to explain."

"It won't get easier so you might as well get it over with." Cal bent down to slide his arms under Meaghan's body. Nick released his grip and Cal lifted her. "I'll take her to the village's guest house. She'll be safe there. For you," he nodded toward the sofa and grinned. "Sweet dreams."

§

SLEEP STOLE Nick from the world before he could consider the worry and exhaustion knotting his muscles. It settled him into a dreamless void, tantalizing him with peaceful silence, and then before no more than two hours had passed, it threw him back with the same haste.

Agony charged through him. His muscles coiled, and he bolted upright with the instinct to flee. He controlled the urge and took a deep breath, closing his eyes to focus on the emotion. It dissipated before he could determine its source. He lay back down and wondered if his body still reacted to Meaghan's ordeal from last night, but when it surged again, he knew better. The pain came from Meaghan. Without a second thought, he jumped from the couch and dashed out the front door.

Bright sunlight burned his eyes. He cupped his hand over his brow and scanned the street for any indication of the guesthouse. Neiszhe's house stood near the end of the road, but several houses remained to the left and another dozen greeted him from the right. The street teemed with people. Some hurried past, busy in their errands, but others took slower steps, eyeing him with curiosity. Meaghan's pain tugged at him again and he turned to his right to follow it, walking with a nonchalance that belied his desire to run. He feared for her safety, but leading people to her identity would only bring Mardróch if traitors resided in the village.

The pain grew stronger, guiding him down a side street to a thatched roof cottage. He opened the house's picket gate, closing it behind him before strolling down the pebble walkway. When he reached the door, he turned the handle, tensing as he sensed for danger, and then entered when he felt nothing more than Meaghan's presence.

Daylight streamed through pale blue curtains, revealing only a single bed and a fireplace. No enemies waited to attack. Instead, Meaghan sat on the floor in the far corner of the room, her feet crossed at her ankles, her knees tucked under her chin. She rocked back and forth, pressing her hands to her ears. A low moan escaped her as he dropped down next to her.

"Meg," he whispered, taking her into his arms. "What's wrong?"

She clutched at him instead of answering, pressing her tear soaked face into his shoulder.

"Meg," he tried again and then remained quiet when her pain

dissolved. He lifted a hand to her head, drawing it down her hair and then her back, repeating the movement until her tight muscles relaxed under his touch. Her sobs subsided, but she remained in his arms for a few minutes longer.

She lifted her head and he thought she would pull back from him, but she pressed her lips into his neck instead. Electricity bulleted through his system. His mind screamed at him to hold back, but he ignored it. Burying his hands in her hair, he drew her closer. She moved her lips along his skin until they tickled his jaw, then she drew them up to graze his lips. Her pressure remained light and he closed his eyes, lost to the warmth she brought him. She placed delicate kisses on each of his eyelids, and then dropped her attention back to his lips. Her pressure turned firmer and he responded, taking her mouth on a sigh.

His heart jolted. His mind panicked. Then he prayed for strength. He dropped his hands to her shoulders and pulled her back. "Meg," he said, opening his eyes, "we can't do this. You know we can't."

"Do I?" She rose to her feet, and then walked across the room to sit on the bed. "You say I do, but you've never told me why. I'm tired of you putting me off, Nick. When will you tell me what I need to know?"

He frowned. "When the time is right."

"When will that be?" She crossed her arms over her chest. "When someone else makes a slip like Neiszhe did? Why did she curtsy anyway? You said you'd explain."

"I will, but not now." He stood and walked to the window. Lifting a curtain, he peered outside. The villagers still scurried about their business, oblivious to Nick and Meaghan's presence. Grateful his foray outside had not drawn attention to the small cottage, he faced Meaghan again. Her eyes held his with a familiar anger and he knew he had pushed her patience too far. Cal's advice echoed through his head, but he ignored it. "I didn't come here to argue. I came because your pain woke me. What happened?"

She lifted her chin, a stubborn gesture he also knew well and he understood she would not answer his question until he answered hers.

"Fine," he said. He turned toward the door. "You need to stay inside until nightfall, so get some sleep. The next few days will be strenuous at best."

He opened the door, took a step outside, and then paused when he heard a noise behind him. It took him a moment to recognize the sound as a single word, "Wait."

He turned back around. Meaghan stood in the center of the room, her hands folded together in front of her. Her anger had disappeared, lost to wide-eyed terror. She tightened her fingers, twisting them around each other. "Don't go."

Closing the door, he shut the village out. Meaghan backed against the bed and sat down again. Her cheeks took on a red tinge. "I didn't mean to wake you."

"It's all right," he said. He sat down beside her. "What happened?"

"I couldn't control it," she whispered. "I feel like I should be able to by now and I tried, but there are too many people. Some pare mad, others are happy. Some are confused and in pain and sad, or worried and stressed. There are dozens of emotions, Nick. Too many of them. They hurt and you weren't close enough for me to focus."

He drew her against him, understanding. He should have realized that would happen. Her mind could not process so many emotions and without the ability to shut them out, they overwhelmed her. He pressed a kiss to her forehead.

"Please don't leave," she begged. "I won't ask any questions. Just don't leave me."

"I won't," he promised. He ran a hand down her bare arm, felt goose bumps and let her go. He stood, and then crossed to the fireplace. Removing small pieces of kindling from the wood box, he tossed them into the hearth.

"You should have told me why you were in pain," he said. He glanced over his shoulder at her, not expecting a verbal answer and she did not disappoint him. Guilt caused her to cast her eyes to her hands, but anger also stiffened her shoulders. "Our travels are dangerous, Meg, and if we expect to live through them, we have to communicate." He turned back to the fireplace and added two small logs, then struck a match and threw it on top. A fire took hold. He waited until it grew strong enough to sustain itself before returning to his seat on the bed.

"Communication starts with me," he said and took her hands in his. "I've built distrust in you since we arrived here and I apologize. You need to ask questions, and I need to keep a promise I made our first night here. I need to answer those questions." He took a deep breath. "What do you want to know first?"

Meaghan sat back. Wrinkles formed between her eyebrows as she pulled them together. "I'm not certain where to start."

"If you don't feel ready, we can wait."

She shook her head. "It's not that. I'm not sure if I am or not, but you've been avoiding this conversation for a reason. Why don't you think I'm ready for the answers?"

"It's not you," he confessed, then sighed. "It's me who isn't ready. I want to protect you."

"That's your job, isn't it?"

"Physically, but not in the way I am. You know I care about you. I won't deny it. And the answers I have for you will make your life difficult. The responsibility you've been given, that I have to give to you, is a lot to bear. I wanted to keep you free of that for as long as possible."

She inclined her head. "You think I can't handle it?"

"Not at all. It's…" he shook his head. Standing, he walked to the fireplace, and then leaned a hand against the mantel as he studied the flames. "It will change things for you," he turned to face her, "and for us."

"I'm not sure I understand."

"I know," he said. Tucking his hands into his pockets, he stared toward the window, his eyes unseeing as his mind worked to tell her the truth he wished more than anything was not true. "Cal told you he guarded the King," he started and forced his eyes to hers. She nodded. "My mother guarded the Queen. They were both at the castle the day Garon's rebellion took place. Neither of them likes to talk about what happened, but I've heard enough. Garon formed an army of Guardians bent on taking control, Guardians who'd been banished for their crimes. They were thieves, murderers, even people who'd tried to overthrow the monarchy in the past. Garon had a Spellmaster design a spell to convert his army's powers into something stronger, something he felt would be unstoppable, and then he killed the Spellmaster to ensure a counter spell couldn't be written."

"The Mardróch," Meaghan realized.

"They weren't his intent, but their powers are unnatural. Since powers are part of a person, the spell not only twisted their magic, but it also twisted what was left of their humanity."

"Couldn't someone else write a spell to stop them?" she asked.

"Only a Spellmaster can give words the power to work as a spell. Garon killed the last known Spellmaster. If a new one has been born, he or she hasn't exhibited the ability yet."

"What do you mean? Aren't people born with their powers?"

"They are, but powers lie dormant until children can handle them. Active powers, those that can be used as weapons, usually don't show up until children are at least eight. A six-month-old Firestarter would be a disaster, for instance, so that power doesn't usually appear until children can understand the damage they cause when they set fires. Powers like yours and mine show up earlier. They're considered passive. They can't cause any physical damage and having them at an early age helps us adapt to them."

"Does it?" she asked, a wry smile crinkling the corners of her lips.

He chuckled. "You're not used to having your full power, but yes, it does. If you hadn't been able to use your power on Earth, you would've had more trouble understanding what you're sensing now.

You wouldn't be able to translate other people's feelings or separate them from your own. As far as controlling your power, you'll learn in time."

"Let's hope so," she said. "I have more questions about powers, but I think I'll reserve those for another day. For now, I'd like to hear more about Garon's attack, if you don't mind."

"Of course." A log popped in the fireplace, scattering sparks over the floor, and Nick turned to draw a screen across the hearth. "The Mardróch used lightning to breach the castle walls," he said, facing Meaghan again. "The stone bricks were thick, and their collapse killed many, including the Queen. She died in her living quarters. The King died in the throne room, by Garon's hand."

Meaghan paled. "The walls fell in first," she said. "Then the smoke came, and the lightning."

"It would appear that way from inside the castle. That's from one of your dreams, isn't it?"

She nodded. "The one with the fire, right before the man rescued me."

"Miles," Nick told her. "He protected the Queen's sister. He's one of the Elders now."

"I remember the woman saying his name. The woman," Meaghan closed her eyes, holding back tears, "with the red hair. That was Mom. Vivian," she corrected.

"Yes, it was." He crossed the room. Pulling her to her feet, he drew her into his arms.

"You knew. Every time I told you about my nightmare. Every time I wondered why it kept coming back to me, you knew the reason." She pushed away from him. "Why didn't you tell me?"

"Would you have believed me?"

"I trusted you. I would have believed you." He raised an eyebrow, and she sighed. "In the same way I believed you about this world at first," she conceded. "How old was I when that happened?"

"Two."

"So if I was in the castle, I'm either the child of a Guardian or part of the royal family."

"You don't have Guardian powers," Nick pointed out.

"And Neiszhe didn't curtsy for you, so I'm royalty. What am I to the King and Queen?"

Nick hesitated, but he could not avoid the truth any longer.

"Nick?"

"You're their daughter."

She stared at him. Her mouth opened, closed, then opened once more before she forced out a whisper. "Are you saying I'm a princess?"

"No." He took her hand in his. "I'm not. I'm saying to anyone who doesn't recognize Garon's rule in this kingdom, you're our Queen."

CHAPTER SIXTEEN

THE AIR grew cold. It hung thick and raw, nipping at Meaghan with sharp ice teeth that turned her skin red. She pulled her cloak tight, grateful Nick had thought to get one for each of them before they had left the village. The thick wool blocked some of the air, warming her skin, though she wished it would do the same for her mind.

They had been walking since the sun fell below the horizon. The moon failed to show its face, leaving only a few brave stars for guidance through the ominous dark. The night stretched out somber before them, its stillness broken only by the occasional reprieve of a songless bird, its soft feathers rustling through the tar black sky. Animals skulked in the shadows, watching them with amber eyes that glinted as she and Nick passed. Their unblinking surveillance seemed to warn of a perilous future, and Meaghan heeded the warning, taking tentative steps to maintain the quiet commanded by the sleeping earth.

Though darkness provided their journey some cover, the fields left them vulnerable for miles, visible to any who wanted to seek them out. The thought tensed her muscles and locked her words into shallow whispers spoken out of strict necessity. Hours stretched silence between her and Nick. Hours in which she had time to focus on the single word numbing her mind.

Queen.

The word carried a weight she had never felt before. She knew nothing of this kingdom, nothing of its practices, its people, its laws, and yet, she had become its leader. The absurd notion poised another argument in her mind for the abolition of monarchies. A leader should have experience and knowledge, age and wisdom. She had none of those things. Her leadership experience extended only to a handful of club offices she had held in high school and a one-time stint as a camp counselor two summers ago. Her knowledge of this world extended to half a week of detrimental days in which survival counted more on luck than expertise.

Cal would have made a better choice to lead, or even Nick, despite his young age, could have done a better job. But because she shared the genetics of the people who had previously run the kingdom, she now owned the responsibility.

She supposed it would have made sense if her parents had raised her. If she had had the luxury of watching them rule every day of her life, of learning from their experiences, she could see taking the role.

But she had never had the chance. She had never known that life or her birthright. Removed from the world well before she could remember living on it, she felt like she belonged in the kingdom as much as she belonged on Mars.

It did not seem fair to the people who looked to her for leadership, and because her adoptive mother—her true mother—had raised her to do the right thing, she knew she had to convince Nick of that fact. If she could convince him she did not belong as Queen, he could convince the Elders. Together, they could figure out a way to replace her.

"Are you okay?"

Nick's question broke through her reverie and she focused her mind again on their surroundings. They walked along the edge of a small cropping of trees, an oasis in the near endless field. He stopped and she did the same.

"Meg, I asked if you were all right."

She nodded in answer, and then turned her gaze toward the horizon. The sun had begun to rise, streaking the sky with pockets of deep red and orange. The surreal scene felt too peaceful for the turmoil within her.

Nick took a step toward her. She returned her eyes to him. "Do you realize I've been talking to you?"

"I....uh," she hesitated. "No. What did you need?"

"Food and shelter," he said, adjusting the backpack on his shoulders. He nodded toward the trees beside them without removing his focus from her. "I was saying this might be a good place to set up for the day. It will be bright soon. And Meg," he lowered his voice when she trailed her eyes away again. "I think it's time for us to finish our conversation."

"There's nothing left to discuss."

"There is. I know you're upset with me. That was obvious when you refused to continue talking yesterday, but you can't ignore this."

"I'm not upset with you. It's a lot to accept."

"It is," he agreed, "and I don't mean to sound callous, but you don't have a choice. You can't change who you are. Did you sleep at all?"

She shook her head. "I couldn't."

"I didn't think so. You need sleep, so we'll definitely stop here. You can take the first sleeping shift."

"Fine," she conceded to the stop, but she did not feel settled by his decree. "I don't understand why I don't have a choice in this though. The idea of me being royalty is," she paused, searching for the right word and then decided to call it as she saw it, "absurd. I don't belong here."

"Absurd," Nick echoed, his voice taking on a chill she had not expected. "We have different views on that, but we'll discuss it after we eat. And we *will* discuss it," he said, holding her with a firm gaze that curbed her instinct to argue. "You've been distracted all day and it's not safe. We need to get this out of the way so you can stay focused."

He turned from her and started walking again. She followed, resuming her silence. Although the trees covered no more than an acre, their dense canopy provided enough coverage to keep them out of sight for the day. Nick threaded his way through the small forest until he found a patch of land clear enough to allow them to set up camp. He eased the backpack from his shoulders, and then dug a hole using a stick. Within the hole, he built a fire. Meaghan removed the blanket from the backpack and spread it out in front of the fire.

"I'll find something to eat," Nick told her when she sat down on the blanket. "Wait here, okay?"

She nodded and he disappeared into the trees. Crossing her legs in front of her, she stretched her hands toward the fire. As her muscles warmed, they relaxed and she struggled to ignore the tiredness tugging at her eyelids. She tried to stay awake by outlining the conversation she wanted to have with Nick. When she had told him how she felt about her leadership role, his anger had surprised her, but she knew him well enough to convince him of her feelings if she approached it the right way. She only had to figure out what approach would work best. She stared at the fire, at the wisps of smoke it created, and drew her knees up to her chin. She felt too weary to think straight, so she allowed the flames to lull her into calm.

The fire's steady flickering took on a deeper glow as it feasted on the fallen limbs Nick had used for fuel. A chilling breeze reached through the forest, and Meaghan tightened her arms around her legs. The smoke grew thicker, and then a log popped. Sparks scattered toward her, dying before they reached the blanket. The fire flared, jumping a foot higher into the air and Meaghan almost did the same. She scrambled to her feet, yanking the blanket away from the fire before another shower of sparks spread across the ground.

"Find the child."

The command came from nowhere and Meaghan startled again, surprised by the sudden noise, but not frightened by it. Although Cal's voice sounded distorted within the element, she recognized it, and she heard the panic in it.

"Who?" she asked, directing her question toward the flames.

"No time. He's in danger. Find him."

Sparks showered across the ground again, singeing a pile of dried leaves and lighting it. Meaghan ran to the budding blaze. Using the blanket, she beat out the flames before they could spread. When she turned back to the fire, it had returned to normal, and she knew Cal had left. She scanned the forest, confused by what he had said, but found nothing that would lead her to the child he had mentioned.

Dropping the blanket to the ground, she frowned down at the scorched grass. Deep brown and black scarring trailed at her feet, pointing toward the woods. Pointing in the shape of a distinguishable arrow. Her heart raced with the realization and she followed it, brushing past Nick as he reentered the clearing.

Cal's command spurred her onward. She ignored Nick's voice calling her and the sound of his feet rustling the ground as he chased her. She ignored fallen tree limbs as they battered her legs and the occasional rock that kicked her ankle. She ignored it all except the need to find the child, and the rancid smell drifting toward her. She knew even before she reached the tree line that Mardróch would greet her, and she knew they would have the child. This time the monsters had not come for her.

When the field came into view, she confirmed her suspicions. A young boy no more than four or five stood in the open, spotlighted by the increasing sun. A gentle breeze lifted a few strands of blonde hair from his head, and tears streaked down his face, but otherwise, he did not move as he remained captive to two Mardróch. They circled him, not attacking, and Meaghan realized they toyed with him.

As one monster broke eye contact, the other came into view. The young child had only seconds to move, enough time to shift a foot forward before he became victim to another set of red eyes. They tortured him with the hope of an impossible escape. The cruel enjoyment the Mardróch gained from their game came across to Meaghan as rotting peat, a putrid odor with a sweet undercurrent that forced her to control her gag reflex.

She approached the edge of the field, speeding up to bolster her courage. She did not have a plan, but hoped one would come to her in time. A dozen steps from clearing the trees, a solid force hit her from behind, tackling her to the ground. She rolled with her attacker until he landed on top of her, pinning her wrists with his hands and her lower body with his legs. She glared up at him.

"Let me go," she commanded, struggling against his grip.

"Keep your voice down," Nick hissed in response. "They'll hear you."

"I intended for them to see me in another minute," she countered, though she whispered in deference to his request. "I have to save the boy."

"He's as good as dead," Nick said. "You can't save him. You'll only get killed in the process."

"I won't." She struggled harder against him, thrashing though he tightened his grip in response. "Cal was in the fire. He said—"

"I don't give a damn what Cal said," Nick shot back, his breath short and his eyes hard with anger. "You're my responsibility and I won't let you go out there."

"I have to."

169

"Not a chance."

Meaghan's wrists hurt from his grip and she stopped struggling. He relaxed his hold, though he kept her pinned.

"So you'll let him die?" she asked. "How can you be so cruel?"

"I'm sorry," he said and she turned her head from him. "Please, Meg, you have to understand—"

"No, I don't." Her eyes met his again, the anger in them matching the venom in her voice. "I don't and I won't."

Taking advantage of his relaxed grip, she made one last attempt at breaking free, resorting to a move she had learned years before in a self-defense course. Planting her feet on the ground, she bent her legs and arched her back upward, throwing him off balance and off her. At the same time, she jerked her arms down, forcing him to break his grip. As he struggled to his feet, she jumped to hers, and fled.

She doubled her pace as she ran, tearing past the remainder of the trees and across the open field toward the boy.

"Get away from him!" she screamed at the monsters.

Surprised by the attack, the Mardróch turned to look at her, breaking their eye contact with the boy. He ran from them, toward Meaghan, and the Mardróch followed. The boy reached her before the Mardróch and she dropped to the ground, scooping him into her arms. The monsters flanked her and the boy buried his head in her shoulder to prevent eye contact with the creatures. Meaghan did not have time to avert her eyes. She stared into their red orbs, surprised to find the color in them swirling, a continuous liquid rather than the solid irises she expected. Her breath caught in her throat and for a moment, she froze.

The odor or rotting flesh overwhelmed her senses, searing her nose. Instinct forced her to inhale to clear it from her airways and she smiled with the realization Nick's theory had been correct. The Mardróch's power had no effect on her. She stood, lifting the boy into her arms.

A hiss of surprise erupted from one of the creatures. "The immune one," he spoke, his voice a guttural mix of road gravel and raspy breath. "We've been looking for you. There's a prize for your death." He let out a rattling noise that sounded like screws bouncing in a tin can. Laughter, Meaghan realized, and her blood chilled. "Run," the creature croaked. "It will make for a better story."

He raised his hands. Blue lightning arced from fingertip to fingertip and Meaghan tightened her grip on the boy, backing away as she looked for a way out. Nick stood a dozen yards from them, unseen by the Mardróch, though he remained frozen as if hypnotized by their power. His face was white and she thought she saw the glint of tears in his eyes. He no longer blocked her. His fear rolled over her, followed by a deep grief that squeezed her heart. She hardened her heart against it, knowing as he did that he could not help her, and kept scanning the field. Nothing offered hope. The trees behind her seemed too far, but they were her only chance. She turned toward them as a flash of lightning blew apart the ground beside her. She felt heat singe her skin and swallowed, controlling her panic as she ran.

Another bolt landed behind her, and then a third and fourth fell to her right. Two more hit at once, missing her to the left as she swerved. The attack came quicker and closer and she feared Nick's warning had been right. Her ill-planned rescue attempt would get them all killed. She swallowed the bile in her throat and pushed her legs harder.

"I'm scared," the boy in her arms whimpered. "Make them stop."

"I can't," she responded between gasps. "I'm sorry."

"They're mean," he said, squeezing his eyes shut and burying his head into her neck. "Mean creatures with red eyes," he whispered. "You're not nice. Freeze and die."

A loud crack echoed behind them followed by an eerie silence. Meaghan could no longer sense Nick's emotions and sorrow washed over her as she feared the worst. She stifled the fear, determined still to save the boy, and continued running. Reaching the trees, she ducked under the canopy, certain the Mardróch could not be far behind, then listened for their pursuit. Only the sound of her own footfalls met her ears. No lightning skirted them. The earth no longer exploded at her heels. The sounds of chase had ceased.

She struggled against her instinct of flight and stopped, turning to look at the field. Less than thirty feet away, two statues stood where only grass had been before, each sculpted with the features of a Mardróch. Nick stood beside them. He traced the stone with his fingers before knocking on one of the creature's heads.

The boy wriggled in her arms and she let him go. He ran to the statues, using the bent arm of one of them to climb up its side, and then swung around to sit on its shoulders. Giggling, he covered the statues' eyes, leaving his hands there before looking up at Meaghan.

Understanding passed between them, and then a grin of pride slowly spread across the boy's face.

CHAPTER SEVENTEEN

"THIS IS amazing."

Meaghan scanned the stone figures in front of her, finding it impossible to disagree with Nick's assessment. The chiseled statues captured every tiny detail, right down to the thin threads of webbing covering the creatures' open mouths. Even the agony contoured on their faces appeared lifelike. Not life*like*, she realized with a shudder. It was life standing before her. Life turned to stone, frozen in death, and the agony had been real.

Freeze and die. The words echoed in her head and she turned her eyes from the Mardróch, feeling sick.

The boy stretched from his perch on the monster's shoulders, reaching his arms toward Nick and Nick lifted him off the statue, then set him on the ground. He circled the statue, trailing his hand along the stone.

"I've never seen this before," Nick said. "I don't think there's a power that can do this. Even the people who can turn things into stone have to be touching the object for their power to work. This isn't possible."

"Obviously it is," Meaghan responded, stopping the boy as he passed. She lifted him into her arms. He squirmed, but settled when she tightened her grip. "What do we do with him?"

"Find his parents," Nick answered. "But we'll have to wait for nightfall. It's not safe for you to be out in the open during the day, especially if there are Mardróch around."

"You don't need to be concerned with my safety," she replied as she turned from him. "We'll take him back to the camp for now, and then we'll figure out what to do."

Before Nick could respond, she walked away from him. He trailed her until they arrived at the campsite. The fire had reduced the wood to embers and he went to it to build it up again. She set the boy down on the blanket. Digging through the backpack for something to distract him, she found only her mother's amulet. It did not seem like the best toy, but it was all she had. She sat down next to the boy and showed it to him.

"That's pretty," he said.

"It is," she agreed. "It used to belong to my mother and now it belongs to me. Do you want to hold it?"

He took it from her. Flipping it in his hands, he traced his fingers along the front, over the glass, and then smiled up at her.

"What's your name?" she asked him.

"Aldin," he answered. "What's yours?"

"Meaghan," she responded and then pointed to Nick. "That's Nick."

"Nice to meet you," the boy responded, his manners automatic, though his eyes remained glued to the amulet. "Mata has pretty things like this, but they aren't this big. Dat makes them."

"Mata and Dat?"

"His mother and father," Nick said, sitting down beside them. Aldin turned the necklace over in his palm before Nick took hold of his left hand. The boy looked up, startled by the intrusion, but giggled when Nick pushed the sleeve of his sweater halfway up his forearm.

"That tickles," he said, and then tried to pull his sweater back down when Nick inched it up further. "Stop," he protested.

Nick held firm. "In a minute, buddy," he said, keeping his voice soft. He met the boy's eyes and smiled. "I only want to see your mark."

"I can't," Aldin said. "Mata said I can't show it to anyone."

"It's okay. You don't have to," Nick said and pulled the sweater back down, letting go of his arm. "Are you hungry?"

"Yes."

"I'll make breakfast then. Stay here and we'll eat soon."

The boy nodded and returned his attention to the amulet. Nick stood. Crossing the clearing, he picked up a pile of thick green branches, then brought them to the fire and tucked them into the dirt under the flames, shifting them so that their ends remained exposed.

He looked up at Meaghan. His face remained impassive, but a strong wave of concern washed over her, contrasting his calm demeanor. She realized he had dropped his guard on purpose to let her know they needed to talk, but she did not care. She refocused her attention on Aldin, and Nick's concern changed to irritation.

Aldin found a small protrusion on the back of the amulet and fidgeted with it, grinning when his prodding opened a thin metal door. He poked his finger into the opening and Meaghan snatched the amulet from him, surprise causing her to take it too fast. She pinched his finger in the hinge in the process.

"Hey!" he protested, puffing out his lip. "That hurt."

"Sorry," she muttered. Aldin stuck his finger in his mouth to suck on the scratch and she locked her eyes on the compartment he had discovered. She only had enough time to see a slip of paper nestled inside before Nick came over. She snapped the compartment closed.

"Did he find something?" Nick asked.

"No. Is the food done?"

Nick frowned. His face darkened, but he nodded in acceptance of her lie. She slipped the chain over her head.

"It's ready," he replied and returned to the fire. He knelt in front of it, pulling the sticks from the soil and piling them on top of a long piece of bark he had laid out. Upon closer inspection, Meaghan realized they looked more like sugar cane than sticks. The long tubes had turned brown while they baked. Nick removed a knife from the backpack and cut the ends off each one before slicing them into smaller segments. Then he picked up a large leaf, and wrapped it around one of the tubes before handing it to her.

"Baktui," he said. "It's essentially a nature-made version of energy gel." He wrapped another leaf around a second one and handed it to Aldin. "Have you had this before?" he asked him. Aldin nodded and pinched his fingers as he ran them up the cane. Thick, yellow goo oozed from one end.

"Careful, it's still hot," Nick warned him.

Aldin pursed his lips, blowing on the goo before he sucked it into his mouth. He repeated the process as Nick picked up a cane of his own, and Meaghan followed Aldin's example, scooping the goo into her mouth with her tongue.

The tube may have looked like sugar cane, but it did not come close to the flavor of the sweet treat. The baktui cane tasted more like a cross between a semi-tart lemon and salt. Its texture felt like crystallized honey. Although it tasted better than the jicab root, she preferred Earth's fabricated, chemical-laden energy gel to the cane. Still, she found it tolerable enough to eat, her hunger drove her to finish it, and a second one Nick handed her. She set the empty shells down, surprised to see Aldin devouring his fourth. The goo coated his cheeks and chin. He stretched his tongue out of his mouth to capture as much of the escaped goo as he could.

Nick chuckled. "You like that, do you bud?" Aldin nodded with enthusiasm and Nick pushed the bark toward him. "Have the last two. I need to talk to Meaghan for a few minutes."

"Mmm'okay," Aldin managed past a sticky mouthful.

Nick stood, offering a hand to Meaghan to pull her up. She left her hands in her lap.

"Don't be like that," Nick said. "We agreed to talk."

"That was before."

"Before what?" he asked, dropping his hand. "Before I made you mad? Or before you made me mad?"

She glared at him. "You have no right to be—"

"Like hell I don't," he snapped, and then glanced down at Aldin.

"I don't want to argue in front of him. Come on." He stuck out his hand again and this time she took it. He drew her to her feet with more force than she expected, and indicated with a nod for her to follow him. He stopped at the edge of the clearing, far enough away from Aldin so he could not hear them if they kept their voices low, but close enough so they could keep him in their sights.

Meaghan faced Nick and crossed her arms. "Go ahead. Talk."

"You first." He matched her posture. "You're obviously furious because I tried to stop you from doing something stupid."

"It wasn't stupid," she spat back, stepping toward him in lieu of raising her voice. "I was trying to do the right thing. I was trying to save the boy. I can't believe you wanted him to die."

"I didn't *want* him to die," Nick responded, his tone turning to ice. "I wanted to keep you safe. You have more responsibility than one boy, Meg. What would have happened to the people of this kingdom if you'd been killed? Did you think of that?"

"No, I didn't. I don't belong here and I certainly don't belong leading a group of people I don't know. You want to talk about stupid? Then let's talk about an entire population who thinks someone with no experience can save them. What do you expect me to do? I can't even control my power. How am I supposed to control a kingdom? How am I supposed to stop a group of unstoppable monsters when no one else has been able to? You people expect too much of me."

"You people," he echoed. "These are your people, not some random group. And when did you stop thinking of me as your friend?"

"When you refused to help him," she said, gesturing toward Aldin. "When you refused to help me."

"I can't help you, Meg. I can't *protect* you if you keep working against me."

"I don't need your protection." She turned to watch the boy as he tossed aside the shell from his fifth baktui cane. "Not at the expense of someone else's life."

"You do need it," he countered, placing a hand on her arm. "You're too valuable to—"

"I'm no more valuable than anyone else," she said, snapping her arm away from his touch. "And it's not like you even tried. You stood there and did nothing. They might as well have frozen you."

"What was I supposed to do? I had no way to attack them."

"You could have tried," she repeated. Turning her eyes back to his, she lifted her chin in defiance. "You didn't, but we did fine on our own."

"You got lucky," he corrected. "Though I'm still not sure how it happened. Do you have any idea?"

She crossed her arms, refusing to respond and he sighed. "You're being childish, Meg." He put his hands on her shoulders and lowered his voice to a near whisper, forcing her to concentrate in order to hear him. "I know you think I was wrong for trying to stop you and I know you think I'm not doing a good job of protecting you, but this is important. Keeping information from me can be dangerous."

"Why?" she asked, holding on to her defiance despite his pleading. "I don't see how it can matter right now."

"Because I know more about this world than you do. I realize that's part of why you don't feel like you belong here. That will change in time, but for now, it matters."

She narrowed her eyes. "What do you know?"

"The names Aldin used for his parents—"

"Mata and Dat?"

"Yes. Those words aren't from here. And neither is he."

Concern emanated from Nick again and Meaghan ceded to it, dropping her arms. "What do you mean?"

"The terms are only used in the northern area of this kingdom, in a territory called Zeiihbu. It's inhabited by people who have chosen to maintain tribal life, guarding and ruling themselves and following old customs and ways."

"Such as?"

"Using single room huts instead of houses. Hunting and gathering for everything they need. Living simple lives with no outside exchange. Each tribal member is marked with a tattoo at birth on the inside of their forearm, close to the elbow."

She nodded, understanding. "Like the one Aldin confirmed he had."

"Exactly. I was hoping to see it so I could recognize which tribe he came from. Some of the tribes are peaceful and others are prone to violence and war. Knowing which he's from would help me figure out why he's here."

She trailed her gaze to Aldin. He remained focused, intent on sucking the last morsels from the cane in his hand. Once he had finished it, he discarded the empty shell and began rooting through the backpack, removing anything that interested him. "He seems innocent enough."

"He's young. He hasn't learned the ways of his tribe yet. But even if he is innocent, he's not alone."

Aldin found a roll of gauze and raveled it around his arm. Meaghan focused on him, feeling no deception or anger in him, no malcontent. He only seemed happy, as a young child of his age should be.

"Cal told me to rescue the boy. I'm sure he wouldn't have told me to do that if he was dangerous."

Nick snorted. "Cal sent you directly into the path of two Mardróch. I'm not sure he's concerned much with danger."

She returned her focus to Nick, her eyes hard again. "Then it's obvious he knows something we don't."

"Cal doesn't know everything, and he's often reckless, but that's beside the point. Aldin shouldn't be here."

"Why not?"

"The people of Zeiihbu are part of this kingdom and they're not. Although they occasionally show up with magical abilities, their powers tend to be minor or weak. They value tactical fighting and manual skills, and are generally better at those than we are. Because of these differences and the cultural ones I've mentioned, they don't consider themselves to be part of the kingdom any more than they consider themselves to be part of the Barren lands bordering them to the north."

"So you're saying it would be unlikely for Aldin's parents to travel through the kingdom?"

"For many reasons," Nick responded and then nodded toward

Aldin. The boy had finished wrapping the roll of gauze around his elbow and forearm, immobilizing it in a casing of white. He held it up, grinning at Nick as he flailed it through the air, flapping it like a bird's wing. Nick waved back.

"He is charming," Nick conceded. "It's too bad all Zeiihbuans aren't like him."

"What are they like?"

"Solitary, unfriendly. We don't know much about them. In the past, attempts to visit their land brought hostility. Few advance parties came back and those who did often lost limbs. They always brought back the message the people of Zeiihbu wished for solitude. Even the peaceful tribes had no issue killing those they deemed as trespassers. Over time, our people got the message and stopped crossing the border. We maintained truce for a century or so, not including a few minor skirmishes at the border villages."

"Then what happened?"

"The Mauraetus tribe came into power. Two brothers led the tribe with mantras of war and visions of taking over all the southern lands, to return them to their glory. The Zeiihbuans consider themselves the original inhabitants of this kingdom. We fought off their raids as long as we could, but eventually we had no choice. We waged war. The battles lasted weeks at times, magic equally matched to their skill, and many good people were lost on both sides. This went on for two decades, until your grandmother died and your mother took the throne."

"My mother?" Meaghan asked, surprised. "I thought monarchies followed the male line."

"Not here," Nick said. "When the Queen weds, she can choose to share the throne, and often does, with her husband. But when your mother inherited the throne, she hadn't met your father yet, so it became solely hers. At nineteen, she was a young ruler, but not without brilliance. She made contact with the leader of the Paecis, the second most powerful tribe in Zeiihbu, and offered to help him become the next Zeiihbuan ruler if he would sign a treaty with her. Zeiihbu would become a part of the kingdom only in name, but they would remain on their own land and we would remain on ours. Essentially, the treaty dictated we would leave each other alone.

"In exchange for joining the kingdom, the Paecis tribe would receive help from the Queen if needed, to ensure they maintained power. Before the ink on the treaty had dried, your mother led an elite force of Guardians to the heart of Zeiihbu for one last battle. They were some of the best Guardians of their generation, but the battle still claimed almost all of them. My father and Cal were two of the Guardians who lived. No one survived from the Mauraetus tribe."

Meaghan turned her attention back to Aldin. He had curled up on the blanket, his bandaged arm cradled under his head as he slept.

"Nobody is allowed to cross the border on either side without permission," Nick continued. "Technically, Garon holds the treaty at the moment. Since he advised your mother to annihilate Zeiihbu and its entire population in order to eliminate the threat of a future war, I doubt he would have granted permission for anyone to cross. That means Aldin's family is either part of a new war, or they've risked their lives to come here for another reason."

"Do you think the statues have something to do with their reason?"

"They might, though no one has ever heard of a Zeiihbu native with powers that strong and a young child with them from any territory is nearly impossible. Did Aldin say or do anything unusual?"

"I didn't think so at the time," she answered. "But I wondered after. He was scared and said a short rhyme that ended with the words 'freeze and die'. Could he have turned them to stone?"

"A rhyme?" Nick asked. His face turned white. "It's not possible."

"What isn't?"

A twig snapped to Meaghan's right. Instead of answering, Nick dove at her, knocking her to the ground. She landed on her back in time to see an arrow lodge into the tree beside her, its feathers quivering with the impact. Both she and Nick scrambled to their feet, turning toward the direction from which the arrow had come.

A tall man stood before them, his flint-colored eyes darkened in loathing as he stared them down, his weathered, olive-toned face set grim beneath a thick head of curly, dirty-blonde hair. Holding a bow in one hand and the feather end of an arrow in the other, he lined up the arrow's stone head for a direct flight into Nick's heart.

"The first shot was a warning," the man said, drawing his bowstring taut. "The second won't miss. Now tell me, why should this day not be your last?"

CHAPTER EIGHTEEN

"YOU HAVE until the count of five to answer my question. One..."

Meaghan swallowed, unable to think of anything to say.

"...two..."

Nick stepped in front of her, shielding her with his body. She thought the effort futile. Once the arrow pierced his heart, he would fall. Another arrow would find her in seconds.

"...three..."

"What do you want?" Nick asked, his voice steady, showing no hint of the fear that robbed Meaghan of her breath.

"The boy," the man answered. "Four."

"What do you want with him?"

"That's my business. Five."

"We saved his life once today," Nick said, holding firm though the man steadied his arm, readying to fire. "We don't intend to hand him over without knowing what you want with him."

"What do you mean, you saved his life?" Though the archer's

fingers tightened on his bow, his gaze wavered. A quick flick of his eyes toward the sleeping boy, a slight increase in fear, and Meaghan realized what the man wanted. She moved to stand beside Nick, taking his hand and squeezing it to let him know she had a plan.

"Two Mardróch attacked him," she answered the man's question. "They didn't harm him, but we didn't know what to do with him so we brought him here to keep him safe."

The man moved his arrow, refocusing it on her. "His arm is injured."

"It isn't. He was playing with gauze. He's okay."

"Stories," the man responded. He drew the arrow tauter against the string. "Lies. Your type never tells the truth. For all I know, you mean to hand him over to the next Mardróch you see."

The man's anger overcame his fear and Meaghan fought to control her own emotions. He was uncertain of his accusations, so he had not killed them yet, but she realized the wrong word would settle his doubt. She tightened her grip on Nick's hand to keep panic from shaking her muscles.

"The Mardróch are after me, too."

The man frowned and she felt his uncertainty growing. "Why?"

"Because I'm meant to rule this kingdom."

Nick inhaled a sharp breath. She ignored it and the reproaching look he shot her. Revealing her identity to a stranger might not be the smartest move, but it was all she had. She only hoped she had not misjudged the man's intent.

The man's eyes locked on hers. For the first time, his arrow wavered. "What's your name?"

"Meaghan," she responded.

"And you?" he inclined his head toward Nick.

"Nick. I'm her Guardian."

The man lowered his bow halfway, though his arrow remained readied within it. "Prove it."

"How do I prove," she began but stopped when she realized. Her power. "You know I'm an Empath?" she asked the man.

"I've heard the Queen is. She's the only one. Do you mean to tell me you can sense what I feel?"

She nodded. "You're afraid. Terrified, in fact, that Aldin might have been hurt or killed. And you feel guilty. I'm guessing you were watching him when he wandered away?"

The man eased his arrow from the bow. She continued. "You're also grateful he's all right, though you're angry that strangers have him. Your love for him is strong and so is your desire to protect him, so I believe you're his father. Am I correct?"

"You are."

"Shall I continue?"

"That won't be necessary." He slid the arrow into a woven basket strapped to his back. Reclaiming his other arrow from the tree, he stowed it before swinging the bow over his shoulder. Then he turned his attention toward Nick. "We agree I can take the boy?"

"He's yours."

The man walked over to the blanket. Kneeling beside Aldin, he laid a hand on the boy's back, giving him a slight shake. Slow and still groggy, Aldin rolled over and opened his eyes. When he saw his father, he sprang to his feet, launching into his father's arms.

"Dat," he squealed, "you found me."

"You shouldn't have wandered off," the man lectured, though the firmness of his tone became muffled in the boy's sweater as he pressed his face into it. "You scared me," he whispered. "I thought I'd lost you."

"I'm okay, Dat." Aldin pushed away from his father so he could look up at him. "Meaghan saved me. She ran out and yelled at the monsters and when they tried to freeze her, she didn't freeze. They were mad." He giggled. "I had to hurt them though." His brow wrinkled and he shifted his eyes away from his father's. "I know you said I shouldn't make my words come true. I didn't mean to, honest. But the monsters scared me."

The man kissed him on the forehead. "It's all right, Aldin. You did the right thing." He hugged his son again before standing, lifting the boy into his arms as he did so. He faced Nick and Meaghan. "Thank you," he said.

Nick nodded in acknowledgement and the man turned to go. He reached the edge of the clearing, hesitated, and then stopped, turning back around. He drew his eyes to Meaghan.

"You're not safe here. If the Mardróch communicated with their kind, more will come. They'll hunt for him, but they'll find you."

"We'll keep moving," Nick responded.

The man's eyes flicked to Nick and then back to Meaghan and she understood. He wanted her to gauge his emotions. He wanted her to read his underlying intent for what he was about to say. "You can't travel during the day. Not here. I'm sure your Guardian knows this?"

"He does."

"Then you'll come with me. Let my family keep you safe for the day and then you can continue your travels tonight, under darkness."

"That isn't necessary," Nick spoke again, his voice stiff with his distrust.

The man's eyes turned to Nick's face again and held there. Meaghan felt the same distrust emanating from him. Although she sensed the emotion had deep roots, seeded and nurtured long ago, his invitation had been open and honest. He would not harm them. Nick did not have the luxury of knowing the man's intent and Meaghan did not get the opportunity to tell him.

"You'd risk your Queen's well-being to continue an old war?" the man asked Nick. "Or are you afraid I aim to start a new one?"

"The thought did cross my mind," Nick said, squaring his shoulders. "You have no obligation to protect her and enough to gain by harming her."

Meaghan pursed her lips, surprised by Nick's accusation. She expected to sense insult coming from the man in front of them, but he simply smiled, his eyes alight with genuine humor.

"That's where you're wrong," he said. "I have everything to lose if she's harmed. I am Faillen."

"Faillen," Nick echoed, "as in the first son of Cadell, the leader of the Paecis and ruler of Zeiihbu?"

"The same," Faillen confirmed. "So you will come," he decreed and, without waiting for further argument, turned and entered the forest.

CHAPTER NINETEEN

THEY FOLLOWED Faillen in silence, their nerves raw, and their senses tuned to the slightest sign of an attack. Once they left the cover of the forest, the field offered no protection and no change in scenery. Miles of grass stretched out before them, green disappearing into the blue of a cloudless horizon. The sun welcomed them from its journey mid-way across the sky, but it failed to provide additional warmth against the crisp wind whipping from the north. Though they remained unprotected, vulnerable in the bright daylight, their one comfort was that the Mardróch had nowhere to stage a sneak attack. Unless they had the ability to turn themselves into field mice, the hunters were as exposed as their prey.

They walked for half an hour before Faillen stopped. Aldin lifted his head from his father's shoulder and stretched out his arms, reaching his hands into the air in greeting.

"Mata," he cried.

A woman ran out of nowhere to scoop him into her arms. She buried him in a hug, her long red hair covering the boy's head before she raised him to smother his face with kisses. Tears streamed freely from her bright green eyes. Joy spread a broad smile across her plump, red lips. "You fool," she said to him, though her words did not carry chastisement. "You fool," she said again, pulling him in for another hug. He giggled, reached up to touch her face and traced a finger down her cheek, connecting freckles.

She lifted her head to look at her husband, love shining on her face, and then turned her attention to the newcomers, her happiness dissolving into surprise.

"Outsiders," she said, her voice hushed. "Faillen." She spoke no more, but the accusation hung in the air, along with a worry that Meaghan did not need her power to see. The risk of exposure Faillen had brought with him had broken a rule, an understanding between them that turned the woman's body rigid and her face stiff.

Instead of responding to her, Faillen took Meaghan's hand in his. "You are welcome here," he said, then turned to Nick and did the same.

As it had with Neiszhe's village, solid matter materialized where only air had been. But here, there was no village. The protection spell hid three huts, no bigger than four hundred square feet each. Their thatched roofs and rough mud stucco spoke of the care taken with their construction.

The woman clutched her son tighter in her arms. Her worry turned to panic, the strength of it almost overwhelming Meaghan's senses. Meaghan stepped forward. The woman stepped back. Meaghan offered a friendly smile, hoping the gesture would ease the woman's mind. The woman did not return it. Instead, her eyes beseeched Faillen for an explanation.

"Our secrets are safe with them," he told her. The statement had the same effect on her as Meaghan's smile. The woman pursed her lips and anger mixed with her worry. Faillen turned to look at Meaghan. She sensed he felt trapped. He needed to offer his wife the truth, but he did not know how much information Meaghan would allow him to share. She nodded, answering his unspoken question and relief washed over him. He addressed his wife. "She is the Queen, my love."

The woman's eyes grew wide. Awe overtook all other emotions. "Are you certain it's her?"

"I'm certain," he responded. "The man is her Guardian. They need a safe place to stay until they can resume their travels tonight."

"Yes, of course," the woman whispered, turning to look at Meaghan. She tucked one foot behind the other, attempting a curtsy, but found it awkward with the boy in her arms.

Meaghan held back a grin, knowing the woman would not see humor in the situation. She nodded and the woman pulled up to her full height again.

"We're still outside the protection," she told them and pointed to the ground. Meaghan saw a line shimmering through the grass, like glass glinting in the sun. It bordered the houses and twenty additional feet of field on three sides. On the fourth side, it bordered a garden full of vegetables. "The spell ends at the line. If you stay within the boundary, you'll be hidden. Come, join us." She stepped across the line and they followed her. Approaching one of the huts, she opened the door, and entered.

Although small, the single room inside served well as a main living area for the family. One side of the room functioned as a kitchen. Pots and pans hung from the walls next to a cupboard and hutch. A basic wood table, built waist high, held the makings of bread. Flour dusted the surface and in the middle of the fine white powder, a lump of dough showed the finger indentation evidence of a worried woman who kneaded to keep her hands busy.

In the center of the back wall, a fire blazed in a large brick fireplace. A hook for hanging pots and a bread oven door indicated the fireplace served several purposes. The other side of the room held a dining table and chairs, and Meaghan realized the area acted as a multi-use family center. A boy who looked to be around twelve or thirteen sat in one of the chairs, studying them. His eyes mirrored his mother's and his short hair had the strawberry-blonde blend of both his mother and father's hair colors.

"Caide," his mother addressed him. "Please put water on for tea."

The boy nodded and jumped from his seat. He had already grown almost to his father's height, though his lanky frame had yet to take on the older man's muscular form. He poured water from a bucket into a kettle and hung it from the hook. Pushing the arm for the hook, he swung it over the fire and then moved to the hutch to gather mugs.

"I know you must be tired," the woman addressed Meaghan and Nick, "but it's been a long time since we've had company. I hope you'll sit with us for a while."

"We can spare an hour," Nick said, "but then we'll need to sleep before we travel."

Faillen's wife smiled in gratitude and extended a hand to him. "I'm Iria, but people call me Ree. Our eldest son is Caide, as I'm sure you heard. And I trust you've already learned Faillen and Aldin's names?"

"We have," Nick responded, shaking her hand. "I'm Nick."

"It's a pleasure," she said, releasing his hand and then cast a smile in Meaghan's direction. "And of course, I know your name, Queen Meaghan. It's rumored the name belonged to one of the first Queens of these lands. I don't think it's been used since then, but it suits you."

"Thank you," Meaghan replied, grimacing at the sound of her formal title. "But please just call me Meaghan. I'd rather not use formalities."

"All right," Ree agreed, and then gestured toward the chairs at the table. "Please sit. I made a fresh pie yesterday, and I suspect we need to talk about a few things."

"I have questions," Nick confirmed. "If you're comfortable answering them."

"We'll hide nothing from you," she responded. Moving to the cupboard, she opened it and took out a pie, setting it on the high table. Dark red berries poked through the latticework crust and Meaghan felt her mouth water at the sight of them.

"As soon as the boys have had their pie," Faillen added. "They'll go out to play after."

Nick nodded in agreement, and as soon as the kettle heated, they sat at the table, enjoying their tea and pie. Caide and Aldin devoured theirs within minutes and excused themselves to play.

"Stay within the boundaries," Faillen reminded them, and then put a hand on Aldin's shoulder, halting him before he could dart out the door. Faillen dropped his voice, a stern tone indicating his sincerity. "Aldin, have you learned your lesson from today?"

Aldin bounced his head in a pronounced nod, his eyes wide.

"Speak the words, son."

"I won't leave the boundary without your permission."

"You were lucky today. Remember that. You won't get lucky twice."

Aldin nodded again and Faillen removed his hand. Free, the boy followed his brother out the door, slamming it behind him.

"The children won't hear us now," Faillen said as he turned back to the table. Though his pie remained half-eaten on his plate, he pushed it aside. For a moment, silence filled the room as the mood shifted. No one touched their mugs or forks while they waited for the serious conversation to start. Finally, Faillen addressed Nick. "Tell us what happened today."

Nick detailed Aldin's rescue, leaving nothing out. When he finished, Ree's soft cries had subsided. She wiped tears from her cheeks as Faillen sat stone still beside her. He drew his eyes to Nick's. Any distrust he had harbored before had been erased.

"Thank you," he said. "Though I expressed my appreciation before, I admit I hadn't truly considered what you'd done for my boy. Since we moved here, he's been a handful. There isn't much space for him. If you hadn't come along," his voice trailed off as he dropped his gaze to the table. He flattened his hands on top of it and Ree took one of them into her own, intertwining their fingers.

"We owe you so much," she said. "I don't know how we can repay you."

"It's not necessary," Nick said. "And frankly, Meaghan is the only one who deserves your gratitude, though I do regret my actions. I didn't think either of them would live."

Meaghan sensed a touch of anger from Ree toward Nick, but Faillen did not hold the same emotion.

"You shouldn't regret what you did," he told Nick. "Though I'm grateful you didn't succeed in your attempt, you were right to try to protect your Queen. I would've acted the same way in your position. Much hinges on her survival, but what you couldn't have known is much hinges on Aldin's survival too."

"I know that now," Nick said. "He's a Spellmaster?"

"Yes," Faillen confirmed.

"He's young to have developed his power. It usually doesn't show up until age ten or so. And in his case, I thought," Nick hesitated, and Meaghan realized he was not certain how to finish his sentence without offending their hosts.

"He shouldn't have a power," Faillen finished for him. "Or if he did, it should be weak. We've fostered that fable with the southerners," he admitted. "But some of us have stronger powers. We just don't covet them the way you do. They get in the way, so we avoid using them."

"Do you have powers?" Nick asked him.

"No." Faillen stood to retrieve the kettle and returned to the table with it. He refilled each of their mugs before sitting back down. "Ree and I don't, but Ree's mother had the power to become invisible.

Her grandmother came from across the border, as others have done throughout the centuries. We suspect they've polluted our gene pool, if you'll forgive the expression."

Nick chuckled. "I think that's an acceptable way of putting it. When did Aldin start using his power?"

"Two months ago. He wanted a toy on a shelf in the sleeping hut and he couldn't reach it. He recited a rhyme and it floated into his hands. Last month, he was playing with a frog and it exploded. We grew concerned and made him promise he wouldn't use his power again. He kept his promise until today."

Meaghan picked up her mug, blowing steam from it before taking a sip. Something felt wrong to her and she could not quite place it, so she studied Faillen over the rim of her mug while she sorted her thoughts. The emotions she sensed seemed buried, so it took her a moment to recognize them as guilt and embarrassment, and to understand they did not come from Faillen, but from his wife. Meaghan diverted her attention to Ree.

"You seem ashamed of Aldin's power," she said.

Ree gripped her own mug as her eyes widened. "I forgot," she said. "You can tell what I feel."

"Yes," Meaghan said. "Why are you ashamed of it?"

"I love Aldin," Ree said, nearly pleading. "I love him no matter what he does."

"No one doubts that," Faillen said. He circled his arm around her waist and drew her close, kissing her on the temple before addressing Meaghan's question. "You have to understand that things are different for us in Zeiihbu. As I said, these powers aren't coveted.

They're considered a disability best kept hidden, but Aldin's isn't so easy to hide." He paused. Lifting his mug to his lips, he took a gulp from it. "My words must appall you."

"They don't," Nick said. "I've been raised to understand your culture is different and to respect it. I can understand your position given that, but the Spellmaster power shouldn't be taken lightly or prevented from maturing. It's rare, maybe the rarest power alive today, and once Aldin gains full control over it, he'll be able to do a tremendous amount of good."

"I know." Faillen lowered his mug and his eyes to the table. "I understand its value. But to us, it's a curse. The Mardróch hunt our family. As a result, we're forced to live here, in fear and near captivity, instead of living in our homeland. Even Zeiihbu suffers because of the power. Garon has stationed Mardróch guards everywhere. They loot and kill as they see fit, holding our citizens captive to their evils and whims. They're slowly destroying us and our way of life."

"I'm sure that was part of Garon's plan well before Aldin was born," Nick said. "Garon has never liked Zeiihbu."

"I'm sure you're right," Faillen conceded, though Meaghan sensed doubt and deceit in him. The deceit was minor, so she did not press an explanation for it.

"I don't mean to sound ungrateful," Faillen continued. "I understand the need for the Spellmaster power, but I fear my country will suffer until the power fully develops. I don't want that for my people."

"I understand," Meaghan said, setting her mug down. "Garon has destroyed many lives, but we'll have retribution for what he's done. Your son's power, though shameful to Zeiihbu now, will bring honor in time."

Faillen met the determination in her eyes with equal conviction. "It's important for your family to be restored," he said. "Your mother brought Zeiihbu a peace it hadn't seen in generations and I want to see that returned. Will you honor the treaty she and my father signed together?"

"I will," Meaghan promised. "And I won't forget your loyalty."

Faillen nodded, and then reached his hand across the table, palm down, fingers splayed. "A Zeiibuan custom," he told her, "to seal the promise we've made today."

She mimicked his gesture. He interlocked their fingers so they both had fingertips above each other's knuckles and then brought his other hand on top of their intertwined hands. She did the same.

"From my lips to the death," he said. "Please repeat it." She did and he smiled, releasing her hand. "A new pact for a new day."

Meaghan leaned back, returning the smile, and then picked up her mug again, resting her elbows on the table as Nick addressed Faillen. "Before the new day can start, we need to ensure your family remains safe. Who else knows you're here?"

"A Guardian named Cal," Faillen responded. "Do you know him?"

"I've known him most of my life. He's trustworthy."

Faillen nodded. "He helped set us up here and he provides supplies we can't make, grow, or hunt. He also gives Aldin lessons for his power."

"Good," Nick said. The news brought relief to his face, but something in Faillen's statement troubled Meaghan. She sipped from her mug again as she mulled over his words.

"Who else knows?" Nick asked.

"There was another man by the name of Delvin," Faillen said. "A Guardian Cal brought to live in the third hut. He left to get supplies one day and never returned. Cal found his body a few miles from here."

"The Mardróch got him?"

Faillen looked away as remorse washed over him. "We believe so. Cal said it was evident by the level of torture on his body that he kept our location secret. No one else knows we're here, not even my father. When the power surfaced and I realized the danger in it, I contacted Cal. I had met him several times when my father and I visited the castle during the good days and I understood his power and loyalty to be strong. He agreed to help and brought us here. He only told Delvin and since his death, Cal is afraid to trust anyone else."

"That's wise," Nick said. "Cal will protect you and so will I, if you need me."

"Thank you. I'll remember that." Faillen stood. "You should sleep. We'll wake you for dinner. There's fresh venison prepared to roast and vegetables ready for harvest."

"That sounds wonderful," Nick said and rose from his chair, but Meaghan remained seated as Faillen's words finally settled into understanding. Cal brought them what they could not grow. Grow. The garden. She realized the source of his deceit.

"The vegetables are ready for harvest?" she asked. "They shouldn't be."

Shame washed over Faillen and he sat down again.

"You said Aldin only started using his power two months ago. Your garden shouldn't be ready yet."

Faillen looked away.

"What are you hiding?"

"I'm not surprised Aldin's powers appeared so early," Faillen said. He brought his eyes to hers and the pain in them matched what she felt from him. It seemed his wife was not the only one ashamed of their son's predicament. "It probably would have taken longer if he didn't know it could be done, but he's fearless and he's always accomplishing things earlier than most kids. I think it's because he likes to mimic what his brother does."

"Caide," Nick whispered, understanding what Faillen meant before Meaghan did.

"Yes," Faillen admitted. "Caide is a Spellmaster too."

CHAPTER TWENTY

NICK'S SKIN poured sweat despite the chill in the air. He threw the pelt off his body and sat up, but the sweat still came, as did the panic driving his heart into frantic beats. He could not make the scene from this morning stop playing in his head. He could not stop seeing the Mardróch in the field as they bore down on Meaghan, as they attacked her with lightning, barely missing her as she ran. He could not stop seeing her fear and feeling his own as he remained frozen and helpless, watching her die. Not her, he realized as he turned his head to confirm. She lay motionless on a straw mattress across the room, a pelt covering her breathing body.

Her breathing body, he repeated, and drew a deep inhale. She still lived.

It was not her he had watched die. Her face had dissolved into another's in his mind and it froze him in his tracks, froze him in his memory when she needed him most. It tore at him that it had happened. He had let her down, but he would not let it happen again.

He closed his eyes, slowed his breathing, and focused on calming his heart, attempting to erase the images from his head in the process. When they faded enough so he could ignore them, he climbed from his mattress. Crossing the room to the door, he opened it, and then leaned against the wood jamb as he examined his surroundings.

The boys still played in the field flanking the Guardian's empty hut. The sky had taken on a crimson red glow as the sun slinked below the horizon. He watched it darken before his eyes and knew he would need to wake Meaghan soon. It would be good to have a hearty meal, and then they would travel again. Another day, if Cal's calculations were right. Or perhaps two, if they were not. Most likely, it would be the latter. Cal had a way of forgetting details he found unpleasant, shortening distances when he did not want to think about how much they would hurt his feet.

Cal's view of the world could be frustrating, and his disregard for common sense and safety downright infuriating, but when it mattered most, he came through. He was one of the most dependable men Nick had ever known, a trait that had served Nick well growing up. Whenever Nick needed the Guide, he only had to call into the wind and within days, Cal would show up. At least he had until the Mardróch made his visits too dangerous.

Nick had been surprised to find Cal in the wilderness after so many years. It seemed fate had a way of offering a helping hand when needed. Although Nick did not feel comfortable relying on that, he appreciated it, especially after this morning.

He looked back at Meaghan, verifying she still slept. He had grown up around Seers his entire life, yet he had had no real understanding of fate until recently. Learning what Vivian had known about her own death had made him realize how fragile the future could be. While the universe could line up opportunities, they could also be misaligned with a single decision. Vivian's understanding of what the wrong decision could do humbled him, and still brought an ache to his heart.

The pairing of Nick and Meaghan's powers also spoke to that. The Elders had had a choice. They could have kept someone else as her Guardian and when she had arrived on this world, she would not have had any way to block the emotions overwhelming her. Nick did not want to think about what would have happened in that case.

His eyes trailed back to the boys playing in the grass. Caide grabbed Aldin's wrists and swung him around. The younger boy flew through the air, squealing with joy. The older grinned, the camaraderie between them serving as evidence of their closeness. Nick could not guess what their fate would be, but he did not doubt the universe had special plans for them. He had never heard of two Spellmasters so close in age and he had heard of only a few times when two were alive at the same time. The fact they were brothers only reinforced his belief that their powers would bring great things. It was only too bad neither of them would be strong enough to help with the war before it was over. It would have been nice to have their aid against Garon's army.

"They're wonderful, aren't they?"

Nick turned his eyes from the boys to view Meaghan, who stood beside him, rubbing the sleep from her eyes. She had slept well and it had eased some of the stress from her face.

"Yes," he agreed, turning back to watch them. Caide dropped Aldin to the ground, falling over in the process, and both boys howled with laughter. Nick turned to face Meaghan. "I owe you an apology," he said.

She made no motion to speak, but instead, watched him, waiting for him to continue. "You were right to want to save him. Not because Cal told you to and not because of his power, but because the Mardróch have already taken too many lives and it was the right thing to do." He tightened his fists at his sides, curbing his renewed fear. "I just didn't want you to be another one of the Mardróch's victims."

She tilted her head, studying his face for a minute and then nodded, accepting his apology. "I know I'm not making your job any easier—"

"It's more than a job," he told her. "You're important—"

"To the people, to the future of this world," she finished for him, and then looked away. "I know."

"To me," he whispered, though he had to force the words out. He did not want to confuse the situation any further by admitting what he felt, but he needed her to realize how her actions affected him. "You're important to me, Meg," he said with more conviction. "It's hard enough to protect you. When I have to worry about what you might do, it makes things worse."

"I know," she said again. This time, remorse filled her voice and tears filled her eyes. She closed them. "This is hard for me, too. I don't know how to react or what to do." Her voice failed and Nick wrapped his arms around her, drawing her into him. She pressed her cheek against his shoulder. "I miss the way it was between us on Earth. I miss my life. I had everything planned out. I was confident in what I was doing and this," she brought her hands to his chest, and then turned her face into his shirt. Her voice came out muffled. "I don't know how to do this."

"You do," he told her, though he doubted his words would convince her. Over time, as she gained experience, she would convince herself. He brought a hand to the back of her head. "You're doing fine, Meg. We just need to figure out how to work together here, as we did on Earth. I don't mind the heroics, but if we intend to save people, we need to consider a careful plan. Losing our lives in the process is not an option."

"We?" she stepped back and rubbed the tears from her face with her palm.

"Of course." He lifted a hand to her shoulder. "You may not believe me right now, but I'm not trying to work against you. I'm here to help you in any way you need me."

She nodded. Her eyes sought the boys again. "I miss my parents," she said, then blew out a frustrated breath. "I hate that I can't call them that anymore."

"You can always call them that around me. I miss them too."

"I need their advice," she continued. "I don't want to lead this kingdom. I don't want to be Queen, and I'm not sure how I would even be able to do what these people need." She shook her head and brought her eyes back to Nick's. "But I don't have a choice, do I?"

"We always have a choice," Nick said, tucking his hands into his pockets. "You can walk away from this, Meg. I don't want you to, but you have the option."

"How?"

"You can abdicate. The people could select another ruler, or you could."

"Wouldn't that be better?" she asked. "There has to be someone with more experience, someone who grew up here, who could do a better job." Nick remained silent. "There must be."

"Aunt Viv didn't think so."

"Why? I know nothing about this world, nothing about being a leader."

Nick shrugged. "She could see the future. More importantly, she could see the present. She watched you grow up and knew your character. You're strong, Meg. You're smart, and you've always done what's right, like today. From what I've heard, those traits also marked Adelina's rule." He paused, studying the doubt on Meaghan's face. "But Aunt Viv didn't simply believe you might be a good ruler. She gave her life protecting you because she was *certain* you would."

Meaghan's eyes grew wide. Her lip trembled but she controlled the reaction, preventing tears from forming again. Though the words were true, Nick wished he had refrained from saying them. He had not intended to cause her pain.

"Few people know you're on this world right now," he told her. "Until you're formally introduced in my village, you won't have to make a decision, so take time to think about it. And trust yourself. You'll make the right decision when you need to."

"I hope so," she said, and turning from him, reentered the sleeping hut.

§

THEIR BELLIES had not held so much food since the night before they left Earth. The feast Ree and Faillen had provided had bulged their eyes and their waistlines. The table had been overloaded with corn and potatoes, salad, green beans, and beets, as well as the promised roast. For dessert, Ree had made a traditional Zeiihbu celebratory cake laden with nuts, dates, and fresh picked apples. The delectable treat had been meant as a good luck gesture, but it weighed on Meaghan as a reminder of the promise she had made to Faillen. What would happen if she abdicated? Would the next leader uphold her promise? She knew even if he did, the foundation she had laid with Faillen in one day, a bond that had formed when she saved his son, could not be repeated by another person, no matter how skilled or knowledgeable that person was as a leader. And she wondered if maybe there was more to being Queen than she had initially thought.

After dinner, she and Nick walked again by moonlight, their words as scarce as they had been the night before. As the sun crested the horizon, they approached a pile of boulders that broke the flat surface of the field. Nick moved around them and then disappeared. At first, Meaghan thought he had found another protected area, but after circling the rocks, she could find no crystals. Her muscles tightened in panic and then she saw the top of his head appear from below the rocks. She jumped in surprise, and then cursed at him.

"Sorry," he chuckled. "I needed to check it out and I didn't want you to come in case it was still inhabited. I should have told you."

"Check what out?"

"The fox hole."

"A fox hole big enough for a human?" she asked, peering down at him, curiosity bypassing her irritation. "Are you kidding?"

"You haven't seen our foxes yet," he said and then laughed when she caught her breath. He ducked his head back down to avoid the playful swat she aimed at him, and then she followed him, moving cautiously in case he was wrong about the inhabitants. After dropping her body into the hole, she stood still for a moment, allowing her eyes to adjust to the minimal light streaming in through the opening.

The space resembled more of an underground cave than a fox hole, with rocks above them and a packed dirt floor below. Although Meaghan could stand upright with an inch or two to spare, Nick had to crouch to avoid hitting his head. He spread out the blanket and sat on the floor. She joined him. There was enough space for them to sit parallel to each other, but not enough to lie down. It would be uncomfortable, but they would be safe.

"Is this really a fox hole?" she asked.

He shrugged and then reached into the backpack to pull out two cloth-wrapped bundles. He handed one to her. "It's hard to say. It is too big for a fox. It could be a bear cave from when these fields were forest, or it could be natural. Either way, it's ours tonight."

He untied the cloth around his bundle, opening it to reveal several hunks of bread and cheese, food Ree had packed for them when they had left. She had apologized for not having more than a meal's worth apiece to give, but Meaghan doubted the family even had this to spare.

Her package contained the same food and she ate it slowly,

enjoying the creamy texture of the homemade cheese and the crunchy crust of the freshly baked bread. No matter how much she missed the convenience of grocery stores, nothing could compare to this. The love and care Ree put into her food came through with each bite.

When she finished, she folded the cloth and stuck it back into the backpack. Nick did the same. For comfort, and out of a habit they had formed while watching movies in his apartment on Earth, she leaned against him, lifting forward so he could slide an arm around her shoulders. Then she rested her head on his chest and fell asleep.

CHAPTER TWENTY-ONE

"**DOES THE** kingdom have a name?"

Nick turned his head to look at Meaghan and smiled, glad a full moon and clear sky kept tonight's journey well-lit. She had begun the night in silence, as she had on the other two nights, but once they had found the cover of trees again, she had started asking questions. Her questions were general at first. She asked about the history of the world and about some of the fruit and plants she saw. But then they had turned more specific. As soon as he finished one answer, she had another question waiting for him. He felt battered by her words and her quick-fire curiosity, but he took it as a good sign and he held hope her interest meant she had begun to accept her new home.

"It does," he answered.

She waited a beat. "You don't expect me to guess, do you?"

He chuckled, and then reached down to pick several bright orange berries from a bush as they passed. He handed them to her. "These are spice berries. Guessing could be fun."

"For you, maybe." She popped one of the berries into her mouth and he could tell the moment the plump fruit exploded. A slow smile spread over her face. "It tastes like cinnamon and nutmeg," she said. "And something else that reminds me of pumpkin pie."

"You should try them with laitte. It's a fruit that looks like a large grape, but it tastes like sweet milk. Every time I had pumpkin pie with whipped cream on Earth, I felt like I was eating fruit salad here."

"Somehow, I can't see fruit being as satisfying as pie," she remarked with a grin. "Do you really expect me to guess the kingdom's name? I'll never get close. I'm sure it's some word I've never heard of, like Amberkassiland."

"What did you say?" Nick turned, walking backward so he could face her. "How did you know?"

Her eyes grew wide at first, and then she tossed a berry at him. He chuckled, ducking to allow the bright fruit to sail over his head.

"I don't want to waste my time guessing. I have more questions."

"I'm sure you do," he continued to tease as he faced forward again. "You're like a one-woman Jeopardy game show."

She stifled a laugh and slipped another berry past her lips. "So what is it?"

"Ærenden."

"Ærenden," she tested the word. "That's nice."

"We think so," he responded. "It's nicer than the names the people of Earth come up with. Like the United States. You can't get more boring than that."

"Hey," she started to protest, and then stopped, huffing out a breath when she realized he was still teasing her. "Nice. You're in a good mood today."

"I guess I am." Adjusting the backpack on his shoulders, he relaxed a little more as the trees surrounding them turned into denser forest. Although it was not as dense as he preferred, it meant they were getting closer to his village and to home. His excitement grew. "What's your next question?"

"I was wondering why your power worked for me," she said. "I've been trying to figure it out, but it doesn't make any sense. I can't use anyone else's power, right?"

"Right." They approached a curtain of vines and he stopped to pick up a stick, tapping on the tendrils, then moving forward when the vines did not react. "To be honest, we don't know much about your power. It hasn't shown up in several generations, but history tells us Empaths have always been born within a few years of a blocking power, and they've always been able to tap into that power."

"How? Powers aren't emotions, and I can't sense them like you do. I've tried."

He chuckled. "I had no doubt you would. There are a few theories, but only two I think might be plausible."

"Which are?"

"The first is it's meant to be."

She rolled her eyes. "That's a cop out."

"Perhaps, but powers have a way of balancing themselves, even if the reasons aren't always apparent. The second theory is when my power blocks you from sensing me, it does so by mimicking an emotion, one that's louder than my other emotions."

"You mean like white noise drowns out other sounds?"

"Exactly."

"So when I focus on it, it overruns the other emotions I sense, provided those emotions aren't too strong. I noticed in Neiszhe's village that the emotions were dulled when I focused on your power, but when it was only Cal in the cave, I couldn't sense his emotions at all."

"That would lend to the theory," Nick said. "But the two theories can work together. Traditionally, our powers are born to children within the same village, which supports the balance theory."

"That makes sense," Meaghan decided, and continued to her next question. "How does the Spellmaster power work? Spells here don't appear to be anything like we portray in fiction on Earth."

"You mean where everyone with a power can perform a spell?" he asked. She nodded. "That isn't entirely untrue. Everyone with a power can invoke a spell, but only Spellmasters can create or alter spells. To do so, they focus on their power, speak in rhyme, and their words come true."

"So how are other people able to use the spells?"

"Spellmasters write them down. When they do, they infuse some of their power into the spell and the spell can then be used by whoever knows it, even after the Spellmaster's death. It's a complicated process. They lose some power each time they do it, but since their power grows stronger each year, it doesn't hurt them."

"So if Caide wanted to write a spell now, he could, and I would be able to recite it?"

"No, you wouldn't. You don't have enough control over your power yet to recite a spell. Even if you did, Caide isn't old enough to write one. Spellmasters begin training with verbal spells and move to written spells as they grow older. They also develop the capability of writing more complex spells as their power gets stronger."

"Like the Mardróch spell?"

"Precisely. Caide won't have enough power to create that type of spell until he's at least fifty. The Spellmaster who wrote it was fifty-six, and it took half a dozen people with strong powers to recite it."

A small rodent scurried across Meaghan's path and she stopped to watch it. Nick lagged behind, waiting for her. The animal looked similar to a squirrel, but it had a thin tail, no thicker than Nick's little finger, and stripes like a tiger's.

"That's a panthmouse," he told Meaghan after it had disappeared. "It's harmless unless you're a worm. That's all it eats."

She nodded, increasing their pace again. "I'm not sure I understand what you mean about needing power to recite a spell," she said. "If the power comes from the Spellmaster, why does it matter who's reciting it?"

"It matters because the power reciting the spell has to be equal to the power the Spellmaster used to create it. The Spellmaster gives words power when he writes them down, but the people reciting them make them alive in the world. Some spells can even vary in the power needed to recite them, if they're written with that intent."

"I see," Meaghan said, though the wrinkles between her brows told Nick some confusion remained.

He tried again. "Think of it as a two-part process that has its own fail-safe. This way a group has to perform the strongest and most destructive spells. It ensures that at least some thought goes into using the spell. It also helps us to understand how many people it took to enact a spell."

"What do you mean?"

"Well," he paused as he thought of an example. "Let's look at the spell we use to protect our villages, the one which makes them invisible to those who aren't invited. Depending on the size of the village, the amount of power needed to make the spell work will increase. Neiszhe's village would have taken eight strong Guardians to enact the spell. The smallest use of the spell takes four people, maybe three if you have someone reciting it like Cal, whose power over the elements is one of the stronger ones."

"Three?" she asked. "If that's the minimum, then that means someone else knows about Faillen and his family."

"Correct," Nick confirmed.

"Doesn't that mean they could be in danger?"

"Not necessarily," he responded. "I know Cal. He would've asked Delvin to help and a third Guardian he trusted to keep his secret, even from the Elders. He would not tell Faillen about that person because he would not want to concern him. But it would make sense for someone else to know in case something happened to Cal. It's redundant protection."

"And you know who the third person is," she guessed.

"There are only two Guardians Cal would trust for this. Neiszhe, of course, and my mother. I doubt he would want to lay that responsibility on his wife, which leaves Mom. I'll confirm that with her when we arrive in my village."

"That makes sense," Meaghan decided. "And I think I understand how the Spellmaster power works now, but I have one more question about it."

"What's that?"

"Since the Spellmasters can create spells that take an accumulation of powers to perform, does that make them the most powerful people?"

"Once their powers have developed enough, yes. That usually happens in their thirties or forties, depending on what age their power surfaced. There used to be stronger powers, but they've gone extinct, such as the powers to transform into animals or objects."

"I see." They exited the trees, stepping into another field that ran along the side of a ravine, and Meaghan lowered her voice. "So Aldin will be stronger than his brother at the same age?"

Nick nodded. "Most likely. Since Aldin has developed his power already, he should be as powerful as a Spellmaster in his thirties by the time he's twenty."

"But he won't be able to help us stop the Mardróch. Neither of them will."

"No, they won't." Nick put a hand on her arm and halted them both. The disappointment on her face tugged at him. "Are you all right?"

"Yes," she said. "I thought I'd figured out how I was supposed to stop this war. I guess I was wrong."

He took a step closer, drawing his hand to her shoulder. "No one said you had to stop the war," he told her. "Not alone anyway."

"But you said—" she began and then shook her head.

"I said," he prompted.

217

"I was the Queen."

"I never said you had to stop the war."

"But I," she faltered, and then her cheeks flared red. "Isn't that what rulers do? Don't they start and stop wars and keep their people safe?"

"Of course," Nick answered. "But they only do it alone if they want to go insane. It's no wonder you've been so scared." He squeezed her shoulder, then dropped his hand and smiled. "Meg, a good leader knows how to surround herself with people who can get things done. Do you realize Guardians are here to help you, not just to protect you? We study tactical planning and fighting as well as defense and protection. You also have advisors and powerful people who are ready to aid you, to teach you, and to follow. As far as the Mardróch," he placed a finger under her chin and lifted it, bringing her eyes to his. "We've been looking for a solution to that problem for a long time. No one expects you to step in and solve it in a week when we haven't been able to do it in more than a decade."

"I guess I didn't think about it that way," she whispered. "I didn't realize—"

A loud whistle echoed from the canyon, startling them both. Before they had a chance to figure out what had made the noise, a light appeared in the sky overhead. Then, it exploded.

CHAPTER TWENTY-TWO

"GET DOWN," Nick yelled, though his voice came across distant, muffled by the sound of ringing in Meaghan's ears. She did not know if he had tackled her or if the impact of the explosion had knocked her to the ground, but she struggled against loose dirt and her own shaky arms as she tried to push back up. Keeping her eyes focused on the trees, she could only think about getting to her feet and running toward safety.

"Stay down!" Nick insisted when she managed to rise to her hands and knees. She continued to struggle, and he pulled her arms out from under her. Her chin knocked against his arm instead of the ground when he softened her fall, but the impact still sent bolts of pain through her head. She rolled onto her back, seeing stars, and she could not tell if they came from the night sky or if they had developed in her vision.

Nick stretched an arm across her stomach, stiffening it to keep her from moving again. She turned her head to look at him. A trickle of blood streamed down the side of his face. He whispered to her, or rather, he sounded as if he spoke underwater. His lips moved again, their efforts lost to her, and then he understood. He pressed his mouth to her ear. This time his voice pushed through the ringing.

"I think there's a battle," he said.

"Where?" she asked, though he seemed to hear her as well as she heard him. He lowered his ear to her lips, waited for her to repeat her question, and then dropped his mouth to the side of her head again.

"In the ravine. Unfortunately, we need to go down there to get home. I'm going to find out what's going on."

He crawled to the edge of the ravine. Bracing his head on his folded arms, he peered over the side. Without waiting for invitation or permission, Meaghan followed, mimicking his movements.

He looked at her and frowned, but instead of lecturing her or trying to make her retreat, he cast an arm over her back. In part, she realized, to keep her from jumping up and in part because the position made it easier for him to whisper in her ear.

"Keep your eyes on me for a minute," he told her.

Although she had yet to look into the ravine, and curiosity begged her to see what took place below them, she did as he asked.

"This isn't fiction," he told her. "It doesn't resemble anything you've seen on television or in movies," he pulled back so he could look at her. The concern on his face touched and scared her at the same time. "It's real." Though she could not hear his last two words, she could read them well enough on his lips. She nodded. He dropped his mouth to her ear again.

"If you decide to look, what you see will change your life. It will change you. You don't have to do this, though. We can wait until the battle ends to go down into the ravine. We'll be safer and then you can avoid seeing it altogether."

"How long does a battle usually last?" she asked.

"Days sometimes. It depends if the armies can get supplies and the strength of the powers involved. If they're not evenly matched, it will be over in a matter of hours."

Days, she thought, and shook her head. Days did not seem like an option for them. She did not want to remain unprotected for so long. But something more tugged at her decision. She raised her head, turning it enough so she could look into Nick's eyes, but still hear him, and he could still hear her. "Is this what it's like for the people in this kingdom? Do these battles happen often?"

"Not every day," he answered. "But the war continues and as Garon tries to capture more villages, we fight back."

"Then I need to see," she decided. "I can't hide from what's happening because it's not easy to deal with. Not if it will help me understand what it's like to live here."

His eyes darkened, but he allowed her to feel his pride in her decision and it touched a brief smile to her face before she turned to look down into the ravine. Its floor sprawled for miles to the left and right, though it was only a few hundred feet wide. Boulders scattered among the patches of grass and bushes hinted that a river once flowed through this area. People fought among those boulders, sometimes using them as a shield against weapons, and she pushed back a few inches, afraid someone would see her.

Despite what Nick had said, the battle seemed fake to her. She could not tell the difference between her allies and her enemies.

Some fell. Some ran. Others tossed objects at each other. They scurried back and forth, no more than ants from the height of her perch. But then she began pulling apart details as she focused on them. The Mardróch's cloaks flew behind them while they chased their prey. Lightning bolts cascaded from their hands, disintegrating bushes and rocks on contact, and sometimes even those they chased. Meaghan watched one man trip and fall in his attempt to escape. Before he could jump to his feet again, a lightning bolt found him.

Closing her eyes, Meaghan pressed her hand to her mouth to keep from crying out, and then forced her eyes back open.

At least a hundred people fought in the ravine and though the Mardróch only accounted for a few dozen of them, the battle raged in sections where no Mardróch fought. A woman tossed rocks at a man, using only her mind. In return, he commanded small animals to scurry around her, clawing and biting. Two men tossed fireballs at each other, while another woman tagged people, turning them into stone. A white orb whistled toward the woman, then exploded at her feet. The stone statues reverted to flesh. Some fell to the ground, dead, while others kept moving.

Nick followed her line of sight and took her hand in his. "Most powers die with their hosts," he told her. "So her victims reverted back to flesh."

"Why did some of them live, but others didn't?"

"They aren't turned to solid stone," he answered. "They're encased in it, so they suffocate. Those who are turned back in time will survive."

Numbness gripped Meaghan and her eyes found the battle again.

"It's not only the Mardróch," she said. "Garon has men and women fighting for him."

"Yes," Nick confirmed. "The Mardróch spell only works on Guardians. Others have chosen to support Garon for one reason or another, and they fight for him."

"Everyone looks the same. If you're fighting, how can you tell who your enemies are?"

"Sometimes you can't. Sometimes you have to guess." Nick looked away, but she caught the shadows haunting his eyes. "We should go."

Nick crawled backward and she put her hand on his arm to stop him. She needed to do one more thing before they left. Taking a deep breath, she steeled her resolve, then fixed her gaze on the ravine.

She had felt little from the battle while she held Nick's power, and she had hoped the distance separating them from the fighting would help dull the emotions coming from the battle. But once she removed her focus from Nick, all hope dissolved. The Mardróch's scent accosted her first. The putrid smell of rotting peat blended with sulfur and somehow she associated the mix with excitement. It rocked her stomach, but she held firm.

Until the human emotions came. Fear and distress approached in waves, drowning her. Exhilaration, satisfaction, and pride bubbled to the surface next and Meaghan understood the emotions came from those who were winning their fights, though the realization came sluggish through the onslaught. Panic met strength. Guilt and shame bordered horror. Hatred bled into anger. And confidence shattered into despair.

Different emotions came from different directions, but the worst emotion—the one ripping through every fiber of her body—came from everywhere. Pain throbbed in her muscles. It ached in her head. It seared her lungs, burned quick through her blood like a starving fire. And when death marched upon those who were injured and helpless, it clawed at her soul, ripping with fine-needled talons that shredded and pierced her mind, tearing apart her sanity.

She tightened her jaw to keep from screaming, felt her stomach pitch, and flipped away from the edge of the ravine in time to release the remains of her breakfast onto the ground at her side.

Her arms and legs refused to move. Her breath came ragged and labored. Her skin felt clammy from sweat. She drew on the last of her strength to seek Nick's power again and then turned her head into the dirt and dissolved into sobs.

"Take a deep breath," Nick whispered in her ear. She felt his arms circle her body. "Breathe, Meg. Just breathe."

She focused on his words and on what he had told her to do. She had started to hyperventilate from sobbing, but as she concentrated on her breath, on drawing it slowly into her lungs and exhaling it with the same control, she found comfort and the edges of calm.

"That's it." He flattened his hand against the side of her face, pushing her hair away and wiping tears from her cheeks. "It's all right," he said. "You're all right."

She nodded, though she could not be certain those words would ever be true again.

CHAPTER TWENTY-THREE

MEAGHAN FROWNED into the mug in her hand, a series of unsavory swear words coursing through her head, but she thought better of voicing any of them. Nick's temper met her from the other side of the small fire he had built, stiffening his face, and she understood any complaint would merit a stern lecture. She had choked down the first mug of jicab tea, and then the second when he had refilled it, but the third seemed impossible. She did not know how much longer she could drink this stuff. Her initial dislike of the brown liquid had now grown to outright hatred with each subsequent dose. It tasted terrible. It looked like mud. It twisted her stomach into protesting knots. It was a vile, nasty, torturous concoction.

And it helped, though she loathed admitting it. It calmed her nerves and eased tension from her body. She brought it to her lips and sipped, hoping Nick would lose interest in watching her soon so she could dump it out.

They were back in the woods. Nick had carried her after she had passed out. She had never roused. Not while he had moved her, not while he had built the fire, and not while more magical bombs had exploded overhead. She had slept, then awoken to daylight and tea.

225

The battle still raged in the ravine below them. A quick release of her link to Nick's power told her as much. She blocked out the emotions again and closed her eyes. Even the brief few seconds she had tapped into the pain and confusion had weighed on her heart.

She felt Nick sit next to her on the log, his thigh brushing hers as his arm circled her waist. Then he removed the mug from her hand and pulled her against him. She opened her eyes, and then turned her head into his shoulder.

"I don't know why you keep doing that," he said. The ringing no longer filled her ears and she could hear him, and the frustration in his voice, clearly. He drew a hand to her cheek. "I can feel your distress," he continued, "even now. Your fear and your pain, too. But they're not yours, are they?" She shook her head, though she knew he did not need the confirmation. "Why did you do it?"

"I wanted to know if they were gone," she whispered.

"You didn't need to. I looked five minutes ago."

"I wanted to check for myself."

He brought his hand to her brow. "And the first time? You were already watching them."

"I needed to know what it felt like. I needed to know what they were going through."

"Why?" he asked.

"Because," she hesitated, not sure how to answer. "Because I felt like I had a responsibility to know."

"Because they're your people?" he guessed. She looked away, not confirming what he had said, but not denying it either. "If you wanted to know what it felt like to be in a battle, I could've told you."

"Hearing about it isn't the same as feeling it."

"It's not," he agreed, "but you felt everyone, Meg. That's not the same either."

"I suppose not," she conceded. Drawing the cup to her lips, she sipped from it before she remembered what it contained. She lowered the mug to the ground. "I didn't realize you'd fought. How many battles have you been in?"

"Three," he responded, then stood and moved to the fire. "Being assigned to you has given me some protection. I've only had to fight in the battles closest to my village. Many of my friends have been in dozens of battles throughout the kingdom."

"Have you had to kill anyone?"

"Yes," he answered. His voice remained neutral, but she caught a glimpse of pain on his face before he turned from her. "We should go," he said, kicking dirt over the flames to suffocate them. "It'll be dark soon."

Meaghan picked up her mug from the ground. After dumping out the remainder of the tea, she stood and went to the backpack, putting the mug away before slinging the bag over her shoulders.

"Can we get down into the ravine?" she asked.

"Past the edge of the battle there's a path leading to the bottom. I've already scouted it out. It should be safe."

He turned and led the way back to the field. Half an hour later, they descended a steep slope into the ravine. A full moon guided their way, unobscured by the few clouds hanging in the sky. Although the bright night provided easier travels along the rocky path, it also gave Meaghan a clear view of the battle. From this far away, she could barely make out the figures as people. Those who remained standing looked like toy soldiers fighting on a board game. And those who lay dead on the ground looked like patches of color blanketing the field. Like wilted wild flowers, she realized and turned her head, disturbed by the image.

"Have they been fighting this whole time?" she asked Nick.

"The Mardróch don't sleep," he responded. "Don't look again. You've seen enough."

She trained her eyes on the earth as her feet moved over it, but her mind remained on the battle. "They must be exhausted."

"They have potions to help them stay awake." Nick stopped walking, placing a hand on her arm to keep her beside him. "You need to focus on something else. This isn't good for you."

"I'm fine."

"You're not. Have you forgotten I can sense your fear?"

"No, I'm—" she started to protest, then turned her eyes to the battle and felt her heart race. Somehow, she had managed to tune out her own emotions. But they still remained. She tore her eyes away. "I didn't realize."

"It's all right. It's hard the first time. We all find a way to cope."

Nick began walking again and Meaghan followed his pace.

"How old were you when you saw your first battle?" she asked.

"Sixteen," he responded, but said no more about it. He took her hand in his and changed the subject. "This reminds me of our first trip to the mountains the week after I moved into the apartment. Do you remember it?"

It still embarrassed her to think about it. "I was horrible to you."

"You were." He squeezed her hand. "Until you and I went hiking alone the second day."

"You mean until we got lost the second day," she said.

"I wasn't lost. I knew where we were."

She narrowed her eyes at him. "Don't lie to me. You were as scared as I was. I could tell."

"I was, but not of being lost. Using my power on Earth was tiring. By the time you thought we were lost in the woods, I had been using it for nearly two days without a break and I was exhausted. Since the emotion I was hiding fit the situation, I dropped my guard."

"What were you afraid of?"

"You," he confessed. "You terrified me."

"I did? But," her eyebrows drew together, "why?"

He shrugged. "Building a bond with you was the only task I'd been given and within a week of meeting you, it was clear I'd failed. You hated me. At least the hike helped. By the end of it, we'd had our first full conversation."

"About Alfred Hitchcock movies," she said and laughed. "How did you even know about him? It's not like you grew up watching the films like I did."

"Uncle James," Nick answered. "I came to Earth a few months before I moved in with him and Viv. They put me up in a hotel on the other side of town and taught me everything they could so I didn't seem out of place when I met you. James told me once they were your favorite movies, so I asked him to bring them to me. I watched all of them at least twice."

The effort Nick had made to get her to like him surprised Meaghan, and it made her feel worse about the way she had treated him.

"I didn't hate you," she said, her voice soft with her shame. "I was angry with my parents for inviting you and I took it out on you. I didn't get much time with them after I started college. Our camping trips were sacred to me and I thought you were an encroaching stranger." She paused as reality changed how she viewed the memory. "I didn't know they were your aunt and uncle. That trip must have meant more to you than it did to me."

"The trip did mean a lot to me," he told her, halting them both once more so he could lower his lips to her forehead. "It was nice to be able to spend with them again. But the trip meant more afterwards when I realized you and I could be friends. Not all Guardians are lucky enough to get along so well with their charges." He released her hand and stepped back. "You impressed me that day, you know, the way you took control and found your way back to the campsite. It was the first time you reminded me of your mother. Or at least of how people describe her."

Her birth mother, Meaghan realized he meant. She swallowed the lump forming in her throat, unsure if she felt fear or pride from his comment, but saved from deciding by a groan coming from below them. She scanned the path ahead and spotted a pile of clothing where the trail met the floor of the ravine. Not clothing, she realized, but a man, broken and bleeding. She ran toward him.

"Meg," Nick called after her in warning. She slowed, letting Nick catch up to her. He gripped her shoulders, pulling her behind him.

"Stay here," he instructed. He approached the man, then knelt down beside him and turned him onto his back. The man's groans turned to cries of pain.

"I need the backpack," Nick told her.

She brought it to him, remaining at his side to examine the man closer. Blood pooled underneath and next to his body, soaking through his clothing and staining his skin. Red coated his face where he had been lying in it, and his white hair stuck to his head with clumps of blood so thick they appeared almost black. A hole gaped in his chest, showing bone and muscle that rose and fell with each breath. She could not understand how he still lived.

Nick opened the backpack and pulled out the jicab root, scraping off three times the amount of bark Cal had told him would be safe. He rolled it between his fingers until it formed a ball. "This will help," he said. The man parted his lips, accepting the bark, and chewed without question or instruction.

"Thank you," he whispered. He turned his gray eyes in Meaghan's direction. The pain in them shined bright, and after a moment, so did the recognition. "Queen Adelina," he choked out, bubbles of blood foaming on his lips. "Have you come to take me to a better place?"

"It's not Adelina," Nick told him. "It's Meaghan."

A wisp of a smile graced the man's mouth, slicing through the agony on his face, and Meaghan knew the root had taken effect. She knelt beside Nick and held the man's hand. Despite her link with Nick's power, she could sense the man's emotions as soon as her fingers brushed his skin. Pain, mostly, which had begun to fade. Pride. And strong happiness. The latter came from his recognition of her. But she felt no fear in him, despite the fact death had made a cruel game of taunting him.

"You've returned," he spoke again, forcing the words from his mouth. "I killed one for you."

At first, she did not understand what he meant, but then Nick put a hand on her shoulder, using his touch to guide her focus to the bushes beside the path. Half-hidden beneath the largest bush, she saw a distinct brown cloak and the grotesque skeletal hand of a Mardróch. She checked her shudder and panic and turned back to Nick. "He killed one? I thought they were unstoppable."

"Their cloaks are impenetrable, but their faces are exposed."

She saw a spear lying on the ground beside the man. Dark blood caked the metal head and streaked thick red rivers down its shaft. She peered into his face and smiled. "Thank you," she said. "Your bravery and sacrifice will not be forgotten."

"You've returned," he said again, his voice no more than a soft breath. "You've returned to save us and now I won't die in vain." His eyes slipped shut. "Thank you, my Queen."

He exhaled one last breath as the root sped him to a painless death and then Meaghan felt only her own grief.

CHAPTER TWENTY-FOUR

THE HOURS slipped by, lost to heavy sorrow as Meaghan and Nick left the ravine behind and wandered into another thick forest. Many miles now separated them from the body of the man they had buried, but he refused to allow Meaghan to leave him behind. Every detail of his death haunted her. She could still feel the pressure of his fingers against her palm. His emotions, though lost in his death, had come back to life within her. His gray eyes still burned their recognition and expectations into hers. And the distinct smell of copper from his blood clung to the inside of her nostrils, reminding her of its presence each time she took a breath. She could not find the words to speak, so she stared ahead, barely noticing the trees as she walked among them. Branches and leaves brushed her face, battered her arms and legs, but she did not care. It seemed only right that her body felt the pain plaguing her heart.

She broke the silence only once, to confess the regret burning most in her mind, "I never asked him his name."

"Dell," Nick told her and his voice carried the same weight as hers. "His name was Dell. He was the Mayor of the village on the other side of the ravine."

Meaghan nodded, settled by knowing at least that fact and offered a wish of peace to the stars for the man's soul. She could not find the will to ask Nick how he knew Dell, and Nick did not offer an explanation. Instead, he took her hand and left her to her thoughts.

When the sun rose again, they exited the woods into a small clearing. A cabin, about half the size of one of Faillen's huts, stood in the center. It looked weather worn. Its plank walls rippled. A thick blanket of moss covered its roof. And its front porch bowed in places. But despite its flaws, it seemed solid and the thought of having a place to sleep indoors replaced Meaghan's emptiness with a sliver of joy.

Nick crossed the clearing, setting the backpack down on the cabin's front porch before turning to stare into the trees. Meaghan followed his gaze, almost missing the crystals hanging in the branches surrounding the cabin. Unlike the ones that had protected them in the cave, these did not glow. Their dull smoke color blended into the receding night sky.

"Is there something wrong with them?" she asked.

"Nothing I can't fix," he told her. Moving to stand underneath one, he extended his hand toward the crystal. Though he was not tall enough to reach it, he kept his hand there and spoke, his words inaudible as his lips moved. After a few seconds, the crystal glowed white.

He moved to the next crystal and she followed him. "What are you doing?" she asked.

"Reciting a spell," he told her. He extended his hand, focused, and repeated the exercise. "The crystals will hold the spell even if I'm not here so the cabin stays protected."

She nodded and he lit the next crystal. "If they hold the spell even after the person who recited it is gone, why did these go dark?"

He looked at her, his eyes masked in shadows and she understood even before he said it. "The Guardian who recited the spell is dead."

More death, she thought and tiredness chased away her joy. What sort of world, what sort of hell had she entered where death dictated every turn? She looked away, toward the forest, and toward the portal that had torn her from home. She felt Nick's hand on her shoulder, but she refused to draw her eyes back to him. His other hand found the small of her back and then she was in his arms.

She pressed her head into his chest and gave into her sorrow. He held her, not speaking as she cried and then his lips found her temple and trailed kisses down her cheek. His touch soothed her, and chased away her tears. He ended his affection at the corner of her lips. Bringing his hands to her cheeks, he stepped back from her.

"Everything will be okay, Meg. I promise," he said. He waited until her eyes met his before he dropped his hands. "I need to finish these crystals. Why don't you see if you can find some food for dinner? If you stay near here, you'll be safe. Just yell if you need me."

Though she did not feel hungry, she left him to search the forest, making a circular pass around the cabin. When she found nothing, she went deeper into the woods. Foliage appeared thick, lush, and green, but bushes that should have held fruit had turned brown, dropping their leaves with the slightest touch. She gave up and returned to the cabin after finding nothing more than two apples on the low branch of a gangly looking tree.

Nick sat on the porch. Next to him, a dying raspberry bush taunted her efforts. This one had held a handful of berries he had already picked. He handed her half of them as she sat down. She gave him one of the apples, setting the other on top of a porch step.

"That's all I could find," she told him.

He shrugged and threw his half of the berries into his mouth. "I'm surprised you found those," he responded. "The castle is about twenty miles from here. We're on the outer border of the land Garon cursed to prevent anyone from living too close. Nothing providing sustenance can grow there."

"More death," she said aloud this time. She rested her forearms on her knees, crushing the berries between her palms, and stared at the ground. The juice stained the edges of her fingers and oozed between them, trailing down her knuckles. She ignored it. "Garon brings nothing but death," she whispered, closing her eyes. "How can you stand it? How can anyone stand to live here?"

Nick did not respond. She heard him move and then felt his fingers touch her hands. Gently, he coaxed one hand from the other and then rubbed something rough against her right hand. She opened her eyes. His fingers wiped raspberry from her skin with green leaves he had plucked from the bush. He concentrated on his task, his face passive, and she wondered if he intended not to answer her question. He discarded the stained leaves and plucked more, wiping the last of the juice from her right hand before moving to her left.

"I was eight when I first saw a man die."

He continued to focus on her hand, wiping with careful strokes and it took her a minute to realize he had spoken. His voice had been so soft his words had nearly dissolved into the air. She felt grief from him, and guilt, and she realized he had dropped his guard so she could fully understand what he needed to say.

"I was similar to Aldin then, more curious than smart. And though I understood the concept of the protective boundary surrounding our village, I didn't always pay attention to it. I would forget it was there and wander outside it, or I would ignore it if I saw something beyond the village I wanted to explore."

He discarded the last of the leaves and then slid his palms over hers. She curled her fingers around his hands. "That day, I ignored it. I saw something in the woods that caught my attention and I thought I had to go to it. I can't even remember what it was now." He raised his eyes to meet hers. His guilt grew stronger. "I was playing somewhere along one of the paths when I felt it for the first time. It was a low heat, a tingling sensation in my stomach I couldn't quite place, and it scared me so much I hid behind a bush. I learned later that it was the automatic warning a Guardian feels when danger is imminent. I'd never faced true danger before that day."

He shrugged and looked away. "They showed up about a minute later. I saw brown cloaks, leathery skin stretched over bone, and those red eyes. They froze me. Even though I never looked into their eyes, my fear froze me."

Nick stopped talking and took in a breath, releasing it with the same calculated measure. Although his eyes remained dry and his voice stayed steady, the pain within him grew. Meaghan moved closer to him, tightening her hold on his hands, and he continued.

"They were looking for me. They'd found out I'd been assigned as your Guardian and had come to kill me. They had been looking for days for the village, but the protection prevented them from finding anything until I ventured across their path." He paused again and she drew a hand to his temple, tracing her fingers through his hair and down his neck. He lifted his hand to cover hers and held them both still.

"They saw him before they found me. He ran from them, leading them away from the village and into the forest. It was there they killed him. They didn't use lightning. They used some sort of spell or strangle power and it took minutes for him to die. I watched him struggle. I watched him fall to the ground. The Mardróch laughed. Their voices echoed around me until they moved away and I could no longer see them.

"I remained frozen where I hid. I waited for my mother to discover I'd escaped my babysitter. I don't think it was long, maybe half an hour, but it felt like an eternity. She organized a search party and they found us both."

Meaghan waited to see if he would continue again, but when he did not, she spoke. "Do you know who the man was?"

"My father," Nick answered. "My mother always assumed I'd gone outside with him, that we'd been ambushed. I've never been able to tell her the truth." He brought their hands down to his lap and stared at them. "I've never told anyone what happened."

"Nick," she whispered, unsure of what to say.

He looked at her again. "Death is a regular part of life here. But it hasn't always been and it won't always be. I'm certain of that. My father died because he believed in that too, and because he believed I could make a difference. So do I. And so does everyone who fights to free the kingdom." He raised a palm to her cheek. Stroking her cheekbone with his thumb, he held her eyes with intensity. "That's how we stand it, Meg. We live on hope and we keep trying to make things better."

She nodded in understanding, but did not shift from his touch. She felt more from him now than she had all week and she did not want to sever the connection. Though his grief and guilt remained, his conviction that they would succeed in what they fought to do overshadowed the darker emotions with hope and faith. She considered his words, painted the image of that dreadful day in her mind, and felt a new type of empathy that had nothing to do with her power.

"Those are good reasons," she said, but then realized how closely the image echoed her own experience. When the Mardróch had chased her through the field while she struggled to protect Aldin, Nick had frozen. She had seen it and did not understand it then, but she did now. She wanted to apologize. She wanted to ease the pain she had caused him. But she could not figure out how to say the words, so she did the only thing that seemed right. She leaned toward him and kissed him.

A spark ignited. The warmth of fire built within her stomach, consuming her. She expected him to pull away. She felt the struggle within him, the longing and fear, but he hesitated for a second. He hesitated, held, and then fed the longing. He touched her face. She traced her fingers through his hair. They grew closer. The fire grew stronger. Then the crystals flickered.

Nick pulled back from her so fast she pitched forward. Panic washed over them both before he succeeded in shutting her out once more. He jumped up, knocking her apple over. It bounced down the stairs and rolled into the clearing. He scanned the trees, the panic disappearing from his eyes as soon as his gaze locked on the white crystals.

"Don't do that again," he told Meaghan, though he refused to look at her. His voice came across as brusque, and she did not understand what had happened. He had enjoyed their brief encounter as much as she had.

"Why not?" she asked.

"Because it's forbidden." He walked down the steps and retrieved her apple. Returning to the porch, he handed it to her, never breaking his stride. Then he disappeared into the cabin, shutting the door behind him.

Several minutes passed. Meaghan stared after him, stunned by his behavior. A breeze picked up from the west, chilling the air around her. She clutched her arms to her sides. The wind grew stronger. Her teeth chattered, her fingers turned to ice, and still, she waited. Embarrassed and angry, she did not want to face him yet. But the wind sliced through her clothes and her cloak. The cold bit her skin, and she could not take it any longer. She picked up the backpack and followed him inside.

Although the outside of the cabin had seemed somewhat run down, the inside looked to be well maintained and clean. Next to the door stood a small table with two chairs. On the far wall, a fireplace waited to give warmth. Flanking the fireplace, two cots invited weary travelers into slumber. Though small, it promised relaxation and safety. They were both too upset to take pleasure in either.

Nick watched her from the foot of one of the cots as she tossed the backpack on the table. "What was that about?" she demanded.

He met her scorching gaze with one of his own. "I told you before. We can't do that."

"I don't recall you fighting me off." She crossed her arms. "It felt more like you were enjoying it."

"It was a mistake," he said. "A moment of weakness. And it can't happen again."

"As I asked before, why not?"

"Because it's forbidden."

"So you said." She pursed her lips. "But you still haven't answered the question."

Nick stood and moved to the fireplace. A wood box to its right held sticks of kindling, and he crouched down next to it. Retrieving the kindling one at a time, he broke them in half before tossing them into the fireplace.

"Guardians are forbidden from falling in love with anyone but another Guardian," he told her. "It's the only way to keep our powers strong."

"I see," she said, her voice as chilly as the air. "So the rest of us aren't good enough for you."

He paused, half a stick locked in his hand as he turned to look at her.

"I'm not good enough for you," she said, dropping her arms. "Is that what you're trying to say?"

"Of course not. Meg—"

"What?" she snapped. "I'm tired of hearing excuses from you. I want the truth."

"There's no point in it," he said. "It doesn't matter what I feel. We can't have a relationship. It's against the rules."

"And there's no way around that?" she asked. When he shook his head, she turned from him. Walking to the cot, she sat down before she looked at him again. Tears burned in her eyes, but she refused to let them fall. "This feels right, Nick. It has since the day we were lost in the woods. I was childish. I wanted to keep hating you, but I found it impossible. I grew to care about you."

"I did too," he confessed. "But the rules have been enacted to protect us. Aunt Viv died to protect us, and I don't want to throw away her sacrifice."

"Why would you?" Meaghan asked. "What aren't you telling me?"

"It's complicated." He turned his attention back to the fireplace. "For now, you'll have to take my word for it. We can never be together."

"Maybe if we—"

"Never," he insisted, his voice stiff with the finality of his decision. He stopped snapping kindling. Waiting for her next protest, she knew, but when she did not offer one, he returned to his task.

She wanted to be angry. She wanted to yell and argue with him, but she could not find the will. Today had been too taxing on her and his rejection tipped her emotional scale. Though she hated showing the weakness in front of him, she buried her head in her hands and cried.

She felt his sorrow join hers and then disappear. He had dropped his guard. It had only lasted a few seconds, but it had been enough for her to know she was not the only one suffering. She looked up at him.

"This isn't fair to you," he said. "I know that, and I want to explain everything, but I don't know how."

He stood, and then placed his hand on the mantel. She began to feel warm. Her eyes turned to the fireplace and she watched the fire he had built spread.

"If I could be with you, I would," he continued. "You're the most remarkable woman I've ever known. You grow stronger each day. I watch it and I'm proud of you for it. You'll be perfect as Ærenden's Queen."

The warmth in her intensified, moving out to her limbs. The fire remained small, and she wondered where the heat came from. It pulsed down her legs, and along her fingertips.

"But your royalty is the reason nothing can happen between us. No matter how much we care about each other, we can never make it work. It's not just against the rules. It's more than that."

She felt feverish. She curled her fingers into her clammy hands and then stretched them out again, bringing them to the burning in her cheeks.

"Meg, please say something."

"I'm sorry," she responded, though the fire filling her brain made it difficult to think, let alone speak. "I'll do whatever you feel is best."

"Thank you," he said. He turned to stare into the fireplace. "For what it's worth," he whispered. "I'm sorry, too."

The warmth she felt boiled, and then it overtook her, searing every fiber of her body before exploding from her, a volcano of heat and light that turned into swirling silver.

A second later, Nick gasped. Blue light poured from him, shooting straight into the air to collide with the silver stream emanating from her. Where the colors met, they swirled together, turning into dark red. Once no more blue and silver existed, the red separated, retreating into Nick and Meaghan in turn. She stared at her hands, at the glow enlivening her skin, and then closed her eyes, sensing steady warmth she had never known before. She felt alive. She felt vibrant. She felt powerful. And for the first time since she had come to this world, she felt right.

Nick sank to the floor in front of the fireplace. "It wasn't supposed to happen that way," he said. He turned to stare at her. Fear haunted his eyes, but she did not need to see it to know. He had stopped hiding his emotions from her again. "We have to touch," he continued, though his words made no sense to her. "That's how it works. It has to be a kiss."

"What do you mean?" she asked. "What happened?"

He closed his eyes and his fear gave way to despair. "It's over," he said. "I have nothing left."

"I don't understand."

"It's over," he repeated and pressed his hands into his forehead. "You took my powers."

CHAPTER TWENTY-FIVE

"I STILL don't understand."

Instead of responding to Meaghan's confusion, Nick stared ahead. At the wall, through it, or maybe he could not see it at all. She did not know. She only knew his emotions harbored both fear and a loss she could not comprehend. He remained on the floor, unmoving for several long minutes that felt like hours before he stood.

"We should sleep," he said and walked to the other cot. After pulling back the rough wool blanket and the crisp white sheet underneath it, he sat down on the edge of the bed and kicked off his shoes.

She watched him, waiting for him to explain, but when he slid under the covers, she realized he did not intend to tell her anything.

"Nick," she began, stopping when he turned to look at her. He had drawn a curtain over his emotions, darkening them, and that frightened her more than anything else.

"I need time," he told her. "Let me sort this out. We can talk about it after we sleep."

She nodded and when he closed his eyes, she rose to add fuel to the fire. The kindling he had lit had nearly burned down and she did not want the flames to go out. Despite the warmth now inhabiting her body, her skin had turned to ice. The temperature felt like it had dropped ten degrees in the last hour.

"Don't," he said when she lifted a log. She turned to face him. His eyes remained closed, a forearm stretched over them, but he had heard her.

"It's cold," she argued.

"We'll live. The smoke will give away our location."

"But we're protected," she protested, though his warning gave her pause. Had she stolen his powers? She looked through the window of the cabin, searching for the glow of the crystals, but could not find anything. Panic rose within her and she settled it. He blocked her Empath power again, so he must be mistaken.

He did not seem to think so. "We're not protected anymore," he said, his tone flat, giving no misinterpretation to his words. "Now go to sleep."

She swallowed her dread, her fear, and now a growing sense of frustration, and did as he asked. She dropped the log back into the wood box before making her way to her own cot. Taking off her cloak, she snapped it flat over the top of the wool blanket, and then slid between the sheets. They felt as icy as the air. Within a few minutes, they insulated her body heat, but not enough. She shivered, clenching her teeth to control the need to chatter them, and waited, hoping sleep would find her despite her accelerated heart rate and overwrought brain.

It did not. An hour crawled by, made unbearable by the increasing cold, and she sighed, giving up on the effort. Though Nick had grown still, his breathing steady, the quiet only made her anxiety worse. She slipped from the bed and found her way to the small table by the entrance. The wind pushed its way through the cracks around the door, making this side of the room feel like a refrigerator, but she ignored it, taking a seat at the table. She shivered, ignoring that too as she dug through the backpack. She focused on one thing, on finding the small object that had brought her comfort night after night while Nick slept—her mother's amulet.

She found it where she had last left it, in the front pocket of the backpack, buried at the bottom. She slipped the amulet from its pouch, and then ran the chain through her fingers. Though it started out as cold as the air, the metal warmed to her touch. She cupped the amulet within her hands and examined it. Each turn of the flowers along the border captivated her. Each twist of metal mesmerized her. Each glint of glass held her eyes transfixed, as it had always done in her dreams. It still amazed her that every detail commanded her memory with accuracy, despite her young age. It must have been important to her birth mother, an importance that had made an impression in Meaghan's mind. And she had not forgotten, despite the years and distance. It still looked the same, except for the glow. It had appeared more beautiful and important when the stone had glowed.

She flipped it over, tracing her finger down the back until she felt the small bump Aldin had found. Pressing it up and then in, she released the catch for the hidden door. Inside laid the paper she had come to cherish each time they had stopped to sleep. With the tip of her finger, she nudged it out of its hiding place and then opened it flat on the table.

When she had first seen the writing on the paper, she had wept. The familiar loop of each cursive letter, the soft touch from a delicate hand, the flowing, graceful characters—they all came together to speak to her. Though the words made no sense and the prophecy— as she had come to decide it must be—escaped her knowledge, the writing brought her happiness. It belonged to Vivian, and it somehow connected Meaghan to her old life and to a peace she could not seem to capture on this world.

She traced the words with her index finger and wondered what her mother had been trying to say. She had no doubt the paper had been hidden within the amulet for her. She just could not figure out why.

"You should be sleeping." Nick's voice broke into her thoughts from across the room. She looked up from the paper to find him sitting up in bed, watching her. His face looked tired, older than it had before he slept, and she turned her eyes back to the paper. Careful to hide her movements, she folded it and tucked it back into the amulet, closing the door over its secret.

"It's too cold," she responded after she put the locket away. "I may go for a walk and see if that warms me up."

"You need to sleep," he said. When she did not respond, he climbed out of bed and came to her. He laid a hand on her shoulder, and then leaned down to press his lips to the top of her head. "This isn't the first time you've spent your hours staring at the amulet instead of sleeping, but you can't keep doing that. Not if you want to stay safe while we travel. You can't stay alert if you're tired."

"I know, but I can't sleep. I don't know what happened between us and I'm scared. I keep thinking something's wrong."

"We'll figure it out," he promised. "Later. For now, come back to bed with me. We can keep each other warm."

She nodded and followed him back to his cot. Though it was small, perhaps too narrow for two people, they made it work. They lay on their sides, facing each other. His arms circled her body. She brought her hands to his chest. And then he did something she did not expect. He kissed her.

His lips were soft, undemanding, and in them, he gave her his acceptance for what they felt for each other. When he drew them up to her forehead, she knew something had changed. She doubted he would tell her what, so she did not bother to ask. Instead, she rested her head next to his and slept.

§

BRIGHT SUNLIGHT streamed through the cabin window, highlighting small particles of dust as they danced in the air. Meaghan frowned. It should have been night, or at the least, dusk. She felt refreshed, so she knew she had not slept only a few hours. But the sunlight told her it was still day.

She did not have to stretch out her hand to know the other half of the small bed lay empty. The warmth of Nick's body had left her. She propped up on her elbows, scanning the room for him. She found him eating an apple at the small table.

Swinging her legs over the side of the bed, she stood. The wood floor did not hold the chill it had earlier. She listened for the wind, but heard only the chirp of birds outside. She hoped that meant the weather would cooperate for their travels today. She stretched to remove the kinks from her body and then reclaimed her shoes, slipping them back onto her feet before she joined Nick at the table. He handed her the remaining apple. She devoured half of it, satisfying a ravenous hunger before she spoke, and then formed words around bites as she continued to eat.

"How long did I sleep?"

"The rest of yesterday and all of last night."

She lowered her apple, her hunger forgotten in surprise. "Why did you let me sleep so long?"

He shrugged, his eyes remaining focused on his own apple, though he had yet to raise it to his lips since she had taken the chair opposite him. She set her apple down.

"Because you needed the rest," he responded. He laid his apple next to hers. "And because we're almost home. Once we arrive there, things will get unpleasant. I didn't want to face that yet."

She laced her fingers together on the table in front of her and studied him. He still refused to meet her eyes. His movements were hesitant and unsure. The confidence that usually held his head high and his shoulders steady had disappeared. He did not act right. He did not look right. It worried her and she tapped the table to get his attention. He lifted his eyes to hers. Pain shone from them. Unlocking her hands, she laid one on top of the table, palm up. He placed his hand on top of hers and grabbled hold, taking comfort as she curled their fingers together.

"You kissed me yesterday," she said.

He nodded. She waited a minute, and then another, and when she thought she would need to prompt him again, he spoke. "Do you remember Christmas last year?" he asked, but before she could answer, he kept talking. "Of course you do. I'm sure you must. It wasn't that long ago." He shook his head, and then grew silent again. She let the seconds pass until he continued. "It was my first Christmas. And my last. I loved every minute of it."

"Except when I woke you at five in the morning to help me make breakfast," she said. "I probably should have let you sleep, but I wanted to spend the time with you."

"I'm glad you did. That was my favorite part of the day." He brought his other hand up to encase hers. "It was sweet of you to want to make breakfast for James and Vivian."

"Mom thought so too, until she saw the mess in her kitchen."

Nick grinned, a genuine gesture that returned a spark of happiness to his eyes. "It was a harmless flour fight," he said. "We cleaned it up."

"And clogged her new vacuum in the process. What was it you got stuck in the hose?"

"A fork." He chuckled. "And a wad of plastic wrap. It took me an hour to figure out how to get the damn thing unclogged, but it was worth it." His smile faded. "Sometimes I wish we could go back there. Even though I knew I couldn't be with you, it was easy to forget on days like that." He let go of her hand, then stood and walked to the fireplace. Shoving his hands into his pockets, he stared into its emptiness. "I loved hearing you sing while we cooked. There was one song in particular that took my breath away. It was a jazz piece, I think. *'s Wonderful?* You were doing the Sarah Vaughan version."

"I was," she confirmed. "I'm surprised you remember that."

"I can't forget." He turned back around to look at her. "That was the moment I knew I was in love with you, and the first time I wanted to kiss you. Yesterday was for that."

The sadness returned to his eyes. She stood, intending to go to him, but he shook his head and she remained rooted to her spot.

"I couldn't kiss you then," he told her, "because I wanted to prevent what happened yesterday."

She wove her hands together in front of her, trying to gather enough strength for the answer to her next question. "What did happen yesterday? You said I took your powers, but you're still able to block me."

"You stole all but my personal power," he answered, "the one power that doesn't make me a Guardian. All of my other powers are specific to my Guardianship. They're a package deal, so to speak, providing me with the ability to protect you. And they need a minimum amount of power to work. An increase in power won't hurt them, but a decrease will destroy them."

"Are you saying I somehow decreased your power?"

"Without meaning to, yes. What happened yesterday was a melding of powers. Our powers combined and then balanced out before returning to us."

He did not have to say any more for Meaghan to understand. Her knees felt weak, so she slid back into her chair. "A Guardian's powers are the strongest on this world, next to a Spellmaster's," she whispered. "When the powers balanced, I got some of your power, didn't I? You're no longer a Guardian."

"Yes," he whispered. "I can't protect you anymore."

And he would no longer be able to protect himself. She closed her eyes against the reality. "How did it happen?"

"Our powers do more than allow us to have special talents," he responded. "They're an extension of our souls. Because of that, they're able to recognize when love is real. And when the time is right," he hesitated. "Well, yesterday happens."

"When the time is right," she echoed, opening her eyes. She gripped the back of her chair, feeling sick. How could the time be right? How could putting Nick's life in danger be right? Nothing could be right about it. She had to have misunderstood him. "Nick, I care for you. I always have. And maybe I feel more, but I couldn't call it love. I wouldn't have said that, so how could my power cause this?"

"I don't know," he responded. He crossed the room and knelt in front of her. Taking her face between his hands, he lifted it so he could press his lips to hers. "I can call what I feel love. But even if what I feel was allowed, I wouldn't have said I was ready for this. None of it makes sense to me. It's only supposed to happen with a kiss, and only then after two people have had time to get to know each other and acknowledge their love." He let go of her. "It doesn't matter now what's supposed to be. And it doesn't matter if we're ready for it or not. It's done, and it can't be undone."

"What's done?" she asked, barely pushing the words past her dry throat. "What happened?"

"Our powers joined us," he told her. "For eternity. We're wed."

CHAPTER TWENTY-SIX

WED.

The word chased through her mind unimpeded, knocking every other thought from recognition. If she had not been sitting, she would have fallen to the floor.

Wed.

No proposal, no ring, no fancy wedding or flowers. No food and family. No dancing and champagne.

Wed.

No church, no reception, no picturesque fairytale celebration. All she had were streams of colors that in no way resembled the decorations she had once planned to the last detail at the age of eleven, and filthy clothes with almost a week's worth of wear that did not even come close to the pristine white dress she had designed in her dreams.

Wed.

Joined in seconds by a force she could not control, by a decision she did not make. Joined forever, or until death, which most likely would come first and not far from now. Joined by magic, not unquestionable love.

Wed.

She buried her face in her hands and squeezed her eyes shut. Was there nothing on this world that made sense? Nick's hands gripped hers. She felt another surge of warmth and then realized maybe one thing did make sense. She raised her head and met his gaze. There was worry there, for her, not for his loss and safety, as well as kindness, and understanding. She smiled. Maybe the dresses and the ceremonies were what did not make sense. And maybe they could find a reason behind the seeming madness of being wed.

"Now that we're married—"

"Not married," he corrected. "It's 'wed' here. A marriage is only the ceremony. We have one similar to yours. But the wedding is the actual act of joining."

She nodded. "Now that we're wed, what happens? You said going back to your village would be unpleasant."

"It won't be easy. The Elders will call a hearing and decide my punishment. Despite what they decide, I'll have to move out of the village. It's for Guardians only. But all of that won't matter if my mother kills me first."

She raised an eyebrow at the joke and then realized he was not kidding. "This is serious, isn't it?" she asked. "Will your mom really be that mad?"

"It's a strict law, and I've made it more unforgiveable because it puts you at risk."

"That doesn't seem fair. How can they expect us to follow the law if our powers make the decision for us?"

"They don't expect you to follow it," he told her and sat back on his heels. "They expect me to, and I'm not exactly blameless. When I first started having feelings for you, I was required to remove myself from the situation, and from being your Guardian. I didn't. I made a choice and they'll hold me accountable for it."

"What will they do to you?"

"Banish me from the kingdom," he answered. "It's only a matter of how long. It could be a year or it could be forever." His body remained relaxed at the decree, but hers tensed. She gripped his hands tighter.

"They can't. They won't."

"We can't stop them. They're the final authority on all Guardians."

She stood. He rose to his feet as well, bringing his hands to her shoulders.

"Even over the Queen?" she asked. "Even if I insist on keeping my husband within my kingdom?"

"Even if." He chuckled. "Though I imagine if you raised enough of a fuss, I'd be safe from permanent banishment."

She lifted her chin. "I intend to."

"Good." He smiled, squeezed her shoulders, and then allowed his smile and the gaiety of the moment to slip away. "Meg, you do understand it's the only thing I'll be safe from. I'm a target already. Without my sensing powers, I won't last long."

"I know," she said, her voice soft. "Are you certain the repercussions aren't a rumor? It wouldn't be the first time a tale became known as reality and if it's always been forbidden—"

"I'm certain. We aren't the first to do this. Before the war, it was a loose warning, a choice—remain a Guardian or follow where love led. Not many chose love, but those who did were living proof of the sacrifice it took to break the rule. After the war started, the Elders declared it a law. A few people have still chosen love over their powers, but none of them have lived long enough to answer to the Elders."

"Have you tried using your powers?" she asked. "There's no danger here, nothing to sense. Maybe—"

"Meg, stop," he interrupted again, a warning of impatience in his tone. He drew his hands to the sides of her neck, and pressed his forehead to hers. "We can't fix this. You need to accept that. It's out of our control."

She covered his hands with her own, closing her eyes as pain washed through her. She had no problem accepting the loss of control. Nothing had been in their control this week. They rode the days like swells in a storm, holding to each other and somehow surviving on wit and luck. Mostly luck. But as long as they made it through, she was okay with it. She was not okay with losing Nick, and she did not intend to accept his death. She could not believe Vivian, with all her wisdom and foresight, would invite Nick to Earth and not understand this might happen. It seemed foolish, and her mother had never been a foolish woman.

A spark of understanding grew within her mind, fed by a few graceful letters and a string of nonsensical lines.

Nonsensical, until they had context.

She pulled away from Nick, stepping back in her excitement without warning. She had to be right. She was certain of it, so certain that she could not keep a smile from her face. Confusion blanketed his.

"They're wrong," she said to him. "You're wrong."

He shook his head. "I know this is hard, but—"

"No, Nick," she turned to the table and the backpack, rummaging through it for the amulet. "It happened differently for us because it *is* different. Mom told me so I wouldn't have to worry about you, but I didn't understand."

"I don't either. You're not making sense."

"I know," she conceded. "It's because I can't find it. Here it is," her fingers wrapped around the velvet pouch and she tugged it from the bag, turning to him. "She left it in here."

She slid the amulet out of the bag into her hand, then flipped it over and popped open the secret door. "Aldin found this," she said, "and this." She poked the paper out of its hole and set the necklace aside. Then she unfolded the paper and handed it to him.

He looked from her to the paper, and then back to her.

"Read it," she insisted.

He dropped his eyes back to the writing and frowned. "This doesn't mean anything. It doesn't negate—"

"You don't recognize the handwriting?" she asked. She took a step closer to him. "How could you not? It's Mom's."

"I recognize it," he said, looking back at the paper. "But it's impossible to tell what she meant by it."

"It's not." She snatched the paper back from him, upset he could not see it as clearly as she could. "When the two houses that cannot be together join as one," she read, "they will become stronger; the world will be reborn and once again have hope." She looked up at him. "That means nothing to you?"

"It can mean whatever I decide it means," he responded. "That's the trouble with prophecies. When you're desperate enough, it becomes what you want instead of being what it is."

She felt heat rise in her cheeks. "Two houses," she pressed forward, "as in the Guardians and everyone else."

"Or two different families," he countered, "or two literal houses, or two villages. As I said, it could be anything."

She crossed her arms, glaring at him. "Until you add the next line, 'That cannot be together join as one'. It can only mean one thing."

"That two feuding tribes need to sign a treaty," he said. "It could have been written long ago for Zeiihbu. At least, that's how I interpret it. But you think it's about us being wed."

"Can you truly argue against that? Mom gave this to me for a reason."

"I can because I've known Guardians who wed and lost their powers. It's hard to ignore that for a piece of paper with fuzzy analogies that, incidentally, could have been put in the amulet at any time. You don't know Vivian meant it for you."

"I do know." She slapped the paper onto the table, raising her voice to punctuate her anger. "But if you're so certain this means nothing, what does it hurt to try using your sensing power? Sense my power. If you can't, then it's settled."

"Fine," he matched her tone with one of equal animosity, and then stared at her with the same heat. A minute dragged forward, then a second before he shook his head. His shoulders slumped. "I'm sorry," he whispered.

Tears welled within her eyes. She dashed them away with the back of her hand, and when he reached for her, she pushed him aside and fled the cabin.

§

NICK LEFT Meaghan alone outside, giving her both space and time to sort out her thoughts. Her reaction had hurt him more than he cared to admit, but he understood. This week had been too much for her. And perhaps it had been too much for him, too.

To keep busy, he tidied up the cabin, ignoring the paper she had left on the table until he had nothing left to distract him. Then he stood over it, studying the small piece of parchment with equal loathing and curiosity. Meaghan had seemed so certain it meant something. He had not wanted to shatter whatever hope she had clung to, but she had left him no choice. And for a moment, his heart had leapt when he thought his sensing power had worked. But the power pushing back to him had felt stronger than anything he had sensed from a single person before. It had more closely matched the level of power three Guardians would produce together. Although Meaghan's power was rare, it was not strong, and he realized that meant his brain had tricked him into feeling something so he would not have to face the grief of feeling emptiness.

He picked the paper up from the table and read it again before setting it back down. He could see how Meaghan could interpret it the way she did. And the promise of hope would lure anyone into

261

believing it applied to them. Hope had been elusive lately. But false hope was worse than having none at all, and he blamed Vivian for instilling that in Meaghan. Although Vivian had been a gifted seer, she had also continually failed in one area. She had never found it important to provide translations for her visions. She would write things or say things in the veiled way she received them, trusting that the person needing the message would understand it at the right time. It was too risky for his taste. It made more sense to make the message clear so there could be no ambiguity, no misinterpretation. Things were not always so obvious to everyone.

Things aren't what they seem.

Parts of his last conversation with Vivian drifted across his mind. She had been right. She usually was. But something about it bothered him. He sat down at the table, staring at the paper as he tried to remember. Why did it feel so important?

Because sometimes she delivered prophecies in plain speak. Had she done that to him? He cleared his thoughts and focused.

They had talked about Meaghan and his attraction for her. She had known, and that had surprised him, but he had not had time to dwell on it. How long had she known? Perhaps longer than he had. She had told him to follow his heart, and he thought she had meant to ignore what he felt for Meaghan, but what if she had meant the opposite? What if she had meant this? She had said something else that had struck him as odd at the time. Something in the prophecy reminded him of it.

He frowned down at her handwriting. The conversation danced around the fringes of his mind, but he could not recall it. In anger, he pressed his hand over the paper, covering it, and then shoved it away. It slid off the table and fluttered to the floor, landing upright at his feet. Taunting him, he thought, and debated setting fire to it. It would disintegrate to ash in seconds, and then he would be done with it.

But he would be no closer to discovering its truth. He leaned down to retrieve it. As his fingers closed around the paper, a single word jumped from it, commanding his attention—*strong*. He crushed the paper in his fist, its presence forgotten as his mind latched on to the memory that had eluded him, on to the words she had spoken.

Sometimes you have to give in to weakness to become stronger.

He uncurled his fingers, and then smoothed the crumpled paper onto the table. "When the two houses that cannot be together join as one, they will become stronger," he read, and understood what Vivian had been trying to tell him. He had to give in to his love for Meaghan for their mission to succeed. He did not know why. He did not know how. But he knew doing so had made Meaghan stronger. Meaghan's interpretation of the first part of the prophecy had been correct. His mind had not tricked him. He had not lost his powers. He had only sensed what had happened to hers.

He stood and went outside to tell her. She sat on the top porch step, her arms wrapped around her knees as one hand stroked an overhanging branch from the raspberry bush. A flicker of light caught his attention from the trees and he paused, surprised by it before he sat down next to her.

"I could use some breakfast," she said, letting go of the branch. "But it would take a miracle to get anything around here." She turned to him. Tears shimmered in her eyes. "Will they let us eat in your village before they take you away?"

"There'll be a feast for my return, and for yours," he promised, then slipped an arm around her shoulders, pulling her close. "They won't take me away from you, though. They'll understand when we tell them. They won't have a choice."

"When we tell them what?" she asked, resting her head against his shoulder. "That we broke the law? That we took a risk which could cost your life?"

"No," he said. "That Vivian predicted our wedding. You were right."

She raised her head and stared at him. "You said it didn't work."

"I thought my sensing power wasn't working because what I sensed from you was too strong. But I was wrong. You're stronger now that we're wed, and so am I. Look," he pointed toward the trees. Sapphire crystals twinkled bright in the sunlight where white had hung the night before. "The color change means they're infused with a stronger power. When they're blue, we're invisible. Someone has to know the cabin is here to use it. With white, anyone who needs it can find it. It takes the power of two strong Guardians to turn the crystals blue. I shouldn't be able to do that on my own."

She smiled. He pressed his lips to her forehead, and then stared over her shoulder, shocked when he saw the raspberry bush that had been close to death the night before. Meaghan tensed at his reaction, and jumped her feet.

"What is it?" she asked, turning to scan the woods. "Is it Mardróch? I don't smell anything."

He took her hand and pulled her back down. "We're invisible," he reminded her. "We're safe."

"Right." She offered him a sheepish grin. "You looked scared."

"I was surprised," he told her. "It seems the second part of Vivian's prophecy was literal."

"What do you mean?"

"The world will be reborn," he recited, placing his hands on Meaghan's shoulders and turning her so she could see the raspberry bush beside the steps. The brown bush had turned green. Its branches now bore dozens of plump red berries. "It seems you have a new power. Shall we eat?"

CHAPTER TWENTY-SEVEN

"I THINK it might be best if we don't mention the wedding," Nick said as they trekked through another thick forest. This one looked no different from the one that had welcomed them to Ærenden. As before, tall trees shaded them, only allowing sunlight to stream through the canopy in pale streaks. Birds rustled leaves as they passed overhead. Animals scurried away from them, their escape heard and never seen. And as Meaghan and Nick had in the first forest, they travelled during the day, using the canopy and overgrowth of the dense woods to cover their movements.

Meaghan knew they were nearing the end of their journey when Nick began coaching her on what to expect in the village. He reiterated that his mother looked identical to Vivian, and that Meaghan must be careful not to refer to Vivian as her mother. He told her the Elders would want an audience with her not long after she arrived, but he would ensure they allowed her time to change and shower, and perhaps eat a snack if she wanted. He would protect her in his own way, even from those who meant her no harm. And then he warned her about the wedding.

"I figured as much," she responded. "And I'm assuming your affections will end as well?"

"My affections?"

The look of confusion on his face amused her into grinning. "Like when you hold me when I'm upset, or kiss my forehead or cheek," she explained. "Or like now. You're holding my hand."

He looked down at their clasped hands and chuckled. "I hadn't realized."

"It must be automatic for you," she said. "You used to do that on Earth, too."

"Did I? Maybe Aunt Viv didn't need to be a Seer to guess how I felt about you after all." He turned his hand to slip his fingers between hers, squeezed, and then let go. "That will definitely have to stop or we'll give ourselves away. I need to find the right time to explain things to the Elders if I want to avoid a trial."

She nodded. "What else should I know?"

"Only that my village is larger than Neiszhe's. It's the primary Guardian village and one of the biggest villages in the kingdom. Most of the people will know who you are because they knew why I went to Earth."

"I understand," she said and then grimaced with a sudden sense of dread. "So there'll be more bowing."

"Some people will bow, mostly those who were too young to have known the royal family or those who are part of the royal guard, but most won't. Most of the people in my village come from families who directly protected your family members. If we bowed all the time, we wouldn't get much done."

"That's a relief," she said and then considered the implication of his words. "I imagine if most of the Guardians in the village protected the royal family, they must be big targets for Garon."

"They are," Nick responded. "Garon destroyed the old village where he grew up, where we used to live, but the new village is protected with the strongest spell available. It took two dozen Guardians to enact it, and after almost fifteen years, it still holds. Garon hasn't found us yet." He stopped in front of a large boulder with a flat top that stretched several feet wide and nearly the same in width. Leaning down he examined a brown, scraggly plant at its base. The plant appeared to be losing its struggle against a thick matting of weeds.

"What is it?" Meaghan asked.

"Tamrin bush," Nick answered. "Both its leaves and nuts are edible when it's bearing." He pulled one of the weeds from the earth and handed it to her. Its roots were twice as thick as the stem of the plant. "This is called grim weed. It twists its roots around the roots of other plants, choking them by cutting off their food source. The nearest I can tell, its sole purpose is to kill everything in its path. It's slow growing, fortunately, but not good for the vegetation if it goes unchecked."

"Handy," Meaghan responded and tossed the plant aside, "if you want to destroy entire forests. We have plants that do similar things on Earth. Is it natural?"

"No. It's another one of Garon's inventions. He has a Gardener in his ranks." Nick leaned down to pick up the weed Meaghan had discarded and threw it on top of the boulder. "They reroot," he told her. "We'll have to burn it. Let's pull the rest so it doesn't spread."

"Is a fire safe?"

"It's dense enough in this part of the woods that a small fire will go unnoticed. We won't have to keep it lit for long to do the job."

"That works for me," she said and then bent down to help him, tearing weeds from the ground in large clumps. "What's a Gardener?" she asked. "Is it anything like it sounds?"

"In a way." He tossed more weeds onto the rock. "A Gardener works with plants, helps them grow, and has the ability to create new species through cross-pollinating, similar to what you're probably used to, but it's all done using a power."

She laughed. "Of course. What else would it be?" Standing, she dropped the weeds she had collected onto the rock. "So this plant was created through magical mutation?"

"Basically," he responded. He pulled the last of the weeds and tossed them on top of the others, then added dried leaves he gathered from a pile at his feet. After dropping the backpack to the ground, he fished a box of matches from it, then struck one on the rock, and touched it to the weeds. The green plants only smoked at first, sending tendrils of gray into the sky, but when Nick leaned down close to them, blowing a steady breath into the pile, the fire took. As the water within the weeds boiled, the plants exploded, giving off satisfying pops and turning the smoke into thick black clouds.

Meaghan watched the fire destroy Garon's vile creation, felt a surge of vindication, and then crouched to examine the weeds' victim. Though she doubted the tamrin bush would live much longer, she saw streaks of green fighting their way through the deepening brown and knew it had life left in it still. Her mind went back to the raspberry bush from this morning and she reached out a hand to touch one of the tamrin bush's branches. She waited a minute, but nothing happened.

Another power she could not control, she thought with frustration, and started to stand, but stopped when Nick placed a hand on her shoulder. She had been so focused on the bush she had not realized he had crouched down beside her.

"You don't know how to do it, do you?" he asked.

She shook her head and then felt dread build again. "What will I do if I can't figure out how to control my powers?" she asked. "You said your village is larger. How will I handle so many emotions if I can't figure this out?"

"Let's take one thing at a time," he said and laid a palm against her cheek. "Until you can control your empathic ability, we'll figure out a way to ensure we don't go too far from each other. If you stay focused on my power, you'll be okay. As far as this new power, it may be stronger, but it should be easier to control since it's dormant."

"Dormant?"

"Not active all the time like your empath power," he explained. "It seems counterintuitive, but a power you access for a particular purpose is easier to control than one that's always working. Because it's constant, it's hard to know where your power stops and you begin."

She did not respond. She turned her attention back to the bush, touching it, and he drew his hand to her back.

"My blocking power was the first thing I learned to control," he told her. "It drove my mother crazy because I would use it to keep her from finding me, particularly when she had chores for me to do." Meaghan smiled, amused, and he moved his hand to the back of her neck. "My ability to sense danger was harder to control. It's active all the time and though it's not usually something I want to subdue, there are times when it's important to do so, like when I'm in battle. Since the danger is everywhere, it inundates me. The power becomes overwhelming and drains my energy."

"Like mine does," Meaghan said.

"Exactly. Guardians learn how to mute their powers around the age of ten, once they've had time to understand how to manipulate their other powers. Even with practice, it's difficult to learn."

"But I don't have ten years to learn how to do it," she protested. "There has to be a quicker way."

"It won't take you long," he promised. "But you won't be able to do it overnight, either. Give yourself time and focus on learning your new power for now. That will help."

She blew out a heavy breath to ease her tension and nodded, conceding. "So what do I do?"

"Start by telling me what you felt when you made the raspberry bush grow."

She took a minute to consider before responding. "I was upset, mostly. I thought I had done something that would get you killed. And I was angry."

"What else?"

"I was hungry, which is why I thought of the bush. Otherwise, I would have left it alone. And I felt warm."

"Warm? It's been cold for days." He drew his brows together and then his eyes widened in understanding. "You felt warmth," he realized, "after we were wed."

"Yes." She turned to study him. "I assumed it was residual from being wed because I felt it first right before the colors started, and it hasn't been as strong today as it was yesterday."

"It's from the wedding and it's not," he said. "What you feel is a concentration of energy. And you feel it less today because your body is growing used to it, not because it's fading."

"What is it?"

He placed his hand on her chest, to the right of her heart. "You feel it emanating from here, right?" She nodded. "It's power, Meg. It's a part of you and you've always had it, which is probably why you never noticed it until it changed. Close your eyes for a minute and focus on it."

She closed her eyes and then hesitated, reopening them. "I don't know how."

"Here," he drew her down to a sitting position and sat facing her. "Do what I do," he told her. "Take in a breath and hold it."

She watched his chest rise, nearly overinflate, and she mimicked him.

"Now close your eyes and focus on exhaling slowly." She did and waited. "Inhale again and hold it," he instructed. When her breath had filled her lungs, he touched two fingers to her chest at the point where she felt the most pressure from holding her breath. "Focus here," he told her. She directed her attention to his fingers, to the sensation of them pressing into her body, and then to her aching lungs as they begged for release. To her surprise, she also felt something else, something warm and radiating. She smiled and released her breath, pleased to discover she could still focus on the warmth.

"You have it?" Nick asked.

"Yes."

"Keep your eyes closed for now, and give me your hand."

Meaghan did as he asked, extending her hand toward his voice. He took her hand in his and then drew it down to her lap. He turned her hand so her palm faced up, and then she felt something rough against it. A branch of the bush, she realized when she closed her fingers around brittle leaves.

"This next part may be difficult to understand," he said. "But try to relax and do it anyway. It should be instinctive, even though you didn't grow up here."

"All right." Though curiosity nearly had her opening her eyes, she remained as she was, tranquil and focused on the warmth. "What next?"

"Send your power to the plant. Exhale it, like you did with your breath."

She frowned, certain what he had instructed could not be possible. Breathing was a physical thing, born to her, and this seemed more abstract. Still, she had agreed to try it, so she willed her doubt away and concentrated harder on her power, commanding it to move. Nothing happened at first, but then it slid. She took in a deep breath, held it, and expelled it again. Then she pictured drawing the warmth across her body and into her hand. When it shifted and did as she pictured, spreading through her and then setting fire to her palm, she gasped. She let go of the plant as her eyes flew open.

Nick grinned, dropping his guard so she could sense his joy. "You did it," he told her, leaning between them to press his lips to hers. "Look at the bush."

She turned her head, amazed to see the plant changing in front of her. It dropped its dry, dead leaves, replacing them with velvet green foliage streaked in orange. It grew, rising from the ground and lifting wilted limbs into the sky as it thickened into a dense bush as large as the raspberry bush by the cabin. When it appeared healthy and full, it sprouted long, thin nuts the size of one of Meaghan's fingers.

Nick plucked a nut from the bush. Snapping it in two, he upended the halves so that several pea-sized filberts emptied into her hand. She tossed them into her mouth, relishing more in their tender flavor than she had anything else before.

"They taste like hazelnuts," she said.

"They do," he agreed. "That's an impressive power you have."

She blushed and reached for another nut, plucking a leaf with it. "You said these were edible, too?"

"They are, but that's more emergency knowledge than anything else. They make jicab root taste like candy."

She dropped the leaf to the ground, shuddering, and he laughed.

They ate until they were full and then moved again. As they came within a mile of the village, Nick quickened his pace, but Meaghan lagged behind, her anxiety growing with each step.

"Are you okay?" he asked after he stopped to let her catch up.

"Yes, it's just," she shrugged. "I'm nervous about this."

"You'll be fine," he told her. "We'll figure out a way to keep your power from overwhelming you."

"I know," she said, and touched a hand to her stomach, feeling queasy. "It's not that though. I'm afraid to meet your mother. She's my mother-in-law now. What if she doesn't like me?"

He grinned. "Considering everything else you've had to face this week, you're worried about that?" She glared at him, and he dropped his grin. "Sorry," he said and wrapped his arms around her. "First of all, we don't have in-laws here. Wedding me means you're her daughter as much as I'm her son."

"That's splitting hairs."

"Perhaps," Nick said. "But even if that weren't true, she won't know we're wed when you meet her. She'll only know you as her Queen."

"I'll know," Meaghan murmured, and pressed her cheek against his shoulder. "And I want her to like me for me, not because she sees me as her Queen. I don't want her to feel like she has to be polite to my face while she secretly hates me behind my back."

"Then you definitely have nothing to worry about," Nick said. "My mother doesn't do polite for the sake of polite. If she doesn't like you, she'll tell you to your face, royalty or not. If she's upset with you for any reason, you'll know."

"Are you sure?"

"I'm certain. She's as direct as one of Faillen's arrows. In fact, she once told off your father, despite the fact he could have thrown her in jail for it."

"Why did she do that?"

"Because he deserved it. He showed up drunk after spending all night at a poker game. It was soon after you were born. You'd been crying non-stop and your mom was exhausted. Your dad strolled through the door of the royal suite, right into my mother's waiting wrath. She badgered him into a corner with an onslaught of well-chosen words and didn't relent for an hour. I can guarantee you she didn't gloss over what she thought of him that day."

Meaghan laughed. "Is that true?"

"Cal claims it is. Of course, he was one of the people at the poker game, so he would know. I understand your dad never did it again."

"I bet he didn't."

Nick rested his chin on top of her head. "Don't worry about my mom, Meg. You'll be fine."

She nodded and closed her eyes, listening to his heart beat slow and steady in his chest. It calmed her more than his words did. "What's your mother like?"

"Stubborn, proud, boisterous, and bossy." He smiled. "It's why we call her May instead of Mai."

"Being bossy is?"

"Yes. Vivian was always the calmer of the two of them, even when they were children. Mom was more of the leader and the protector, though it came across as pushy, which Viv hated. Mom tells me she used her older sister status as an excuse to keep Viv in line."

"I thought they were twins."

"She's older by forty-three minutes. It's enough for Mom to believe it matters."

Meaghan laughed and Nick continued his story. "As the older sister, Mom would make Viv ask permission to do everything. Viv did it to keep the peace, but she found her own way of resisting. She narrowed her eyes, planted her hands on her hips, and said '*May* I' when asking permission. Then she used the same posture and tone, calling my mother May instead of Mai during conversations. It annoyed my mother so much she eventually stopped being so controlling of Viv, but the name stuck and Mom grew to like it. Everyone calls her that now."

Meaghan laughed again, and then pulled back from Nick to wipe a tear from her eye. "That sounds like Mom. Vivian," she corrected. "She always knew how to get her way. She was one of the smartest people I've ever known."

"My mom is too. And like Vivian, she's also fiercely loyal and loving. She'll do anything to help, whether you're family or a complete stranger. And she's as free with wisdom or a hug. She's well-loved and respected in the village, and she's pretty much the best person to have around in a crisis."

"Like you," Meaghan said.

"I like to think I got some of her best qualities," Nick agreed. "Are you ready?"

She nodded. They walked further and when they crested a hill, he turned to her and took her hand. "You are welcome here," he said to her. The trees in front of her disappeared and in their place, a village materialized, surrounded by open fields. As Nick had stated, it was larger than Neiszhe's village. Four times larger at least, but before panic had time to settle over her, a movement in the field distracted her. A boy ran toward them, his brown hair streaked back from his face by his speed, his cheeks flushed with exertion. He kicked up dirt as he skidded to a stop in front of them.

"Nick," he cried through gasps. "May sent me. She said she could sense you close by and I had to get you." He stopped talking. Bending over to press his hands to his knees, he worked to catch his breath.

"What's wrong, Alcent?" Nick asked. "Is my mother all right?"

Alcent nodded and looked up, seeming to notice Meaghan for the first time. His tawny eyes grew wide. "Is she—?

"Yes," Nick interrupted. "What did my mother say?"

"She said," he panted, tried again. "She said she needs your help with a patient. Right away. She said to go to her house."

Meaghan barely had time to look at Nick before he grabbed her hand and took off running toward the village.

CHAPTER TWENTY-EIGHT

THEY SPED down wide roads paved in stone, through alleys lined in gravel, and past colorful, multi-story houses. They blended together, one into another, until they were no more than a streak of color and movement. People stepped out of houses and shops. Some watched them with obvious stares, their curiosity piqued as she and Nick ran past. Others waved and called out to Nick in recognition. And one elderly man on his front porch whistled, hollering at them to slow down before they knocked someone over.

Nick ignored them all, dragging her along a route he knew by memory until they reached a two-story house that looked almost identical to the one Vivian and James had built on Earth, except that a small guest cottage stood to the right of the house instead of a garage.

Nick did not bother to knock on the front door. He opened it and charged in, threading his way through a living room overstuffed with furniture and knickknacks to a door opposite the entrance. Meaghan did not have to wonder how he knew where to find his

279

mother. She could hear the shouting as well as he could.

He pushed open the door, stepped into a kitchen also similar to the one on Earth, and then came to an abrupt stop. Meaghan squeezed into the room behind him, pausing when she saw the source of the noise.

Nick's mother stood on one side of a kitchen island. A man stood on the other, brandishing a knife in his hand. His mouth moved constantly, spewing unintelligible words. His eyes shown bright and wild, and each time May took a step toward him, he screamed, slashing the knife through the air in warning.

The man's shrill cries commanded Meaghan's attention for a moment, but soon her eyes locked on May and froze. Although Nick had warned Meaghan about the identical appearance between Vivian and her sister, seeing May standing in a near copy of the room Vivian had cherished stole Meaghan's breath. If May's hair had been long like Vivian's instead of cropped short at her ears, or if the kitchen had housed the gleaming white appliances Vivian had found so comforting instead of the more rustic tools May owned, Meaghan would not have been able to separate the past from the present. She checked her impulse to run to the woman, and then fought the equally strong impulse to cry, faking calm by folding her hands together in front of her.

"What's going on?" Nick asked his mother.

"I don't know," May responded. "His name's Abbott. He's a Guardian assigned to a village a few days' walk from here. The village was attacked last week. Someone found him unconscious in the field this morning and brought him to me, but I can't find anything wrong with him." Abbott screamed again and May sighed. "That's getting old," she told her patient, then spoke to Nick again. "When he woke up, he ran from me and came in here. He's been screaming and babbling ever since."

"How long has he been doing this?"

"Two hours now. I can't get close enough to sedate him."

"I could try sneaking around if you think you could distract him."

The man turned his knife toward Nick, slashing again as he argued in his senseless language.

"Or not," Nick said. "We could let him keep going like this. He'll get tired eventually and pass out."

May shook her head. "That could take days. I have better things to do with my time than babysit him. Any other ideas?"

"Did anyone else live through the attack?"

"About half of the village survived," May responded. "A quarter of those are still recovering from injuries. Are you thinking he was driven mad by the violence?"

"He wouldn't be the first," Nick reasoned. "Give me the needle. I'll take my chances against his knife."

May slipped a syringe from her pocket and handed it to him. Nick picked up a cookie sheet from the counter, weighing it in his hands before extending it out like a shield. He inched forward and Abbott's protests filled the room once more.

Meaghan released her hold on Nick's power. A rush of emotions from the surrounding village assaulted her, but she gritted her teeth, and held her gaze steady on Abbott. Although the other emotions remained, they became no more than background noise when

Abbott's eyes met hers. His emotions surged forward, strong and commanding, and she curled her fingers into her palms, standing her ground against them. It only took her a moment to realize what they meant.

"Wait," she said.

Nick kept the cookie sheet in front of him, but followed her request and stopped walking.

"He's not insane," she told him.

"How do you know?"

"Because he's terrified. I can feel it, but the emotion isn't natural. It feels forced."

"You mean like it's induced?" May asked.

"Maybe. Though it seems to surge when he looks at you."

"He could be hallucinating," May said.

Meaghan focused more of her power on Abbott. Although his fear seemed to overwhelm him, something else surfaced through the chaos. She took a step forward, stopping when Nick took hold of her arm.

"That's enough," he said. "I don't want you near him. And stop using your power. There are too many people within sensing distance."

"I'm fine. The other emotions aren't as strong as long as I focus on him."

"You're not fine. You're white and you're sweating."

Meaghan raised a hand to her forehead. As soon as her fingers met her brow, beads of sweat rolled over them. She rubbed the moisture between her fingertips, surprised by it, but shook her head.

"I'm okay."

Nick's grip tightened. "Turn off your power before you get hurt."

"Not yet. I can help." She turned her gaze to Nick, pleading with him to believe her and he nodded. His hold slackened and she started moving toward Abbott again. She only managed a few steps before another emotion surged from her left, stronger than the ones in the village and it broke her concentration. Anger, she realized, and flicked her eyes toward the redheaded woman who had moved to block her path. The heat in May's green eyes matched the emotion Meaghan sensed.

"Nick told you not to take another step," she said.

"Abbott understands I'm safe," Meaghan assured her. "He's fighting his fear."

"There's no way you could possibly—"

"Trust her," Nick interrupted. "Meaghan knows what she's doing. Do you have something that could help Abbott based on what she described?"

May blew out a hot breath and Meaghan felt certain she would continue arguing, but she only nodded. "He might be under the influence of a serum. I've heard Garon had one created to magnify a person's fears, but I didn't think the rumors were true."

The room grew quiet and Meaghan realized Abbott had stopped babbling. She glanced at him again. His eyes locked on hers. Relief now fought with his fear.

"You're right," Meaghan said. "He's calm because you figured it out."

May pursed her lips. Her hands came to her hips, but she

conceded once more. "He may have been trying to explain all along. It's possible the serum also masks speech."

"Can you do anything for him?" Nick asked.

May cocked her head to the side, studying her patient, and then returned her focus to her son. "I think so. I have a few potions that should work."

"Get them," Nick said and set the cookie sheet down on the counter. After his mother left the room, he faced Meaghan. "I don't want you getting any closer," he told her. "If Abbott knows we're safe, I'll approach. I need to sedate him."

"All right," Meaghan agreed and addressed Abbott. "Will you allow him to help you?"

Abbott nodded and Nick inched around the island, his movements cautious, though Abbot's gaze never left Meaghan's face. Not even when Nick slipped the needle into his arm.

§

MEAGHAN SAT on the couch in the living room, waiting as Nick and his mother worked. She felt ill and she preferred not to show how much her efforts in the kitchen had exhausted her. She needed May to see her strength, not her weakness, as much for their relationship as for the other reason that had occurred to her when the woman had confronted her in the kitchen. May was an Elder. Although Meaghan felt certain May's role as a mother came first, she could not disregard the fear that if the Elder saw Meaghan as unable to control her power, the choice to remove Nick as Guardian would be as much for his protection as hers. So Meaghan watched them work and willed her shaking muscles to relax.

Nick pinned Abbott's shoulders to the floor. May held down his feet. Although the patient remained unconscious, his body thrashed in response to the potions warring for possession of his blood. When his arms jerked out, Nick used his knees to hold the man's shoulders, and then moved his hands to the man's arms, locking them at his sides. Every few minutes, May immobilized his feet in a similar manner and relieved Nick of his awkward position by taking Abbott's hands.

When Abbott's breath grew labored, they both let go. Nick lifted the patient's upper body while May listened to his heart, feeding him more potions or laying her hands on his chest and closing her eyes to heal him. No words passed between Nick and his mother. They had choreographed this dance many years before.

It took well over an hour before Abbott's body stopped flailing and his breathing normalized. After checking his vital signs once more, May stood.

"Take him to the guest room," she instructed Nick. He disappeared up the stairs with the patient and May turned to face Meaghan. A frown dug shadows into her cheeks and Meaghan swallowed the sudden urge to shrink back into the couch.

"You were foolish," May said. Her tone took on the heat her eyes had earlier. "You shouldn't have approached Abbott. You couldn't be certain of what he was seeing or that he understood what you were saying. With his babbling—"

"I could feel his trust," Meaghan protested. "I can tell enough about basic emotions to guess—"

"You can tell about emotions on *Earth*," May stressed the last word with distaste and Meaghan bit the inside of her cheek. "Don't make the mistake of thinking you know anything about this world. Garon's potion could have masked Abbott's emotions in the same way it distorted his speech. It could have been a trick to trap you." She placed her hands firmly on her hips. "I'm amazed you and Nick are still alive. With your foolish Earth tendencies, I'm surprised you didn't get him—"

"Don't you dare finish that sentence," Nick's voice commanded from the top of the stairs. May dropped her arms and he descended the steps. "I take it Cal told you what happened."

May's lower lip trembled, but she raised her chin, facing him. "This doesn't have anything to do with—"

"It obviously does. And it seems you've forgotten who you're talking to."

"If you mean I shouldn't speak to royalty that way, you're mistaken. I know who her parents were. I loved them as much as I could love any family member."

"I'm aware," he said, his tone turning hard. "And you know that isn't what I meant. You've forgotten Meaghan is no more from Earth than you are. Even if she was, creatures from Ærenden are to blame. I realize you wish to see it differently, but I can't allow you to take it out on her."

A tear escaped May's control. She wiped it away, but failed to catch the others that had begun coursing down her cheeks. Nick continued without wavering. "You've also forgotten I was there when Viv and James died. I watched it happen and *we*," he stressed the word to ensure May could not ignore what he said, "did everything we could. Vivian made her choice long ago. We couldn't stop it, so if you want to blame someone, blame her. Or blame me if you must. But don't ever blame Meaghan for this."

May's shoulders slumped and Nick wrapped his arms around her. Meaghan felt moisture fill her own eyes, but she refused to cry. This moment belonged to Nick and his mother, and she did not want to interrupt.

"Vivian made the right choice," Nick said. His eyes found Meaghan's over his mother's shoulder and she understood he spoke to her, too.

"She made the right choice because she made it out of love for the woman she saw as her daughter. She made it because she realized Meaghan's future, and ours, was worth saving."

And in those words, Meaghan realized the true depth of Vivian's sacrifice. She buried her face in her hands and wept.

CHAPTER TWENTY-NINE

A SHOWER had never felt so good in Meaghan's life. She soaked up the warm water, relishing in each drop for longer than she knew she should. As the minutes passed, she felt the remnants of her journey dissolve from her body and her mind, washed down the drain with the last remnants of dried sweat and grime. She stayed in the shower until it turned her arms and legs into beets and her fingers into prunes, and then forced herself to turn off the water and step out of the tub. Cold air brought the hairs on her arms to attention, but even that felt like a blessing bestowed on baptized skin.

Sighing with relief, she wrapped a large towel around her body, and then fingered the wool dress May had given her. The finely woven blue and white material sparkled with the simplest movement, reminding her of a crystal lake in full sunlight. She slipped the dress over her head, smiled as it flowed over her skin, and then drew a hand up to the elegant neckline to finger the white lace along the edge. The same lace edged the sleeves and the bottom of the dress.

Nick had told her making clothes took a special power, but she had understood it through her limited knowledge to be a talent, similar to clothing designers on Earth. She had not realized until now how breathtaking that power could be. No regular tailor could spin material like this. She turned to look in the mirror. The dress made the copper in her eyes dance. Like fall leaves swaying above the water, she thought, and opened the bathroom door to exit.

As soon as she saw Nick standing in the hall, she froze. Her gaze locked on the warning in his eyes, and her good mood disappeared. He glanced toward the stairs and she nodded. She could hear his mother's voice drifting up from the living room, as well as the voices of several men she did not recognize. She waited for Nick to speak.

"They sent me to get you," he said, his easy tone betraying no hint of the worry she saw on his face, and now felt within him. Worry, anger, confusion, and even joy washed over her from downstairs, though the emotions felt faint, as did the dozens of other emotions filtering through the walls of the house. She raised an eyebrow at Nick in question and he stepped forward so she could hear him whisper.

"My power is muted half-way," he told her. "But it's difficult to maintain at that level, so it can't last long. Hopefully it will be enough for you to read them."

Meaghan raised an eyebrow. "Who?"

"The Elders," Nick responded and stepped back from her. Her heart dropped. "They want to speak with you. I've already given them my report of everything that's happened since the Mardróch came to Earth."

"Of course," she said and then mouthed, "Everything?"

Nick shook his head and she knew he had not told them about the wedding. She nodded and when he inclined his head toward the stairs, she took the lead. Pausing at the bottom of the staircase, she surveyed the room.

May sat in the chair closest to the stairs, her face grim as she clutched a coffee cup in her hand. Meaghan sensed worry and a small amount of anger emanating from her.

On May's left sat an older man sporting a short, white beard and snowy hair cropped tight above his ears. His portly body seemed molded to his seat as if he had spent half his life in it. His steel blue eyes studied Meaghan from a face etched with laugh lines and fine red veins. She felt curiosity and concern from him, but no negative emotions.

Unlike the man to his left, Meaghan realized, and caught her breath when the man's resentment battered her power with such strength she could not ignore the implication of it. He detested her presence and he did not bother to hide it.

His copper eyes sparked with anger. He stretched long arms in front of him and then folded them together, a silent hint of defiance. A frown drew shadows along his dark, willowy beard, but he settled back into his chair, his emotions now contained, and she chased away the discomfort she had felt under his gaze and moved her attention to the last man in the room.

Although years had added a few pounds to his muscular frame and his wavy black hair had turned to salt and pepper, his round face remained clean shaven and devoid of heavy lines. She could not ignore the familiarity she felt looking at it, or the memories flooding her mind when she stared into his dark gray eyes. A smile stretched across his lips and she returned it, her joy matching his.

"Miles," she said.

He nodded. "You remember?"

"Some. You saved my life. Then you gave me to," she hesitated, then swallowed the word readied on her lips, replacing it with the one required of her. "Vivian."

"I did," Miles responded. "You've had a difficult journey. Sit, please. We aren't here to judge you."

All four pairs of eyes flicked to Nick when he came to stand beside her and she understood, even before May's anger strengthened, that Miles had not lied. The Elders had not come to judge her. They had come to judge Nick.

Meaghan forced a smile, nodded, and found her way to the couch. Nick sat on the opposite end. "So this is a social call?" she asked, crossing her legs and lacing her hands over her knee. "A meet the Queen and see if she'll be a pain in the ass type of thing?"

The white haired man chuckled and gripped the arms of his seat, pushing forward to study her. "Do you intend to be a pain?"

"That depends," she said. "Who are you?"

"Sam," he responded. "Do you?"

"If you intend to replace Nick, I promise I will be."

Sam's chuckle turned to guffaws of laughter and he slapped a hand on his knee. "I love it. She's Adelina through and through." He turned to the man who sat to his left. "You had nothing to worry about, Angus. Earth didn't soften her at all. Seems the royal family's trademark tenacity's in the blood."

Angus' frowned. "And it also seems she has no manners. She's using her power."

Meaghan bristled. "Does it matter?"

"It does," Miles responded. "As Elders, we've earned a certain amount of respect. Spying on our emotions doesn't fall in line with that."

"Then I recommend you don't do things behind my back," she said, her tone turning stiff with her anger at the reprimand. "Were you planning on telling me this meeting had an alternate purpose, or were you hoping to trick me into helping you hang Nick?"

Guilt flickered through Miles and she realized the Elders had intended to do exactly that. She leaned forward, pinning him with a glare. "Wrong answer," she said. "It's my understanding we'll be working together if you intend for me to be Queen. We can't do that if you think you can manipulate me."

"Meaghan," May warned from across the room, but Miles held up his hand, halting her. His eyes remained on Meaghan.

"That's fair," he said. "Nick tells us you've grown stronger in the days since you left Earth, and you're ready to be Queen, but it's difficult for us to accept. You're little more than a stranger to us."

"As are you to me," Meaghan told him. "But our safety depends on us communicating, and at least attempting to trust each other."

Miles nodded. "That's also fair. In the interest of that trust, I'll be frank with you. Nick's status as your Guardian is our decision. As Queen, you have authority over us on many things, but not this. If we feel he needs to be replaced, we'll replace him."

"I would prefer you didn't."

"I understand you're comfortable with him, but we have your safety in mind. And Nick's. From what he's told us, you have a tendency of seeking out danger."

Meaghan frowned. "That's not his fault. I can be headstrong, but I'm getting better at listening to him."

"It's his job to protect you," Sam pointed out. "Even if it's against your will. If you didn't listen to him, he should have stopped you anyway. Like when you saved that village boy. Nick never should have let you get close to the Mardróch. A Guardian should have more control over his charge."

The village boy? Meaghan wondered and then realized he meant Aldin. He had told them about her rescue attempt, but not how it had ended. She deferred to Nick's decision to keep Faillen a secret and deflected from the incident, taking a gamble she hoped would pay off. She directed her next question at May, seeking the woman's alignment in protecting her son. "Was my mother so easy to control?"

May's cheeks flushed in embarrassment, but she answered. "No," she said. "She bypassed my efforts to protect her more times than not."

"Yet you remained her Guardian, as I sense you feel Nick should stay as mine."

May nodded. "Nick has kept you safe, like I always kept Adelina safe."

"Until her demise," Angus said. His words shot pain through May and she looked away. "If the Elders had replaced you," he continued, "do you suppose Adelina would still be alive?"

"I couldn't have stopped that," May argued, though Meaghan felt doubt in her. "Even if I did have better control over Adelina, I was fighting the army at the perimeter, like nearly everyone else. None of us knew Garon had assigned us there to further his plan. Even Vivian didn't get her vision until it was too late to save them."

"We all know that," Sam said and took May's hand in his. "Don't let Angus rile you. You were always good at protecting Adelina and she appreciated it." He squeezed May's hand before letting it go and then addressed Meaghan. "There'll be a full debate before Nick is removed, if he is. We don't take these decisions lightly."

"Good," Meaghan said.

"I'm glad you agree." Sam narrowed his eyes. "And if it helps, I'm not entirely convinced you're controllable. As strong as I used to be before old age caught up with me, the most I could've done in Nick's position is shut you up."

"Shut me—?" Meaghan started to ask, but despite her best efforts, she could not finish the sentence. She spoke the word, but no sound left her throat.

"You knew to ask May that question because you were reading her emotions," Sam said. "As an old man, I value respect, so I'll make a deal with you. If you stop using your power, I'll stop using mine. We'll try the trust route and keep you in the loop and you'll stop spying on us. Deal?"

Meaghan nodded and Sam released her voice before turning to Nick and grinning. "Bet you wish you had that power."

"Some days," Nick admitted and turned his power on fully, acknowledging the deal Meaghan had made. "Though I think mine's been more helpful so far."

"Agreed," Miles said. "And it could continue to be until she learns to control her power. We'll take that into account when we make our decision." He stood and clutched his hands behind his back. "Before we can do anything else, there is one other thing we need to address."

Meaghan leaned back against the couch, working hard not to give in to her panic. She did not need her power to know what would be coming next.

"What is it?" she asked, hoping she was wrong.

"Nick told us you may want to abdicate."

And there it was. Decision time had come.

"If you do, it's your right," Miles continued. "But you have to tell us now. If we introduce you to the people, if we raise their hopes, you won't be able to back out. These people have been through enough. If their Queen returned to them, only to leave them later, their spirit would not survive. And neither, in turn, would they. Holding their resolve and their hopes together in this war has been delicate. We can't allow you to disrupt that."

Meaghan pressed her lips together and wished her decision would spring from her without thought. It did not. Nor did it readily come to mind. Her grief still sat like a stone in her heart. The sorrow she had felt while watching Dell die in the ravine still gripped her. The physical pain that had ripped through her during much of her journey, the emotions that had overwhelmed her while watching the battle, the worry she felt for Nick's safety—it all swelled within her and begged her to take the escape she had been offered. If she abdicated, if she allowed someone more experienced to take over, if she walked away from the horror of this world, what harm would come of it? None she could see. And perhaps everyone could gain from her decision. This world would have the leader it needed, and she could go back to Earth. The last thought stalled her breath, but she could not decide if joy or fear had caused the reaction.

"People have seen me already," she responded. "How do you plan on telling them I abdicated?"

Miles' gaze turned hard. "We wouldn't. People only saw you running through the village, heading toward the Healer. As far as they know, you're injured. We can sneak you out tonight and tell them you died. You'd become a martyr to them."

"Where would I go?"

"Back to Earth."

"And Nick?"

"Would be reassigned here. Since you would no longer be royalty, you would forego any protection." She nodded and Miles frowned. "Is that your decision then? Are you abdicating?"

Home, she thought, and swallowed the immediate reaction to say yes to his question. She wanted the comfort of it again, but would it ever be the same? She had no family left except for Nick, and he would have to stay here. He would be safer, though, and he would never have to explain the wedding. The Mardróch might follow her, but she doubted she would be worth the effort without her title. She would live a safe life, a life in the world she knew. But what would she do with her life? Go back to school and follow a career path she no longer felt certain she wanted?

"You can't," a voice spoke from the stairs. It came out as no more than a whisper, but all heads turned toward it. Abbott clutched the railing, his knuckles as white as his face, his body shaking, but his eyes remained steady on Meaghan's. "I've seen it," he spoke again. "I've seen it both ways. She showed it to me."

"Who did?" Nick asked.

"Vivian," Abbott told him. "I'm a Dreamer. That's how I got away from the village. I dreamed of the attack the night it happened. I got out a few steps ahead of the army. I was faster than they were, but the poison is delivered in darts." He turned his gaze to May for a moment and she nodded, accepting his unspoken gratitude. His attention drifted back to Meaghan. "You can't leave us to die."

"I don't understand," Meaghan said. "Vivian is dead."

"She sent the message a month ago," Abbott responded. "She didn't want you to waste her sacrifice."

Meaghan stiffened. Her eyes grew hot with tears. "You don't know me. How can you assume I'd forget what she did? How could you," a hand gripped her arm, stopping her from continuing. She looked from the familiar fingers to Nick's face.

"Meaghan," he said, and the use of her full name tightened the tension in her stomach. Although she knew he could not use her nickname in front of the Elders, it felt as wrong as everything else right now. "Dreamers are similar to Seers only they can't receive predictions during the day like Seers can. They receive them in their dreams. And unlike Seers, they can receive direct messages from Seers or other Dreamers. Vivian reached out to him because she wanted to get a message to you. She knew he would be here now, when you needed to make this decision. She wanted you to make the right one."

She nodded and then faced Abbott again, forcing her next question past a throat too tight and too dry for proper use. "What did you see?"

"I saw the results of your decision," he told her. "Both sides. If you choose to leave, you'll be safe on Earth, but the kingdom will be sacrificed. Garon will annihilate those who don't support him. I've seen the bodies of everyone in this room, lost in battle. But if you choose to stay, the kingdom will reclaim its glory and Garon will be defeated. I've seen," he hesitated, his eyes flicked to Nick for a brief second, and then moved back to her. No one else in the room caught the movement. "Your King," he continued, "sitting on the throne during his coronation and I see the joy of the people as they watch it."

"And what of Meaghan?" Nick asked. "Is she there?"

"I wasn't given that vision," he answered, though Meaghan felt a chill at his response. "I have no doubt she'll succeed if she chooses to stay."

But she may not live, Meaghan realized and tore her eyes from Abbott to search the room. The hope she saw on May's face reminded her of Faillen, of the hope that had emanated from him when they shook hands to seal their pact. Sam balanced on the edge of his seat, anxious as he watched her. He would be ready to die for her, as Dell had. She closed her eyes over the memory. She understood then, as she saw clearly now, the extent of Dell's sacrifice. The happiness she had felt within him when he recognized her still haunted her. She opened her eyes and made her decision, the same one she knew Vivian had made years before. It did not matter if she lived or died. It only mattered that they succeeded in defeating Garon. Hundreds of thousands of lives would be spared in exchange for hers. Hundreds of thousands of futures would be allowed to continue. And a King worthy of their respect would lead them.

She brought her attention back to Miles and said the words she knew would change the course of her life forever.

"I am the Queen of Ærenden," she announced. No doubt remained within her. "I have returned to take my rightful place and I will lead my people to victory."

CHAPTER THIRTY

MILES INTRODUCED her as Queen Meaghan that night in the village. White lights lined the shops surrounding the main courtyard at the center of town, sparkling in unison with the crowd's cheers and applause. The clock hanging over the town hall chimed in celebration. And as Nick had promised, a feast followed the formal announcement. Several spits lined the town square. A boar roasted on one, a deer on another, and an enormous buffalo weighted down a third. Tables surrounded the spits, each laden with platters of food. There was more than she could ever have tasted. Well-wishers and proud cooks handed vegetables, fruit, breads, and even desserts to her. She did her best to eat everything, but soon her stomach could hold no more.

As Nick had also told her, only half the people bowed to her. It still felt like too many. She nodded until she thought her head would jump off her neck and then exhaled a sigh of relief when a band started playing. Joyful tunes filled the air from a variety of instruments she did not recognize and a few she did. An old man danced around with a banjo in his hand. A young woman adeptly fiddled away, her eyes bright as her fingers blurred across the strings. A boy who seemed no older than thirteen mesmerized the crowd with a trumpet. And Miles joined in on a guitar.

As tables disappeared from the courtyard, people began dancing. Some dances Meaghan did not recognize, though their effortlessness spoke of generations of teaching. Everyone moved in unison, choreographed from tradition and flawless from habit. Other dances seemed no different from what she had learned on Earth.

When a fast dance resembling a waltz circled the impromptu dance floor, Nick took her arm and insisted she join him. He led her around, the pressure of his hands light, his step graceful, and she did her best to follow. She had never been good at dancing, but the grin on his face kept her going. It also lightened the darkness that had shadowed her mind since her meeting with the Elders. Her decision, now final, felt like iron chains binding her soul. She knew she had made the right choice, but that knowledge did not ease her burden. Meeting the villagers tonight had only added to that weight, putting faces to the responsibility and lives to the kingdom she now directed.

Reality pushed in around her and every time she felt claustrophobic from it, she focused on Nick's face. His joy grew as each person greeted them. While they bowed to her or shook her hand to show their respect, they offered him hugs. He knew them all and they loved him well. Many even had tears in their eyes when they saw him, their worry lifted in knowing he had arrived home safely.

Home, she thought. His home, his life. He had grown up in this place and it showed in his relaxed posture, in the laughter bubbling through his lips, in the stories he shared with old friends, and in his smile as he taught her the steps to a dance he had no doubt learned in childhood. She had seen him as responsible and reserved, only occasionally relaxing his guard. She had never seen him this free. And though she could not sense his joy, she could feel it when she looked up at him.

The song stopped and another, slower tune followed. Nick led her off the dance floor. "You weren't too bad," he said.

"I'm not sure your toes agree," she responded with a grin.

He laughed, squeezed her hand, and then released it as a couple approached. The man stood at Nick's height. His blond hair fell in waves to his shoulders. His blue eyes sparkled in what appeared to be permanent amusement. And when he smiled, he exuded charisma and Meaghan responded with a smile of her own. The willowy woman holding his hand held a smile more bashful. Big tawny eyes and long blonde hair graced a porcelain face highlighted by full lips and rosy cheeks. Nick engulfed them both in a hug.

"I'm sure you've come to meet Meaghan," he said once he had let them go.

A sly grin spread across the man's face. "Of course. Did you think we wanted to see your ugly face again? I thought we'd finally gotten rid of you."

Nick chuckled. "It's nice to be loved."

"Don't listen to him," the woman said and slapped the man on the stomach. "He's jealous you got to explore a new world and he got stuck here training the ten-year-olds in combat maneuvers." She extended a hand to Meaghan. "I'm Cissiline. Please call me Cissy."

Meaghan took her hand and shook it. Cissy pointed to the man next to her. "This is Maxillion—"

"Who definitely does not go by that," the man said. "I'm Max." He took Meaghan's hand in a firm grip. His gaze felt almost as firm as he cocked his head to the side to study her. "I'm afraid you don't live up to your legend."

"Oh?" Meaghan raised an eyebrow. "I have a legend?"

Max let go of her hand. "You bet. According to the stories, you're ten feet tall. You wield a sword of iron, which is capable of decapitating legions of Mardróch at a time. And you breathe fire." He stepped closer and lowered his voice. "If the last part is true, I have a neighbor who complains nonstop. Apparently, I even sneeze too loud. I'd love it if you could teach him a lesson."

Meaghan laughed and liked him instantly. "I'm afraid not," she said. "The most I can do is tell him what his emotions are."

"That's no good," he replied. "He's always grouchy and everybody already knows that." He flicked his eyes from Meaghan to Nick and then back to her again. "Now that you've stolen Nick from us for over a year, do you plan on giving him back? Or have you already wed him?"

Meaghan felt her heart leap, but Nick chuckled. "I'm a catch," he responded. "But I'm afraid it's against the rules."

"Since when do you pay attention to rules? I seem to recall you breaking them a time or two when we were younger."

Nick raised an eyebrow. "I did nothing worth mentioning."

"Oh no? Then what do you call skipping training? Or how about the time you stole pies from the baker every week until he set a trap for you that you had you dangling in the air by your feet? Or better yet, do you really consider sneaking off with his daughter not worth mentioning?" Max grinned. "Of course, *that* crime was well worth being hung up in the air."

Nick scowled, though Meaghan did not miss the levity in his voice when he responded. "I was eleven. It was a lot more innocent than you make it sound."

"I'm only pointing out your track record in case you're trying to hide it," Max said. "Our new Queen should know what sort of ill repute she has as her guard."

Nick rolled his eyes, and brushed off the ribbing with a shrug of his shoulders. Hooking his thumbs into his pockets, he nodded toward Cissy and Max's linked hands. "Speaking of hiding things, how long has this been going on?"

"Since before you left," Cissy told him and drew a hand up to Max's bicep. "We kept it a secret for a while, but it's been long enough."

"Long enough for," Nick started and then grinned. "A wedding," he realized. He clapped Max on the shoulder. "Congratulations. I always thought you'd make a good match."

"So did I," Max confessed and nodded toward Cissy. "She took a bit more convincing though. Along those lines, are you seriously trying to tell me there's nothing between you two? I saw you dancing out there. Maybe no one else would notice the way you looked at each other, but you can't slip it by me. I'm your oldest friend after all."

Nick frowned. "There's nothing between us, and I'd appreciate it if you didn't talk like that. All it takes is one person overhearing for rumors to get started. I'm under review at the moment and that could be enough to jeopardize everything."

The grin died on Max's face. "I didn't know," he said. "I was joking. What happened?"

"It's a long story."

"I have time," Max said. "Cissy can watch out for Meaghan and maybe if you tell me, I can help. Just like old times," he added when Nick hesitated.

Nick nodded, conceding, and turned to Meaghan. "Is it okay? I won't go far."

"I'll be fine," she assured him. The two men walked away and Meaghan kept her eyes glued on Nick and her power focused on his. The further away he moved, the weaker his power got. She swallowed her panic, ignored the emotions seeping through his power, and drew her eyes to the woman who stood beside her.

"Are you okay?" Cissy asked. "You look like you're about to be sick."

"Yes." Meaghan tightened a smile across her face. "How long have you been wed?"

"Two months," Cissy responded. Her face glowed with a light Meaghan had seen on many of her newlywed friends in school. Some things remained constant no matter what world they happened on. "It was wonderful. The night was clear like this one. The stars and the moon basked everything in a soft glow. Max had packed a picnic and we snuck into the field to enjoy it together. When he leaned in to kiss me, the colors, they," she shrugged. "It's hard to explain. When it happens to you, you'll understand."

"I'm sure I will," Meaghan said, her smile turning genuine. "It sounds lovely."

"It was perfect. Are you sure you're feeling okay?"

The emotions had grown stronger, battering at Meaghan's resolve. Hundreds of them swirled within her, gripping her stomach, pounding within her head. She ached, but she clutched her hands together in front of her and nodded. "How long have you and Nick been friends?"

"Since the village was built," Cissy said. "Max knew him from the last village, but my family came from another one. I guess we were about eight at the time. I knew him shortly before his father died." She frowned and placed a hand on Meaghan's arm. "You look green."

"I'm fine," Meaghan insisted, and then felt the ache in her head swell. Squeezing her eyes shut, she pressed her fingers to her temples. Cissy's hand tightened on her arm, pulling her away from the crowd, and from Nick. The emotions broke through the remainder of her hold on his power, flooding her senses. Her mind screamed. Her stomach rolled. Her eyes flew open. And then she pulled from Cissy's grip and ran.

She did not know where she was going. She only hoped no one saw her. The Queen fleeing in panic would not help the spirits of the people. But vomiting in front of them and then curling up into a fetal ball certainly would not help either. She ran down one street and then another. When the emotions still chased her, she dashed down an alley, turned a corner, and then met a dead end. A building blocked her from advancing. The emotions behind her kept her from going back the way she had come. She turned, pressed her body against the wall, and sank down to the ground. Burying her face in her hands, she prayed for the pain to stop.

Her breathing came in quick, uneven bursts as she tried to fight off the assault. She focused on the warmth by her heart. She tried to pull on it, to move or dull it, but no efforts to control her power helped. Several minutes passed and then she felt hands grip her arms.

"I'm here," Nick's voice broke through the swell of emotions. "Focus on me, Meg. I'm here."

She did as he instructed. Her breathing slowed. "Good," he said. She heard other voices, though they came across as muffled through the pain still throbbing within her head. "She'll be okay," Nick said and she realized he had responded to whoever had spoken. "Go back to the party and tell everyone she was tired so I took her home. And please don't tell anyone about this. It's best if no one knows she can't control her power yet."

"We understand," Cissy's voice finally broke through the pain. "Do you need us to send your mother?"

"No. I have this under control."

"All right," a man said and Meaghan recognized him as Max. "Good luck. Let us know if you need anything."

Footsteps retreated from the alley. Nick drew his hands down Meaghan's arms and linked his fingers with hers. "How do you feel?" he asked.

"Sick," she responded. Resting her head against the wall, she opened her eyes. "That was almost as bad as the battle. There were too many emotions. I had to get away."

"I know." Releasing his grip on one of her hands, Nick raised his fingers to her face, and stroked his thumb across her cheekbone. "I don't sense your pain any longer. Is it gone?" She nodded. "What happened?"

"I don't know. You weren't far away, but I couldn't hold on to your power. I panicked." She sighed and closed her eyes again. "Did anyone see me?"

"I don't think so. Cissy thought you were sick so she brought you to an area out of view." He leaned in to press his lips to her forehead. "It's been a long day. I should have realized."

"Realized what?"

"How tired you are. I'm sure that's why you couldn't maintain focus on my power from a distance. I'm sorry I left you."

"It's not your fault," she said and struggled to her feet. He stood with her. "I need to be able to control this on my own. You can't stay next to me forever."

"No," he agreed, "but control will come soon enough. The Elders have decided to put you through training. They feel the same techniques Guardians use to control their sensing powers will help you."

"Training?" she asked. "Like school?"

"More like boot camp, but with pre-teens."

She grimaced and he laughed, drawing her in for a hug. "Are you okay to head back to my mom's place? You're staying in the guesthouse next to it. I can stay with you until you fall asleep."

"That would be nice," she said, smiling when he drew his hands up her back. He pulled her in for a kiss, then slipped an arm around her waist and led her down the alley. They had only managed a few steps before he stiffened. Meaghan stopped to look up at him. "What's wrong?"

Nick's eyes remained fixed on the shadows lining the street in front of the alley. He frowned. "I thought I saw something move."

"What?"

He shook his head. "I'm not sure, but I don't sense any danger. It's probably my imagination. Let's go."

Urging her forward again, he quickened their pace back to the guest cottage.

CHAPTER THIRTY-ONE

MEAGHAN AWOKE to anger. The emotion screamed at her from outside the guest cottage, pounding its way into her dreams and disrupting her rest. When her heart doubled its pace in response, despite her efforts to calm it, she gave up on sleeping and threw off her blankets. The emotion felt strong, yet she could tell it came from only two people. The rest of the village remained quiet. She focused on the anger and then on the mix of other emotions hidden beneath it. Confusion, hurt, and frustration swirled with the anger in a familiar way, and she realized the people were arguing. She also realized it might be some time before they finished. She dragged her tired body out of bed, and then exchanged her nightgown for her dress. She did not feel like waking Nick to use his power. He needed his rest as much as she did. Instead, she decided to take a walk for an hour. She hoped it would be enough time for the argument to reach a conclusion, and then she could return to sleep.

Finding her shoes by the door, she put them on, and exited the cottage. The emotions came from her left, so she turned right to avoid them, but halted when the breeze carried part of the argument her way.

"It wasn't like that."

She frowned, recognizing Nick's voice, then turned and walked to the corner of the cottage so she could peer around it. Nick had his back to her, but his mother faced Meaghan's hiding place. Her eyes blazed in the moonlight.

"I'm not a fool! I saw the way you held her, the way you kissed her. Are you trying to get yourself killed?"

"No, Mom. Please, let's go inside. I'd like to explain in—"

"What is there to explain? You're being stupid. If I'd known this would happen, I never would have let you to go to Earth when Vivian sent for you."

"Which is probably why she didn't tell you," Nick said.

"She knew?" May's eyes narrowed and she planted her fists on her hips. "Then she's the bigger idiot. What was it she said to convince you? Did she claim there was a prophecy involved? Or did she appeal to you with the promise of ruling the kingdom?"

The accusation spiked Nick's anger and he took a step closer to her. His voice rose. "Viv didn't have to convince me of anything. What I feel for Meg is—"

"Meg?" May interrupted. "Where do you get off calling your Queen such an informal name?"

"It's what Viv and James called her."

"And they're dead," May snapped. "You will be too if you don't detach from her. There's a reason these relationships are forbidden."

"You don't think I know that?" he asked. He dug his hands into his pockets. "You don't think I considered that before—"

"Before what?" May pressed forward, standing toe-to-toe with her son. "What did you do?" Without waiting for Nick's response, she threw up her hands. "Forget it. I don't want to know. You've lost your mind, and if you won't do the right thing, I will. As of tomorrow morning, the Elders will be removing you as her Guardian."

"If you'll let me explain—"

She spun away from him and entered her house through the side door, slamming it behind her. Nick rubbed the back of his neck as he turned to stare in Meaghan's direction. "That didn't go well, did it?"

Certain he could not see her, she remained silent. He approached. "I know you're there, Meg. You have a habit of spying, you know. I'd rather you didn't do that to me."

She stepped around the corner. "How did you know I was listening?"

"It's another one of my sensing abilities," he told her. "Guardians can sense the presence of their charges."

"You never mentioned that before."

"It slipped my mind."

"Or you wanted to be able to use it against me."

"Maybe," he confessed. For a moment, levity cocked a smile on his face before it faded. "Guardians can also sense their children, which is what got us in trouble tonight. Mom tracked us down after we left the party. She saw us in the alley."

"How much have you been able to tell her?"

"Not much. I tried to tell her why Vivian brought me to Earth, and she cut me off. I tried to tell her about the prophecy, but she wouldn't listen. And now, well, you heard."

"So she doesn't know we're wed yet?" she asked. He shook his head. "I suppose that's good news, but we need to get the whole story across or we'll have a mess to clean up by morning. Will she try to contact the Elders now?"

"No. She needs to cool down first and she knows it."

"Then let's get this over with while we still can." Meaghan led the way to the kitchen door and knocked. The door swung open to the beginning of another argument.

"If you think you'll be able to talk me into going along with whatever idiotic idea you've come up with, then you're as much of a fool as my damned sister. If I had known she planned this…" the rest of the words froze on May's lips when she saw Meaghan standing in front of her. Her eyes whipped to her son, who stood a step behind. "Why is she here?"

"She overheard us," Nick responded. "Can we come in?"

"So you're in on this?" she asked Meaghan. "Are you that irresponsible? Of course you are. Viv raised you. It seems her judgment was—"

Meaghan grabbed May's arm. Her glare pinned May's mouth shut. "I won't tolerate that," she said. Her voice remained low, but the ice in it conveyed her anger well enough. "I know I'm not allowed to call Vivian my mother any longer, but she was a wonderful woman and I will not allow you to continue to speak about her that way. The only person having judgment problems at the moment is you." She released her grip, but not her glare. "Did you want to let us in or did you intend to continue giving your neighbors a show? Some of them are awake and curious."

May nodded and stepped aside. After Meaghan and Nick entered, she shut the door behind them. "Would you like some tea?" she asked.

"That's not necessary, Mom," Nick responded.

"Let her make it," Meaghan said. "She's nervous. It will help her."

"Thanks," May said and put a kettle on top of the stove before keeping busy by collecting dishes.

Meaghan found a seat at the kitchen table where a ceramic pot held a sickly looking plant. She could not tell what it had been in its life, but near-death, it looked like a twig. She ran her finger along the pot's rim while Nick paced the room. Minutes passed in silence before the teakettle whistled. May poured the tea to steep and then brought the cups to the table. When she sat, the conversation began again.

"Why are you here?" she asked Meaghan. "Do you know how my son feels about you?"

"I do."

"Do you feel the same way?"

Meaghan hesitated, considering how she wanted to respond. "I care about him," she said. "But so much has happened since we left Earth that I haven't had time to figure out how deep those emotions run."

May's relief came out as a sigh. "Then there's still time to fix this," she decided and drew a cup to her lips. She took a sip and then clutched the cup in front of her. "I don't know if Nick has told you

314

about our weddings, but it's important you don't see each other anymore. If you were to fall in love, he would lose his powers. That could get him killed."

"I know," Meaghan said. "He—"

"You know?" May asked. Her hands tightened around her teacup and her anger swelled again. Behind it, panic surfaced. "Then why did you fight to keep him as your Guardian? How could you willingly put him in danger?"

"Because we're already wed."

Color drained from May's face, and then her cup fell from her hands. Tea flooded the table. Nick stood to get a towel from the counter.

"Please tell me you're not serious," May whispered. She turned her eyes toward her son, beseeching him to deny it. He remained silent as he wiped up the tea. "Nick," she pled.

"I'm fine, Mom. I promise you."

"That's not possible." Tears filled her eyes and Meaghan thought she would cry, but she jumped from her seat instead. "How could you do this to him?" she demanded of Meaghan. "Do you not understand you'll be burying him within a year? Do you not realize how that will feel?" She faced Nick, grabbing his arm. "She said she didn't love you, Nick. She told me. How could she lie about that? How could you tolerate it?"

"Mom—" he started, but May overran him with another tirade.

"How could you do this to me? To us? Your job as her Guardian meant everything. Meaghan's our future. Vivian died for her. We've all sacrificed for her. And you've invited your own death and risked

Meaghan's life in the process. How could you? How—"

"May, stop." The authority in Meaghan's voice cut through May's yelling better than any counterattack ever could. May turned her head and nodded. She sat again at the table. "You're good at acting angry," Meaghan told her, "but I know anger isn't your driving emotion. You're scared, terrified even, of losing Nick, but you don't need to be. If you'll let him talk, he can explain everything to you."

"I don't see how anything he can say will fix this."

"There's nothing to fix." Meaghan covered May's hand with one of her own. "Listen, okay?"

The older woman nodded. Nick discarded the towel, and then slid into the seat next to Meaghan, taking her other hand and linking their fingers together. "Aunt Viv asked me to come to Earth because she knew she had to die and because she knew I had to build a relationship with Meaghan before I brought her home. Meaghan had to trust me enough to follow me."

"Yes, of course. That makes sense. But I fail to see—"

"He isn't finished," Meaghan interrupted.

May pursed her lips and then sighed. "Continue."

"Vivian had a prophecy," Nick said. "She hid it in Adelina's amulet so we would find it when we got here. It spoke of our wedding and of why it needed to happen."

"What did it say?" May asked.

Nick pulled a slip of paper from his pocket and handed it to her. She read it, smoothed it out on the table, and read it again. Then she looked up at him. "It isn't clear. It could be about anything. Please tell me you didn't wed based on this."

"We didn't," Nick said. "In fact, I didn't see it for the first time until after the wedding. It didn't matter, though. It happened anyway."

"Happened?" she asked, narrowing her eyes. "Don't you mean you kissed her anyway? You took the risk anyway?"

"No, I don't. I mean it happened. We were standing across the room from each other and it happened. I know that's hard to believe, but—"

"Across the room," May whispered and stared at the paper again. "You weren't kissing?"

"We weren't even touching. As I said—"

"Did anything else happen?" she asked, turning her attention toward Meaghan. No anger remained within her. Even her worry had disappeared. In its place, and laced within her voice, she held only excitement. "If I'm reading this prophecy correctly, something did. Am I right?"

"Yes," Nick confirmed. He frowned at his mother. "I'm confused. Why aren't you upset anymore?"

"I'll explain in a minute. What happened to Meaghan after you wed?"

"She received a new power."

May's eyes flew back to Meaghan's. "Show it to me," she commanded. "I need to see it."

Meaghan hesitated. "I'm not certain I can. I don't have much control over it."

"You can do it," Nick said. "Focus. You'll be fine."

"All right," Meaghan agreed, and turned her attention to the clay pot on the table. She touched the grayish-brown plant within it and then focused on the warmth harboring next to her heart. She tugged on it, sent it down her arm, through her fingers, and then sat back when the plant came to life. It grew tall and green. It sprouted leaves, and at the top of the thin, delicate stalk now standing where the brown twig had been, a white flower budded and blossomed. She gasped in recognition. "It's an orchid. I didn't know those grew here."

"They don't," May told her. "Vivian brought it to me the last time I saw her. The local Gardener has kept it alive, but he's never been able to get it to grow." She turned to her son. "Your powers became stronger, didn't they?"

"How did you know?"

"Because Meaghan's power is stronger than yours. It's why you didn't lose your powers when you wed. You took some of her power."

"How is that possible?" Meaghan asked. "I thought the only power stronger than a Guardian's was a Spellmaster's, and then only when the Spellmaster grew older."

"That's supposed to be true," May agreed. "And your revival power is supposed to have gone extinct centuries ago, but obviously that's incorrect."

"Revival power?" Nick asked. "I've never heard of it. I thought we learned about all the extinct powers in school."

"Not this one," May replied. Standing, she picked up her teacup and brought it to the stove to refill it. "It only ran through the royal line. It was also extremely rare, so common knowledge of it went away with the power."

"Then how do you know about it?"

May turned to face them again. She brought the teacup to her lips and blew the steam from it. "As Adelina's Guardian," she responded after taking a sip, "I overheard some of the royal family secrets which were kept from the rest of the kingdom. I've maintained those secrets, as was required of me, but I think it's also required of me to share them with you. I wish I knew them all. I'm afraid most of them died with your mother."

Meaghan nodded and felt sorrow in her statement. "What do you know about the revival power?"

"Not much. I don't know why it came to you later than your empath power, and I don't know the full scope of what it can do. But it seems to play a part in this prophecy so I'm guessing there's more to it than it appears." She set her cup down on the counter, and then rejoined them at the table. "I'm sorry I doubted you," she told Nick, clasping his hands between her own. "I should've realized you never would have taken the risk. You deserve this, though. You deserve to be happy, and I'm glad you are. And you," she turned to Meaghan. "Don't worry too much about what you feel. Love will come to you in time. The other prophesied weddings have proven that."

"There are others?" Meaghan asked.

"There were. When I saw you tonight, you'd fled to the alley because of your empath power, correct?"

"Unfortunately."

"That means Nick needs to be closer to you than I realized. You start training tomorrow, as I'm sure he's told you. Until you have better control over your power, he should stay with you in the guest cottage."

"That won't look right," Nick protested. "People here gossip too easily and since I'm already under review—"

"You're wed now," she reminded him.

"No one knows."

"We'll fix that in the morning. The Elders will understand. For now, your priority is protecting Meaghan, even if it's from her own power. The best way you can do that is to stay at her side."

Nick stood. "Then I think it's time we slept. Especially if we intend to talk to the Elders in the morning. I'm certain that won't be easy."

"They'll understand," May repeated and rose from her seat. Crossing the room to a bookcase, she slid a brown journal from the shelf and brought it back to the table. Without opening it, she handed it to Meaghan. "As I said, you aren't the first to have a prophesied wedding. This book will explain the rest, but don't open it until you're alone. The story was penned by a Writer."

"What's a Writer?" Meaghan asked.

"Someone who can infuse words with life," Nick explained. "You aren't just reading the words, you're watching the story the way it happened. You're living it."

"I see," Meaghan said and looked down at the book in her hands. At best, it appeared nondescript, nothing more than a cloth journal she could find in any bookstore, but she had a feeling its appearance belied its importance. "So this book is based on a true story?"

"About your family," May said. Meaghan's heart jumped, but she had no time to ask any further questions before May pulled her from her seat. "Go to bed," May said. "You have an early day tomorrow."

And with those last words, she scooted them out the door.

CHAPTER THIRTY-TWO

THE NEW day had already started when they returned to the guest cottage. Meaghan could hear the clock in the town square chime the one o'clock hour. Though she wanted to read the book May had given her, Nick removed it from her hands, and ushered her to bed. He did not have to say anything. She knew they needed rest. But her body still reeled from the day, and her mind still clung to what May had told them. The answers were in the book and Meaghan had to learn them. When Nick's breathing deepened into sleep, she climbed from bed and retrieved the book from the small table where Nick had left it. Tucking it under her arm, she found a seat beneath the window, and then opened it to read by the patch of moonlight streaming into the room.

As soon as her eyes fell on the first words, the cottage surrounding her disappeared. Much like the sensation she had felt while being teleported, her world shifted, and she landed in another place, watching two women from another time hurry past.

§

QUEEN ADELINA threaded her way through the maze of stone hallways, easily avoiding the pools of stagnant water that hid in the shadows lining the underbelly of the castle. Few people would have guessed the glistening quartz walls and colorful gardens housing the royal family could harbor such a dark and dreary place. But few people could understand the need for such a place. Most prisoners, those convicted of petty crimes, were housed in village facilities, kept well, and provided standard comforts until they had served their terms.

Those brought here and tossed into the dredges of the Pit, as this place had been nicknamed by the guards, held worse intentions in their hearts. They were repeat criminals, murderers, rapists, and traitors. The Pit housed them until trial. If proven innocent, they found freedom. If not, banishment or death became their fate.

Few received an innocent verdict, though that came as no surprise. A criminal's guilt had to be almost certain for the person to gain entrance into the Pit. Punishment was inherent in its design.

Stale air lay thick and oppressive over an endless maze. Stone walls coated in water from long-forgotten leaks had sprouted black mold and white chalk. Prison cells offered no beds or blankets to keep the prisoners warm. And meals, though provided three times a day, did no more than sustain minimum life. Bland porridge started the morning. Bread and a hunk of horsemeat marked the noon hour. A hash of vegetables and potatoes came at the day's end. Water accompanied each meal, though Adelina loathed calling it that. Tinged a light shade of gray, she questioned not only its quality but also its cruelty.

The place appalled Adelina. She considered it a violation of basic human rights. When she had first discovered it as a teenager, she had demanded her mother shut it down. She and her father had argued over it for weeks. She had sulked, pouted, and used every manipulation technique in her arsenal. In the end, her father had used only one. He had made her sit through the trial of a murderer housed within the Pit.

The prisoner had been a Healer with a specialty in potions. Known to be both conniving and ambitious, his goal had been to create a potion that would allow him to advance on the royal family and take over. He had never had the chance to fulfill his goal. Because of the secretive nature of his plan, he had tested his potions on himself. One concoction had snapped his sanity and he had gone on a rampage, killing not only his entire family with a butcher knife, but everyone who happened to be within throwing distance of his house. By the time the village Guardians had detained him, twelve bodies lay at his feet, including four children, two of which were not his own.

Declared insane, even though he had arrived at that condition by his own hand, the laws would not allow the judging panel to execute him. He had been banished, sent into the wilderness where Adelina felt certain he had met his death. The punishment seemed fitting for the crime. She had never forgotten the sobbing of the surviving villagers as they described the carnage they had witnessed, nor the despondency of the couple who had lost their children. No punishment could make right their grief or make whole their loss. She had never forgotten that lesson, and she had never forgotten the name of the white haired man who had sat through his trial with a crooked smile on his face and malice in his eyes. Finnil.

For Finnil, she had allowed the Pit to continue housing the unworthy. And to ease her own guilt, she had vowed never to set foot in the dungeon again.

A rat scurried across her boot and she froze in her path, checking the shudder creeping up her spine. Strength, she remembered. She must only show strength in the presence of others. Especially those she could not trust. Although the Guardian who walked a step behind her had come with high regards from the Elders, Adelina could not find the will to trust her. She missed Ellida too much. The woman had been her mother's Guardian for forty years and Adelina's since she was born. But Adelina had no control over who guarded her. The Elders dictated those assignments, for good reason, and it had been determined that Ellida had earned a peaceful retirement. Translation: Adelina had proven to be too much of a handful for the seventy-year-old woman. Since Adelina's mother had been dead for a year, Ellida had moved back to the Guardian village and her granddaughter had taken the job.

Adelina did not dislike her new Guardian. She found the woman capable and smart. She just did not see the point in having a Guardian. There was nothing she could not do on her own. She had wielded a sword since childhood. She could race horses with the best soldiers in the kingdom. She had even fought in a battle during the Zeiihbu War. The latter, of course, had happened despite Ellida's protests. Adelina had ridden off without her personal Guardian, protected by the youngest and strongest of the royal army. And she suspected that decision had something to do with the elder Guardian's retirement. The thought tugged at her heart, but she knew she had done the right thing. She had needed to meet with the leader of the Paecis in person for her plan to succeed. And she had needed her plan to succeed to bring peace to the northern kingdom.

Her participation in the battle had been incidental, an error of timing. She had intended to return before the battle started, but the Zeiihbu ruler she had wanted to overthrow had a different strategy in mind. He forced the battle early and she fought in it. She supposed she could have heeded the head of the royal army's command to hide, but she had not felt right about it. They fought for her vision, and so should she.

When she returned from the battle, Ellida's face had looked more lined, her hair whiter than it had when Adelina left. Of course, it had not helped that the majority of the royal army who had flanked Adelina when she rode out had not returned with her. Their deaths also tugged at her heart. At night, she remembered them and mourned for them. But during the day, she remained as passive as her role as Queen required. As passive as she also felt she needed to be around her newly appointed Guardian.

She entered the cellblock housing the vilest of the prisoners and her stomach pitched when the stench of body odor, rot, and feces greeted her. She clenched her jaw to prevent her supper from abandoning her and pushed forward. The cell she wanted was last on the block. She needed to see him. She needed to lay eyes on the man who ruled the tribe known as the Raiders.

The Raiders had existed longer than Adelina had been alive. They roamed the country in the north, robbing villages, burning what they left behind, and taking women at their will. The villagers who resisted were murdered, their throats slit without hesitation. As far as Adelina could tell, the Raiders had no home and no origin. And though they had been a bane for her parents, the Zeiihbu War had kept everyone's focus off them. They thought themselves untouchable. But now Adelina had brought peace to Zeiihbu, and she refused to stop there. Her focus had been set on ending the Raiders' plundering. Three months ago, the royal army had killed the head of the tribe, and today, they had captured his son.

She had been riding when she received word the prisoner had arrived at the Pit. In her excitement, she had rushed her horse to the castle and bounded down the stairs to the dungeon, her feet barely touching the stone as she ran. She did not bother to change her clothes. Though mud had now dried on her riding slacks, and her jacket held a thin coat of dust, she did not care. A prisoner of the Pit deserved no decorum. She also ignored her vow not to set foot in the dungeons. Today would be a one-time exception. Today she had to see the face of the last enemy against her plan for peace.

No sunlight reached the inhabitants in this part of the Pit. They were too far underground. The only light came from a few torches standing like sentries against the dark. Instead of adding warmth, their flames added eerie shadows to the chill clinging to the walls. She felt no less horror in this place than she had the first time she had set foot in it. But that was the point—to remind the prisoners of the gravity of their crimes, of the sorrow they had caused. This environment served that purpose.

She located the last cell, squared her shoulders, and prepared for the verbal battle she wanted. Although the Raider had not been here long, only hours, she expected to see misery on his face, remorse in his voice. She expected him to beg for his life, and she intended to capitalize on that to put a stop to the rest of his tribe. She did not expect to hear him singing.

She froze in her tracks outside visual range of the cell. She had heard many noises down here the last time she had visited. She had expected those, and steeled her heart in preparation for them. Wailing, crying, moaning—those were the standard sounds in this place. But not singing, and certainly not a joyful song about love. She listened, recognizing the song from her childhood.

Her mother used to sing it to her. The lyrics told the tale of the great love that had flourished between the first King and Queen of these lands, of the peace their love had brought and of how their love had lived with them into old age when they died in each other's arms. Her mother had been a soprano. Her beautiful voice had drifted on the air as delicate as a leaf on the autumn breeze, captivating her audience. The voice Adelina heard now held the same command, as did the stringed instrument accompanying it. It brought Adelina back to her childhood, and it drew a smile across her face. She waited, and listened, though she knew she should not. This man did not deserve her devout attention, but she could not help the reaction. His voice chased away the cold of this dreadful place, warming her, and she held on to the feeling as long as she could.

When the song ended, she felt disappointment, but discarded it. She was Queen now, and had no time for such foolishness. Nor did she have the luxury of allowing a prisoner to sway her resolve, even if he did have a wonderful voice.

She approached the bars, surprised to find him waiting close behind them. His eyes studied her. They were crystal blue, clear, with no hint of the evil she had expected. He had the olive complexion of a Zeiihbu native. His dark hair was not dirty and unkempt, as she had imagined for a roaming man. Instead, he kept it clean and tidy. It ran long to his shoulders, but it seemed freshly trimmed. Even his clothes appeared neat. The only scruff on him came in the form of stubble along his jaw. It looked nice, she thought, and frowned to cover the sudden attraction. It had no place here. A murderer, no matter how charming, could not be considered handsome.

He smiled at her, a gesture both natural and genuine, and bowed. Her frown deepened to a scowl and she did not bother to nod in return. "My Queen," he said, rising slowly as he continued to study her. "Have you no courtesy for one of your own people?"

"I do not consider Raiders to be my people any more than I consider animals in the forest to be mine."

"You consider us animals?" he asked and approached the bars. "That's a shame. I had hoped you might help us achieve peace in the same way you helped the Zeiihbu. Word of your bravery and wisdom has even reached us in our travels."

"Travels?" she snorted. "Crimes is more like it."

"Crimes," he echoed, and his shoulders slumped forward. "Then you've already sentenced me. Why not execute me now? What do you wait for?" He turned from her and walked to the far wall. Bending over, he picked up the instrument he had been playing. A

329

dulcet guitar, she realized. Only this one looked homemade. A soft red gleam shone from the polished wood half-tube serving as its shell. The pearl tabs holding all seven strings in place appeared worn from constant adjustment and play. He turned in time to catch her looking at them and a smile returned to his lips. "Do you like it? I made it."

"You were playing it a minute ago."

"Yes," he confirmed. "Music is a gift."

"Your power?" she asked, bringing her eyes back to his.

"No. Just a gift."

She nodded in agreement before she realized she had done so and covered the mistake with indignation. "How did you get that instrument?"

"I told you," he responded, his smile unfaltering. "I made it."

"You know what I meant. The guards should have taken it from you when they brought you here."

"Threw me in here is more like it," he said. "But don't worry. Your guards haven't forgotten their protocols. They took it, and I took it back."

"How?"

"That's my secret to keep. I turned myself in. I would think letting me keep my instrument would be a fitting gesture in return."

"Even if that were true," she told him, "prisoners are not allowed personal effects. I'll ask you to hand it over or I'll send the guards in to get it."

"It is true," he said, but extended the instrument through the bars anyway. She reached out to take it, but her Guardian snatched it from his hands before she could touch it.

"Careful," he protested. "It took me weeks to make."

"And likely it took so long because it hides a weapon," the Guardian said. "I won't leave her exposed to your murderous plots."

"I'm no murderer. I came to talk to her."

"We know what Raiders do."

He gripped the bars. The heat in his eyes turned dangerous. "And what is it we do?"

"Rob, steal—"

"Only what we need to survive," he countered.

The Guardian narrowed her eyes and continued. "Murder, rape, burn villages to the ground."

"Lies," he snapped. "We take food to eat. We take clothes to survive the winter. We aren't savages."

"I don't lie," she shot back. "I saw the bodies in the villages below Clear Mountain. I helped heal the men your people stabbed, the women you—"

"May," Adelina interrupted, conveying her authority without raising her voice. May stopped talking and Adelina tilted her head, curious as she studied the man in front of her. She saw pain on his face. Unmistakable pain that did not fit with the ruthless men May described. Anger also lived in the hard set of his lips and the tightening of his knuckles on the bars. He knew of Clear Mountain, but he also knew something she did not.

Knowledge was the most important tool a Queen could have, she remembered her mother telling her, and opened her mind to learning from this man. She took a step forward and then another, holding his gaze with one of equal intensity. When she stood in front of him, she placed her hands below his on the bars. May gasped in protest, but Adelina ignored the noise. "You say you turned yourself in. You came to speak to me."

"I did."

"Then I require honesty. You claim the men who terrorized Clear Mountain were not Raiders, but we know they were. How can they be both?"

"Have you no criminals among your people?" he asked in response. Her eyes left his to stare into the bleak shadows of his cell for only a brief second, but when she met his gaze again, she knew he had not missed the reaction. He nodded. "You have this place, of course, so you must. You don't like it though."

"It serves a purpose."

"Not as swift a purpose as execution," he replied. "The men who fulfilled their whims on the villages of Clear Mountain were part of my father's tribe once. I won't deny that. But they were no more human than you think I am. They broke away and formed a band of their own, performing the acts May mentioned, but they do not represent my people."

"What happened to them?"

His hand slipped down the bar, coming to rest against hers. He took comfort from the touch, she realized, and knew what he was about to say. "I tracked them down and took care of them."

"And you said you weren't a murderer," May growled from the shadows.

His eyes snapped away from Adelina. Anger returned to them. "It was no less than they deserved. You saw what they did, and so did I. The people from those villages deserved justice."

"Without a trial?" May countered. "That makes you no better than your so-called criminals."

"Perhaps that's true." He removed his hands from the bars. "But you're no better than I am. Your trials are a farce if you conduct them with preconceived notions. I'd even wager you'd hang me now if you could."

"You're right. I would," May said with a chilling smile. "Because I don't believe a word you've said, except for the last part. Those people do deserve justice, and the Raiders will pay for what they've done."

"So be it," he responded and turned from them. "Leave me. There's no point in talking any longer."

He was right, Adelina decided. There was no point. She watched the man withdraw to the far side of his cell and vowed to give her new Guardian a firm lecture when they returned to the privacy of the royal quarters. She could have gained more information from this conversation, maybe even found a solution to keep the peace, but May had effectively killed the chance. For today, at least. Adelina would try again tomorrow.

She turned to go, stopping when she saw the dulcet guitar clutched between May's hands. She reached out to take it, meeting resistance from her Guardian. Already angry, she raised her eyes to May's, ensuring the woman received the message. She would give in on this one thing, or she would suffer for it. Although Adelina could not control who stood as her guard, she could control how she reacted to that person, and how miserable she made the Elders' lives. As far as she was concerned, May was a breath away from understanding the full impact of Adelina's will.

May's throat constricted and her hands released the instrument. Turning back to the Raider, Adelina approached the bars one last time. He remained at the back wall, unwilling to meet her. She did not blame him. She slipped the instrument through the bars and laid it on the cleanest pile of hay she could find. "I'm sorry," she said.

"I am too," he told her.

Unsure of what else to say, she nodded and stepped back. Then it happened. Her heart heated, and then her body. The closest she had ever felt to this level of warmth had been when she had caught fever as a child. She had been ill for two weeks, with spots covering her skin. It had been uncomfortable, but this felt almost pleasant. Before she had time to figure out what it was, the color shot from her. Yellow rose into the air to slam into the stream of green coming from him. Then, the colors turned to rich crimson, split, and poured back into both of them. When it was over, she felt confused, weak, and betrayed.

"What have you done?" she hissed at him.

"I didn't do anything," he said. His eyes grew wide with his own confusion, but she ignored it. This had to be a trick, a spell or power to convince her the colors had been real. She refused to believe the alternative.

"I swear I didn't do this," he insisted when she turned from him.

"Swear to it in court," she said. "We'll add it to your list of crimes."

He cursed. She disappeared into the shadows, but not before his final taunt reached her ears.

"You mean to tell me you'd execute your own husband?"

CHAPTER THIRTY-THREE

HE HATED the words as soon as they left his lips. They echoed off the walls, mocking him with the absurdity of his desperation well after Adelina's footsteps had faded. Within the hour, the guards came to extinguish the torches. He understood that to mean bedtime had come, though sleep seemed laughable in this place. The dungeon brought only discomfort to mind. The little bit of hay lining his cell smelled of sweat, urine, and death. The stone beneath it bled moisture through his clothes, soaking his skin and causing him to shiver with cold. He ground his teeth, controlling the need to chatter, but his muscles would not obey the same command. They shook in the effort to stay warm and convulsed from the pain the unyielding stone brought to them.

More than once his misery drove him to wonder why he remained subjected to this, and why he did not leave. And more than once, he reminded himself he had come to seek help for his people and he still had not received it.

Of course, he had never expected to stay overnight in this sty. He had known convincing the Queen to align with him would be difficult, but he had naively believed he could achieve it in one afternoon.

A scream tore down the hall. He brought his hands to his ears, blocking the sound out, and with it, the urge to run. His people also screamed in their makeshift camp, lost to a plague that had taken many since his father's death. He needed a talented Healer like the one guarding the Queen to save them. Yet the woman would sooner kill him than help him, he realized, and squeezed his eyes shut.

Things may not have gone according to plan so far, but he could not give up. No matter the cost, he had to convince Adelina's Guardian to visit the camp. Once she arrived, she would change her mind. How could she not? It would take someone callous to look at the skeletal bodies of the children or see the bloody eyes of those who could not eat, could not sleep, and let them suffer.

It would take someone callous or someone who had seen the destruction the rogue men had wrought. The Healer had witnessed the worst of their crimes and it had poisoned her. He had felt no less angry the first time he had seen what they had done. And since his people had spent the majority of their existence hiding in the woods and mountains, at least until the war had depleted their resources, the woman could not know these men were deviants. She could only see them as an example of the norm.

His father's decision to steal from the villagers instead of seeking their assistance did not help matters. He had wanted to remain separate. He had wanted to maintain his pride. In the end, that decision and that same pride had brought his death. And it might also cause the deaths of everyone who had trusted him.

"Are you hungry?" The voice drifted to him as no more than a whisper, but it seemed like a yell in the darkness.

He scrambled to his feet. "Who's there?"

"It's only me," the voice said and this time he recognized her. The Queen. He heard the sound of steel striking flint, saw a spark, and then the torch lit and he could see her. Although earlier she had worn what looked to be riding gear, she had changed into a dress, a simple cotton and lace garment that highlighted her lean body.

"Is it morning?" he asked.

"Not quite, but close," she responded and turned to face him. Though he had heard stories of her bravery in the war, and heard tales of the cunning plan she had executed to win peace in Zeiihbu, he had never heard anyone mention her beauty. He wished he had. At least then he would have been prepared for the way it had stopped his heart yesterday.

Her dark brown hair looked almost black. It cascaded down her back in silken waves that called for him to run his fingers through it. Her eyes shone copper. With gold flecks. He had noticed it when she stood in front of him. The color in them sparked, ignited, and burned all thought from his brain. Her skin was smooth and milk white, dotted with freckles, and he ached to touch it. He had given into that urge for a moment yesterday when he had needed the contact most. His hand had only brushed hers, but the warmth had started building, and it had not eased until they had been wed.

The mistake had been his, and he did not blame her for being upset. It confused him as well. The wedding had not been ordinary.

But neither was the woman who stood in front of him. If they had met under different circumstances, he had no doubt he would have loved her. He leaned against the wall and felt the stone cold reality of their current circumstance pressing against his back.

"Are you hungry?" she asked again.

"Do you aim to poison me?"

She laughed. Walking to the bars, she stopped where they had stood together the day before and shook her head. "I only aim to feed you." She slipped her hand through the bars and extended it. A small paper package lay on her palm. "It's cheese," she said. "I'll be able to get you more once I authorize your release."

He studied the parcel she offered him. His stomach grumbled in anticipation for it, but he did not move toward her. "Why would you do that?"

"Because I won't execute my husband," she responded. "Please eat. I know the food in here is terrible, and I also know they haven't given any of it to you yet. They usually wait a day or two to provide the first meal."

He approached and removed the cheese from her hand. After unwrapping it, he tore a chunk from it and offered the morsel to her first.

"Still think I want to poison you?" she asked. He smiled in response and she took the cheese, tossed it into her mouth and swallowed. "Satisfied?"

"Yes," he said and started eating. "Where's your guard?"

"Past the light, in the shadows," she nodded her head toward the hallway. "I made her wait there so we could talk."

"You mean so she wouldn't interrupt again," he quipped and heard a growl from the darkness. He laughed. "She can hear, apparently. Aren't you afraid I'll try to hurt you?"

"You won't. I'm certain our powers wouldn't have joined us if you meant me harm."

"Then you believe me? You believe I'm not trying to trick you?"

"I know you aren't. I knew it yesterday, but the wedding took me by surprise. I shouldn't have treated you that way."

"You knew?" he asked. "How could you have known? It's not as if it's happened before. If our roles were reversed, I would think the worst of you."

"No, you wouldn't." She leaned against the bars, wrapping her hands around them. "If you held my role, you would know the secrets I know."

He finished the last of the cheese and joined her at the bars. He wrapped his hands around hers. "And what secrets do you know?"

"Royal ones," she replied. "That song you sang yesterday isn't just a tale. It's history. My family's history."

"I've heard that before. It's not a secret."

"How they fell in love is. They belonged to rival tribes, the two largest in these parts before the kingdom came about. There were wars at the time. Each tribe had gathered the smaller tribes to their sides, essentially dividing the lands in two. One war lasted for decades. Some say fifty years or more, but I don't know for certain if that's true. It could have been longer. It could have been shorter." She shrugged. "The tribes were too evenly matched. Either they had to eliminate each other, or they had to reach a truce. They never had the chance to decide which they wanted to do. They called a meeting of the elder tribesmen and their families. As soon as everyone arrived at the gathering point, the powers of the opposing Chiefs' children wed them. They say it happened so fast the bride fainted."

"You're serious?" he asked. "Why would your family hide that?"

"Because it tells better as a love story. The Chiefs' children hated each other at first. They wanted to continue the war, but the Chiefs took the wedding as a sign they must make peace. They did. The kingdom was formed and eventually the anointed King and Queen grew to love each other in the way we know them in song." She paused and studied him, her head tilted in curiosity. "A Seer later prophesied there would be more weddings in the same fashion, weddings brought about with purpose instead of love."

"So what do you think our purpose is?"

"I don't know. Perhaps we'll never know. It could be something we need to do together, or it could be we need to create a descendant. The only thing we can know for certain is we're bound to each other."

"I hope someday you'll be happy with that," he told her. "The original King and Queen found love. Maybe we can too."

She smiled and turned from him. "I'll have the guard release you. It won't be long."

"Wait," he called out to her. "Queen Adelina, please don't go yet. I came for a reason."

She faced him again. "Adelina," she said and returned to the bars. "Just Adelina. I'm no more Queen over you than you're King over me."

"I'm not a," he started and then felt his heart race in panic. "Adelina, I'm not meant to be a king. I only lead my people because they need help."

"All people need help," she told him and reached through the bars to lay a palm against his cheek. "You'll make a fine king, I assure you. Now what is it you needed from me?"

"My people," he forced the words from his mouth. "We're not like you."

"What do you mean?"

"We were from Zeiihbu once, a long time ago. We left the lands there to live south of the border, in the forests and mountains. We've always been nomads, living off the land and making what we need. But the Zeiihbu War made our regular territory unsafe and depleted our resources."

"Which is why you started raiding the villages," she said.

"My father made that decision. I never agreed with it."

"But you didn't come to me before and you didn't go to my mother. What brings you here now?"

"We're not like you," he said again. "Once we ventured into the villages, we caught diseases we'd never been exposed to before. Some only harmed us until we built immunities. Others killed whoever caught them. Until recently, the deaths were minimal, though, limited to a few people at a time. Now we've caught something that's killing everyone it touches. I think it's a plague. We've lost a third of our population already, and I can't save the rest of them without your help."

"What are the symptoms?" The question came from the shadows

and he turned his head in time to see May step out of them. "I need to know them in order to figure out what type of plague it is."

He raised an eyebrow, surprised at the relaxed manner in which she asked the question. She seemed to want to help. "It starts with a stomach ache and bloody eyes, and then the pain becomes so bad the infected can no longer eat or sleep. We force water into them to keep them alive, but it hurts them. They scream the whole time."

"And eventually they starve to death," she said.

"Yes."

"It's not a disease. It's the Famine Curse. It's a bad spell designed to mimic disease, which is why it didn't hit everyone at once. "

"Where did it come from?"

"The short answer?" May asked. "It stems from revenge. I'm guessing your people do more than raid villages. They rob travelers too."

"Sometimes," he admitted. "How did you know?"

"Because I know of the Spellmaster who created this spell and you can't get into his village, which means your people had to have robbed him or he wouldn't have bothered to cast the curse. He used the same spell on the Zeiihbuans during the war. I helped my mother come up with the cure for it."

"You helped the Zeiihbu people when you were at war with them? Why?"

"I won't allow people to suffer if I can help them. It's not in my nature."

"I can understand that," he said and regarded her with a new respect he would never have thought possible in their first meeting.

"I would do the same."

She nodded. "I believe you. And I'm sorry for the way I treated you yesterday. I can be wrong occasionally. Even about Raiders."

"I hate that name. I wish you wouldn't use it."

"What do you want to be called?"

"My people don't have a name, but you can call me Ed. It's short for Edáire."

"Ed it is then," she agreed. "I'll organize the Healers and as soon as you're released, you can show me where your people live. You'll also need to take the potion or it won't be long before you fall to the spell."

"I understand. Thank you." He turned back to Adelina. "How soon can I go?"

"I'll need to explain this to the head guard and then probably the Guardian Elders. It could take half a day or so."

"And if I had a way of leaving here sooner, would you allow it?"

"Of course. What did you have in mind?"

"You asked me how I got my instrument back yesterday. I used my power and retrieved it from the guard station where they left it."

"What is your power?"

Instead of telling her, he showed her. He passed his arms and then his entire body through the bars, walking through them as if they were no more than beams of sunlight. Adelina's mouth hung open and it was all Ed could do not to laugh at the reaction.

"I can move through objects," he told her. "Now it's only a matter of getting out of here without lighting the torches along the hallways. The guards are bound to notice my escape if we do that."

"Why would we light the torches?" she asked and shook her head. "There's no need."

"How did you get down here then? It's impossible to see anything without them."

"Not if you have my power," she said and turned to extinguish the torch. He felt her hand grip his. "I can see in the dark."

§

MEAGHAN CLOSED the book and sighed as tears streamed down her face. Her parents had seemed so real. She had watched them move, heard their thoughts, felt their breath as they took it in and let it go, and sensed their emotions as if they were standing in the room with her. No one could describe them to her the way she had just seen them. The book was a gift. But it was also a curse to be this close to them and not be able to touch them, to feel their presence and not have them feel hers, and to know they would die too young and not be able to warn them. She had hated the story as much as she had loved it.

She stood and slipped the book into the backpack. Running her hand over the bag's rip-stop material, the irony did not escape her that she was using the last reminder of one father to house the only memory she had of the other. Weary, she climbed back into bed with Nick, and closed her eyes. As she drifted to sleep, she wondered if Queen Adelina and King Edáire had ever discovered the purpose of their wedding. Had they found a Seer who knew their only child would experience a prophesied wedding as well? Had it crossed their minds that their purpose might have been to create that child?

Meaghan doubted it, but they had not needed to know for it to matter. She knew. And she would not let them down.

CHAPTER THIRTY-FOUR

SOMETHING SLICED into Meaghan's stomach. The pain came hot and swift, ripping through her from her belly button to her breastbone. Then, as fast as it had started, it stopped. Before she could catch her breath, pain squeezed at her neck and panic joined it. Terror matching no other she had ever felt overcame all else and then faded into nothing.

She forced her eyes open, and then squinted as the pink haze of a new day greeted her. It chased some of the shadows from the cottage, leaving those that remained to shrink into the corners, and she knew she had not been asleep long, maybe a few hours at most. She sat up and a new round of pain began. The first strike came as a blow to the temple that exploded like sharp fingers across her head. Before it faded, the second seized her arm, splintering up to her elbow from her wrist. A sharp needle stabbed her heart next, and then flames seared her lungs. When pain burned her skin, she screamed.

Nick startled awake beside her. "There's danger," he muttered, and then faced her. She felt his panic and his fingers on her arm before she tumbled from bed. The pain continued to roll. Her legs hurt. Her feet felt like they were on fire. Her lungs convulsed, and then her stomach turned. She tried to stand, but could only pull up to her knees before she fell back down, landing on her palms. Desperate, she crawled across the floor, making it as far as the trash can before a wave of nausea overcame her.

"Meg!" Nick called from beside her. His hands gripped her shoulders, holding her when she convulsed again. "I sense danger. We have to leave."

She could not speak. Her muscles felt weak and she collapsed to the floor. Drawing her knees to her chest, she wrapped her arms around them, and prayed for the pain to stop.

"Meg," Nick begged her, laying a hand on her back. "What's wrong? Your pain, it's—"

"Everywhere," she moaned. "Everywhere," she repeated, and then the screams started outside. Nick's panic changed into a chilling fear that only added to her misery. His touch disappeared and she heard him moving around the cottage. He returned to her a moment later. After slipping her nightgown over her head, he dressed her in her travel clothes, and then lifted her into his arms. She felt the rough material of the backpack strap brush against her cheek and struggled to comprehend its meaning through the excruciating pain now echoing within her body. She felt the pain from tears and breaks, from sharp stabs, and agonizing burns. And she felt them stop, only to start again from another direction. They rolled over each other, a constant battering of rough waves that drowned her. She forced a painful breath into her lungs, struggled to hold her focus on her own feelings, her own sensations, and lost. She felt dizzy, or was Nick running? She could not tell. She screamed from the agony, or were those the voices of the villagers? The sounds and pain blended together and she could not tell if they belonged to someone else or if they were her own. Even the warmth of Nick's body melded with the burning pain searing her skin. She heard talking and wondered if she had begun to hallucinate.

"What are you doing here? You should've gotten her out. She's more important than I am."

"She won't survive without you. She's feeling all of this. It's too much."

"But your power—"

"I can't get her to focus on it. Grab your kit. Do you think we can teleport without being tracked?"

"We can't risk it. Set her down."

Meaghan felt the unyielding wood of a chair, and then the sharp smell of burning rubber as it assaulted her nose. She recoiled from the odor, regretting the reaction when her head slammed against the back of the chair. Pressing a hand to the base of her skull, she winced when she felt a welt.

Fingers covered hers. "It's all right," May's voice came from beside Meaghan's ear. "It's only a minor injury."

"Good," Nick responded. "Meg, open your eyes."

She did as he asked and his face filled her vision. "Focus on my power," he said. Her eyes drifted from him to his mother, who knelt beside the chair. Nick placed a hand on her cheek and guided her focus back to him. "Do it, Meg. It won't be long before you're overwhelmed."

She closed her eyes again. She could already feel the emotions pushing their way past the fringes of her control, clawing at her sanity—another sharp blow to her gut, another slash of pain in her mind, a fire of agony spreading across her legs. They swelled and then they faded, dissolving as soon as she found Nick's power.

She opened her eyes, but not all of the emotions left her. Her own panic and fear built each time another scream pierced the air. Through the window of May's kitchen, Meaghan could see fires devouring buildings and villagers running through the streets as they tried to escape. One man stopped to stare at them. Blood coursed down his face, streaming from a gash in his temple. His eyes met Meaghan's, and then he turned from her. He stumbled a few more steps before he collapsed to the ground. A bolt of lightning streaked by, illuminating a woman in the distance and then she, too, was gone.

Meaghan felt fingers clutch her arms. They dug in and pulled her to her feet, but she did not look at them until they shook her.

"Meaghan!"

Meaghan's gaze trailed from the fingers up arms clad in flannel sleeves to the ashen skin of May's face.

"Can you walk?" May asked.

"I think so." Meaghan's hand shook, but it obeyed her command as she drew it up to grasp May's arm. If it worked, her legs should too. She tried not to notice the fire springing to life outside the window. The guest cottage roof had sparked. The house would not be far behind.

"We need to run for the woods," May instructed. Her grip disappeared, replaced by another, more familiar touch. Nick urged Meaghan forward, tugging her through the kitchen and the living room, then out the front door.

It happened again, as it had little more than a week before. The brisk air slapped her face, shattering the numbness encasing her. She followed Nick. She ran from the house resembling the one where she had grown up and she could not separate the past from the present, Earth from Ærenden. In her mind, night turned to day. The scent of snow filled the air instead of ash. Clouds filled the sky instead of stars. Death filled the living room behind her instead of flames.

She sought the SUV, but found the blood-spattered faces of children littering the grass where the driveway should have been. They stared at her, frozen like dolls discarded in play. She wanted to scream, but her voice remained trapped in her throat.

The ground exploded beside her, showering her in dirt and she snapped her eyes from the bodies to the cloaked figure to her right. He held no club. Blue electricity served as his weapon, and she knew she would not evade death so easily this time. She caught her breath, then surged forward as Nick's hand pulled hard on hers. The ground heaved where she had stood, blown apart by the bolt meant for her.

They fled, chased again by three Mardróch. Meaghan saw them each time she glanced over her shoulder, but they appeared as creatures in a dream. Nick dragged her behind him through village streets and alleys, twisting their way to an escape.

Fire consumed all but a few buildings. It cascaded light through the sky, reflecting orange against thick, black smoke. Meaghan traced her gaze along the roofline, past chimneys crumbling under their own weight, and windows exploding from heat. She saw men jumping from balconies, and women wailing over the bodies of their loved ones. She felt numb to it, distanced from the horror and the belief of it.

Her eyes turned from a brick wall scarred black and splattered with blood, and came to rest on the only face that could soothe her. Her mother stared back at her. Vivian had cut her hair. The long, red locks she had cherished now framed her face as a delicate bob, but her eyes remained the same. They narrowed at Meaghan, and then widened with alarm.

A scream shattered the sky from their left, another from their right. A child's cry for his father bounced down a side street, following them as they broke through the back line of houses and chased the moon across the field. They had almost reached the forest. Meaghan wondered how they had arrived here so quickly without a car. It had taken Nick hours the first time.

She lost his hand as he surged forward, but she kept his pace. She followed him into the tree line, deviating to avoid a log, and her feet hit something solid.

She tumbled forward. Small stones and twigs bit her palms, and then her body came to rest over whatever had tripped her.

Rolling off the object, she scrambled around so she could see it, then caught her breath when moonlight illuminated blonde hair and a beautiful face that did not belong here. Tawny eyes stared wide at Meaghan, though they had lost the capacity to see.

"Cissy," Meaghan whispered, her voice no more than the small breath she could manage. Her fingers touched the cold, pale cheek of the woman she had met only hours before, and reality settled over her. This was not the past on Earth. This was the present, and the people of Ærenden were dying around her.

She sucked in a breath, then another, and in her panic, let go of her hold on Nick's power. May's grief and anger assaulted Meaghan first, then pain flooded out all other emotions. It burned, a bath of acid, and Meaghan screamed before she collapsed to the ground.

"Can you carry her?" May asked.

"Yes," Nick responded. "The vitalizing salts won't work again?"

"I'm afraid not," May said, though her voice had begun to fade. "She's too far gone this time. Tilt her head back."

Meaghan felt fingers behind her neck before the glass rim of a small vial pressed against her lips. Bitter liquid filled her mouth. She swallowed from instinct and within seconds, the world faded into blackness.

§

"WHAT THE hell happened?"

Meaghan kept her eyes closed. She turned her head, heard the backpack rustle underneath her, and stopped moving, afraid the noise would give her away. Holding her breath, she tried to sense the emotions surrounding her. Aggravation, concern, and fear came from those talking. Pain still came from many different directions, although it had dwindled to only a few dozen people. One stopped and then another dulled into death. She curled her fingers, felt dry leaves crush into her palm, and realized she lay on the ground.

Pain built within her again. When fresh agony stabbed through her head, she reached for Nick's power, trusting he would be there and emotional silence rewarded that trust. It washed over her, calming her, and she almost wept with relief.

"The raid overwhelmed her power," she heard May respond to the question.

"She's unconscious," said another voice.

"I gave her something. She'll be awake soon."

"But not able," a third voice spoke. Meaghan recognized the gravel in it, and realized the Elders were talking about her. "I think we may have introduced her as our Queen prematurely," Angus continued. "We should have waited to ensure she could do the job."

"She's the Queen," May told him. "Waiting to introduce her wouldn't have changed that."

"Because of her lineage? That's not a good enough reason. She isn't capable. We need to replace her."

"With whom?" May shot back. "Or are you volunteering?"

"I have as much right to the throne as she does," Angus replied.

"Not anymore. You haven't since your mother—"

"This isn't up for debate," Miles interrupted. His voice held a warning that hung in the air, silencing even the song of a bird high in the trees. "She's our Queen and that's final. The only thing that needs to be decided now is who will be her Guardian."

"Nick—" May began.

"Has proven his power can't truly help her," Miles interrupted. "Since he also can't control her, we need someone more experienced to take over. We need someone who can train her so something like this doesn't happen again."

"You can't. They have to stay together."

"Why?" Miles asked. "What aren't you telling us?"

May sighed. "They're wed."

Meaghan's eyes snapped open. Nick glanced at her and she realized he had sensed she had awakened. His hand moved a fraction of an inch at his side, and she obeyed his request to stay still.

Miles stared at May for a moment before he spoke. "That's not possible. Nick wouldn't—"

"They're prophesied."

Miles hissed in a breath of air in surprise at the news, but Angus only smiled. "She no longer has a claim to the throne then," he said. "As my mother did, Meaghan has to give it up for wedding a Guardian."

"Not if their wedding was prophesied," Sam told him. "They didn't have a choice in the matter."

"You can't be certain it was," Angus argued. "There's no proof."

"Nick still has his powers," May said. "The impossibility of that is proof enough."

Angus narrowed his eyes. "He *says* he has his powers."

"How dare you! My son doesn't—"

Miles placed a hand on May's arm to calm her. "I've known Nick since he was an infant. I don't doubt his integrity. He wouldn't lie if it would put Meaghan in danger."

Angus pressed his lips together. "I'm not so easily convinced. He hid the wedding from us for a reason."

"He didn't know about the prophecy yet," May objected. "The

secret was held by the royal family."

"He still should have told us," Miles said. "After seeing the confusion Adelina and Ed's wedding caused them, I'm willing to overlook his transgression, but it does make me certain of the need to replace him as Meaghan's Guardian."

May shook her head. "Please don't punish him for that. He planned on telling you today."

"I'm not punishing him," Miles responded. "Meaghan needs more experienced protection. She needs someone who understands the importance of sharing everything with the Elders."

"Who did you have in mind?" Sam asked.

"May. Unless you want the job."

"I don't, but we need to put this to a vote. Nick is—"

"Lucky to be alive after this past week," Angus said. "He's young and foolish, and she's no different. They're a good fit. Let him protect her. If he gets her killed, it's better for all of us."

"Angus," Miles warned.

"Are you really going to keep defending her?" Angus snapped. "Her presence cost several dozen lives tonight, maybe more. Not to mention your entire family. Is their sacrifice meaningless to you?"

Anger flashed over Miles' face, turning the corners of his mouth hard. He grabbed the front of Angus' shirt. "You don't think I know what this night cost us? You don't think I harbor that pain? All of us do. Sam lost his daughter. Nick lost one of his closest friends. But it's not our Queen's fault. It's the fault of whoever let the Mardróch into the village. If anything, the fact they came for her tells us they consider her a threat. Why do you suppose that is?"

"Because they don't realize how useless she is," Angus countered. He locked his hand over Miles' wrist and twisted, forcing the other man to let go. "They will soon. How many lives do you think her incompetency will cost us in the meantime?"

"She's not incompetent," Nick said and stepped into the circle of Elders. Sam moved out of the way to make room for him, but Miles frowned at the intrusion. "She's only been on this world a week and a half, and she's learned a lot during that time. More than you could, I'm certain."

Angus swept his hand through the air, pushing Nick back with the gesture. "How dare you talk to me that way," he said. "Have you forgotten your place? Do you truly think you can question an Elder's judgment because you guard that joke of a Queen?" He moved his hand again, and knocked Nick off his feet. When he raised his hand a third time, May stepped in front of her son.

"Enough," she hissed. "You've made your point. And so has he. It's a valid one. Meaghan needs more time."

"Time we don't have," Angus replied.

"The final battle isn't upon us," Sam told him. "She has time and I'm willing to give it to her. As to her Guardian's status, protocol calls for a vote."

Nick rose to his feet, nodding in concession before stepping back. Meaghan drew up to her knees.

"A vote then," Miles agreed. "I think Nick has done the best job he can, but this situation needs a more experienced Guardian. I vote that May takes his place."

"Fine," Angus said, and slipped his hands into his pockets. "I concede to the Head Elder's judgment."

May crossed her arms over her chest. "Well I don't. Miles is wrong."

"Noted," Miles said and turned to Sam. "And you? Where does your vote lie?"

"Between the two options," he responded. "Nick is a good Guardian and I think a lot can be said for the trust he instills in Meaghan."

"But?" Angus prompted.

"But he lacks the experience May holds. I think removing Nick might prove to be a mistake, but for now, it's a necessity."

"Then it shall be," Miles determined. He turned to Nick and held up his hand. His palm appeared to shimmer white as he spoke. "Nick, from this point forward, you are relieved of your duties as Guardian over the Queen." He addressed May next. "You are henceforth granted the powers of Guardian over Meaghan."

No sooner had the words left his mouth then May frowned and Meaghan realized her new Guardian now sensed her. "She's awake," May muttered.

All eyes found Meaghan. With their focus on her, only Meaghan saw Angus slip his left hand from his pocket. A flash of purple radiated from between his fingers and Nick's eyes widened with fear and confusion, matching the emotions Meaghan sensed from him.

He did not have to say anything for her to understand what had happened. She felt it. She felt everything from him and from everyone else.

This time, there could be no mistake. He had lost his powers.

CHAPTER THIRTY-FIVE

"SPYING AGAIN?" Miles asked Meaghan, not bothering to mask the displeasure in his voice. "How long have you been awake?"

"Long enough," she responded and stood. She could feel the pain building. It tore at her muscles and pounded within her head, but she ignored it. She fought past it, focusing on the threat in front of her instead. "What did you do?" she asked Angus.

"It wasn't his choice alone," Sam said, stepping forward to lay a hand on her shoulder. "We voted to remove Nick as your Guardian."

She kept her eyes pinned on Angus. "Tell me," she said. "Tell me what you did to him."

"I didn't do anything," he responded. "You're mistaken."

"Don't lie to me." She advanced on him, her steps slow and deliberate. Angus began backing away. She smiled, though the gesture held menace instead of joy, and his Adam's apple bobbed fast in his throat.

"You don't think I can sense your deceit?" she asked him. "Your hatred toward me? Your *fear*?"

"I'd never—"

"Did you bring the Mardróch too? Was the raid your idea?"

He shook his head. "Please, my Queen, I—"

"No more lies!"

Angus backed into a tree and froze. Meaghan pressed forward.

"Did you think I wouldn't figure out your plan?" she asked. "Did you truly believe I wouldn't sense your betrayal?"

"I haven't done anything," Angus protested. His eyes grew wide with innocence, but she could sense the anger and panic he fought to hide.

She halted her advance in front of him and he shrank against the tree. "If I'm wrong, then show me your left hand," she said. "Show everyone your hand so they can see what you hold."

"But I..." His throat constricted. His panic swelled, and he tore his eyes from Meaghan's face to seek out May's. "Please," he begged. "She's gone crazy. Control her."

"I'd be happy to," May responded. "Just show us your hand first."

Angus tightened his fist around the object in question. His eyes darted to Miles, beseeching. "You can't expect me to entertain her request, can you? It's insulting."

Miles nodded. "He's right. Meaghan's not making much sense. Angus has been with us from the beginning. He's given us no reason to doubt him."

"He hasn't," Sam agreed. "But she's our Queen. Insulting or not, it's a simple request. Show us your hand, Angus."

Angus' eyes widened again, his fear no longer guarded, and Miles nodded his consent for the request. Angus raised his hand, but rather than open it, he pushed it forward. A wave of power hit Meaghan like a surge of water, knocking her backwards. She landed flat on the ground. Air rushed from her lungs. White stars flashed in front of her eyes. Her head screamed, pain surging from the lump that had formed earlier. She heard Angus running away and rolled onto her side, but did not get the chance to rise to her feet before she began sliding. She flipped onto her stomach, struggling against an invisible force as Angus drew her behind him with his power.

Clawing at the ground, she sought anything that would slow her movement. Leaves crumbled beneath her fingers. Limbs brushed by, scratching her arms. Nick and the Elders chased after her, but Angus ran faster. Desperate, she dug into the dirt, sifting through grass and pebbles until her hands grasped the withered, brown rope of a dying vine. She gripped hard. The vine wriggled around her fingers, but lost the will to fight as Angus' pull increased.

She felt his power tug her ankles, yank on her legs, then finally lock on her waist. She twisted the vine around her arms, using it to anchor her. Pain surged through her body as Angus increased his power, and then the pressure suddenly eased. Nick caught up to her. He pulled her to her feet, unraveling the vine from her arms to show red welts indented into her skin.

"Angus! You traitor!" Miles bellowed. He raised his hands and Meaghan turned in time to see the air shimmer in front of Angus. Angus skidded to a stop, and then turned to face them.

"I only do what's best for the kingdom," he said. "She'll bring our deaths."

"Don't confuse her with Garon," Sam responded. "Meaghan is the rightful heir. She has the blood of your ancestors, and the wisdom."

"Not my ancestors," Angus growled. "My mother was the true heir and now I am. Adelina was an imprudent offshoot of the family line, an impulsive ruler who brought about her own death and the deaths of many others. Meaghan's no different."

"Istera would never have made a good ruler," Miles said. "She was selfish. She chose your father over the kingdom and its people."

"You have no right," Angus barked, punching a fist forward. Miles staggered back a step, but held his ground. "You betray my mother by speaking of her in that way."

"I guarded her for many years," Miles said. "I knew her better than you did, and I also know she chose her love over the throne because she felt Adelina would make the better ruler. She knew her own selfishness, and she had enough wisdom to recognize it. That wisdom would do you well."

"You lie!" With a flick of his wrist, Angus launched a rock through the air. It sailed toward Miles' head, but the Elder did not move. He raised a hand instead, and the air shimmered again. The rock met his force field and fell to the ground.

"You know I'm telling the truth," Miles replied. "And you also know you can't win this fight. If you try, you'll pay with your life."

"We'll see about that," Angus responded and lifted his hand. Miles did the same, pushing back a barrage of stones with another quick force field. A boulder and a log met his shield with the same ease. Angus narrowed his eyes. His face flashed red with anger, and then he raised his hand once more. Miles did the same, but before he had the chance to use his power, Angus turned and fled.

"No!" Meaghan cried after him. She did not care if he escaped justice. Nor did she care that he had tried to kill her. She only cared about the object he still clutched in his hand, and what it would do to Nick if Angus got away. "Use your force field," she told Miles.

Miles raised his hand. The air shimmered in front of Angus, but he dodged it. A second force field hit a tree to Angus' left. By the time a third missed its mark, Meghan realized Miles' power would be useless in catching Angus. But hers would not.

She dropped to her knees in the grass, waited until Angus had run a few more steps, then grabbed onto the creeper vine, surging her revival power through it. The thin, brown plant turned green, and then lashed from her grip, snapping in anger. Angus' next step landed beside the vine. It whipped around his ankle, yanking him to the ground. He writhed, snakelike, as he tried to escape, then grew still when the vine cocooned his body to his shoulders.

Meaghan jumped to her feet and ran toward him. Bending over him, she dug through the vines to clear his hand, and then pulled at his fingers. He tightened them.

"Give it to me," she commanded.

In response, he spit at her. The vines crawled up his neck. His breathing turned to wheezing. His eyes closed halfway and his grip loosened. The object fell to the ground, but before Meaghan could reach for it, she flew backward.

"His hand is free," Nick yelled and she understood her error. She had unbound Angus' hand, allowing him the chance to use his power. She rolled onto her elbows in time to see a large tree branch lift from the ground and fly at her head. With no way to escape, she moved to cover her face with her arms, stopping when the air shimmered in front of her. The branch hit the ground.

Miles walked around her, holding his hand in front of him as the shimmering pushed toward Angus. "Did you bring the Mardróch?" Miles asked. "You didn't answer her question."

"Not this time," Angus snarled in response. May gasped and charged toward him, but Nick caught her. He locked his arms around her waist. She struggled, but could not break from his grasp.

"You killed them," she sobbed, her grief sharp in her voice. "How could you? They trusted you!"

"I was after Meaghan. Vivian and James got in the way."

"Monster!" She surged forward again, but when Nick did not let her go, she collapsed against his chest.

Sam moved to May's side to console her. Miles glanced over at her, and while both men remained distracted, Angus inched across the ground. Though the vines tightened their hold on him again, he fought them, stretching his hand toward the object he had dropped. It wiggled, sliding across the dirt in response to his power, and Meaghan dove underneath Miles' shield, reaching the object a moment before Angus did. Her fingers tightened around it. His fingers closed around her wrist.

He smiled, and then the forest disappeared.

CHAPTER THIRTY-SIX

THE WORLD bled back into focus, streaking across Meaghan's vision in patches before turning solid. Trees stood tall in front of her, ominous in their posture. Dried leaves and the scent of fresh dirt greeted her from a forest floor no different from the one she had left. The grip on her wrist released, but she knew the reprieve would not last long. Angus had teleported her away from the others. She had no protection and no way to escape, but she would fight. She had too much of Adelina's personality within her to allow Angus to kill her so easily.

Tensing, she flipped onto her back, set to spring to her feet, but paused when four faces she did not expect stared back at her.

Nick pulled her to her feet and she felt relief wash through him. "That was stupid," he said. "You're lucky I was able to pull you out of Angus' grip before he could finish teleporting you. You could have been in the middle of a volcano by now."

She pressed her lips together at the thought, but chased it and the image of molten lava from her mind as fast as it had formed. The hard object locked within her fingers reminded her she had done the right thing. "I didn't have a choice," she told him. "I had to save your powers."

"And you almost lost your life in the process," he lectured before nodding at the ground. "Watch out for the creeper."

Meaghan looked down at the tangled mass of wriggling vines, and then stepped to the side when a tentacle shot toward her. Another snapped at her leg and she moved out of its range before opening her hand. A five-sided gem lay on her palm, glinting varying shades of amethyst in the sunlight. She focused on it, on the heat emanating from it, and it flashed. Nick smiled and the emotions fighting to overwhelm Meaghan's mind ceased to exist.

"Is that what I think it is?" May asked. "Is that the Reaper Stone?"

"It is," Sam replied, stepping to May's side to examine the object. "Do you think Angus has had it this whole time?"

"Most likely," Miles answered, and then addressed Meaghan, though he kept his eyes locked on the stone. "How did you know he had it?"

"I saw it flash. I think he took Nick's powers with it."

Miles frowned. "I didn't realize," he said, looking up at her. "I'm sure he planned on killing Nick after he killed you. Have you returned Nick's powers to him?"

Meaghan curled her fingers around the stone. The warmth continued to pulse against her skin. "I did, but I don't know how I did it."

"Perhaps the ability is innate." Miles said. "I'm sure you'll learn how to control it in time. For now, keep it well. You'll need it on your journey."

"What journey?"

Miles looked from her fingers to her face. "You aren't safe with us any longer. You need to go."

"Go?" she asked, though her voice sounded hollow to her. "Go where?"

"It doesn't matter." Miles turned his gaze on Nick. "You need to leave, too."

"I understand," Nick said, slipping an arm around Meaghan's shoulders. The thought of travelling again, of spending nights in the woods and days attempting to avoid death made her feel week. She leaned against him to keep steady.

"I don't," she said. "There are people here who can protect us—"

"And one of them tried to kill you tonight," Miles reminded her. "Unless Angus was lying about letting the Mardróch into the village. Was he?"

Meaghan did not respond. She did not want to utter the truth, but Miles nodded and she knew her face had given him the answer. "I was afraid of that," he said and turned to Nick's mother, "do you have your commcrystals?"

"I do."

"Bring them here. We don't have much time. Angus will return soon if he has reinforcements."

"Time for what?" Nick asked.

"We have two things to accomplish before you go. I need to gather the villagers so you can teleport safely. I'll send groups in different directions."

"And the other thing?"

"We need to ensure your safety," Miles answered. May returned and he took two oblong crystals from her, rubbing them together with a flick of his wrists. They shifted from smoke-gray to bright white, then back again, and he handed one to Nick before giving the other back to May. "Two people can hide better than three. I'm reassigning you as Meaghan's Guardian, but I expect you to be smarter about it this time. Stay firm with her safety, and use the crystal to communicate with your mother. Keep us up-to-date on everything, save for one secret you'll be required to keep."

Nick clutched the crystal between his hands. "What's that?"

"Your location. Only tell us if danger requires it. May will be your Guardian going forward."

"My Guardian?" Nick shook his head. "I don't need a—"

"The King always needs one," Miles interrupted. He took Meaghan's hand in his, lifting it so he could see the stone still nestled in her palm. It flashed again.

"But I'm not," Nick started to protest, stopping when Sam chuckled. Nick's eyes grew wide before falling on Meaghan.

"This stone belongs to your family," Miles said, drawing Meaghan's hand closer. "It was taken from Adelina's amulet the day she was murdered. We believe it's for protection though no one outside the royal family knew its full purpose or its origin."

"So it does more than steal powers?" Meaghan asked.

Miles nodded. "Istera told me as much."

"Shouldn't we destroy it then? It could be dangerous if Garon ever got it."

"He wouldn't be able to use it. It only works for members of the royal family. There are only two of you left, about to be three." Miles gestured toward Nick. "Place your hand on the stone, please."

Though Nick's hand trembled, he did as Miles requested of him, covering Meaghan's fingers with his own. Miles pressed his hand on top of Nick's, and the stone flashed, sending light through his fingers. It glowed for a full minute before the light went out and Miles released their hands. "It's done."

"What is?" Nick asked.

"The stone has recognized you as the rightful King. It can't be used against a royal family member, so you're now immune to it." Miles passed his hand in front of his waist and bowed low. A smile spread across his face. "And now it's my honor to officially recognize you. Welcome, King of Ærenden."

EPILOGUE

THEY LANDED in another endless forest. Rough bark blended into dark shadows and Meaghan closed her eyes against it. She had hoped Nick knew of a place where they could settle, a place where a bed would greet them when they were weary, and a fireplace would warm them when they were cold. But they were back in the woods, which meant they were back to misery until she learned to control her powers. She pressed her lips together, releasing them with a heavy breath when Nick kissed her forehead.

"We're alone here," he said, drawing her against him. "Would it be okay if I didn't use my power?"

She nodded and then sensed him again as she had on Earth. His emotions lay open to her. She felt relief and understood it well. It had been no small accomplishment to live through today. And she felt grief, too.

"I'm sorry about Cissy," she whispered.

Nick tightened his hold on her, but said nothing. She reached for the amulet now sparkling around her neck and closed her fingers around it. There would be more dead before this war was over. She turned her head to press it against Nick's chest. His heart beat a steady rhythm and it paired with the calm she sensed from him. She held on to that. They stood still and quiet before his lips found the top of her head. Then he let her go.

"We shouldn't stay here," he told her, and laced his fingers together with hers. "Do you smell anything?"

She closed her eyes and inhaled. Her stomach rumbled. "Something's roasting," she said.

He laughed. "I meant anything bad. I don't sense any Mardróch, but you can sense them better than I can."

She shook her head. "They're not around. Where are we?"

In response, he tugged her behind him through a group of trees and into a clearing. A small cabin appeared. Smoke curled from the chimney and sitting on the front porch, several packages waited. A quick scan of the surrounding woods revealed a dozen crystals glowing blue against the sky.

Nick smiled. "I didn't want to teleport directly here in case there were Mardróch around, but I couldn't think of a safer place for us."

"Neither could I," Meaghan responded. Her eyes drew to the smoke again and her hunger responded to the roast she had no doubt would be waiting inside. "Who's been here?"

"You mean you haven't guessed?" Nick asked. She shook her head. "Cal. I'm certain he's known all along where we would end up. And I'm just as certain we won't see him for some time, because he'll also know I intend to find out what else Vivian told him. Come on." He led the way across the clearing, and then scooped up the packages from the porch step. "He left clothing and supplies, all the comforts of home."

She sighed. "I'll kiss him next time I see him."

"Another reason he'll stay away," Nick joked. "Let's eat and then watch the sun set. We need a break after today."

Meaghan nodded. Swinging open the cabin door, she stepped aside to let him pass. "And tomorrow?" she asked.

"Tomorrow," he said and paused on the threshold long enough to study her. His eyes locked with hers. "I'm going to turn you into a warrior."

The adventure continues with

ÆRENDEN: THE GILDONAE ALLIANCE

Coming Soon!

ABOUT THE AUTHOR

Born in Bangor, Maine, Kristen Taber spent her childhood at the feet of an Irish storytelling grandfather, learning to blend fact with fiction and imagination with reality. She lived within the realms of the worlds that captivated her, breathing life into characters and crafting stories even before she could read. Those stories have since turned into a wide range of short tales, poems, and manuscripts in both Young Adult and Adult genres. Currently, she is working on the Ærenden series from her home in the suburbs of Washington, D.C.

Learn more about Kristen and her work at www.kristentaber.com.